RACHEL RAY

RACHEL RAY

by

Anthony Trollope

DOVER PUBLICATIONS, INC.
NEW YORK

Published in Canada by General Publishing Company, Ltd.,
30 Lesmill Road, Don Mills, Toronto, Ontario.

Published in the United Kingdom by Constable and Company, Ltd., 10 Orange Street, London WC2H 7EG.

This Dover edition, first published in 1980, is an unabridged
republication of the work first published by Chapman & Hall,
London, in 1863.

International Standard Book Number: 0-486-23930-6
Library of Congress Catalog Card Number: 79-56319

Manufactured in the United States of America
Dover Publications, Inc.
180 Varick Street
New York, N.Y. 10014

CONTENTS

RACHEL RAY

RACHEL RAY

CHAPTER I

The Ray Family

THERE ARE WOMEN who cannot grow alone as standard trees;—
for whom the support and warmth of some wall, some paling,
some post, is absolutely necessary;—who, in their growth, will
blend and incline themselves towards some such prop for their
life, creeping with their tendrils along the ground till they
reach it when the circumstances of life have brought no such
prop within their natural and immediate reach. Of most women
it may be said that it would be well for them that they should
marry,—as indeed of most men also, seeing that man and wife
will each lend the other strength, and yet in lending lose none;
but to the women of whom I now speak some kind of marriage is quite indispensable, and by them some kind of marriage is always made, though the union is often unnatural. A
woman in want of a wall against which to nail herself will
swear conjugal obedience sometimes to her cook, sometimes to
her grandchild, sometimes to her lawyer. Any standing corner,
post, or stump strong enough to bear her weight will suffice;
but to some standing corner, post, or stump, she will find her
way and attach herself, and there will she be married.

Such a woman was our Mrs. Ray. As her name imports, she
had been married in the way most popular among ladies, with
bell, book, and parson. She had been like a young peach tree
that, in its early days, is carefully taught to grow against a
propitious southern wall. Her natural prop had been found for
her, and all had been well. But her heaven had been made
black with storms; the heavy winds had come, and the warm
sheltering covert against which she had felt herself so safe had

been torn away from her branches as they were spreading themselves forth to the fulness of life. She had been married at eighteen, and then, after ten years of wedded security, she had become a widow.

Her husband had been some years older than herself,—a steady, sober, hardworking, earnest man, well fitted to act as a protecting screen to such a woman as he had chosen. They had lived in Exeter, both of them having belonged to Devonshire from their birth; and Mr. Ray, though not a clergyman himself, had been employed in matters ecclesiastical. He was a lawyer,—but a lawyer of that sort that is so nearly akin to the sacerdotal profession, as to make him quite clerical and almost a clergyman. He managed the property of the dean and chapter, and knew what were the rights, and also what were the wrongs, of prebendaries and minor canons,—of vicars choral, and even of choristers. But he had been dead many years before our story commences, and so much as this is now said of him simply to explain under what circumstances Mrs. Ray had received the first tinge of that colouring which was given to her life by church matters.

They had been married somewhat over ten years when he died, and she was left with two surviving daughters, the eldest and the youngest of the children she had borne. The eldest, Dorothea, was then more than nine years old, and as she took much after her father, being stern, sober, and steady, Mrs. Ray immediately married herself to her eldest child. Dorothea became the prop against which she would henceforth grow. And against Dorothea she had grown ever since, with the exception of one short year. In that year Dorothea had taken a husband to herself and had lost him;—so that there were two widows in the same house. She, like her mother, had married early, having joined her lot to that of a young clergyman near Baslehurst; but he had lived but a few months, and Mrs. Ray's eldest child had come back to her mother's cottage, black, and stiff, and stern, in widow's weeds,—Mrs. Prime by name. Black, and stiff, and stern, in widow's weeds, she had remained since, for nine years following, and those nine years will bring us to the beginning of our story.

As regards Mrs. Ray herself, I think it was well that poor Mr. Prime had died. It assured to her the support which she needed. It must, however, be acknowledged that Mrs. Prime was a harder taskmaster than Dorothea Ray had been, and that the mother might have undergone a gentler ruling had the daughter never become a wife. I think there was much in the hardness of the weeds she wore. It seemed as though Mrs. Prime in selecting her crape, her bombazine, and the models of her caps, had resolved to repress all ideas of feminine soft-ness;—as though she had sworn to herself, with a great oath, that man should never again look on her with gratified eyes. The materials she wore have made other widows very pleasant to be seen,—with a sad thoughtful pleasantness indeed, but still very pleasant. There was nothing of that with Mrs. Prime. When she came back to her mother's cottage near Baslehurst she was not yet twenty years old, but she was rough with weeds. Her caps were lumpy, heavy, full of woe, and clean only as decency might require,—not nicely clean with feminine care. The very stuff of which they were made was brown, rather than white, and her dress was always the same. It was rough, and black, and clinging,—disagreeable to the eye in its shape, as will always be the dress of any woman which is worn day after day through all hours. By nature and education Mrs. Prime was a prim, tidy woman, but it seemed that her peculiar ideas of duty required her to militate against her nature and education, at any rate in appearance. And this was her lot in life before she had yet reached her twentieth year!

Dorothea Ray had not been wanting in some feminine at-traction. She had ever been brown and homely, but her fea-tures had been well-formed, and her eyes had been bright. Now, as she approached to thirty years of age, she might have been as well-looking as at any earlier period of her life if it had been her wish to possess good looks. But she had had no such wish. On the contrary, her desire had been to be ugly, forbid-

ding, unattractive, almost repulsive; so that, in very truth, she
might be known to be a widow indeed. And here I must not
be misunderstood. There was nothing hypocritical about Mrs.
Prime, nor did she make any attempt to appear before men to
be weighted with a deeper sorrow than that which she truly
bore; hypocrisy was by no means her fault. Her fault was this;
that she had taught herself to believe that cheerfulness was a
sin, and that the more she became morose, the nearer would
she be to the fruition of those hopes of future happiness on
which her heart was set. In all her words and thoughts she was
genuine; but, then, in so very many of them she was mistaken!
This was the wall against which Mrs. Ray had allowed herself
to be fastened for many years past, and though the support was
strong it must be admitted that it could hardly have been at all
times pleasant.

Mrs. Ray had become a widow before she was thirty; and
she had grieved for her husband with truest sorrow, pouring
herself out at first in tears, and afterwards expending herself in
long hours of vain regrets. But she had never been rough or
hard in her widowhood. It had ever been her nature to be soft.
She was a woman all over, and had about her so much of a
woman's prettiness, that she had not altogether divested herself
of it, even when her weepers had been of the broadest. To ob-
tain favour in men's eyes had never been in her mind since she
had first obtained favour in the eyes of him who had been her
lord; but yet she had never absolutely divested herself of her
woman charms, of that look half retreating, half beseeching,
which had won the heart of the ecclesiastical lawyer. Gradually
her weeds and her deep heavy crapes had fallen away from her,
and then, without much thought on the matter, she dressed herself much as did other women of forty or forty-five,—being
driven, however, on certain occasions by her daughter to a degree of dinginess, not by any means rivalling that of the daughter herself, but which she would not have achieved had she
been left to her own devices. She was a sweet-tempered, good-
humoured, loving, timid woman, ever listening and believing

and learning, with a certain aptitude for gentle mirth at her heart which, however, was always being repressed and controlled by the circumstances of her life. She could gossip over a cup of tea, and enjoy buttered toast and hot cake very thoroughly, if only there was no one near her to whisper into her ear that any such enjoyment was wicked. In spite of the sorrows she had suffered she would have taught herself to believe this world to be a pleasant place, were it not so often preached into her ears that it is a vale of tribulation in which no satisfaction can abide. And it may be said of Mrs. Ray that her religion, though it sufficed her, tormented her grievously. It sufficed her; and if on such a subject I may venture to give an opinion, I think it was of a nature to suffice her in that great strait for which it had been prepared. But in this world it tormented her, carrying her hither and thither, and leaving her in grievous doubt, not as to its own truth in any of its details, but as to her own conduct under its injunctions, and also as to her own mode of believing in it. In truth she believed too much. She could never divide the minister from the Bible;— nay, the very clerk in the church was sacred to her while exercising his functions therein. It never occurred to her to question any word that was said to her. If a linen-draper were to tell her that one coloured calico was better for her than another, she would take that point as settled by the man's word, and for the time would be free from all doubt on that heading. So also when the clergyman in his sermon told her that she should live simply and altogether for heaven, that all thoughts as to this world were wicked thoughts, and that nothing belonging to this world could be other than painful, full of sorrow and vexations, she would go home believing him absolutely, and with tear-laden eyes would bethink herself how utterly she was a castaway, because of that tea, and cake, and innocent tittle tattle with which the hours of her Saturday evening had been beguiled. She would weakly resolve that she would laugh no more, and that she would live in truth in a valley of tears. But then as the bright sun came upon her, and the birds sang around her, and some one that she loved would cling to her and kiss her, she would be happy in her own despite, and would laugh with a low musical sweet tone, forgetting that such laughter was a sin.

And then that very clergyman himself would torment her; —he that told her from the pulpit on Sundays how frightfully vain were all attempts at worldly happiness. He would come to her on the Monday with a good-natured, rather rubicund face, and would ask after all her little worldly belongings,— for he knew of her history and her means,—and he would joke with her, and tell her comfortably of his grown sons and daughters, who were prospering in worldly matters, and express the fondest solicitude as to their worldly advancement. Twice or thrice a year Mrs. Ray would go to the parsonage, and such evenings would be by no means hours of wailing. Tea and buttered toast on such occasions would be very manifestly in the ascendant. Mrs. Ray never questioned the propriety of her clergyman's life, nor taught herself to see a discrepancy between his doctrine and his conduct. But she believed in both, and was unconsciously troubled at having her belief so varied. She never thought about it, or discovered that her friend allowed himself to be carried away in his sermons by his zeal, and that he condemned this world in all things, hoping that he might thereby teach his hearers to condemn it in some things. Mrs. Ray would allow herself the privilege of no such argument as that. It was all gospel to her. The parson in the church, and the parson out of the church, were alike gospels to her sweet, white, credulous mind; but these differing gospels troubled her and tormented her.

Of that particular clergyman, I may as well here say that he was the Rev. Charles Comfort, and that he was rector of Cawston, a parish in Devonshire, about two miles out of Baslehurst. Mr. Prime had for a year or two been his curate, and during that term of curacy he had married Dorothea Ray. Then he had died, and his widow had returned from the house her husband had occupied near the church to her mother's cottage. Mr. Prime had been possessed of some property, and when he died he left his widow in the uncontrolled possession of two hundred a year. As it was well known that Mrs. Ray's income was considerably less than this, the people of Baslehurst and Cawston had declared how comfortable for Mrs. Ray would be this accession of wealth to the family. But Mrs. Ray had not become much the richer. Mrs. Prime did no doubt pay her fair quota towards the maintenance of the humble cottage at Bragg's End, for such was the name of the spot at which Mrs. Ray lived. But she did not do more than this. She established a Dorcas society at Baslehurst, of which she became permanent president, and spent her money in carrying on this institution in the manner most pleasing to herself. I fear that Mrs. Prime liked to be more powerful at these charitable meetings than her sister labourers in the same vineyard, and that she achieved this power by the means of her money. I do not bring this as a heavy accusation against her. In such institutions there is generally need of a strong, stirring, leading mind. If some one would not assume power, the power needed would not be exercised. Such a one as Mrs. Prime is often necessary. But we all have our own pet temptations, and I think that Mrs. Prime's temptation was a love of power.

It will be understood that Baslehurst is a town,—a town with a market, and hotels, and a big brewery, and a square, and street; whereas Cawston is a village, or rather a rural parish, three miles out of Baslehurst, north of it, lying on the river Avon. But Bragg's End, though within the parish of Cawston, lies about a mile and a half from the church and village, on the road to Baslehurst, and partakes therefore almost as much of the township of Baslehurst as it does of the rusticity of Cawston. How Bragg came to such an end, or why this corner of the parish came to be thus united for ever to Bragg's name, no one in the parish knew. The place consisted of a little green, and a little wooden bridge, over a little stream that trickled away into the Avon. Here were clustered half a dozen labourers' cottages, and a beer or cider shop. Standing back from the green was the house and homestead of Farmer Sturt, and close upon the green, with its garden hedge running down to the bridge, was the pretty cottage of Mrs. Ray. Mr. Comfort had known her husband, and he had found for her this quiet home. It was a pretty place, with one small sitting-room opening back upon the little garden, and with another somewhat larger fronting towards the road and the green. In the front room Mrs. Ray lived, looking out upon so much of the world as Bragg's End green afforded to her view. The other seemed to be kept with some faint expectation of company that never came. Many of the widow's neatest belongings were here preserved in most perfect order; but one may say that they were altogether thrown away,—unless indeed they afforded solace to their owner in the very act of dusting them. Here there were four or five books, prettily bound, with gilt leaves, arranged in shapes on the small round table. Here also was deposited a spangled mat of wondrous brightness, made of short white sticks of glass strung together. It must have taken care and time in its manufacture, but was, I should say, but of little efficacy either for domestic use or domestic ornament. There were shells on the chimneypiece, and two or three china figures. There was a birdcage hung in the window but without a bird. It was all very clean, but the room conveyed at the first glance an overpowering idea of its own absolute inutility and vanity. It was capable of answering no purpose for which men and women use rooms; but he who could have said so to Mrs. Ray must have been a cruel and a hardhearted man.

The other room which looked out upon the green was snug enough, and sufficed for all the widow's wants. There was a little book-case laden with books. There was the family table at which they ate their meals; and there was the little table near the window at which Mrs. Ray worked. There was an old sofa, and an old arm-chair; and there was, also, a carpet, alas, so old that the poor woman had become painfully aware that she must soon have either no carpet or a new one. A word or two had already been said between her and Mrs. Prime on that matter, but the word or two had not as yet been comfortable. Then, over the fire, there was an old round mirror; and, having told of that, I believe I need not further describe the furniture of the sitting-room at Bragg's End.

But I have not as yet described the whole of Mrs. Ray's family. Had I done so, her life would indeed have been sour, and sorrowful, for she was a woman who especially needed companionship. Though I have hitherto spoken but of one daughter, I have said that two had been left with her when her husband died. She had one whom she feared and obeyed, seeing that a master was necessary to her; but she had another whom she loved and caressed, and I may declare, that some such object for her tenderness was as necessary to her as the master. She could not have lived without something to kiss, something to tend, something to which she might speak in short, loving, pet terms of affection. This youngest girl, Rachel, had been only two years old when her father died, and now, at the time of this story, was not yet quite twenty. Her sister was, in truth, only seven years her senior, but in all the facts and ways of life, she seemed to be the elder by at least half a century. Rachel indeed, at the time, felt herself to be much nearer of an age with her mother. With her mother she could laugh and talk, ay, and form little wicked whispered schemes behind the tyrant's back, during some of those Dorcas hours, in which Mrs. Prime would be employed at Baslehurst; schemes, however, for the final perpetration of which, the courage of the elder widow would too frequently be found insufficient.

Rachel Ray was a fair-haired, well-grown, comely girl,— very like her mother in all but this, that whereas about the mother's eyes there was always a look of weakness, there was a shadowing of coming strength of character round those of the daughter. On her brow there was written a capacity for sustained purpose which was wanting to Mrs. Ray. Not that the reader is to suppose that she was masterful like her sister. She had been brought up under Mrs. Prime's directions, and had

not, as yet, learned to rebel. Nor was she in any way prone to
domineer. A little wickedness now and then, to the extent, perhaps, of a vain walk into Baslehurst on a summer evening, a
little obstinacy in refusing to explain whither she had been and
whom she had seen, a yawn in church, or a word of complaint
as to the length of the second Sunday sermon,—these were her
sins; and when rebuked for them by her sister, she would of
late toss her head, and look slily across to her mother, with an
eye that was not penitent. Then Mrs. Prime would become
black and angry, and would foretell hard things for her sister,
denouncing her as fashioning herself wilfully in the world's
ways. On such occasions Mrs. Ray would become very unhappy, believing first in the one child and then in the other.
She would defend Rachel, till her weak defence would be
knocked to shivers, and her poor vacillating words taken from
out of her mouth. Then, when forced to acknowledge that Rachel was in danger of backsliding, she would kiss her and cry
over her, and beg her to listen to the sermons. Rachel hitherto
had never rebelled. She had never declared that a walk into
Baslehurst was better than a sermon. She had never said out
boldly that she liked the world and its wickednesses. But an observer of physiognomy, had such observer been there, might
have seen that the days of such rebellion were coming.

She was a fair-haired girl, with hair, not flaxen, but of light-
brown tint,—thick, and full, and glossy, so that its charms
could not all be hidden away let Mrs. Prime do what she would
to effect such hiding. She was well made, being tall and
straight, with great appearance of health and strength. She
walked as though the motion were pleasant to her, and easy,—
as though the very act of walking were a pleasure. She was
bright too, and clever in their little cottage, striving hard with
her needle to make things look well, and not sparing her
strength in giving household assistance. One little maiden Mrs.
Ray employed, and a gardener came to her for half a day once
a week;—but I doubt whether the maiden in the house, or the
gardener out of the house, did as much hard work as Rachel.

How she had toiled over that carpet, patching it and piecing it! Even Dorothea could not accuse her of idleness. Therefore Dorothea accused her of profitless industry, because she would not attend more frequently at those Dorcas meetings.

"But, Dolly, how on earth am I to make my own things, and look after mamma's? Charity begins at home." Then had Dorothea put down her huge Dorcas basket, and explained to her sister, at considerable length, her reading of that text of Scripture. "One's own clothes must be made all the same," Rachel said when the female preacher had finished. "And I don't suppose even you would like mamma to go to church without a decent gown." Then Dorothea had seized up her huge basket angrily, and had trudged off into Baselhurst at a quick pace,— at a pace much too quick when the summer's heat is considered;—and as she went, unhappy thoughts filled her mind. A coloured dress belonging to Rachel herself had met her eye, and she had heard tidings of—a young man!

Such tidings, to her ears, were tidings of iniquity, of vanity, of terrible sin; they were tidings which hardly admitted of being discussed with decency, and which had to be spoken of below the breath. A young man! Could it be that such disgrace had fallen upon her sister! She had not as yet mentioned the subject to Rachel, but she had given a dark hint to their afflicted mother.

"No, I didn't see it myself, but I heard it from Miss Pucker."

"She that was to have been married to William Whitecoat, the baker's son, only he went away to Torquay and picked up with somebody else. People said he did it because she does squint so dreadfully."

"Mother!"—and Dorothea spoke very sternly as she answered—"what does it matter to us about William Whitecoat, or Miss Pucker's squint? She is a woman eager in doing good."

"It's only since he left Baselhurst, my dear."

"Mother!—does that matter to Rachel? Will that save her if she be in danger? I tell you that Miss Pucker saw her walking with that young man from the brewery!"

Though Mrs. Ray had been strongly inclined to throw what odium she could upon Miss Pucker, and though she hated Miss Pucker in her heart,—at this special moment,—for having carried tales against her darling, she could not deny, even to herself, that a terrible state of things had arrived if it were really true that Rachel had been seen walking with a young man. She was not bitter on the subject as was Mrs. Prime and poor Miss Pucker, but she was filled full of indefinite horror with regard to young men in general. They were all regarded by her as wolves,—as wolves, either with or without sheep's clothing. I doubt whether she ever brought it home to herself that those whom she now recognized as the established and well-credited lords of the creation had ever been young men themselves. When she heard of a wedding,—when she learned that some struggling son of Adam had taken to himself a wife, and had settled himself down to the sober work of the world, she rejoiced greatly, thinking that the son of Adam had done well to get himself married. But whenever it was whispered into her ear that any young man was looking after a young woman,— that he was taking the only step by which he could hope to find a wife for himself,—she was instantly shocked at the wickedness of the world, and prayed inwardly that the girl at least might be saved like a brand from the burning. A young man, in her estimation, was a wicked wild beast, seeking after young women to devour them, as a cat seeks after mice. This at least was her established idea,—the idea on which she worked, unless some other idea on any special occasion were put into her head. When young Butler Cornbury, the eldest son of the neighbouring squire, came to Cawston after pretty Patty Comfort,—for Patty Comfort was said to have been the prettiest girl in Devonshire;—and when Patty Comfort had been allowed to go to the assemblies at Torquay almost on purpose to meet him, Mrs. Ray had thought it all right, because it had been presented to her mind as all right by the rector. Butler Cornbury had married Patty Comfort and it was all right. But had she heard of Patty's dancings without the assistance of a few hints from Mr. Comfort himself, her mind would have worked in a different way.

She certainly desired that her own child Rachel should some day find a husband, and Rachel was already older than she had been when she married, or than Mrs. Prime had been at her wedding; but, nevertheless, there was something terrible in the very thought of—a young man; and she, though she would fain have defended her child, hardly knew how to do so otherwise than by discrediting the words of Miss Pucker. "She always was very ill-natured, you know," Mrs. Ray ventured to hint.

"Mother!" said Mrs. Prime, in that peculiarly stern voice of hers. "There can be no reason for supposing that Miss Pucker wishes to malign the child. It is my belief that Rachel will be in Baslehurst this evening. If so, she probably intends to meet him again."

"I know she is going into Baslehurst after tea," said Mrs. Ray, "because she has promised to walk with the Miss Tappitts. She told me so."

"Exactly!—with the brewery girls! Oh, mother!" Now it is certainly true that the three Miss Tappitts were the daughters of Bungall and Tappitt, the old-established brewers of Baslehurst. They were, at least, the actual children of Mr. Tappitt, who was the sole surviving partner in the brewery. The name of Bungall had for many years been used merely to give solidity and standing to the Tappitt family. The Miss Tappitts certainly came from the brewery, and Miss Pucker had said that the young man came from the same quarter. There was ground in this for much suspicion, and Mrs. Ray became uneasy. This conversation between the two widows had occurred before dinner at the cottage on a Saturday;—and it was after dinner that the elder sister had endeavoured to persuade the younger one to accompany her to the Dorcas workshop;—but had endeavoured in vain.

CHAPTER II

The Young Man from the Brewery

THERE WERE during the summer months four Dorcas after-
noons held weekly in Baslehurst, at all of which Mrs. Prime
presided. It was her custom to start soon after dinner, so as to
reach the working-room before three o'clock, and there she
would remain till nine, or as long as the daylight remained.
The meeting was held in a sitting-room belonging to Miss
Pucker, for the use of which the Institution paid some moderate rent. The other ladies, all belonging to Baslehurst, were
accustomed to go home to tea in the middle of their labours;
but, as Mrs. Prime could not do this because of the distance,
she remained with Miss Pucker, paying for such refreshment
as she needed. In this way there came to be a great friendship
between Mrs. Prime and Miss Pucker;—or rather, perhaps,
Mrs. Prime thus obtained the services of a most obedient
minister.

Rachel had on various occasions gone with her sister to the
Dorcas meetings, and once or twice had remained at Miss
Pucker's house, drinking tea there. But this she greatly disliked. She was aware, when she did so, that her sister paid for
her, and she thought that Dorothea showed by her behaviour
that she was mistress of the entertainment. And then Rachel
greatly disliked Miss Pucker. She disliked that lady's squint,
she disliked the tone of her voice, she disliked her subservi-
ence to Mrs. Prime, and she especially disliked the vehemence
of her objection to—young men. When Rachel had last left Miss
Pucker's room she had resolved that she would never again
drink tea there. She had not said to herself positively that she
would attend no more of the Dorcas meetings;—but as regarded their summer arrangement this resolve against the tea-
drinking amounted almost to the same thing.

It was on this account, I protest, and by no means on account of that young man from the brewery, that Rachel had with determination opposed her sister's request on this special Saturday. And the refusal had been made in an unaccustomed manner, owing to the request also having been pressed with unusual vigour.

"Rachel, I particularly wish it, and I think that you ought to come," Dorothea had said.

"I had rather not come, Dolly."

"That means," continued Mrs. Prime, "that you prefer your pleasure to your duty;—that you boldly declare yourself determined to neglect that which you know you ought to do."

"I don't know any such thing," said Rachel.

"If you think of it you will know it," said Mrs. Prime.

"At any rate I don't mean to go to Miss Pucker's that afternoon."—Then Rachel left the room.

It was immediately after this conversation that Mrs. Prime uttered to Mrs. Ray that terrible hint about the young man; and at the same time uttered another hint by which she strove to impress upon her mother that Rachel ought to be kept in subordination,—in fact, that the power should not belong to Rachel of choosing whether she would or would not go to Dorcas meetings. In all such matters, according to Dorothea's view of the case, Rachel should do as she was bidden. But then how was Rachel to be made to do as she was bidden? How was her sister to enforce her attendance? Obedience in this world depends as frequently on the weakness of him who is governed as on the strength of him who governs. That man who was going to the left is ordered by you with some voice of command to go to the right. When he hesitates you put more command into your voice, more command into your eyes, —and then he obeys. Mrs. Prime had tried this, but Rachel had not turned to the right. When Mrs. Prime applied for aid to their mother, it was a sign that the power of command was going from herself. After dinner the elder sister made another little futile attempt, and then, when she had again failed, she trudged off with her basket.

Mrs. Ray and Rachel were left sitting at the open window, looking out upon the mignonette. It was now in July, when the summer sun is at the hottest,—and in those southern parts of Devonshire the summer sun in July is very hot. There is no other part of England like it. The lanes are low and narrow, and not a breath of air stirs through them. The ground rises in hills on all sides, so that every spot is a sheltered nook. The rich red earth drinks in the heat and holds it, and no breezes come up from the southern torpid sea. Of all counties in England Devonshire is the fairest to the eye; but, having known it in its summer glory, I must confess that those southern regions are not fitted for much noonday summer walking.

"I'm afraid she'll find it very hot with that big basket," said Mrs. Ray, after a short pause. It must not be supposed that either she or Rachel were idle because they remained at home. They both had their needles in their hands, and Rachel was at work, not on that coloured frock of her own which had roused her sister's suspicion, but on needful aid to her mother's Sunday gown.

"She might have left it in Baslehurst if she liked," said Rachel, "or I would have carried it for her as far as the bridge, only that she was so angry with me when she went."

"I don't think she was exactly angry, Rachel."

"Oh, but she was, mamma;—very angry. I know by her way of flinging out of the house."

"I think she was sorry because you would not go with her."

"But I don't like going there, mamma. I don't like that Miss Pucker. I can't go without staying to tea, and I don't like drinking tea there." Then there was a little pause. "You don't want me to go;—do you, mamma? How would the things get done here? and you can't like having your tea alone."

"No; I don't like that at all," said Mrs. Ray. But she hardly thought of what she was saying. Her mind was away, working on the subject of that young man. She felt that it was her duty to say something to Rachel, and yet she did not know what to say. Was she to quote Miss Pucker? It went, moreover, sorely against the grain with her to disturb the comfort of their present happy moments by any disagreeable allusion. The world gave her nothing better than those hours in which Rachel was alone with her,—in which Rachel tended her and comforted her. No word had been said on a subject so wicked and full of vanity, but Mrs. Ray knew that her evening meal would be brought in at half-past five in the shape of a little feast,—a feast which would not be spread if Mrs. Prime had remained at home. At five o'clock Rachel would slip away and make hot toast, and would run over the Green to Farmer Sturt's wife for a little thick cream, and there would be a batter cake, and so there would be a feast. Rachel was excellent at the preparation of such banquets, knowing how to coax the teapot into a good drawing humour, and being very clever in little comforts; and she would hover about her mother, in a way very delightful to that lady, making the widow feel for the time that there was a gleam of sunshine in the valley of tribulation. All that must be over for this afternoon if she spoke of Miss Pucker and the young man. Yes; and must it not be over for many an afternoon to come? If there were to be distrust between her and Rachel what would her life be worth to her?

But yet there was her duty! As she sat there looking out into the garden indistinct ideas of what were a mother's duties to her child lay heavy on her mind,—ideas which were very indistinct, but which were not on that account the less powerful in their operation. She knew that it behoved her to sacrifice everything to her child's welfare, but she did not know what special sacrifice she was at this moment called upon to make. Would it be well that she should leave this matter altogether in the hands of Mrs. Prime, and thus, as it were, abdicate her own authority? Mrs. Prime would undertake such a task with much more skill and power of language than she could use. But then would this be fair to Rachel, and would Rachel obey her sister? Any explicit direction from herself,—if only she could bring herself to give any,—Rachel would, she thought, obey. In this way she resolved that she would break the ice and do her duty.

"Are you going into Baslehurst this evening, dear?" she said.

"Yes, mamma; I shall walk in after tea;—that is if you don't want me. I told the Miss Tappitts I would meet them."

"No; I shan't want you. But Rachel——"

"Well, mamma?"

Mrs. Ray did not know how to do it. The matter was surrounded with difficulties. How was she to begin, so as to introduce the subject of the young man without shocking her child and showing an amount of distrust which she did not feel? "Do you like those Miss Tappitts?" she said.

"Yes;—in a sort of a way. They are very good-natured, and one likes to know somebody. I think they are nicer than Miss Pucker."

"Oh, yes;—I never did like Miss Pucker myself. But, Rachel——"

"What is it, mamma? I know you've something to say, and that you don't half like to say it. Dolly has been telling tales about me, and you want to lecture me, only you haven't got the heart. Isn't that it, mamma?" Then she put down her work, and coming close up to her mother, knelt before her and looked up into her face. "You want to scold me, and you haven't got the heart to do it."

"My darling, my darling," said the mother, stroking her child's soft smooth hair. "I don't want to scold you;—I never want to scold you. I hate scolding anybody."

"I know you do, mamma."

"But they have told me something which has frightened me."

"They! who are they?"

"Your sister told me, and Miss Pucker told her."

"Oh, Miss Pucker! What business has Miss Pucker with me? If she is to come between us all our happiness will be over." Then Rachel rose from her knees and began to look angry, whereupon her mother was more frightened than ever. "But let me hear it, mamma. I've no doubt it is something very awful."

Mrs. Ray looked at her daughter with beseeching eyes, as though praying to be forgiven for having introduced a subject so disagreeable. "Dorothea says that on Wednesday evening you were walking under the churchyard elms with—that young man from the brewery."

At any rate everything had been said now. The extent of the depravity with which Rachel was to be charged had been made known to her in the very plainest terms. Mrs. Ray as she uttered the terrible words turned first pale and then red,— pale with fear and red with shame. As soon as she had spoken them she wished the words unsaid. Her dislike to Miss Pucker amounted almost to hatred. She felt bitterly even towards her own eldest daughter. She looked timidly into Rachel's face and unconsciously construed into their true meaning those lines which formed themselves on the girl's brow and over her eyes.

"Well, mamma; and what else?" said Rachel.

"Dorothea thinks that perhaps you are going into Baslehurst to meet him again."

"And suppose I am?"

From the tone in which this question was asked it was clear to Mrs. Ray that she was expected to answer it. And yet what answer could she make?

It had never occurred to her that her child would take upon herself to defend such conduct as that imputed to her, or that any question would be raised as to the propriety or impropriety of the proceeding. She was by no means prepared to show why it was so very terrible and iniquitous. She regarded it as a sin,—known to be a sin generally,—as is stealing or lying. "Suppose I am going to walk with him again? what then?"

"Oh, Rachel, who is he? I don't even know his name. I didn't believe it, when Dorothea told me; only as she did tell me I thought I ought to mention it. Oh dear, oh dear! I hope there is nothing wrong. You were always so good;—I can't believe anything wrong of you."

"No, mamma;—don't. Don't think evil of me."

"I never did, my darling."

"I am not going into Baslehurst to walk with Mr. Rowan;—for I suppose it is him you mean."

"I don't know, my dear; I never heard the young man's name."

"It is Mr. Rowan. I did walk with him along the churchyard path when that woman with her sharp squinting eyes saw me. He does belong to the brewery. He is related in some way to the Tappitts, and was a nephew of old Mrs. Bungall's. He is there as a clerk, and they say he is to be a partner,—only I don't think he ever will, for he quarrels with Mr. Tappitt."

"Dear, dear!" said Mrs. Ray.

"And now, mamma, you know as much about him as I do; only this, that he went to Exeter this morning, and does not come back till Monday, so that it is impossible that I should meet him in Baslehurst this evening;—and it was very unkind of Dolly to say so; very unkind indeed." Then Rachel gave way and began to cry.

It certainly did seem to Mrs. Ray that Rachel knew a good deal about Mr. Rowan. She knew of his kith and kin, she knew of his prospects and what was like to mar his prospects, and she knew also of his immediate proceedings, whereabouts, and intentions. Mrs. Ray did not logically draw any conclusion from these premises, but she became uncomfortably assured that there did exist a considerable intimacy between Mr. Rowan and her daughter. And how had it come to pass that this had been allowed to form itself without any knowledge on her part? Miss Pucker might be odious and disagreeable;—Mrs. Ray was inclined to think that the lady in question was very odious and disagreeable;—but must it not be admitted that her little story about the young man had proved itself to be true?

"I never will go to those nasty rag meetings any more."

"Oh Rachel, don't speak in that way."

"But I won't. I will never put my foot in that woman's room again. They talk nothing but scandal all the time they are there, and speak any ill they can of the poor young girls whom they talk about. If you don't mind my knowing Mr. Rowan, what is it to them?"

But this was assuming a great deal. Mrs. Ray was by no means prepared to say that she did not object to her daughter's acquaintance with Mr. Rowan. "But I don't know anything about him, my dear. I never heard his name before."

"No, mamma; you never did. And I know very little of him; so little that there has been nothing to tell,—at least next to nothing. I don't want to have any secrets from you, mamma."

"But, Rachel,—he isn't, is he——? I mean there isn't anything particular between him and you? How was it you were walking with him alone?"

"I wasn't walking with him alone;—at least only for a little way. He had been out with his cousins and we had all been together, and when they went in, of course I was obliged to come home. I couldn't help his coming along the churchyard path with me. And what if he did, mamma? He couldn't bite me."

"But my dear——"

"Oh mamma;—don't be afraid of me." Then she came across, and again knelt at her mother's feet. "If you'll trust me I'll tell you everything."

Upon hearing this assurance, Mrs. Ray of course promised Rachel that she would trust her, and expected in return to be told everything then, at the moment. But she perceived that her daughter did not mean to tell her anything further at that time. Rachel, when she had received her mother's promise, embraced her warmly, caressing her and petting her as was her custom, and then after a while she resumed her work. Mrs. Ray was delighted to have the evil thing over, but she could not but feel that the conversation had not terminated as it should have done.

Soon after that the hour arrived for their little feast, and Rachel went about her work just as merrily and kindly as though there had been no words about the young man. She went across for the cream, and stayed gossiping for some few minutes with Mrs. Sturt. Then she bustled about the kitchen making the tea and toasting the bread. She had never been more anxious to make everything comfortable for her mother, and never more eager in her coaxing way of doing honour to the good things which she had prepared; but, through it all, her mother was aware that everything was not right; there was something in Rachel's voice which betrayed inward uneasiness;—something in the vivacity of her movements that was not quite true to her usual nature. Mrs. Ray felt that it was so, and could not therefore be altogether at her ease. She pretended to enjoy herself;—but Rachel knew that her joy was not real. Nothing further, however, was said, either regarding that evening's walk into Baslehurst, or touching that other walk as to which Miss Pucker's tale had been told. Mrs. Ray had done as much as her courage enabled her to attempt on that occasion.

When the tea-drinking was over, and the cups and spoons had been tidily put away, Rachel prepared herself for her walk. She had been very careful that nothing should be hurried,— that there should be no apparent anxiety on her part to leave her mother quickly. And even when all was done, she would not go without some assurance of her mother's goodwill. "If you have any wish that I should stay, mamma, I don't care in the least about going."

"No, my dear; I don't want you to stay at all."

"Your dress is finished."

"Thank you, my dear; you have been very good."

"I haven't been good at all; but I will be good if you'll trust me."

"I will trust you."

"At any rate you need not be afraid to-night, for I am only going to take a walk with those three girls across the church meadows. They're always very civil, and I don't like to turn my back upon them."

"I don't wish you to turn your back upon them."

"It's stupid not to know anybody; isn't it?"

"I dare say it is," said Mrs. Ray. Then Rachel had finished tying on her hat, and she walked forth.

For more than two hours after that the widow sat alone, thinking of her children. As regarded Mrs. Prime, there was at any rate no cause for trembling, timid thoughts. She might be regarded as being safe from the world's wicked allurements. She was founded like a strong rock, and was, with her stedfast earnestness, a staff on which her weaker mother might lean with security. But then she was so stern,—and her very strength was so oppressive! Rachel was weaker, more worldly, given terribly to vain desires and thoughts that were almost wicked; but then it was so pleasant to live with her! And Rachel, though weak and worldly and almost wicked, was so very good and kind and sweet! As Mrs. Ray thought of this she began to doubt whether, after all, the world was so very bad a place, and whether the wickedness of tea and toast, and of other creature comforts, could be so very great. "I wonder what sort of a young man he is," she said to herself.

Mrs. Prime's return was always timed with the regularity of clockwork. At this period of the year she invariably came in exactly at half-past nine. Mrs. Ray was very anxious that Rachel should come in first, so that nothing should be said of her walk on this evening. She had been unwilling to imply distrust by making any special request on this occasion, and had therefore said nothing on the subject as Rachel went; but she had carefully watched the clock, and had become uneasy as the time came round for Mrs. Prime's appearance. Exactly at half-past nine she entered the house, bringing with her the heavy basket laden with work, and bringing with her also a face full of the deepest displeasure. She said nothing as she seated herself wearily on a chair against the wall; but her manner was such as to make it impossible that her mother should not notice it. "Is there anything wrong, Dorothea?" she said.

"Rachel has not come home yet, of course?" said Mrs. Prime.

"No; not yet. She is with the Miss Tappitts."

"No, mother, she is not with the Miss Tappitts": and her voice, as she said these words, was dreadful to the mother's ears.

"Isn't she? I thought she was. Do you know where she is?"

"Who is to say where she is? Half an hour since I saw her alone with——"

"With whom? Not with that young man from the brewery, for he is at Exeter."

"Mother, he is here,—in Baslehurst! Half an hour since he and Rachel were standing alone together beneath the elms in the churchyard. I saw them with my own eyes."

CHAPTER III

The Arm in the Clouds

THERE WAS PLENTY OF TIME for full inquiry and full reply between Mrs. Ray and Mrs. Prime before Rachel opened the cottage door, and interrupted them. It was then nearly half-past ten. Rachel had never been so late before. The last streak of the sun's reflection in the east had vanished, the last ruddy line of evening light had gone, and the darkness of the coming night was upon them. The hour was late for any girl such as Rachel Ray to be out alone.

There had been a long discussion between the mother and the elder daughter; and Mrs. Ray, believing implicitly in the last announcements made to her, was full of fears for her child. The utmost rigour of self-denying propriety should have been exercised by Rachel, whereas her conduct had been too dreadful almost to be described. Two or three hours since Mrs. Ray had fondly promised that she would trust her younger daughter, and had let her forth alone, proud in seeing her so comely as she went. An idea had almost entered her mind that if the young man was very steady, such an acquaintance might perhaps be not altogether wicked. But everything was changed now. All the happiness of her trust was gone. All her sweet hopes were crushed. Her heart was filled with fear, and her face was pale with sorrow.

"Why should she know where he was to be?" Dorothea had asked. "But he is not at Exeter;—he is here, and she was with him." Then the two had sat gloomily together till Rachel returned. As she came in there was a little forced laugh upon her face. "I am late; am I not?" she said. "Oh, Rachel, very late!" said her mother. "It is half-past ten," said Mrs. Prime. "Oh, Dolly, don't speak with that terrible voice, as though the world were coming to an end," said Rachel; and she looked up almost savagely, showing that she was resolved to fight.

But it may be as well to say a few words about the firm of Messrs. Bungall and Tappitt, about the Tappitt family generally, and about Mr. Luke Rowan, before any further portion of the history of that evening is written.

Why there should have been any brewery at all at Baslehurst, seeing that everybody in that part of the world drinks cider, or how, under such circumstances, Messrs. Bungall and Tappitt had managed to live upon the proceeds of their trade, I cannot pretend to say. Baslehurst is in the heart of the Devonshire cider country. It is surrounded by orchards, and farmers talk there of their apples as they do of their cheese in Cheshire, or their wheat in Essex, or their sheep in Lincolnshire. Men drink cider by the gallon,—by the gallon daily; cider presses are to be found at every squire's house, at every parsonage, and every farm homestead. The trade of a brewer at Baslehurst would seem to be as profitless as that of a breeches-maker in the Highlands, or a shoemaker in Connaught;—but nevertheless Bungall and Tappitt had been brewers in Baslehurst for the last fifty years, and had managed to live out of their brewery.

It is not to be supposed that they were great men like the

mighty men of beer known of old,—such as Barclay and Per-
kins, or Reid and Co. Nor were they new, and pink, and prosperous, going into Parliament for this borough and that, just
as they pleased, like the modern heroes of the bitter cask.
When the student at Oxford was asked what man had most
benefited humanity, and when he answered "Bass," I think that
he should not have been plucked. It was a fair average answer.
But no student at any university could have said as much for
Bungall and Tappitt without deserving utter disgrace, and
whatever penance an outraged examiner could inflict. It was
a sour and muddy stream that flowed from their vats; a beverage disagreeable to the palate, and very cold and uncomfortable to the stomach. Who drank it I could never learn. It
was to be found at no respectable inn. It was admitted at no
private gentleman's table. The farmers knew nothing of it. The
labourers drenched themselves habitually with cider. Nevertheless the brewery of Messrs. Bungall and Tappitt was kept
going, and the large ugly square brick house in which the Tappitt family lived was warm and comfortable. There is something in the very name of beer that makes money.

Old Bungall, he who first established the house, was still remembered by the seniors of Baslehurst, but he had been dead
more than twenty years before the period of my story. He had
been a short, fat old man, not much above five feet high, very
silent, very hard, and very ignorant. But he had understood
business, and had established the firm on a solid foundation.
Late in life he had taken into partnership his nephew Tappitt,
and during his life had been a severe taskmaster to his partner.
Indeed the firm had only assumed its present name on the
demise of Bungall. As long as he had lived it had been Bungall's brewery. When the days of mourning were over, then—
and not till then—Mr. Tappitt had put up a board with the
joint names of the firm as at present called.

It was believed in Baslehurst that Mr. Bungall had not bequeathed his undivided interest in the concern to his nephew.
Indeed people went so far as to say that he had left away from

Mr. Tappitt all that he could leave. The truth in that respect may as well be told at once. His widow had possessed a third of the profits of the concern, in lieu of her right to a full half share in the concern, which would have carried with it the onus of a full half share of the work. That third and those rights she had left to her nephew,—or rather to her great-nephew, Luke Rowan. It was not, however, in this young man's power to walk into the brewery and claim a seat there as a partner. It was not in his power to do so, even if such should be his wish. When old Mrs. Bungall died at Dawlish at the very advanced age of ninety-seven, there came to be, as was natural, some little dispute between Mr. Tappitt and his distant connection, Luke Rowan. Mr. Tappitt suggested that Luke should take a thousand pounds down, and walk forth free from all contamination of malt and hops. Luke's attorney asked for ten thousand. Luke Rowan at the time was articled to a lawyer in London, and as the dinginess of the chambers which he frequented in Lincoln's Inn Fields appeared to him less attractive than the beautiful rivers of Devonshire, he offered to go into the brewery as a partner. It was at last settled that he should place himself there as a clerk for twelve months, drawing a certain moderate income out of the concern; and that if at the end of the year he should show himself to be able, and feel himself to be willing, to act as a partner, the firm should be changed to Tappitt and Rowan, and he should be established permanently as a Baslehurst brewer. Some information, however, beyond this has already been given to the reader respecting Mr. Rowan's prospects. "I don't think he ever will be a partner," Rachel had said to her mother, "because he quarrels with Mr. Tappitt." She had been very accurate in her statement. Mr. Rowan had now been three months at Baslehurst, and had not altogether found the ways of his relative pleasant. Mr. Tappitt wished to treat him as a clerk, whereas he wished to be treated as a partner. And Mr. Tappitt had by no means found the ways of the young man to be pleasant. Young Rowan was not idle, nor did he lack intelligence; in-

deed he possessed more energy and cleverness than, in Tappitt's opinion, were necessary to the position of a brewer in
Baslehurst; but he was by no means willing to use these good
gifts in the manner indicated by the sole existing owner of the
concern. Mr. Tappitt wished that Rowan should learn brewing
seated on a stool, and that the lessons should be purely arith-
metical. Luke was instructed as to the use of certain dull,
dingy, disagreeable ledgers, and informed that in them lay the
natural work of a brewer. But he desired to learn the chemical
action of malt and hops upon each other, and had not been a
fortnight in the concern before he suggested to Mr. Tappitt
that by a salutary process, which he described, the liquor might
be made less muddy. "Let us brew good beer," he had said;
and then Tappitt had known that it would not do. "Yes," said
Tappitt, "and sell for twopence a pint what will cost you three-
pence to make!" "That's what we've got to look to," said
Rowan. "I believe it can be done for the money,—only one
must learn how to do it." "I've been at it all my life," Tappitt
said. "Yes, Mr. Tappitt; but it is only now that men are beginning to appreciate all that chemistry can do for them. If you'll
allow me I'll make an experiment on a small scale." After that
Mr. Tappitt had declared emphatically to his wife that Luke
Rowan should never become a partner of his. "He would ruin
any business in the world," said Tappitt. "And as to conceit!"
It is true that Rowan was conceited, and perhaps true also that
he would have ruined the brewery had he been allowed to
have his own way.

But Mrs. Tappitt by no means held him in such aversion as
did her husband. He was a well-grown, good-looking young
man for whom his friends had made comfortable provision, and
Mrs. Tappitt had three marriageable daughters. Her ideas
on the subject of young men in general were by no means iden-
tical with those held by Mrs. Ray. She was aware how frequently it happened that a young partner would marry a
daughter of the senior in the house, and it seemed to her that
special provision for such an arrangement was made in this

case. Young Rowan was living in her house, and was naturally thrown into great intimacy with her girls. It was clear to her quick eye that he was of a susceptible disposition, fond of ladies' society, and altogether prone to those pleasant pre-matrimonial conversations, from the effects of which it is so difficult for an inexperienced young man to make his escape. Mrs. Tappitt was minded to devote to him Augusta, the second of her flock,—but not so minded with any obstinacy of resolution. If Luke should prefer Martha, the elder, or Cherry, the younger girl, Mrs. Tappitt would make no objection; but she expected that he should do his duty by taking one of them. "Laws, T., don't be so foolish," she said to her husband, when he made his complaint to her. She always called her husband T., unless when the solemnity of some special occasion justified her in addressing him as Mr. Tappitt. To have called him Tom or Thomas, would, in her estimation, have been very vulgar. "Don't be so foolish. Did you never have to do with a young man before? Those tantrums will all blow off when he gets himself into harness." The tantrums spoken of were Rowan's insane desire to brew good beer, but they were of so fatal a nature that Tappitt was determined not to submit himself to them. Luke Rowan should never be partner of his,—not though he had twenty daughters waiting to be married!

Rachel had been acquainted with the Tappitts before young Rowan had come to Baslehurst, and had been made known to him by them all collectively. Had they shared their mother's prudence they would probably not have done anything so rash. Rachel was better-looking than either of them,—though that fact perhaps might not have been known to them. But in justice to them all I must say that they lacked their mother's prudence. They were good-humoured, laughing, ordinary girls,— very much alike, with long brown curls, fresh complexions, large mouths, and thick noses. Augusta was rather the taller of the three, and therefore, in her mother's eyes, the beauty. But the girls themselves, when their distant cousin had come amongst them, had not thought of appropriating him. When, after the first day, they became intimate with him, they promised to introduce him to the beauties of the neighbourhood, and Cherry had declared her conviction that he would fall in love with Rachel Ray directly he saw her. "She is tall, you know," said Cherry, "a great deal taller than us." "Then I'm sure I shan't like her," Luke had said. "Oh, but you must like her, because she is a friend of ours," Cherry had answered; "and I shouldn't be a bit surprised if you fell violently in love with her." Mrs. Tappitt did not hear all this, but, nevertheless, she began to entertain a dislike to Rachel. It must not be supposed that she admitted her daughter Augusta to any participation in her plans. Mrs. Tappitt could scheme for her child, but she could not teach her child to scheme. As regarded the girl, it must all fall out after the natural, pleasant, everyday fashion of such things; but Mrs. Tappitt considered that her own natural advantages were so great that she could make the thing fall out as she wished. When she was informed about a fortnight after Rowan's arrival in Baslehurst that Rachel Ray had been walking with the party from the brewery, she could not prevent herself from saying an ill-natured word or two. "Rachel Ray is all very well," she said, "but she is not the person whom you should show off to a stranger as your particular friend."

"Why not, mamma?" said Cherry.

"Why not, my dear! There are reasons why not. Mrs. Ray is very well in her way, but——"

"Her husband was a gentleman," said Martha, "and a great friend of Mr. Comfort's."

"My dear, I have nothing to say against her," said the mother, "only this; that she does not go among the people we know. There is Mrs. Prime, the other daughter; her great friend is Miss Pucker. I don't suppose you want to be very intimate with Miss Pucker." The brewer's wife had a position in Baslehurst and wished that her daughters should maintain it.

It will now be understood in what way Rachel had formed her acquaintance with Luke Rowan, and I think it may certainly be admitted that she had been guilty of no great impropriety;—unless, indeed, she had been wrong in saying nothing of the acquaintance to her mother. Previous to those ill-natured tidings brought home as to the first churchyard meeting, Rachel had seen him but twice. On the first occasion she had thought but little of it,—but little of Luke himself or of her acquaintance with him. In simple truth the matter had passed from her mind, and therefore she had not spoken of it. When they met the second time, Luke had walked much of the way home with her,—with her alone,—having joined himself to her when the Tappitt girls went into their house as Rachel had afterwards described to her mother. In all that she had said she had spoken absolutely the truth; but it cannot be pleaded on her behalf that after this second meeting with Mr. Rowan she had said nothing of him because she had thought nothing. She had indeed thought much, but it had seemed well to her to keep her thoughts to herself.

The Tappitt girls had by no means given up their friend because their mother had objected to Miss Pucker; and when Rachel met them on that Saturday evening,—that fatal Saturday, —they were very gracious to her. The brewery at Baslehurst stood on the outskirts of the town, in a narrow lane which led from the church into the High Street. This lane,—Brewery Lane, as it was called,—was not the main approach to the church; but from the lane there was a stile into the churchyard, and a gate, opened on Sundays, by which people on that side reached the church. From the opposite side of the churchyard a road led away to the foot of the High Street, and out towards the bridge which divided the town from the parish of Cawston. Along one side of this road there was a double row of elms, having a footpath beneath them. This old avenue began within the churchyard, running across the lower end of it, and was continued for some two hundred yards beyond its precincts. This, then, would be the way which Rachel would naturally take in going home, after leaving the Miss Tappitts at their door; but it was by no means the way which was the nearest for Mrs. Prime after leaving Miss Pucker's lodgings in the High Street, seeing that the High Street itself ran direct to Cawston bridge.

And it must also be explained that there was a third path out of the churchyard, not leading into any road, but going right away across the fields. The church stood rather high, so that the land sloped away from it towards the west, and the view there was very pretty. The path led down through a small field, with high hedgerows, and by orchards, to two little hamlets belonging to Baslehurst, and this was a favourite walk with the people of the town. It was here that Rachel had walked with the Miss Tappitts on that evening when Luke Rowan had first accompanied her as far as Cawston bridge, and it was here that they agreed to walk again on the Saturday when Rowan was supposed to be away at Exeter. Rachel was to come along under the elms, and was to meet her friends there, or in the churchyard, or, if not so, then she was to call for them at the brewery.

She found the three girls leaning against the rails near the churchyard stile. "We have been waiting ever so long," said Cherry, who was more specially Rachel's friend.

"Oh, but I said you were not to wait," said Rachel, "for I never am quite sure whether I can come."

"We knew you'd come," said Augusta, "because——"

"Because what?" asked Rachel.

"Because nothing," said Cherry. "She's only joking."

Rachel said nothing more, not having understood the point of the joke. The joke was this,—that Luke Rowan had come back from Exeter, and that Rachel was supposed to have heard of his return, and therefore that her coming for the walk was certain. But Augusta had not intended to be ill-natured, and had not really believed what she had been about to insinuate. "The fact is," said Martha, "that Mr. Rowan has come home; but I don't suppose we shall see anything of him this evening as he is busy with papa."

Rachel for a few minutes became silent and thoughtful. Her mind had not yet freed itself from the effects of her conversation with her mother, and she had been thinking of this young man during the whole of her solitary walk into town. But she had been thinking of him as we think of matters which need not put us to any immediate trouble. He was away at Exeter, and she would have time to decide whether or no she would admit his proffered intimacy before she should see him again. "I do so hope we shall be friends," he had said to her as he gave her his hand when they parted on Cawston bridge. And then he had muttered something, which she had not quite caught, as to Baslehurst being altogether another place to him since he had seen her. She had hurried home on that occasion with a feeling, half pleasant and half painful, that something out of the usual course had occurred to her. But, after all, it amounted to nothing. What was there that she could tell her mother? She had no special tale to tell, and yet she could not speak of young Rowan as she would have spoken of a chance acquaintance. Was she not conscious that he had pressed her hand warmly as he parted from her?

Rachel herself entertained much of that indefinite fear of young men which so strongly pervaded her mother's mind, and which, as regarded her sister, had altogether ceased to be indefinite. Rachel knew that they were the natural enemies of her special class, and that any kind of friendship might be allowed to her, except a friendship with any of them. And as she was a good girl, loving her mother, anxious to do well, guided by pure thoughts, she felt aware that Mr. Rowan should be shunned. Had it not been that he himself had told her that he was to be in Exeter, she would not have come out to walk with the brewery girls on that evening. What she might hereafter decide upon doing, how these affairs might be made to arrange themselves, she by no means could foresee;—but on that evening she had thought she would be safe, and therefore she had come out to walk.

"What do you think?" said Cherry; "we are going to have a party next week."

"It won't be till the week after," said Augusta.

"At any rate, we are going to have a party, and you must come. You'll get a regular invite, you know, when they're sent out. Mr. Rowan's mother and sister are coming down on a visit to us for a few days, and so we're going to be quite smart."

"I don't know about going to a party. I suppose it is for a dance?"

"Of course it is for a dance," said Martha.

"And of course you'll come and dance with Luke Rowan," said Cherry. Nothing could be more imprudent than Cherry Tappitt, and Augusta was beginning to be aware of this, though she had not been allowed to participate in her mother's schemes. After that, there was much talking about the party, but the conversation was chiefly kept up by the Tappitt girls. Rachel was almost sure that her mother would not like her to go to a dance, and was quite sure that her sister would oppose such iniquity with all her power; therefore she made no promise. But she listened as the list was repeated of those who were expected to come, and asked some few questions as to Mrs. Rowan and her daughter. Then, at a sudden turn of a lane, a lane that led back to the town by another route, they met Luke Rowan himself.

He was a cousin of the Tappitts, and therefore, though the relationship was not near, he had already assumed the privilege of calling them by their Christian names; and Martha, who was nearly thirty years old, and four years his senior, had taught herself to call him Luke; with the other two he was as yet Mr. Rowan. The greeting was of course very friendly, and he returned with them on their path. To Rachel he raised his hat, and then offered his hand. She had felt herself to be confused the moment she saw him,—so confused that she was not able to ask him how he was with ordinary composure. She was very angry with herself, and heartily wished that she was seated with the Dorcas women at Miss Pucker's. Any position would have been better for her than this, in which she was disgracing herself and showing that she could not bear herself

before this young man as though he were no more than an ordinary acquaintance. Her mind would revert to that hand-
squeezing, to those muttered words, and to her mother's caution. When he remarked to her that he had come back earlier
than he expected, she could not take his words as though they
signified nothing. His sudden return was a momentous fact to
her, putting her out of her usual quiet mode of thought. She
said little or nothing, and he, at any rate, did not observe that
she was confused; but she was herself so conscious of it, that
it seemed to her that all of them must have seen it.

Thus they sauntered along, back to the outskirts of the
town, and so into the brewery lane, by a route opposite to that
of the churchyard. The whole way they talked of nothing but
the party. Was Miss Rowan fond of dancing? Then by degrees
the girls called her Mary, declaring that as she was a cousin
they intended so to do. And Luke said that he ought to be
called by his Christian name; and the two younger girls agreed
that he was entitled to the privilege, only they would ask
mamma first; and in this way they were becoming very intimate. Rachel said but little, and perhaps not much that was
said was addressed specially to her, but she seemed to feel that
she was included in the friendliness of the gathering. Every
now and then Luke Rowan would address her, and his voice
was pleasant to her ears. He had made an effort to walk next
to her,—an attempt almost too slight to be called an effort,
which she had, almost unconsciously, frustrated, by so placing
herself that Augusta should be between them. Augusta was not
quite in a good humour, and said one or two words which were
slightly snubbing in their tendency; but this was more than
atoned for by Cherry's high good humour.

When they reached the brewery they all declared themselves to be very much astonished on learning that it was already past nine. Rachel's surprise, at any rate, was real. "I must
go home at once," she said; "I don't know what mamma will
think of me." And then, wishing them all good-bye, without
further delay she hurried on into the churchyard.

"I'll see you safe through the ghosts at any rate," said Rowan.

"I'm not a bit afraid of churchyard ghosts," said Rachel, moving on. But Rowan followed her.

"I've got to go into town to meet your father," said he to the other girls, "and I'll be back with him."

Augusta saw with some annoyance that he had overtaken Rachel before she had passed over the stile, and stood lingering at the door long enough to be aware that Luke was over first. "That girl is a flirt, after all," she said to her sister Martha.

Luke was over the stile first, and then turned round to assist Miss Ray. She could not refuse him her hand in such a position; or if she could have done so she lacked the presence of mind that was necessary for such refusal. "You must let me walk home with you," he said.

"Indeed I will do no such thing. You told Augusta that you were going to her papa in the town."

"So I am, but I will see you first as far as the bridge; you can't refuse me that."

" Indeed I can, and indeed I will. I beg you won't come. I am sure you would not wish to annoy me."

"Look," said he, pointing to the west; "did you ever see such a setting sun as that? Did you ever see such blood-red colour?" The light was very wonderful, for the sun had just gone down and all the western heavens were crimson with its departing glory. In the few moments that they stood there gazing it might almost have been believed that some portentous miracle had happened, so deep and dark, and yet so bright, were the hues of the horizon. It seemed as though the lands below the hill were bathed in blood. The elm trees interrupted their view, so that they could only look out through the spaces between their trunks. "Come to the stile," said he. "If you were to live a thousand years you might never again see such a sunset as that. You would never forgive yourself if you missed it, just that you might save three minutes."

Rachel stepped with him towards the stile; but it was not

solely his entreaty that made her do so. As he spoke of the sun's glory her sharp ear caught the sound of a woman's foot close to the stile over which she had passed, and knowing that she could not escape at once from Luke Rowan, she had left the main path through the churchyard, in order that the new comer might not see her there talking to him. So she accompanied him on till they stood between the trees, and then they remained encompassed as it were in the full light of the sun's rays. But if her ears had been sharp, so were the eyes of this new comer. And while she stood there with Rowan beneath the elms, her sister stood a while also on the churchyard path and recognized the figures of them both.

"Rachel," said he, after they had remained there in silence for a moment, "live as long as you may, never on God's earth will you look on any sight more lovely than that. Ah! do you see the man's arm, as it were; the deep purple cloud, like a huge hand stretched out from some other world to take you? Do you see it?"

The sound of his voice was very pleasant. His words to her young ears seemed full of poetry and sweet mysterious romance. He spoke to her as no one,—no man or woman,—had ever spoken to her before. She had a feeling, as painful as it was delicious, that the man's words were sweet with a sweetness which she had known in her dreams. He had asked her a question, and repeated it, so that she was all but driven to answer him; but still she was full of the one great fact that he had called her Rachel, and that he must be rebuked for so calling her. But how could she rebuke a man who had bid her look at God's beautiful works in such language as he had used?

"Yes, I see it; it is very grand; but——"

"There were the fingers, but you see how they are melting away. The arm is there still, but the hand is gone. You and I can trace it because we saw it when it was clear, but we could not now show it to another. I wonder whether any one else saw that hand and arm, or only you and I. I should like to think that it was shown to us, and us only."

It was impossible for her now to go back upon that word Rachel. She must pass it by as though she had not heard it. "All the world might have seen it had they looked," said she.

"Perhaps not. Do you think that all eyes can see alike?"

"Well, yes; I suppose so."

"All eyes will see a loaf of bread alike, or a churchyard stile, but all eyes will not see the clouds alike. Do you not often find worlds among the clouds? I do."

"Worlds!" she said, amazed at his energy; and then she bethought herself that he was right. She would never have seen that hand and arm had he not been there to show it her. So she gazed down upon the changing colours of the horizon, and almost forgot that she should not have lingered there a moment.

And yet there was a strong feeling upon her that she was sinking,—sinking,—sinking away into iniquity. She ought not to have stood there an instant, she ought not to have been there with him at all;—and yet she lingered. Now that she was there she hardly knew how to move herself away.

"Yes; worlds among the clouds," he continued; but before he did so there had been silence between them for a minute or two. "Do you never feel that you look into other worlds beyond this one in which you eat, and drink, and sleep? Have you no other worlds in your dreams?" Yes; such dreams she had known, and now, she almost thought that she could remember to have seen strange forms in the clouds. She knew that henceforth she would watch the clouds and find them there. She looked down into the flood of light beneath her, with a full consciousness that he was close to her, touching her; with a full consciousness that every moment that she lingered there was a new sin; with a full consciousness, too, that the beauty of those fading colours seen thus in his presence possessed a charm, a sense of soft delight, which she had never known before. At last she uttered a long sigh.

"Why, what ails you?" said he.

"Oh, I must go; I have been so wrong to stand here. Goodbye; pray, pray do not come with me."

"But you will shake hands with me." Then he got her hand, and held it. "Why should it be wrong for you to stand and look at the sunset? Am I an ogre? Have I done anything that should make you afraid of me?"

"Do not hold me. Mr. Rowan, I did not think you would behave like that." The gloom of the evening was now coming on, and though but a few minutes had passed since Mrs. Prime had walked through the churchyard, she would not have been able to recognize them had she walked there now. "It is getting dark, and I must go instantly."

"Let me go with you, then, as far as the bridge."

"No, no, no. Pray do not vex me."

"I will not. You shall go alone. But stand while I say one word to you. Why should you be afraid of me?"

"I am not afraid of you,—at least,—you know what I mean."

"I wonder,—I wonder whether—you dislike me."

"I don't dislike anybody. Good night."

He had however again got her hand. "I'll tell you why I ask; —because I like you so much, so very much! Why should we not be friends? Well; there. I will not trouble you now. I will not stir from here till you are out of sight. But mind,—remember this; I intend that you shall like me."

She was gone from him, fleeing away along the path in a run while the last words were being spoken; and yet, though they were spoken in a low voice, she heard and remembered every syllable. What did the man mean by saying that he intended that she should like him? Like him! How could she fail of liking him? Only was it not incumbent on her to take some steps which might save her from ever seeing him again? Like him, indeed! What was the meaning of the word? Had he intended to ask her to love him? And if so, what answer must she make?

How beautiful had been those clouds! As soon as she was beyond the church wall, so that she could look again to the west, she gazed with all her eyes to see if there were still a remnant left of that arm. No; it had all melted into a monstrous shape, indistinct and gloomy, partaking of the darkness of night. The brightness of the vision was gone. But he bade her look into the clouds for new worlds, and she seemed to feel that there was a hidden meaning in his words. As she looked out into the coming darkness, a mystery crept over her, a sense of something wonderful that was out there, away,—of something so full of mystery that she could not tell whether she was thinking of the hidden distances of the horizon, or of the distances of her own future life, which were still further off and more closely hidden. She found herself trembling, sighing, almost sobbing, and then she ran again. He had wrapped her in his influence, and filled her full of the magnetism of his own being. Her woman's weakness,—the peculiar susceptibility of her nature, had never before been touched. She had now heard the first word of romance that had ever reached her ears, and it had fallen upon her with so great a power that she was overwhelmed.

Words of romance! Words direct from the Evil One, Mrs. Prime would have called them! And in saying so she would have spoken the belief of many a good woman and many a good man. She herself was a good woman,—a sincere, honest, hard-working, self-denying woman; a woman who struggled hard to do her duty as she believed it had been taught to her. She, as she walked through the churchyard,—having come down the brewery lane with some inkling that her sister might be there,—had been struck with horror at seeing Rachel standing with that man. What should she do? She paused a moment to ask herself whether she should return for her; but she said to herself that her sister was obstinate, that a scene would be occasioned, that she would do no good,—and so she passed on. Words of romance, indeed! Must not all such words be words from the Father of Lies, seeing that they are words of falseness? Some such thoughts passed through her mind as she walked home, thinking of her sister's iniquity,—of her sister who must be saved, like a brand from the fire, but whose saving could now be effected only by the sternest of discipline.

The hours at the Dorcas meetings must be made longer, and Rachel must always be there.

In the mean time Rachel hurried home with her spirits all a-tremble. Of her immediately-coming encounter with her mother and her sister she hardly thought much before she reached the door. She thought only of him, how beautiful he was, how grand,—and how dangerous; of him and of his words, how beautiful they were, how grand, and how terribly danger-ous! She knew that it was very late and she hurried her steps. She knew that her mother must be appeased, and her sister must be opposed,—but neither to her mother or to her sister was given the depth of her thoughts. She was still thinking of him, and of the man's arm in the clouds, when she opened the door of the cottage at Bragg's End.

CHAPTER IV

What Shall Be Done about It?

RACHEL WAS STILL THINKING of Luke Rowan and of the man's arm when she opened the cottage door, but the sight of her sister's face, and the tone of her sister's voice, soon brought her back to a full consciousness of her immediate present posi-tion. "Oh, Dolly, do not speak with that terrible voice, as though the world were coming to an end," she said, in answer to the first note of objurgation that was uttered; but the notes that came afterwards were so much more terrible, so much more severe, that Rachel found herself quite unable to stop them by any would-be joking tone.

Mrs. Prime was desirous that her mother should speak the words of censure that must be spoken. She would have pre-ferred herself to remain silent, knowing that she could be as se-vere in her silence as in her speech, if only her mother would use the occasion as it should be used. Mrs. Ray had been made to feel how great was the necessity for outspoken severity; but when the moment came, and her dear beautiful child stood there before her, she could not utter the words with which she had been already prompted. "Oh, Rachel," she said, "Dorothea tells me——" and then she stopped.

"What has Dorothea told you?" asked Rachel.

"I have told her," said Mrs. Prime, now speaking out, "that I saw you standing alone an hour since with that young man, —in the churchyard. And yet you had said that he was to have been away in Exeter!"

Rachel's cheeks and forehead were now suffused with red. We used to think, when we pretended to read the faces of our neighbours, that a rising blush betrayed a conscious falsehood. For the most part we know better now, and have learned to decipher more accurately the outward signs which are given by the impulses of the heart. An unmerited accusation of untruth will ever bring the blood to the face of the young and innocent. But Mrs. Ray was among the ignorant in this matter, and she groaned inwardly when she saw her child's confusion.

"Oh, Rachel, is it true?" she said.

"Is what true, mamma? It is true that Mr. Rowan spoke to me in the churchyard, though I did not know that Dorothea was acting as a spy on me."

"Rachel, Rachel!" said the mother.

"It is very necessary that some one should act the spy on you," said the sister. "A spy, indeed! You think to anger me by using such a word, but I will not be angered by any words. I went there to look after you, fearing that there was occasion,— fearing it, but hardly thinking it. Now we know that there was occasion."

"There was no occasion," said Rachel, looking into her sister's face with eyes of which the incipient strength was becoming manifest. "There was no occasion. Oh, mamma, you do not think there was an occasion for watching me?"

"Why did you say that that young man was at Exeter?" asked Mrs. Prime.

"Because he had told me that he would be there;—he had told us all so, as we were walking together. He came to-day instead of coming to-morrow. What would you say if I questioned you in that way about your friends?" Then, when the words had passed from her lips, she remembered that she should not have called Mr. Rowan her friend. She had never called him so, in thinking of him, to herself. She had never admitted that she had any regard for him. She had acknowledged to herself that it would be very dangerous to entertain friendship for such as he.

"Friend, Rachel!" said Mrs. Prime. "If you look for such friendship as that, who can say what will come to you?"

"I haven't looked for it. I haven't looked for anything. People do get to know each other without any looking, and they can't help it."

Then Mrs. Prime took off her bonnet and her shawl, and Rachel laid down her hat and her little light summer cloak; but it must not be supposed that the war was suspended during these operations. Mrs. Prime was aware that a great deal more must be said, but she was very anxious that her mother should say it. Rachel also knew that much more would be said, and she was by no means anxious that the subject should be dropped, if only she could talk her mother over to her side.

"If mother thinks it right," exclaimed Mrs. Prime, "that you should be standing alone with a young man after nightfall in the churchyard, then I have done. In that case I will say no more. But I must tell her, and I must tell you also, that if it is to be so, I cannot remain at the cottage any longer."

"Oh, Dorothea!" said Mrs. Ray.

"Indeed, mother, I cannot. If Rachel is not hindered from such meetings by her own sense of what is right, she must be hindered by the authority of those older than herself."

"Hindered,—hindered from what?" said Rachel, who felt that her tears were coming, but struggled hard to retain them. "Mamma, I have done nothing that was wrong. Mamma, you will believe me, will you not?"

Mrs. Ray did not know what to say. She strove to believe both of them, though the words of one were directly at variance with the words of the other.

"Do you mean to claim it as your right," said Mrs. Prime, "to be standing out there alone at any hour of the night, with any young man that you please? If so, you cannot be my sister."

"I do not want to be your sister if you think such hard things," said Rachel, whose tears now could no longer be restrained. Honi soit qui mal y pense. She did not, at the moment, remember the words to speak them, but they contain exactly the purport of her thought. And now, having become conscious of her own weakness by reason of these tears which would overwhelm her, she determined that she would say nothing further till she pleaded her cause before her mother alone. How could she describe before her sister the way in which that interview at the churchyard stile had been brought about? But she could kneel at her mother's feet and tell her everything;— she thought, at least, that she could tell her mother everything. She occupied generally the same bedroom as her sister; but, on certain occasions,—if her mother was unwell or the like,— she would sleep in her mother's room. "Mamma," she said, "you will let me sleep with you to-night. I will go now, and when you come I will tell you everything. Good night to you, Dolly."

"Good night, Rachel"; and the voice of Mrs. Prime, as she bade her sister adieu for the evening, sounded as the voice of the ravens.

The two widows sat in silence for a while, each waiting for the other to speak. Then Mrs. Prime got up and folded her shawl very carefully, and carefully put her bonnet and gloves down upon it. It was her habit to be very careful with her clothes, but in her anger she had almost thrown them upon the little sofa. "Will you have anything before you go to bed, Dorothea?" said Mrs. Ray. "Nothing, thank you," said Mrs. Prime; and her voice was very like the voice of the ravens. Then Mrs. Ray began to think it possible that she might escape away to Rachel without any further words. "I am very tired," she said, "and I think I will go, Dorothea."

"Mother," said Mrs. Prime, "something must be done about this."

"Yes, my dear; she will talk to me to-night, and tell it me all."

"But will she tell you the truth?"

"She never told me a falsehood yet, Dorothea. I'm sure she didn't know that the young man was to be here. You know if he did come back from Exeter before he said he would she couldn't help it."

"And do you mean that she couldn't help being with him there,—all alone? Mother, what would you think of any other girl of whom you heard such a thing?"

Mrs. Ray shuddered; and then some thought, some shadow perhaps of a remembrance, flitted across her mind, which seemed to have the effect of palliating her child's iniquity. "Suppose—" she said. "Suppose what?" said Mrs. Prime, sternly. But Mrs. Ray did not dare to go on with her supposition. She did not dare to suggest that Mr. Rowan might perhaps be a very proper young man, and that the two young people might be growing fond of each other in a proper sort of way. She hardly believed in any such propriety herself, and she knew that her daughter would scout it to the winds. "Suppose what?" said Mrs. Prime again, more sternly than before. "If the other girls left her and went away to the brewery, perhaps she could not have helped it," said Mrs. Ray.

"But she was not walking with him. Her face was not turned towards home even. They were standing together under the trees, and, judging from the time at which I got home, they must have remained together for nearly half an hour afterwards. And this with a perfect stranger, mother,—a man whose name she had never mentioned to us till she was told how Miss Pucker had seen them together! You cannot suppose that I want to make her out worse than she is. She is your child, and my sister; and we are bound together for weal or for woe."

"You talked about going away and leaving us," said Mrs. Ray, speaking in soreness rather than in anger.

"So I did; and so I must, unless something be done. It could not be right that I should remain here, seeing such things, if my voice is not allowed to be heard. But though I did go, she would still be my sister. I should still share the sorrow,—and the shame."

"Oh, Dorothea, do not say such words."

"But they must be said, mother. Is it not from such meetings that shame comes,—shame, and sorrow, and sin? You love her dearly, and so do I; and are we therefore to allow her to be a castaway? Those whom you love you must chastise. I have no authority over her,—as she has told me, more than once already,—and therefore I say again, that unless all this be stopped, I must leave the cottage. Good night, now, mother. I hope you will speak to her in earnest." Then Mrs. Prime took her candle and went her way.

For ten minutes the mother sat herself down, thinking of the condition of her youngest daughter, and trying to think what words she would use when she found herself in her daughter's presence. Sorrow, and Shame, and Sin! Her child a castaway! What terrible words they were! And yet there had been nothing that she could allege in answer to them. That comfortable idea of a decent husband for her child had been banished from her mind almost before it had been entertained. Then she thought of Rachel's eyes, and knew that she would not be able to assume a perfect mastery over her girl. When the ten minutes were over she had made up her mind to nothing, and then she also took up her candle and went to her room. When she first entered it she did not see Rachel. She had silently closed the door and come some steps within the chamber before her child showed herself from behind the bed. "Mamma," she said, "put down the candle that I may speak to you." Whereupon Mrs. Ray put down the candle, and Rachel took hold of both her arms. "Mamma, you do not believe ill of me; do you? You do not think of me the things that Dorothea says? Say that you do not, or I shall die."

"My darling, I have never thought anything bad of you before."

"And do you think bad of me now? Did you not tell me before I went out that you would trust me, and have you so soon forgotten your trust? Look at me, mamma. What have I ever done that you should think me to be such as she says?"

"I do not think that you have done anything; but you are very young, Rachel."

"Young, mamma! I am older than you were when you married, and older than Dolly was. I am old enough to know what is wrong. Shall I tell you what happened this evening? He came and met us all in the fields. I knew before that he had come back, for the girls had said so, but I thought that he was in Exeter when I left here. Had I not believed that, I should not have gone. I think I should not have gone."

"Then you are afraid of him?"

"No, mamma; I am not afraid of him. But he says such strange things to me; and I would not purposely have gone out to meet him. He came to us in the fields, and then we returned up the lane to the brewery, and there we left the girls. As I went through the churchyard he came there too, and then the sun was setting, and he stopped me to look at it; I did stop with him,—for a few moments, and I felt ashamed of myself; but how was I to help it? Mamma, if I could remember them I would tell you every word he said to me, and every look of his face. He asked me to be his friend. Mamma, if you will believe in me I will tell you everything. I will never deceive you."

She was still holding her mother's arms while she spoke. Now she held her very close and nestled in against her bosom, and gradually got her cheek against her mother's cheek, and her lips against her mother's neck. How could any mother refuse such a caress as that, or remain hard and stern against such signs of love? Mrs. Ray, at any rate, was not possessed of strength to do so. She was vanquished, and put her arm round her girl and embraced her. She spoke soft words, and told Rachel that she was her dear, dear, dearest darling. She was still awed and dismayed by the tidings which she had heard of the young man; she still thought there was some terrible danger against which it behoved them all to be on their guard. But she no longer felt herself divided from her child, and had ceased to believe in the necessity of those terrible words which Mrs. Prime had used.

"You will believe me?" said Rachel. "You will not think that I am making up stories to deceive you?" Then the mother assured the daughter with many kisses that she would believe her.

After that they sat long into the night, discussing all that Luke Rowan had said, and the discussion certainly took place after a fashion that would not have been considered satisfactory by Mrs. Prime had she heard it. Mrs. Ray was soon led into talking about Mr. Rowan as though he were not a wolf,— as though he might possibly be neither a wolf ravenous with his native wolfish fur and open wolfish greed; or, worse than that, a wolf, more ravenous still, in sheep's clothing. There was no word spoken of him as a lover; but Rachel told her mother that the man had called her by her Christian name, and Mrs. Ray had fully understood the sign. "My darling, you mustn't let him do that." "No, mamma; I won't. But he went on talking so fast that I had not time to stop him, and after that it was not worth while." The project of the party was also told to Mrs. Ray, and Rachel, sitting now with her head upon her mother's lap, owned that she would like to go to it. "Parties are not always wicked, mamma," she said. To this assertion Mrs. Ray expressed an undecided assent, but intimated her decided belief that very many parties were wicked. "There will be dancing, and I do not like that," said Mrs. Ray. "Yet I was taught dancing at school," said Rachel. When the matter had gone so far as this it must be acknowledged that Rachel had done much towards securing her share of mastery over her mother. "He will be there, of course," said Mrs. Ray. "Oh, yes;

he will be there," said Rachel. "But why should I be afraid of him? Why should I live as though I were afraid to meet him? Dolly thinks that I should be shut up close, to be taken care of; but you do not think of me like that. If I was minded to be bad, shutting me up would not keep me from it." Such arguments as these from Rachel's mouth sounded, at first, very terrible to Mrs. Ray, but yet she yielded to them.

On the next morning Rachel was down first, and was found by her sister fast engaged on the usual work of the house, as though nothing out of the way had occurred on the previous evening. "Good morning, Dolly," she said, and then went on arranging the things on the breakfast-table. "Good morning, Rachel," said Mrs. Prime, still speaking like a raven. There was not a word said between them about the young man or the churchyard, and at nine o'clock Mrs. Ray came down to them, dressed ready for church. They seated themselves and ate their breakfast together, and still not a word was said.

It was Mrs. Prime's custom to go to morning service at one of the churches in Baslehurst; not at the old parish church which stood in the churchyard near the brewery, but at a new church which had been built as auxiliary to the other, and at which the Rev. Samuel Prong was the ministering clergyman. As we shall have occasion to know Mr. Prong it may be as well to explain here that he was not simply a curate to old Dr. Harford, the rector of Baslehurst. He had a separate district of his own, which had been divided from the old parish, not exactly in accordance with the rector's good pleasure. Dr. Harford had held the living for more than forty years; he had held it for nearly forty years before the division had been made, and he had thought that the parish should remain a parish entire, —more especially as the presentation to the new benefice was not conceded to him. Therefore Dr. Harford did not love Mr. Prong.

But Mrs. Prime did love him,—with that sort of love which devout women bestow upon the church minister of their choice. Mr. Prong was an energetic, severe, hard-working, and,

I fear, intolerant young man, who bestowed very much laudable care upon his sermons. The care and industry were laudable, but not so the pride with which he thought of them and their results. He spoke much of preaching the Gospel, and was sincere beyond all doubt in his desire to do so; but he allowed himself to be led away into a belief that his brethren in the ministry around him did not preach the Gospel,—that they were careless shepherds, or shepherds' dogs indifferent to the wolf, and in this way he had made himself unpopular among the clergy and gentry of the neighbourhood. It may well be understood that such a man coming down upon a district, cut out almost from the centre of Dr. Harford's parish, would be a thorn in the side of that old man. But Mr. Prong had his circle of friends, of very ardent friends, and among them Mrs. Prime was one of the most ardent. For the last year or two she had always attended morning service at his church, and very frequently had gone there twice in the day, though the walk was long and tedious, taking her the whole length of the town of Baslehurst. And there had been some little uneasiness between Mrs. Ray and Mrs. Prime on the matter of this church attendance. Mrs. Prime had wished her mother and sister to have the benefit of Mr. Prong's eloquence; but Mrs. Ray, though she was weak in morals, was strong in her determination to adhere to Mr. Comfort of Cawston. It had been matter of great sorrow to her that her daughter should leave Mr. Comfort's church, and she had positively declined to be taken out of her own parish. Rachel had, of course, stuck to her mother in this controversy, and had said some sharp things about Mr. Prong. She declared that Mr. Prong had been educated at Islington, and that sometimes he forgot his "h's." When such things were said Mrs. Prime would wax very angry, and would declare that no one could be saved by the perfection of Dr. Harford's pronunciation. But there was no question as to Dr. Harford, and no justification for the introduction of his name into the dispute. Mrs. Prime, however, did not choose to say anything against Mr. Comfort, with whom her husband had been curate, and who, in her younger days, had been a light to her own feet. Mr. Comfort was by no means such a one as Dr. Harford, though the two old men were friends. Mr. Comfort had been regarded as a Calvinist when he was young, as Evangelical in middle life, and was still known as a Low Churchman in his old age. Therefore Mrs. Prime would spare him in her sneers, though she left his ministry. He had become lukewarm, but not absolutely stone cold, like the old rector at Baslehurst. So said Mrs. Prime. Old men would become lukewarm, and therefore she could pardon Mr. Comfort. But Dr. Harford had never been warm at all,—had never been warm with the warmth which she valued. Therefore she scorned him and sneered at him. In return for which Rachel scorned Mr. Prong and sneered at him.

But though it was Mrs. Prime's custom to go to church at Baslehurst, on this special Sunday she declared her intention of accompanying her mother to Cawston. Not a word had been said about the young man, and they all started off on their walk together in silence and gloom. With such thoughts as they had in their mind it was impossible that they should make the journey pleasantly. Rachel had counted on the walk with her mother, and had determined that everything should be pleasant. She would have said a word or two about Luke Rowan, and would have gradually reconciled her mother to his name. But as it was she said nothing; and it may be feared that her mind, during the period of her worship, was not at charity with her sister. Mr. Comfort preached his half-hour as usual, and then they all walked home. Dr. Harford never exceeded twenty minutes, and had often been known to finish his discourse within ten. What might be the length of a sermon of Mr. Prong's no man or woman could foretell, but he never spared himself or his congregation much under an hour.

They all walked home gloomily to their dinner, and ate their cold mutton and potatoes in sorrow and sadness. It seemed as though no sort of conversation was open to them. They could not talk of their usual Sunday subjects. Their minds were full of one matter, and it seemed that that matter was by common consent to be banished from their lips for the day. In the evening, after tea, the two sisters again went up to Cawston church, leaving their mother with her Bible;— but hardly a word was spoken between them, and in the same silence they sat till bed-time. To Mrs. Ray and to Rachel it had been one of the saddest, dreariest days that either of them had ever known. I doubt whether the suffering of Mrs. Prime was so great. She was kept up by the excitement of feeling that some great crisis was at hand. If Rachel were not made amenable to authority she would leave the cottage.

When Rachel had run with hurrying steps from the stile in the churchyard, she left Luke Rowan still standing there. He watched her till she crossed into the lane, and then he turned and again looked out upon the still ruddy line of the horizon. The blaze of light was gone, but there were left, high up in the heavens, those wonderful hues which tinge with softly-changing colour the edges of the clouds when the brightness of some glorious sunset has passed away. He sat himself on the wooden rail, watching till all of it should be over, and thinking, with lazy half-formed thoughts, of Rachel Ray. He did not ask himself what he meant by assuring her of his friendship, and by claiming hers, but he declared to himself that she was very lovely,—more lovely than beautiful, and then smiled inwardly at the prettiness of her perturbed spirit. He remembered well that he had called her Rachel, and that she had allowed his doing so to pass by without notice; but he understood also how and why she had done so. He knew that she had been flurried, and that she had skipped the thing because she had not known the moment at which to make her stand. He gave himself credit for no undue triumph, nor her discredit for any undue easiness. "What a woman she is!" he said to himself; "so womanly in everything." Then his mind rambled away to other subjects, possibly to the practicability of making good beer instead of bad.

He was a young man, by no means of a bad sort, meaning

to do well, with high hopes in life, one who had never wronged a woman, or been untrue to a friend, full of energy and hope and pride. But he was conceited, prone to sarcasm, sometimes cynical, and perhaps sometimes affected. It may be that he was not altogether devoid of that Byronic weakness which was so much more prevalent among young men twenty years since than it is now. His two trades had been those of an attorney and a brewer, and yet he dabbled in romance, and probably wrote poetry in his bedroom. Nevertheless, there were worse young men about Baslehurst than Luke Rowan.

"And now for Mr. Tappitt," said he, as he slowly took his legs from off the railing.

CHAPTER V

Mr. Comfort Gives His Advice

MRS. TAPPITT was very full of her party. It had grown in her mind as those things do grow, till it had come to assume almost the dimensions of a ball. When Mrs. Tappitt first consulted her husband and obtained his permission for the gathering, it was simply intended that a few of her daughters' friends should be brought together to make the visit cheerful for Miss Rowan; but the mistress of the house had become ambitious; two fiddles, with a German horn, were to be introduced because the piano would be troublesome; the drawing-room carpet was to be taken up, and there was to be a supper in the dining-room. The thing in its altered shape loomed large by degrees upon Mr. Tappitt, and he found himself unable to stop its growth. The word "ball" would have been fatal; but Mrs. Tappitt was too good a general, and the girls were too judicious as lieutenants, to commit themselves by the presumption of any such term. It was still Mrs. Tappitt's evening tea-party, but it was understood in Baslehurst that Mrs. Tappitt's evening tea-party was to be something considerable.

A great success had attended this lady at the onset of her
scheme. Mrs. Butler Cornbury had called at the brewery, and
had promised that she would come, and that she would bring
some of the Cornbury family. Now Mr. Butler Cornbury was
the eldest son of the most puissant squire within five miles of
Baslehurst, and was indeed almost as good as squire himself,
his father being a very old man. Mrs. Butler Cornbury had, it
is true, not been esteemed as holding any very high rank while
shining as a beauty under the name of Patty Comfort; but she
had taken kindly to her new honours, and was now reckoned
as a considerable magnate in that part of the county. She did
not customarily join in the festivities of the town, and held herself aloof from people even of higher standing than the Tappitts. But she was an ambitious woman, and had inspired her
lord with the desire of representing Baslehurst in Parliament.
There would be an election at Baslehurst in the coming au-
tumn, and Mrs. Cornbury was already preparing for the fight.
Hence had arisen her visit at the brewery, and hence also her
ready acquiescence in Mrs. Tappitt's half-pronounced request.

The party was to be celebrated on a Tuesday,—Tuesday
week after that Sunday which was passed so uncomfortably at
Bragg's End; and on the Monday Mrs. Tappitt and her daughters sat conning over the list of their expected guests, and preparing their invitations. It must be understood that the Rowan
family had somewhat grown upon them in estimation since
Luke had been living with them. They had not known much
of him till he came among them, and had been prepared to
patronise him; but they found him a young man not to be
patronised by any means, and imperceptibly they learned to
feel that his mother and sister would have to be esteemed by
them rather as great ladies. Luke was in nowise given to boasting, and had no intention of magnifying his mother and sister;
but things had been said which made the Tappitts feel that
Mrs. Rowan must have the best bedroom, and that Mary
Rowan must be provided with the best partners.

"And what shall we do about Rachel Ray?" said Martha,

who was sitting with the list before her. Augusta, who was leaning over her sister, puckered up her mouth and said nothing. She had watched from the house door on that Saturday evening, and had been perfectly aware that Luke Rowan had taken Rachel off towards the stile under the trees. She could not bring herself to say anything against Rachel, but she certainly wished that she might be excluded.

"Of course she must be asked," said Cherry. Cherry was sitting opposite to the other girls writing on a lot of envelopes the addresses of the notes which were afterwards to be prepared. "We told her we should ask her." And as she spoke she addressed a cover to "Miss Ray, Bragg's End Cottage, Cawston."

"Stop a moment, my dear," said Mrs. Tappitt from the corner of the sofa on which she was sitting. "Put that aside, Cherry. Rachel Ray is all very well, but considering all things I am not sure that she will quite do for Tuesday night. It's not quite in her line, I think."

"But we have mentioned it to her already, mamma," said Martha.

"Of course we did," said Cherry. "It would be the meanest thing in the world not to ask her now!"

"I am not at all sure that Mrs. Rowan would like it," said Mrs. Tappitt.

"And I don't think that Rachel is quite up to what Mary has been used to," said Augusta.

"If she has half a mind to flirt with Luke already," said Mrs. Tappitt, "I ought not to encourage it."

"That is such nonsense, mamma," said Cherry. "If he likes her he'll find her somewhere if he doesn't find her here."

"My dear, you shouldn't say that what I say is nonsense," said Mrs. Tappitt.

"But, mamma, when we have already asked her!—Besides, she is a lady," said Cherry.

"I can't say that I think Mrs. Butler Cornbury would wish to meet her," said Mrs. Tappitt.

"Mrs. Butler Cornbury's father is their particular friend,"
said Martha. "Mrs. Ray always goes to Mr. Comfort's parties."

In this way the matter was discussed, and at last Cherry's
eagerness and Martha's sense of justice carried the day. The
envelope which Cherry had addressed was brought into use,
and the note to Rachel was deposited in the post with all those
other notes, the destination of which was too far to be reached
by the brewery boy without detrimental interference with the
brewery work. We will continue our story by following the
note which was delivered by the Cawston postman at Bragg's
End about seven o'clock on the Tuesday morning. It was delivered into Rachel's own hand, and read by her as she stood
by the kitchen dresser before either her mother or Mrs. Prime
had come down from their rooms. There still was sadness and
gloom at Bragg's End. During all the Monday there had been
no comfort in the house, and Rachel had continued to share
her mother's bedroom. At intervals, when Rachel had been
away, much had been said between Mrs. Ray and Mrs. Prime;
but no conclusion had been reached; no line of conduct had
received their joint adhesion; and the threat remained that
Mrs. Prime would leave the cottage. Mrs. Ray, while listening
to her elder daughter's words, still continued to fear that evil
spirits were hovering around them; but yet she would not consent to order Rachel to become a devout attendant at the Dorcas meetings. Monday had not been a Dorcas day, and therefore it had been very dull and very tedious.

Rachel stood a while with the note in her hand, fearing
that the contest must be brought on again and fought out to
an end before she could send her answer to it. She had told
her mother that she was to be invited, and Mrs. Ray had lacked
the courage at the moment which would have been necessary
for an absolute and immediate rejection of the proposition. If
Mrs. Prime had not been with them in the house, Rachel little
doubted but that she might have gone to the party. If Mrs.
Prime had not been there, Rachel, as she was now gradually
becoming aware, might have had her own way almost in ev-

erything. Without the support which Mrs. Prime gave her,
Mrs. Ray would have gradually slid down from that stern code
of morals which she had been induced to adopt by the teaching of those around her, and would have entered upon a new
school of teaching under Rachel's tutelage. But Mrs. Prime was
still there, and Rachel herself was not inclined to fight, if fighting could be avoided. So she put the note into her pocket, and
neither answered it or spoke of it till Mrs. Prime had started
on her after-dinner walk into Baslehurst. Then she brought it
forth and read it to her mother. "I suppose I ought to answer
it by the post this evening, mamma?"

"Oh, dear, this evening! that's very short."

"It can be put off till to-morrow if there's any good in putting it off," said Rachel. Mrs. Ray seemed to think that there
might be good in putting it off, or rather that there would be
harm in doing it at once.

"Do you particularly want to go, my dear?" Mrs. Ray said,
after a pause.

"Yes, mamma; I should like to go." Then Mrs. Ray uttered
a little sound which betokened uneasiness, and was again silent for a while.

"I can't understand why you want to go to this place,—so
particularly. You never used to care about such things. You
know your sister won't like it, and I'm not at all sure that you
ought to go."

"I'll tell you why I wish it particularly, only——"

"Well, my dear."

"I don't know whether I can make you understand just
what I mean."

"If you tell me, I shall understand, I suppose."

Rachel considered her words for a moment or two before
she spoke, and then she endeavoured to explain herself. "It
isn't that I care for this party especially, mamma, though I own
that, after what the girls have said, I should like to be there;
but I feel——"

"You feel what, my dear?"

"It is this, mamma. Dolly and I do not agree about these things, and I don't intend to let her manage me just in the way she thinks right."

"Oh, Rachel!"

"Well, mamma, would you wish it? If you could tell me that you really think it wrong to go to parties, I would give them up. Indeed it wouldn't be very much to give up, for I don't often get the chance. But you don't say so. You only say that I had better not go, because Dolly doesn't like it. Now, I won't be ruled by her. Don't look at me in that way, mamma. Is it right that I should be?"

"You have heard what she says about going away."

"I shall be very sorry if she goes, and I hope she won't; but I can't think that her threatening you in that way ought to make any difference. And—I'll tell you more; I do particularly wish to go to Mrs. Tappitt's, because of all that Dolly has said about,—about Mr. Rowan. I wish to show her and you that I am not afraid to meet him. Why should I be afraid of any one?"

"You should be afraid of doing wrong."

"Yes; and if it were wrong to meet any other young man I ought not to go; but there is nothing specially wrong in my meeting him. She has said very unkind things about it, and I intend that she shall know that I will not notice them." As Rachel spoke Mrs. Ray looked up at her, and was surprised by the expression of unrelenting purpose which she saw there. There had come over her face that motion in her eyes and that arching of her brows which Mrs. Ray had seen before, but which hitherto she had hardly construed into their true meaning. Now she was beginning to construe these signs aright, and to understand that there would be difficulty in managing her little family.

The conversation ended in an undertaking on Rachel's part that she would not answer the note till the following day. "Of course that means," said Rachel, "that I am to answer it just as Dolly thinks fit." But she repented of these words as

soon as they were spoken, and repented of them almost in
ashes when her mother declared, with tears in her eyes, that it
was not her intention to be guided by Dorothea in this matter.
"You ought not to say such things as that, Rachel," she said.
"No, mamma, I ought not; for there is no one so good as you
are; and if you'll say that you think I ought not to go, I'll write
to Cherry, and explain it to her at once. I don't care a bit about
the party,—as far as the party is concerned." But Mrs. Ray
would not now pronounce any injunction on the matter. She
had made up her mind as to what she would do. She would
call upon Mr. Comfort at the parsonage, explain the whole
thing to him, and be guided altogether by his counsel.

Not a word was said in the cottage about the invitation
when Mrs. Prime came back in the evening, nor was a word
said on the following morning. Mrs. Ray had declared her intention of going up to the parsonage, and neither of her daughters had asked her why she was going. Rachel had no need to
ask, for she well understood her mother's purpose. As to Mrs.
Prime, she was in these days black and full of gloom, asking
but few questions, watching the progress of events with the
eyes of an evil-singing prophetess, but keeping back her words
till the moment should come in which she would be driven by
her inner impulses to speak them forth with terrible strength.
When the breakfast was over, Mrs. Ray took her bonnet and
started forth to the parsonage.

I do not know that a widow, circumstanced as was Mrs.
Ray, could do better than go to her clergyman for advice, but
nevertheless, when she got to Mr. Comfort's gate she felt that
the task of explaining her purpose would not be without difficulty. It would be necessary to tell everything; how Rachel had
become suddenly an object of interest to Mr. Luke Rowan,
how Dorothea suspected terrible things, and how Rachel was
anxious for the world's vanities. The more she thought over it,
the more sure she felt that Mr. Comfort would put an embargo upon the party. It seemed but yesterday that he had
been telling her, with all his pulpit unction, that the pleasures

of this world should never be allowed to creep near the heart. With doubting feet and doubting heart she walked up to the parsonage door, and almost immediately found herself in the presence of her husband's old friend.

Whatever faults there might be in Mr. Comfort's character, he was at any rate good-natured and patient. That he was sincere, too, no one who knew him well had ever doubted,—sincere, that is, as far as his intentions went. When he endeavoured to teach his flock that they should despise money, he thought that he despised it himself. When he told the little children that this world should be as nothing to them, he did not remember that he himself enjoyed keenly the good things of this world. If he had a fault it was perhaps this,—that he was a hard man at a bargain. He liked to have all his temporalities, and make them go as far as they could be stretched. There was the less excuse for this, seeing that his children were well, and even richly, settled in life, and that his wife, should she ever be left a widow, would have ample provision for her few remaining years. He had given his daughter a considerable fortune, without which perhaps the Cornbury Grange people would not have welcomed her so kindly as they had done, and now, as he was still growing rich, it was supposed that he would leave her more.

He listened to Mrs. Ray with the greatest attention, having first begged her to recruit her strength with a glass of wine. As she continued to tell her story he interrupted her from time to time with good-natured little words, and then, when she had done, he asked after Luke Rowan's worldly means. "The young man has got something, I suppose," said he.

"Got something!" repeated Mrs. Ray, not exactly catching his meaning.

"He has some share in the brewery, hasn't he?"

"I believe he has, or is to have. So Rachel told me."

"Yes,—yes; I've heard of him before. If Tappitt doesn't take him into the concern he'll have to give him a very serious bit of money. There's no doubt about the young man having means. Well, Mrs. Ray, I don't suppose Rachel could do better than take him."

"Take him!"

"Yes,—why not? Between you and me, Rachel is growing into a very handsome girl,—a very handsome girl indeed. I'd no idea she'd be so tall, and carry herself so well."

"Oh, Mr. Comfort, good looks are very dangerous for a young woman."

"Well, yes; indeed they are. But still, you know, handsome girls very often do very well; and if this young man fancies Miss Rachel——"

"But, Mr. Comfort, there hasn't been anything of that. I don't suppose he has ever thought of it, and I'm sure she hasn't."

"But young people get to think of it. I shouldn't be disposed to prevent their coming together in a proper sort of way. I don't like night walkings in churchyards, certainly, but I really think that was only an accident."

"I'm sure Rachel didn't mean it."

"I'm quite sure she didn't mean anything improper. And as for him, if he admires her, it was natural enough that he should go after her. If you ask my advice, Mrs. Ray, I should just tell her to be cautious, but I shouldn't be especially careful to separate them. Marriage is the happiest condition for a young woman, and for a young man, too. And how are young people to get married if they are not allowed to see each other?"

"And about the party, Mr. Comfort?"

"Oh, let her go; there'll be no harm. And I'll tell you what, Mrs. Ray; my daughter, Mrs. Cornbury, is going from here, and she shall pick her up and bring her home. It's always well for a young girl to go with a married woman." Then Mrs. Ray did take her glass of sherry, and walked back to Bragg's End, wondering a good deal, and not altogether at ease in her mind as to that great question,—what line of moral conduct might best befit a devout Christian.

Something also had been said at the interview about Mrs. Prime. Mrs. Ray had intimated that Mrs. Prime would separate herself from her mother and her sister unless her views were allowed to prevail in this question regarding the young man from the brewery. But Mr. Comfort, in what few words he had said on this part of the subject, had shown no consideration whatever for Mrs. Prime. "Then she'll behave very wickedly," he had said. "But I'm afraid Mrs. Prime has learned to think too much of her own opinion lately. If that's what she has got by going to Mr. Prong she had better have remained in her own parish." After that, nothing more was said about Mrs. Prime.

"Oh, let her go; there'll be no harm." That had been Mr. Comfort's dictum about the evening party. Such as it was, Mrs. Ray felt herself bound to be guided by it. She had told Rachel that she would ask the clergyman's advice, and take it, whatever it might be. Nevertheless she did not find herself to be easy as she walked home. Mr. Comfort's latter teachings tended to upset all the convictions of her life. According to his teaching, as uttered in the sanctum of his own study, young men were not to be regarded as ravening wolves. And that meeting in the churchyard, which had utterly overwhelmed Dorothea by the weight of its iniquity, and which even to her had been very terrible, was a mere nothing;—a venial accident on Rachel's part, and the most natural proceeding in the world on the part of Luke Rowan! That it was natural enough for a wolf Mrs. Ray could understand; but she was now told that the lamb might go out and meet the wolf without any danger! And then those questions about Rowan's share in the brewery, and Mr. Comfort's ready assertion that the young wolf,—man or wolf, as the case might be,—was well to do in the world! In fact Mrs. Ray's interview with her clergyman had not gone exactly as she had expected, and she was bewildered; and the path into evil,—if it was a path into evil,—was made so easy and pleasant! Mrs. Ray had already considered the difficult question of Rachel's journey to the party, and journey home again; but provision was now made for all that in a way that was indeed very comfortable, but which might make Rachel

very vain. She was to be ushered into Mrs. Tappitt's drawing-
room under the wing of the most august lady of the neighbourhood. After that, for the remaining half-hour of her walk home,
Mrs. Ray gave her mind up to the consideration of what dress
Rachel should wear.

When Mrs. Ray reached her own gate, Rachel was in the
garden waiting for her. "Well, mamma?" she said. "Is Dorothea
at home?" Mrs. Ray asked; and on being informed that Dorothea was at work within, she desired Rachel to follow her up
to her bedroom. When there she told her budget of news,—
not stinting her child of the gratification which it was sure to
give. She said nothing about Luke Rowan and his means, keeping that portion of Mr. Comfort's recommendation to herself;
but she declared it out as a fact, that Rachel was to accept the
invitation, and to be carried to the party by Mrs. Butler Cornbury. "Oh, mamma! Dear mamma!" said Rachel, who was leaning against the side of the bed. Then she gave a long sigh, and
a bright colour came over her face,—almost as though she were
blushing. But she said no more at the moment, but allowed her
mind to run off and revel in its own thoughts. She had indeed
longed to go to this party, though she had taught herself to
believe that she could bear being told that she was not to go
without disappointment. "And now we must let Dorothea
know," said Mrs. Ray. "Yes,—we must let her know," said Rachel; but her mind was away, straying, I fear, under the
churchyard elms with Luke Rowan, and looking at the arm
amidst the clouds. He had said that it was stretched out as
though to take her; and she had never shaken off from her imagination the idea that it was his arm on which she had been
bidden to look,—the arm which had afterwards held her when
she strove to go.

It was tea-time before courage was mustered for telling the
facts to Mrs. Prime. Mrs. Prime, after dinner, had gone into
Baslehurst; but the meeting at Miss Pucker's had not been a
regular full gathering, and Mrs. Prime had come back to tea.
There was no hot toast, and no clotted cream. It may appear

selfish on the part of Mrs. Ray and Rachel that they should have kept such good things for their only little private banquets, but, in truth, such delicacies did not suit Mrs. Prime. Nice things aggravated her spirits and made her fretful. She liked the tea to be stringy and bitter, and she liked the bread to be stale;—as she preferred also that her weeds should be battered and old. She was approaching that stage of discipline at which ashes become pleasant eating, and sackcloth is grateful to the skin. The self-indulgences of the saints in this respect often exceed anything that is done by the sinners.

"Dorothea," said Mrs. Ray, and she looked down upon the dark dingy fluid in her cup as she spoke, "I have been up to Mr. Comfort's to-day."

"Yes; I heard you say you were going there."

"I went to ask him for advice."

"Oh."

"As I was in much doubt, I thought it right to go to the clergyman of my parish."

"I don't think much about parishes myself. Mr. Comfort is an old man now, and I fear he does not give himself up to the Gospel as he used to do. If people were called upon to bind themselves down to parishes, what would those poor creatures do who have over them such a pastor as Dr. Harford?"

"Dr. Harford is a very good man, I believe," said Rachel, "and he keeps two curates."

"I'm afraid, Rachel, you know but little about it. He does keep two curates,—but what are they? They go to cricket-matches, and among young women with bows and arrows! If you had really wanted advice, mamma, I would sooner have heard that you had gone to Mr. Prong."

"But I didn't go to Mr. Prong, my dear;—and I don't mean. Mr. Prong is all very well, I dare say, but I've known Mr. Comfort for nearly thirty years, and I don't like sudden changes." Then Mrs. Ray stirred her tea with rather a quick motion of her hand. Rachel said not a word, but her mother's sharp speech and spirited manner was very pleasant to her.

She was quite contented now that Mr. Comfort should be regarded as the family counsellor. She remembered how well she had loved Mr. Comfort always, and thought of days when Patty Comfort had been very good-natured to her as a child.

"Oh, very well," said Mrs. Prime. "Of course, mamma, you must judge for yourself."

"Yes, my dear, I must; or rather, as I didn't wish to trust my own judgment, I went to Mr. Comfort for advice. He says that he sees no harm in Rachel going to this party."

"Party! what party?" almost screamed Mrs. Prime. Mrs. Ray had forgotten that nothing had as yet been said to Dorothea about the invitation.

"Mrs. Tappitt is going to give a party at the brewery," said Rachel, in her very softest voice, "and she has asked me."

"And you are going? You mean to let her go?" Mrs. Prime had asked two questions, and she received two answers. "Yes," said Rachel; "I suppose I shall go, as mamma says so." "Mr. Comfort says there is no harm in it," said Mrs. Ray; "and Mrs. Butler Cornbury is to come from the parsonage to take her up." All question as to Dorcas discipline to be inflicted daily upon Rachel on account of that sin of which she had been guilty in standing under the elms with a young man was utterly lost in this terrible proposition! Instead of being sent to Miss Pucker in her oldest merino dress, Rachel was to be decked in muslin and finery, and sent out to a dancing party at which this young man was to be the hero! It was altogether too much for Dorothea Prime. She slowly wiped the crumbs from off her dingy crape, and with creaking noise pushed back her chair. "Mother," she said, "I couldn't have believed it! I could not have believed it!" Then she withdrew to her own chamber.

Mrs. Ray was much afflicted; but not the less did Rachel look out for the returning postman, on his road into Baslehurst, that she might send her little note to Mrs. Tappitt, signifying her acceptance of that lady's kind invitation.

CHAPTER VI

Preparations for Mrs. Tappitt's Party

I AM DISPOSED to think that Mrs. Butler Cornbury did Mrs. Tappitt an injury when she with so much ready good nature accepted the invitation for the party, and that Mrs. Tappitt was aware of this before the night of the party arrived. She was put on her mettle in a way that was disagreeable to her, and forced into an amount of submissive supplication to Mr. Tappitt for funds, which was vexatious to her spirit. Mrs. Tappitt was a good wife, who never ran her husband into debt, and kept nothing secret from him in the management of her household, —nothing at least which it behoved him to know. But she understood the privileges of her position, and could it have been possible for her to have carried through this party without extra household moneys, or without any violent departure from her usual customs of life, she could have snubbed her husband's objections comfortably, and have put him into the background for the occasion without any inconvenience to herself or power of remonstrance from him. But when Mrs. Butler Cornbury had been gracious, and when the fiddles and horn had become a fact to be accomplished, when Mrs. Rowan and Mary began to loom large on her imagination and a regular supper was projected, then Mrs. Tappitt felt the necessity of superior aid, and found herself called upon to reconcile her lord.

And this work was the more difficult and the more disagreeable to her feelings because she had already pooh-poohed her husband when he asked a question about the party. "Just a few friends got together by the girls," she had said. "Leave it all to them, my dear. It's not very often they see anybody at home."

"I believe I see my friends as often as most people in Baslehurst," Mr. Tappitt had replied indignantly, "and I suppose my friends are their friends." So there had been a little soreness which made the lady's submission the more disagreeable to her.

"Butler Cornbury! He's a puppy. I don't want to see him, and what's more, I won't vote for him."

"You need not tell her so, my dear; and he's not coming. I suppose you like your girls to hold their heads up in the place; and if they show that they've respectable people with them at home, respectable people will be glad to notice them."

"Respectable! If our girls are to be made respectable by giving grand dances, I'd rather not have them respectable. How much is the whole thing to cost?"

"Well, very little, T.; not much more than one of your Christmas dinner-parties. There'll be just the music, and the lights, and a bit of something to eat. What people drink at such times comes to nothing,—just a little negus and lemonade. We might possibly have a bottle or two of champagne at the supper-table, for the look of the thing."

"Champagne!" exclaimed the brewer. He had never yet incurred the cost of a bottle of champagne within his own house, though he thought nothing of it at public dinners. The idea was too much for him; and Mrs. Tappitt, feeling how the ground lay, gave that up,—at any rate for the present. She gave up the champagne; but in abandoning that, she obtained the marital sanction, a quasi sanction which he was too honourable as a husband afterwards to repudiate, for the music and the eatables. Mrs. Tappitt knew that she had done well, and prepared for his dinner that day a beef-steak pie, made with her own hands. Tappitt was not altogether a dull man, and understood these little signs. "Ah," said he, "I wonder how much that pie is to cost me?"

"Oh, T., how can you say such things! As if you didn't have beef-steak pie as often as it's good for you." The pie, however, had its effect, as also did the exceeding "boilishness" of the water which was brought in for his gin-toddy that night; and it was known throughout the establishment that papa was in a good humour, and that mamma had been very clever.

"The girls must have had new dresses anyway before the month was out," Mrs. Tappitt said to her husband the next morning before he had left the conjugal chamber.

"Do you mean to say that they're to have gowns made on purpose for this party?" said the brewer; and it seemed by the tone of his voice that the hot gin and water had lost its kindly effects.

"My dear, they must be dressed, you know. I'm sure no girls in Baslehurst cost less in the way of finery. In the ordinary way they'd have had new frocks almost immediately."

"Bother!" Mr. Tappitt was shaving just at this moment, and dashed aside his razor for a moment to utter this one word. He intended to signify how perfectly well he was aware that a muslin frock prepared for an evening party would not fill the place of a substantial morning dress.

"Well, my dear, I'm sure the girls ain't unreasonable; nor am I. Five-and-thirty shillings apiece for them would do it all. And I shan't want anything myself this year in September." Now Mr. Tappitt, who was a man of sentiment, always gave his wife some costly article of raiment on the 1st of September, calling her his partridge and his bird,—for on that day they had been married. Mrs. Tappitt had frequently offered to intromit the ceremony when calling upon his generosity for other purposes, but the September gift had always been forthcoming.

"Will thirty-five shillings apiece do it?" said he, turning round with his face all covered with lather. Then again he went to work with his razor just under his right ear.

"Well, yes; I think it will. Two pounds each for the three shall do it anyway."

Mr. Tappitt gave a little jump at this increased demand for fifteen shillings, and not being in a good position for jumping, encountered an unpleasant accident, and uttered a somewhat vehement exclamation. "There," said he, "now I've cut myself, and it's your fault. Oh dear; oh dear! When I cut myself there it never stops. It's no good doing that, Margaret; it only makes it worse. There; now you've got the soap and blood all down inside my shirt."

Mrs. Tappitt on this occasion was subjected to some trouble, for the wound on Mr. Tappitt's cheek-bone declined to be stanched at once; but she gained her object, and got the dresses for her daughters. It was not taken by them as a drawback on their happiness that they had to make the dresses themselves, for they were accustomed to such work; but this necessity joined to all other preparations for the party made them very busy. Till twelve at night on three evenings they sat with their smart new things in their laps and their needles in their hands; but they did not begrudge this, as Mrs. Butler Cornbury was coming to the brewery. They were very anxious to get the heavy part of the work done before the Rowans should arrive, doubting whether they would become sufficiently intimate with Mary to tell her all their little domestic secrets, and do their work in the presence of their new friend during the first day of her sojourn in the house. So they toiled like slaves on the Wednesday and Thursday in order that they might walk about like ladies on the Friday and Saturday.

But the list of their guests gave them more trouble than aught else. Whom should they get to meet Mrs. Butler Cornbury? At one time Mrs. Tappitt had proposed to word certain of her invitations with a special view to this end. Had her idea been carried out people who might not otherwise have come were to be tempted by a notification that they were especially asked to meet Mrs. Butler Cornbury. But Martha had said that this she thought would not do for a dance. "People do do it, my dear," Mrs. Tappitt had pleaded.

"Not for dancing, mamma," said Martha. "Besides, she would be sure to hear of it, and perhaps she might not like it."

"Well, I don't know," said Mrs. Tappitt. "It would show that we appreciated her kindness." The plan, however, was abandoned.

Of the Baslehurst folk there were so few that were fitted to meet Mrs. Butler Cornbury! There was old Miss Harford, the rector's daughter. She was fit to meet anybody in the county, and, as she was good-natured, might probably come. But she was an old maid, and was never very bright in her attire. "Perhaps Captain Gordon's lady would come," Mrs. Tappitt suggested. But at this proposition all the girls shook their heads. Captain Gordon had lately taken a villa close to Baslehurst, but had shown himself averse to any intercourse with the townspeople. Mrs. Tappitt had called on his "lady," and the call had not even been returned, a card having been sent by post in an envelope.

"It would be no good, mamma," said Martha, "and she would only make us uncomfortable if she did come."

"She is always awfully stuck up in church," said Augusta.

"And her nose is red at the end," said Cherry.

Therefore no invitation was sent to Captain Gordon's house.

"If we could only get the Fawcetts," said Augusta. The Fawcetts were a large family living in the centre of Baslehurst, in which there were four daughters, all noted for dancing, and noted also for being the merriest, nicest, and most popular girls in Devonshire. There was a fat good-natured mother, and a thin good-natured father who had once been a banker at Exeter. Everybody desired to know the Fawcetts, and they were the especial favourites of Mrs. Butler Cornbury. But then Mrs. Fawcett did not visit Mrs. Tappitt. The girls and the mothers had a bowing acquaintance, and were always very gracious to each other. Old Fawcett and old Tappitt saw each other in town daily, and knew each other as well as they knew the cross in the butter market; but none of the two families ever went into each other's houses. It had been tacitly admitted among them that the Fawcetts were above the Tappitts, and so the matter had rested. But now, if anything could be done? "Mrs. Butler Cornbury is all very well, of course," said Augusta, "but it would be so nice for Mary Rowan to see the Miss Fawcetts dancing here."

Martha shook her head, but at last she did write a note in the mother's name. "My girls are having a little dance, to welcome a friend from London, and they would feel so much obliged if your young ladies would come. Mrs. Butler Cornbury has been kind enough to say that she would join us, &c., &c., &c." Mrs. Tappitt and Augusta were in a seventh heaven of happiness when Mrs. Fawcett wrote to say that three of her girls would be delighted to accept the invitation; and even the discreet Martha and the less ambitious Cherry were well pleased.

"I declare I think we've been very fortunate," said Mrs. Tappitt.

"Only the Miss Fawcetts will get all the best partners," said Cherry.

"I'm not so sure of that," said Augusta, holding up her head.

But there had been yet another trouble. It was difficult for them to get people proper to meet Mrs. Butler Cornbury; but what must they do as to those people who must come and who were by no means proper to meet her? There were the Griggses for instance, who lived out of town in a wonderfully red brick house, the family of a retired Baslehurst grocer. They had been asked before Mrs. Cornbury's call had been made, or, I fear, their chance of coming to the party would have been small. There was one young Griggs, a man very terrible in his vulgarity, loud, rampant, conspicuous with villainous jewellery, and odious with the worst abominations of perfumery. He was loathsome even to the Tappitt girls; but then the Griggses and the Tappitts had known each other for half a century, and among their ordinary acquaintances Adolphus Griggs might have been endured. But what should they do when he asked to be introduced to Josceline Fawcett? Of all men he was the most unconscious of his own defects. He had once shown some symptoms of admiration for Cherry, by whom he was hated with an intensity of dislike that had amounted to a passion. She had begged that he might be omitted from the list; but Mrs. Tappitt had been afraid of angering their father.

The Rules also would be much in the way. Old Joshua Rule was a maltster, living in Cawston, and his wife and daughter had been asked before the accession of the Butler Cornbury dignity. Old Rule had supplied the brewery with malt almost ever since it had been a brewery; and no more harmless people than Mrs. Rule and her daughter existed in the neighbourhood; —but they were close neighbours of the Comforts, of Mrs. Cornbury's father and mother, and Mr. Comfort would have as soon asked his sexton to dine with him as the Rules. The Rules never expected such a thing, and therefore lived on very good terms with the clergyman. "I'm afraid she won't like meeting Mrs. Rule," Augusta had said to her mother; and then the mother had shaken her head.

Early in the week, before Rachel had accepted the invitation, Cherry had written to her friend. "Of course you'll come," Cherry had said; "and as you may have some difficulty in getting here and home again, I'll ask old Mrs. Rule to call for you. I know she'll have a place in the fly, and she's very good-natured." In answer to this Rachel had written a separate note to Cherry, telling her friend in the least boastful words which she could use that provision had been already made for her coming and going. "Mamma was up at Mr. Comfort's yesterday," Rachel wrote, "and he was so kind as to say that Mrs. Butler Cornbury would take me and bring me back. I am very much obliged to you all the same, and to Mrs. Rule."

"What do you think?" said Cherry, who had received her note in the midst of one of the family conferences; "Augusta said that Mrs. Butler Cornbury would not like to meet Rachel Ray; but she is going to bring her in her own carriage."

"I never said anything of the kind," said Augusta.

"Oh, but you did, Augusta; or mamma did, or somebody. How nice for Rachel to be chaperoned by Mrs. Butler Cornbury!"

"I wonder what she'll wear," said Mrs. Tappitt, who had on that morning achieved her victory over the wounded brewer in the matter of the three dresses.

On the Friday morning Mrs. Rowan came with her daughter, Luke having met them at Exeter on the Thursday. Mrs.

Rowan was a somewhat stately lady, slow in her movements and careful in her speech, so that the girls were at first very glad that they had valiantly worked up their finery before her coming. But Mary was by no means stately; she was younger than them, very willing to be pleased, with pleasant round eager eyes, and a kindly voice. Before she had been three hours in the house Cherry had claimed Mary for her own, had told her all about the party, all about the dresses, all about Mrs. Butler Cornbury and the Miss Fawcetts, and a word or two also about Rachel Ray. "I can tell you somebody that's almost in love with her." "You don't mean Luke?" said Mary. "Yes, but I do," said Cherry; "but of course I'm only in fun." On the Saturday Mary was hard at work herself assisting in the decoration of the drawing-room, and before the all-important Tuesday came even Mrs. Rowan and Mrs. Tappitt were confidential. Mrs. Rowan perceived at once that Mrs. Tappitt was provincial,—as she told her son, but she was a good motherly woman, and on the whole, Mrs. Rowan condescended to be gracious to her.

At Bragg's End the preparations for the party required almost as much thought as did those at the brewery, and involved perhaps deeper care. It may be remembered that Mrs. Prime, when her ears were first astounded by that unexpected revelation, wiped the crumbs from out of her lap and walked off, wounded in spirit, to her own room. On that evening Rachel saw no more of her sister. Mrs. Ray went up to her daughter's bedroom, but stayed there only a minute or two. "What does she say?" asked Rachel, almost in a whisper. "She is very unhappy. She says that unless I can be made to think better of this she must leave the cottage. I told her what Mr. Comfort says, but she only sneers at Mr. Comfort. I'm sure I'm endeavouring to do the best I can."

"It wouldn't do, mamma, to say that she should manage everything, otherwise I'm sure I'd give up the party."

"No, my dear; I don't want you to do that,—not after what Mr. Comfort says." Mrs. Ray had in truth gone to the clergyman feeling sure that he would have given his word against the party, and that, so strengthened, she could have taken a course that would have been offensive to neither of her daughters. She had expected, too, that she would have returned home armed with such clerical thunders against the young man as would have quieted Rachel and have satisfied Dorothea. But in all this she had been,—I may hardly say disappointed,—but dismayed and bewildered by advice the very opposite to that which she had expected. It was perplexing, but she seemed to be aware that she had no alternative now, but to fight the battle on Rachel's side. She had cut herself off from all anchorage except that given by Mr. Comfort, and therefore it behoved her to cling to that with absolute tenacity. Rachel must go to the party, even though Dorothea should carry out her threat. On that night nothing more was said about Dorothea, and Mrs. Ray allowed herself to be gradually drawn into a mild discussion about Rachel's dress.

But there was nearly a week left to them of this sort of life. Early on the following morning Mrs. Prime left the cottage, saying that she should dine with Miss Pucker, and betook herself at once to a small house in a back street of the town, behind the new church, in which lived Mr. Prong. Have I as yet said that Mr. Prong was a bachelor? Such was the fact; and there were not wanting those in Baslehurst who declared that he would amend the fault by marrying Mrs. Prime. But this rumour, if it ever reached her, had no effect upon her. The world would be nothing to her if she were to be debarred by the wickedness of loose tongues from visiting the clergyman of her choice. She went, therefore, in her present difficulty to Mr. Prong.

Mr. Samuel Prong was a little man, over thirty, with scanty, light-brown hair, with a small, rather upturned nose, with eyes by no means deficient in light and expression, but with a mean mouth. His forehead was good, and had it not been for his mouth his face would have been expressive of intellect and of some firmness. But there was about his lips an assumption of character and dignity which his countenance and body generally failed to maintain; and there was a something in the carriage of his head and in the occasional projection of his chin, which was intended to add to his dignity, but which did, I think, only make the failure more palpable. He was a devout, good man; not self-indulgent; perhaps not more self-ambitious than it becomes a man to be; sincere, hard-working, sufficiently intelligent, true in most things to the instincts of his calling,—but deficient in one vital qualification for a clergyman of the Church of England; he was not a gentleman. May I not call it a necessary qualification for a clergyman of any church? He was not a gentleman. I do not mean to say that he was a thief or a liar; nor do I mean hereby to complain that he picked his teeth with his fork and misplaced his "h's." I am by no means prepared to define what I do mean,—thinking, however, that most men and most women will understand me. Nor do I speak of this deficiency in his clerical aptitudes as being injurious to him simply,—or even chiefly,—among folk who are themselves gentle; but that his efficiency for clerical purposes was marred altogether, among high and low, by his misfortune in this respect. It is not the owner of a good coat that sees and admires its beauty. It is not even they who have good coats themselves who recognize the article on the back of another. They who have not good coats themselves have the keenest eyes for the coats of their better-clad neighbours. As it is with coats, so it is with that which we call gentility. It is caught at a word, it is seen at a glance, it is appreciated unconsciously at a touch by those who have none of it themselves. It is the greatest of all aids to the doctor, the lawyer, the member of Parliament,—though in that position a man may perhaps prosper without it, —and to the statesman; but to the clergyman it is a vital necessity. Now Mr. Prong was not a gentleman.

Mrs. Prime told her tale to Mr. Prong, as Mrs. Ray had told hers to Mr. Comfort. It need not be told again here. I fear that she made the most of her sister's imprudence, but she did not do so with intentional injustice. She declared her conviction

that Rachel might still be made to go in a straight course, if
only she could be guided by a hand sufficiently strict and armed
with absolute power. Then she went on to tell Mr. Prong how
Mrs. Ray had gone off to Mr. Comfort, as she herself had now
come to him. It was hard,—was it not?—for poor Rachel that
the story of her few minutes' whispering under the elm tree
should thus be bruited about among the ecclesiastical council-
lors of the locality. Mr. Prong sat with patient face and with
mild demeanour while the simple story of Rachel's conduct was
being told; but when to this was added the iniquity of Mr.
Comfort's advice, the mouth assumed the would-be grandeur,
the chin came out, and to any one less infatuated than Mrs.
Prime it would have been apparent that the purse was not made
of silk, but that a coarser material had come to hand in the
manufacture.

"What shall the sheep do," said Mr. Prong, "when the shepherd slumbers in the folds?" Then he shook his head and puckered up his mouth.

"Ah!" said Mrs. Prime; "it is well for the sheep that there are
still left a few who do not run from their work, even in the
heat of the noonday sun."

Mr. Prong closed his eyes and bowed his head, and then
reassumed that peculiarly disagreeable look about his mouth
by which he thought to assert his dignity, intending thereby to
signify that he would willingly reject the compliment as unnecessary, were he not forced to accept it as being true. He
knew himself to be a shepherd who did not fear the noonday
heat; but he was wrong in this,—that he suspected all other
shepherds of stinting their work. It appeared to him that no
sheep could nibble his grass in wholesome content, unless some
shepherd were at work at him constantly with his crook. It was
for the shepherd, as he thought, to know what tufts of grass
were rank, and in what spots the herbage might be bitten down
to the bare ground. A shepherd who would allow his flock to
feed at large under his eye, merely watching his fences and
folding his ewes and lambs at night, was a truant who feared

the noonday sun. Such a one had Mr. Comfort become, and therefore Mr. Prong despised him in his heart. All sheep will not endure such ardent shepherding as that practised by Mr. Prong, and therefore he was driven to seek out for himself a peculiar flock. These to him were the elect of Baslehurst, and of his elect, Mrs. Prime was the most elect. Now this fault is not uncommon among young ardent clergymen.

I will not repeat the conversation that took place between the two, because they used holy words and spoke on holy subjects. In doing so they were both sincere, and not, as regarded their language, fairly subject to ridicule. In their judgment I think they were defective. He sustained Mrs. Prime in her resolution to quit the cottage unless she could induce her mother to put a stop to that great iniquity of the brewery. "The Tappitts," he said, "were worldly people,—very worldly people; utterly unfit to be the associates of the sister of his friend. As to the 'young man,' he thought that nothing further should be said at present, but that Rachel should be closely watched,— very closely watched." Mrs. Prime asked him to call upon her mother and explain his views, but he declined to do this. "He would have been most willing,—so willing! but he could not force himself where he would be unwelcome!" Mrs. Prime was, if necessary, to quit the cottage and take up her temporary residence with Miss Pucker; but Mr. Prong was inclined to think, knowing something of Mrs. Ray's customary softness of character, that if Mrs. Prime were firm, things would not be driven to such a pass as that. Mrs. Prime said that she would be firm, and she looked as though she intended to keep her word.

Mr. Prong's manner as he bade adieu to his favourite sheep was certainly of a nature to justify that rumour to which allusion has been made. He pressed Mrs. Prime's hand very closely, and invoked a blessing on her head in a warm whisper. But such signs among such people do not bear the meaning which they have in the outer world. These people are demonstrative and unctuous,—whereas the outer world is reticent and dry. They are perhaps too free with their love, but the fault is bet-

ter than that other fault of no love at all. Mr. Prong was a little free with his love, but Mrs. Prime took it all in good part,
and answered him with an equal fervour. "If I can help you,
dear friend,"—and he still held her hand in his,—"come to me
always. You never can come too often."

"You can help me, and I will come, always," she said, returning his pressure with mutual warmth. But there was no
touch of earthly affection in her pressure; and if there was any
in his at its close, there had, at any rate, been none at its commencement.

While Mrs. Prime was thus employed, Rachel and her
mother became warm upon the subject of the dress, and when
the younger widow returned home to the cottage, the elder
widow was actually engaged in Baslehurst on the purchase of
trappings and vanities. Her little hoard was opened, and some
pretty piece of muslin was purchased by aid of which, with the
needful ribbons, Rachel might be made, not fit, indeed, for
Mrs. Butler Cornbury's carriage,—no such august fitness was
at all contemplated by herself,—but nice and tidy, so that her
presence need not be a disgrace. And it was pretty to see how
Mrs. Ray revelled in these little gauds for her daughter now
that the barrier of her religious awe was broken down, and
that the waters of the world had made their way in upon her.
She still had a feeling that she was being drowned, but she
confessed that such drowning was very pleasant. She almost
felt that such drowning was good for her. At any rate it had
been ordered by Mr. Comfort, and if things went astray Mr.
Comfort must bear the blame. When the bright muslin was
laid out on the counter before her, she looked at it with a
pleased eye and touched it with a willing hand. She held the
ribbon against the muslin, leaning her head on one side, and
enjoyed herself. Now and again she would turn her face upon
Rachel's figure, and she would almost indulge a wish that this
young man might like her child in the new dress. Ah!—that was
surely wicked. But if so, how wicked are most mothers in this
Christian land!

The morning had gone very comfortably with them during Dorothea's absence. Mrs. Prime had hardly taken her departure before a note came from Mrs. Butler Cornbury, confirming Mr. Comfort's offer as to the carriage. "Oh, papa, what have you done?"—she had said when her father first told her. "Now I must stay there all the night, for of course she'll want to go on to the last dance!" But, like her father, she was good-natured, and therefore, though she would hardly have chosen the task, she resolved, when her first groans were over, to do it well. She wrote a kind note, saying how happy she should be, naming her hour,—and saying that Rachel should name the hour for her return.

"It will be very nice," said Rachel, rejoicing more than she should have done in thinking of the comfortable grandeur of Mrs. Butler Cornbury's carriage.

"And are you determined?" Mrs. Prime asked her mother that evening.

"It is too late to go back now, Dorothea," said Mrs. Ray, almost crying.

"Then I cannot remain in the house," said Dorothea. "I shall go to Miss Pucker's,—but not till that morning; so that if you think better of it, all may be prevented yet."

But Mrs. Ray would not think better of it, and it was thus that the preparations were made for Mrs. Tappitt's—ball. The word "party" had now been dropped by common consent throughout Baslehurst.

CHAPTER VII

An Account of Mrs. Tappitt's Ball—
Commenced

Mrs. Butler Cornbury was a very pretty woman. She possessed that peculiar prettiness which is so often seen in England, and which is rarely seen anywhere else. She was bright,

well-featured, with speaking lustrous eyes, with perfect com-
plexion, and full bust, with head of glorious shape and figure
like a Juno;—and yet with all her beauty she had ever about
her an air of homeliness which made the sweetness of her wom-
anhood almost more attractive than the loveliness of her personal charms. I have seen in Italy and in America women perhaps as beautiful as any that I have seen in England, but in
neither country does it seem that such beauty is intended for
domestic use. In Italy the beauty is soft, and of the flesh. In
America it is hard, and of the mind. Here it is of the heart, I
think, and as such is the happiest of the three. I do not say that
Mrs. Butler Cornbury was a woman of very strong feeling; but
her strongest feelings were home feelings. She was going to
Mrs. Tappitt's party because it might serve her husband's purposes; she was going to burden herself with Rachel Ray because her father had asked her; and her greatest ambition was
to improve the worldly position of the squires of Cornbury
Grange. She was already calculating whether it might not
some day be brought about that her little Butler should sit in
Parliament for his county.

At nine o'clock exactly on that much to be remembered
Tuesday the Cornbury carriage stopped at the gate of the cottage at Bragg's End, and Rachel, ready dressed, blushing, nerv-
ous, but yet happy, came out, and mounting on to the step was
almost fearful to take her share of the seat. "Make yourself
comfortable, my dear," said Mrs. Cornbury; "you can't crush
me. Or rather I always make myself crushable on such occasions as this. I suppose we are going to have a great crowd?"
Rachel merely said that she didn't know. She supposed there
would be a good many persons. Then she tried to thank
Mrs. Cornbury for being so good to her, and of course broke
down. "I'm delighted,—quite delighted," said Mrs. Cornbury.
"It's so good of you to come with me. Now that I don't dance
myself, there's nothing I like so much as taking out girls
that do."

"And don't you dance at all?"

"I stand up for a quadrille sometimes. When a woman has five children I don't think she ought to do more than that."

"Oh, I shall not do more than that, Mrs. Cornbury."

"You mean to say you won't waltz?"

"Mamma never said anything about it, but I'm sure she would not like it. Besides—"

"Well—"

"I don't think I know how. I did learn once, when I was very little; but I've forgotten."

"It will soon come again to you if you like to try. I was very fond of waltzing before I was married." And this was the daughter of Mr. Comfort, the clergyman who preached with such strenuous eloquence against worldly vanities! Even Rachel was a little puzzled, and was almost afraid that her head was sinking beneath the waters.

There was a great fuss made when Mrs. Butler Cornbury's carriage drove up to the brewery door, and Rachel almost felt that she could have made her way up to the drawing-room more comfortably under Mrs. Rule's mild protection. All the servants seemed to rush at her, and when she found herself in the hall and was conducted into some inner room, she was not allowed to shake herself into shape without the aid of a maid-servant. Mrs. Cornbury,—who took everything as a matter of course and was ready in a minute,—had turned the maid over to the young lady with a kind idea that the young lady's toilet was more important than that of the married woman. Rachel was losing her head and knew that she was doing so. When she was again taken into the hall she hardly remembered where she was, and when Mrs. Cornbury took her by the arm and began to walk up-stairs with her, her strongest feeling was a wish that she was at home again. On the first landing,—for the danc-ing-room was up-stairs,—they encountered Mr. Tappitt, con-spicuous in a blue satin waistcoat; and on the second landing they found Mrs. Tappitt, magnificent in a green Irish poplin. "Oh, Mrs. Cornbury, we are so delighted. The Miss Fawcetts are here; they are just come. How kind of you to bring Rachel

Ray. How do you do, Rachel?" Then Mrs. Cornbury moved easily on into the drawing-room, and Rachel still found herself carried with her. She was half afraid that she ought to have slunk away from her magnificent chaperon as soon as she was conveyed safely within the house, and that she was encroaching as she thus went on; but still she could not find the moment in which to take herself off. In the drawing-room,—the room from which the carpets had been taken,—they were at once encountered by the Tappitt girls, with whom the Fawcett girls on the present occasion were so intermingled that Rachel hardly knew who was who. Mrs. Butler Cornbury was soon surrounded, and a clatter of words went on. Rachel was in the middle of the fray, and some voices were addressed also to her; but her presence of mind was gone, and she never could remember what she said on the occasion.

There had already been a dance,—the commencing operation of the night's work,—a thin quadrille, in which the early comers had taken part without much animation, and to which they had been driven up unwillingly. At its close the Fawcett girls had come in, as had now Mrs. Cornbury, so that it may be said that the evening was beginning again. What had been as yet done was but the tuning of the fiddles before the commencement of the opera. No one likes to be in at the tuning, but there are those who never are able to avoid this annoyance. As it was, Rachel, under Mrs. Cornbury's care, had been brought upon the scene just at the right moment. As soon as the great clatter had ceased, she found herself taken by the hand by Cherry, and led a little on one side. "You must have a card, you know," said Cherry handing her a ticket on which was printed the dances as they were to succeed each other. "That first one is over. Such a dull thing. I danced with Adolphus Griggs, just because I couldn't escape him for one quadrille." Rachel took the card, but never having seen such a thing before did not in the least understand its object. "As you get engaged for the dances you must put down their names in this way, you see,"—and Cherry showed her card, which already bore the designations of several cavaliers, scrawled in hieroglyphics which were intelligible to herself. "Haven't you got a pencil? Well, you can come to me. I have one hanging here, you know." Rachel was beginning to understand, and to think that she should not have very much need for the pencil, when Mrs. Cornbury returned to her, bringing a young man in her wake. "I want to introduce my cousin to you, Walter Cornbury," said she. Mrs. Cornbury was a woman who knew her duty as a chaperon, and who would not neglect it. "He waltzes delightfully," said Mrs. Cornbury, whispering, "and you needn't be afraid of being a little astray with him at first. He always does what I tell him." Then the introduction was made; but Rachel had no opportunity of repeating her fears, or of saying again that she thought she had better not waltz. What to say to Mr. Walter Cornbury she hardly knew; but before she had really said anything he had pricked her down for two dances,—for the first waltz, which was just going to begin, and some not long future quadrille. "She is very pretty," Mrs. Butler Cornbury had said to her cousin, "and I want to be kind to her." "I'll take her in hand and pull her through," said Walter. "What a tribe of people they've got here, haven't they?" "Yes, and you must dance with them all. Every time you stand up may be as good as a vote." "Oh," said Walter, "I'm not particular;—I'll dance as long as they keep the house open." Then he went back to Rachel, who had already been at work with Cherry's pencil.

"If there isn't Rachel Ray going to waltz with Walter Cornbury," said Augusta to her mother. Augusta had just refused the odious Griggs, and was about to stand up with a clerk in the brewery, who was almost as odious.

"It's because she came in the carriage," said Mrs. Tappitt; "but I don't think she can waltz." Then she hurried off to welcome other comers.

Rachel had hardly been left alone for a minute, and had been so much bewildered by the lights and crowd and strangeness of everything around her, that she had been unable to turn her thoughts to the one subject on which during the last week her mind had rested constantly. She had not even looked round the room for Luke Rowan. She had just seen Mary Rowan in the crowd, but had not spoken to her. She had only known her from the manner in which Cherry Tappitt had spoken to her, and it must be explained that Rachel had not seen young Rowan since that parting under the elm trees. Indeed, since then she had seen none of the Tappitt family. Her mother had said no word to her, cautioning her that she had better not seek them in her evening walks; but she had felt herself debarred from going into Baslehurst by all that her sister had said, and in avoiding Luke Rowan she had avoided the whole party from the brewery.

Now the room was partially cleared, the non-dancers being pressed back into a border round the walks, and the music began. Rachel, with her heart in her mouth, was claimed by her partner, and was carried forward towards the ground for dancing, tacitly assenting to her fate because she lacked words in which to explain to Mr. Cornbury how very much she would have preferred to be left in obscurity behind the wall of crinoline.

"Pray wait a minute or two," said she, almost panting.

"Oh, certainly. There's no hurry, only we'll stand where we can get our place when we like it. You need not be a bit afraid of going on with me. Patty has told me all about it, and we'll make it right in a brace of turns." There was something very good-natured in his voice, and she almost felt that she could ask him to let her sit down.

"I don't think I can," she said.

"Oh yes; come, we'll try!" Then he took her by the waist, and away they went. Twice round the room he took her, very gently, as he thought; but her head had gone from her instantly in a whirl of amazement! Of her feet and their movements she had known nothing; though she had followed the music with fair accuracy, she had done so unconsciously, and when he allowed her to stop she did not know which way she had been going, or at which end of the room she stood. And yet she had liked it, and felt some little triumph as a conviction came upon her that she had not conspicuously disgraced herself.

"That's charming," said he. She essayed to speak a word in answer, but her want of breath did not as yet permit it.

"Charming!" he went on. "The music's perhaps a little slow, but we'll hurry them up presently." Slow! It seemed to her that she had been carried round in a vortex, of which the rapidity, though pleasant, had been almost frightful. "Come; we'll have another start," said he; and she was carried away again before she had spoken a word. "I'd no idea that girl could waltz," said Mrs. Tappitt to old Mrs. Rule. "I don't think her mother would like it if she saw it," said Mrs. Rule. "And what would Mrs. Prime say?" said Mrs. Tappitt. However the ice was broken, and Rachel, when she was given to understand that that dance was done, felt herself to be aware that the world of waltzing was open to her, at any rate for that night. Was it very wicked? She had her doubts. If anybody had suggested to her, before Mrs. Cornbury's carriage had called for her, that she would waltz on that evening, she would have repudiated the idea almost with horror. How easy is the path down the shores of the Avernus! but then,—was she going down the shores of the Avernus?

She was still walking through the crowd, leaning on her partner's arm, and answering his good-natured questions almost in monosyllables, when she was gently touched on the arm by a fan, and on turning found herself confronted by Luke Rowan and his sister. "I've been trying to get at you so long," said he, making some sort of half apology to Cornbury, "and haven't been able; though once I very nearly danced you down without your knowing it."

"We're so much obliged to you for letting us escape," said Cornbury; "are we not, Miss Ray?"

"We carried heavy metal, I can tell you," said Rowan. "But I must introduce you to my sister. Where on earth have you been for these ten days?" Then the introduction was made, and young Cornbury, finding that his partner was in the hands of another lady, slipped away.

"I have heard a great deal about you, Miss Ray," said Mary Rowan.

"Have you? I don't know who should say much about me." The words sounded uncivil, but she did not know what words to choose.

"Oh, from Cherry especially;—and—and from my brother."

"I'm very glad to make your acquaintance," said Rachel.

"He told me that you would have been sure to come and walk with us, and we have all been saying that you had disappeared."

"I have been kept at home," said Rachel, who could not help remembering all the words of the churchyard interview, and feeling them down to her finger-nails. He must have known why she had not again joined the girls from the brewery in their walks. Or had he forgotten that he had called her Rachel, and held her fast by the hand? Perhaps he did these things so often to other girls that he thought nothing of them!

"You have been keeping yourself up for the ball," said Rowan. "Precious people are right to make themselves scarce. And now what vacancies have you got for me?"

"Vacancies!" said Rachel.

"You don't mean to say you've got none. Look here, I've kept all these on purpose for you, although twenty girls have begged me to dispose of them in their favour."

"Oh, Luke, how can you tell such fibs?" said his sister.

"Well;—here they are," and he showed his card.

"I'm not engaged to anybody," said Rachel; "except for one quadrille to Mr. Cornbury,—that gentleman who just went away."

"Then you've no excuse for not filling up my vacancies,— kept on purpose for you, mind." And immediately her name was put down for she knew not what dances. Then he took her card and scrawled his own name on it in various places. She knew that she was weak to let him thus have his way in everything; but he was strong and she could not hinder him.

She was soon left with Mary Rowan, as Luke went off to fulfil the first of his numerous engagements. "Do you like my brother?" said she. "But of course I don't mean you to answer that question. We all think him so very clever."

"I'm sure he is very clever."

"A great deal too clever to be a brewer. But you mustn't say that I said so. I wanted him to go into the army."

"I shouldn't at all like that for my brother—if I had one."

"And what would you like?"

"Oh, I don't know. I never had a brother;—perhaps to be a clergyman."

"Yes; that would be very nice; but Luke would never be a clergyman. He was going to be an attorney, but he didn't like that at all. He says there's a great deal of poetry in brewing beer, but of course he's only quizzing us. Oh, here's my partner. I do so hope I shall see you very often while I'm at Baslehurst." Then Rachel was alone, but Mrs. Tappitt came up to her in a minute. "My dear," said she, "Mr. Griggs desires the honour of your hand for a quadrille." And thus Rachel found herself standing up with the odious Mr. Griggs. "I do so pity you," said Cherry, coming behind her for a moment. "Remember, you need not do it more than once. I don't mean to do it again."

After that she was allowed to sit still while a polka was being performed. Mrs. Cornbury came to her saying a word or two; but she did not stay with her long, so that Rachel could think about Luke Rowan, and try to make up her mind as to what words she should say to him. She furtively looked down upon her card and found that he had written his own name to five dances, ending with Sir Roger de Coverley at the close of the evening. It was quite impossible that she should dance five dances with him, so she thought that she would mark out two with her nail. The very next was one of them, and during that she would explain to him what she had done. The whole thing loomed large in her thoughts and made her feel anxious. She would have been unhappy if he had not come to her at all, and now she was unhappy because he had thrust himself upon her so violently,—or if not unhappy, she was at any rate uneasy. And what should she say about the elm trees? Nothing, unless he spoke to her about them. She fancied that he would say something about the arm in the cloud, and if so, she must endeavour to make him understand that—that—that—— She did not know how to fix her thoughts. Would it be possible to make him understand that he ought not to have called her Rachel?

While she was thinking of all this Mr. Tappitt came and sat beside her. "Very pretty; isn't it?" said he. "Very pretty indeed, I call it."

"Oh yes, very pretty. I had no idea it would be so nice." To Mr. Tappitt in his blue waistcoat she could speak without hesitation. Ah me! It is the young men who receive all the reverence that the world has to pay;—all the reverence that is worth receiving. When a man is turned forty and has become fat, anybody can speak to him without awe!

"Yes, it is nice," said Mr. Tappitt, who, however, was not quite easy in his mind. He had been into the supper-room, and had found the waiter handling long-necked bottles, arranging them in rows, apparently by the dozen. "What's that?" said he, sharply. "The champagne, sir! there should have been ice, sir, but I suppose they forgot it." Where had Mrs. T. procured all that wine? It was very plain to him that she had got the better of him by some deceit. He would smile, and smile, and smile during the evening; but he would have it out with Mrs. Tappitt before he would allow that lady to have any rest. He lingered in the room, pretending that he was overlooking the arrangements, but in truth he was counting the bottles. After all there was but a dozen. He knew that at Griggs's they sold it for sixty shillings. "Three pounds!" he said to himself. "Three pounds more; dear, dear!"

"Yes, it is nice!" he said to Rachel. "Mind you get a glass of champagne when you go in to supper. By-the-by, shall I get a partner for you? Here, Buckett, come and dance the next dance with Miss Ray." Buckett was the clerk in the brewery. Rachel had nothing to say for herself; so Buckett's name was put down on the card, though she would rather not have danced with Buckett. A week or two ago, before she had been taken up into Mrs. Cornbury's carriage, or had waltzed with Mrs. Cornbury's cousin, or had looked at the setting sun with Luke Rowan, she would have been sufficiently contented to dance with Mr. Buckett,—if in those days she had ever dreamed of dancing with any one. Then Mrs. Cornbury came to her again, bringing other cavaliers, and Rachel's card began to be filled. "The quadrille before supper you dance with me," said Walter Cornbury. "That's settled, you know." Oh, what a new world it was, and so different from the Dorcas meetings at Miss Pucker's rooms!

Then came the moment of the evening which, of all the moments, was the most trying to her. Luke Rowan came to claim her hand for the next quadrille. She had already spoken to him,—or rather he to her; but that had been in the presence of a third person, when, of course, nothing could be said about the sunset and the clouds,—nothing about that promise of friendship. But now she would have to stand again with him in solitude,—a solitude of another kind,—in a solitude which was authorized, during which he might whisper what words he pleased to her, and from which she could not even run away. It had been thought to be a great sin on her part to have remained a moment with him by the stile; but now she was to stand up with him beneath the glare of the lights, dressed in her best, on purpose that he might whisper to her what words he pleased. But she was sure—she thought that she was sure, that he would utter no words so sweet, so full of meaning, as those in which he bade her watch the arm in the clouds.

Till the first figure was over for them he hardly spoke to her. "Tell me," said he then, "why has nobody seen you since Saturday week last?"

"I have been at home."

"Ah; but tell me the truth. Remember what we said as we parted,—about being friends. One tells one's friend the real truth. But I suppose you do not remember what we said?"

"I don't think I said anything, Mr. Rowan."

"Did you not? Then I must have been dreaming. I thought you promised me your friendship." He paused for her answer, but she said nothing. She could not declare to him that she would not be his friend. "But you have not told me yet why it was that you remained at home. Come;—answer me a fair question fairly. Had I offended you?" Again she paused and made him no reply. It seemed to her that the room was going round her, and that the music made her dizzy. If she told him that he had not offended her would she not thereby justify him in having called her Rachel?

"Then I did offend you?" said he.

"Oh, Mr. Rowan,—never mind now; you must go on with the figure," and thus for a moment she was saved from her difficulty. When he had done his work of dancing, she began hers, and as she placed both her hands in his to make the final turn, she flattered herself that he would not go back to the subject.

Nor did he while the quadrille lasted. As they continued to dance he said very little to her, and before the last figure was over she had almost settled down to enjoyment. He merely spoke a word or two about Mrs. Cornbury's dress, and another word about the singular arrangement of Mr. Griggs's jewellery, at which word she almost laughed outright, and then a third word laudatory of the Tappitt girls. "As for Cherry," said he, "I'm quite in love with her for her pure good nature and hearty manners; and of all living female human beings Martha is the most honest and just."

"Oh! I'll tell her that," said Rachel. "She will so like it."

"No, you mustn't. You mustn't repeat any of the things I tell you in confidence." That word "confidence" again silenced her, and nothing more was said till he had offered her his arm at the end of the dance.

"Come away and have some negus on the stairs," he said.

"The reason I like these sort of parties is, that one is allowed to go into such queer places. You see that little room with the door open. That's where Mr. Tappitt keeps his old boots and the whip with which he drives his grey horse. There are four men playing cards there now, and one is seated on the end of an upturned portmanteau."

"And where are the old boots?"

"Packed away on the top of Mrs. Tappitt's bed. I helped to put them there. Some are stuck under the grate because there are no fires now. Look here; there's a seat in the window." Then he placed her in the inclosure of an old window on the staircase landing, and brought her lemonade, and when she had drunk it he sat down beside her.

"Hadn't we better go back to the dancing?"

"They won't begin for a few minutes. They're only tuning up again. You should always escape from the hot air for a moment or two. Besides, you must answer me that question. Did I offend you?"

"Please don't talk of it. Please don't. It's all over now."

"Ah, but it is not all over. I knew you were angry with me because,—shall I say why?"

"No, Mr. Rowan, don't say anything about it."

"At any rate, I may think that you have forgiven me. But what if I offend in the same way again? What if I ask permission to do it, so that it may be no offence? Only think; if I am to live here in Baslehurst all my life, is it not reasonable that I should wish you to be my friend? Are you going to separate yourself from Cherry Tappitt because you are afraid of me?"

"Oh, no."

"But is not that what you have done during the last week, Miss Ray;—if it must be Miss Ray?" Then he paused, but still she said nothing. "Rachel is such a pretty name."

"Oh, I think it so ugly."

"It's the prettiest name in the Bible, and the name most fit for poetic use. Who does not remember Rachel weeping for her children?"

"That's the idea, and not the name. Ruth is twice prettier, and Mary the sweetest of all."

"I never knew anybody before called Rachel," said he.

"And I never knew anybody called Luke."

"That's a coincidence, is it not?—a coincidence that ought to make us friends. I may call you Rachel then?"

"Oh, no; please don't. What would people think?"

"Perhaps they would think the truth," said he. "Perhaps they would imagine that I called you so because I liked you. But perhaps they might think also that you let me do so because you liked me. People do make such mistakes."

At this moment up came to them, with flushed face, Mr. Buckett. "I have been looking for you everywhere," said he to Rachel. "It's nearly over now."

"I am so sorry," said Rachel, "but I quite forgot."

"So I presume," said Mr. Buckett angrily, but at the same time he gave his arm to Rachel and led her away. The fag end of some waltz remained, and he might get a turn with her. People in his hearing had spoken of her as the belle of the room, and he did not like to lose his chance. "Oh, Mr. Rowan," said Rachel, looking back as she was being led away. "I must speak one word to Mr. Rowan." Then she separated herself, and returning a step or two almost whispered to her late partner— "You have put me down for ever so many dances. You must scratch out two or three of them."

"Not one," said he. "An engagement is an engagement."

"Oh, but I really can't."

"Of course I cannot make you, but I will scratch out nothing,—and forget nothing."

Then she rejoined Mr. Buckett, and was told by him that young Rowan was not liked in the brewery at all. "We think him conceited, you know. He pretends to know more than anybody else."

CHAPTER VIII

An Account of Mrs. Tappitt's Ball— Concluded

It came to be voted by public acclamation that Rachel Ray was the belle of the evening. I think this was brought about quite as much by Mrs. Butler Cornbury's powerful influence as by Rachel's beauty. Mrs. Butler Cornbury having begun the work of chaperon carried it on heartily, and talked her young friend up to the top of the tree. Long before supper her card was quite full, but filled in a manner that was not comfortable to herself,—for she knew that she had made mistakes. As to those spaces on which the letter R was written, she kept them very sacred. She was quite resolved that she would not stand up with him on all those occasions,—that she would omit at any rate two; but she would accept no one else for those two dances, not choosing to select any special period for throwing him over. She endeavoured to explain this when she waltzed with him, shortly before supper; but her explanation did not come easy, and she wanted all her attention for the immediate work she had in hand. "If you'd only give yourself to it a little more eagerly," he said, "you'd waltz beautifully."

"I shall never do it well," she answered. "I don't suppose I shall ever try again."

"But you like it?"

"Oh yes; I like it excessively. But one can't do everything that one likes."

"No; I can't. You won't let me do what I like."

"Don't talk in that way, Mr. Rowan. If you do you'll destroy all my pleasure. You should let me enjoy it while it lasts." In this way she was becoming intimate with him.

"How very nicely your house does for a dance," said Mrs. Cornbury to Mrs. Tappitt.

"Oh dear,—I don't think so. Our rooms are so small. But

it's very kind of you to say so. Indeed, I never can be sufficiently obliged——"

"By-the-by," said Mrs. Cornbury, "what a nice girl Rachel
Ray has grown."

"Yes, indeed," said Mrs. Tappitt.

"And dances so well! I'd no idea of it. The young men seem
rather taken with her. Don't you think so?"

"I declare I think they are. I always fancy that is rather a
misfortune to a young girl,—particularly when it must mean
nothing, as of course it can't with poor Rachel."

"I don't see that at all."

"Her mother, you know, Mrs. Cornbury;—they are not in
the way of seeing any company. It was so kind of you to bring
her here, and really she does look very nice. My girls are very
good-natured to her. I only hope her head won't be turned.
Here's Mr. Tappitt. You must go down, Mrs. Cornbury, and
eat a little bit of supper." Then Mr. Tappitt in his blue waistcoat led Mrs. Cornbury away.

"I am a very bad hand at supper," said the lady.

"You must take just one glass of champagne," said the gentleman. Now that the wine was there, Mr. Tappitt appreciated
the importance of the occasion.

For the last dance before supper,—or that which was intended to be the last,—Rachel had by long agreement been
the partner of Walter Cornbury. But now that it was over,
the majority of the performers could not go into the supper-
room because of the crowd. Young Cornbury therefore proposed that they should loiter about till their time came. He was
very well inclined for such loitering with Rachel.

"You're flirting with that girl, Master Walter," said Mrs.
Cornbury.

"I suppose that's what she came for," said the cousin.

"By no means, and she's under my care; therefore I beg
you'll talk no nonsense to her."

Walter Cornbury probably did talk a little nonsense to her,
but it was very innocent nonsense. Most of such flirtations if

they were done out loud would be very innocent. Young men are not nearly so pointed in their compliments as their elders, and generally confine themselves to remarks of which neither mothers nor grandmothers could disapprove if they heard them. The romance lies rather in the thoughts than in the words of those concerned. Walter Cornbury believed that he was flirting and felt himself to be happy, but he had uttered nothing warmer to Rachel than a hope that he might meet her at the next Torquay ball.

"I never go to public balls," said Rachel.

"But why not, Miss Ray?" said Walter.

"I never went to a dance of any description before this."

"But now that you've begun of course you'll go on." Mr. Cornbury's flirtation never reached a higher pitch than that.

When he had got as far as that Luke Rowan played him a trick,—an inhospitable trick, seeing that he, Rowan, was in some sort at home, and that the people about him were bound to obey him. He desired the musicians to strike up again while the elders were eating their supper,—and then claimed Rachel's hand, so that he might have the pleasure of serving her with cold chicken and champagne.

"Miss Ray is going in to supper with me," said Cornbury.

"But supper is not ready," said Rowan, "and Miss Ray is engaged to dance with me."

"Quite a mistake on your part," said Cornbury.

"No mistake at all," said Rowan.

"Indeed it is. Come, Miss Ray, we'll take a turn down into the hall, and see if places are ready for us." Cornbury rather despised Rowan, as being a brewer and mechanical; and probably he showed that he did so.

"Places are not ready, so you need not trouble Miss Ray to go down as yet. But a couple is wanted for a quadrille, and therefore I'm sure she'll stand up."

"Come along, Rachel," said Cherry. "We just want you. This will be the nicest of all, because we shall have room."

Rachel had become unhappy seeing that the two men were

in earnest. Had not Cherry spoken she would have remained with Mr. Cornbury, thinking that to be her safer conduct; but Cherry's voice had overpowered her, and she gave her arm to young Rowan, moving away with slow, hesitating step.

"Of course Miss Ray will do as she pleases," said Cornbury.

"Of course she will," said Rowan.

"I am so sorry," said Rachel, "but I was engaged, and it seems I am really wanted." Walter Cornbury bowed very stiffly, and there was an end of his flirtation. "That's the sort of thing that always happens when a fellow comes among this sort of people!" It was thus he consoled himself as he went down solitary to his supper.

"That's all right," said Rowan; "now we've Cherry for our vis-à-vis, and after that we'll go down to supper comfortably."

"But I said I'd go with him."

"You can't now, for he has gone without you. What a brick Cherry is! Do you know what she said of you?"

"No; do tell me."

"I won't. It will make you vain."

"Oh, dear no; but I want Cherry to like me, because I am so fond of her."

"She says you're by far—— But I won't tell you. I hate compliments, and that would look like one. Come, who's forgetting the figure now? I shouldn't wonder if young Cornbury went into the brewery and drowned himself in one of the vats."

It was very nice,—very nice indeed. This was her third dance with Luke Rowan, and she was beginning to think that the other two might perhaps come off without any marked impropriety on her part. She was a little unhappy about Mr. Cornbury,—on his cousin's account rather than on his own. Mrs. Cornbury had been so kind to her that she ought to have remained with Walter when he desired it. So she told herself; —but yet she liked being taken down to supper by Luke Rowan. She had one other cause of uneasiness. She constantly caught Mrs. Tappitt's eye fixed upon herself, and whenever she did so Mrs. Tappitt's eye seemed to look unkindly at her. She had also an instinctive feeling that Augusta did not regard her with favour, and that this disfavour arose from Mr. Rowan's attentions. It was all very nice; but still she felt that there was danger around her, and sometimes she would pause a moment in her happiness, and almost tremble as she thought of things. She was dividing herself poles asunder from Mrs. Prime.

"And now we'll go to supper," said Rowan. "Come, Cherry; do you and Boyd go on first." Boyd was a friend of Rowan's. "Do you know, I've done such a clever trick. This is my second descent among the eatables. As I belong in a manner to the house I took down Miss Harford, and hovered about her for five minutes. Then I managed to lose myself in the crowd, and coming up here got the music up. The fellows were just going off. We've plenty of time now, because they're in the kitchen eating and drinking. I contrived all that dodge that I might give you this glass of wine with my own hands."

"Oh, Mr. Rowan, it was very wrong!"

"And that's my reward! I don't care about its being wrong as long as it's pleasant."

"What shocking morality!"

"All is fair in—— Well, never mind, you'll own it is pleasant."

"Oh, yes; it's very pleasant."

"Then I'm contented, and will leave the moral of it for Mr. Cornbury. I'll tell you something further if you'll let me."

"Pray don't tell me anything that you ought not."

"I've done all I could to get up this party on purpose that we might have you here."

"Nonsense."

"But I have. I have cared about it just because it would enable me to say one word to you;—and now I'm afraid to say it."

She was sitting there close to him, and she couldn't go away. She couldn't run as she had done from the stile. She couldn't show any feeling of offence before all those who were around her; and yet,—was it not her duty to do something to stop him? "Pray don't say such things," she whispered.

"I tell you that I'm afraid to say it. Here; give me some wine. You'll take some more. No? Well; shall we go? I am afraid to say it." They were now out in the hall, standing idly there, with their backs to another door. "I wonder what answer you would make me!"   •

"We had better go up-stairs. Indeed we had."

"Stop a moment, Miss Ray. Why is it that you are so unwilling even to stay a moment with me?"

"I'm not unwilling. Only we had better go now."

"Do you remember when I held your arm at the stile?"

"No; I don't remember anything about it. You ought not to have done it. Do you know, I think you are very cruel." As she made the accusation, she looked down upon the floor, and spoke in a low, trembling voice that almost convinced him that she was in earnest.

"Cruel!" said he. "That's hard too."

"Or you wouldn't prevent me enjoying myself while I am here, by saying things which you ought to know I don't like."

"I have hardly thought whether you would like what I say or not; but I know this; I would give anything in the world to make myself sure that you would ever look back upon this evening as a happy one."

"I will if you'll come up-stairs, and——"

"And what?"

"And go on without—without seeming to mind me so much."

"Ah, but I do mind you. Rachel—no; you shall not go for a minute. Listen to me for one moment." Then he tried to stand before her, but she was off from him, and ran up-stairs by herself. What was it that he wished to say to her? She knew that she would have liked to have heard it;—nay, that she was longing to hear it. But she was startled and afraid of him, and as she gently crept in at the door of the dancing-room, she determined that she would tell Mrs. Cornbury that she was quite ready for the carriage. It was impossible that she should go through those other two dances with Luke Rowan; and as for her other engagements, they must be allowed to shift for themselves. One had been made early in the evening with Mr. Griggs. It would be a great thing to escape dancing with Mr. Griggs. She would ask Cherry to make her apologies to everybody. As she entered the room she felt ashamed of herself, and unable to take any place. She was oppressed by an idea that she ought not to be walking about without some gentleman with her, and that people would observe her. She was still very near the door when she perceived that Mr. Rowan was also coming in. She determined to avoid him if she could, feeling sure that she could not stop him in anything that he might say, while so many people would be close around them. And yet she felt almost disappointment when she heard his voice as he talked merrily with some one at the door. At that moment Mrs. Cornbury came up to her, walking across the room on purpose to join her.

"What, all alone! I thought your hand was promised for every dance up to five o'clock."

"I believe I'm engaged to some one now, but I declare I don't know who it is. I dare say he has forgotten."

"Ah, yes; people do get confused a little just about this time. Will you come and sit down?"

"Thank you, I should like that. But, Mrs. Cornbury, when you're ready to go away, I am,—quite ready."

"Go away! Why I thought you intended to dance at least for the next two hours."

In answer to this, Rachel declared that she was tired. "And, Mrs. Cornbury, I want to avoid that man," and she pointed out Mr. Griggs by a glance of her eye. "I think he'll say I'm engaged to him for the next waltz, and—I don't like him."

"Poor man; he doesn't look very nice, certainly; but if that's all I'll get you out of the scrape without running away." Then Mr. Griggs came up, and, with a very low bow, stuck out the point of his elbow towards Rachel, expecting her immediately to put her hand within it.

"I'm afraid, sir, you must excuse Miss Ray just at present. She's too tired to dance immediately."

Mr. Griggs looked at his card, then looked at Rachel, then looked at Mrs. Cornbury, and stood twiddling the bunch of little gilt playthings that hung from his chain. "That is too hard," said he; "deuced hard."

"I'm very sorry," said Rachel.

"So shall I be,—uncommon. Really, Mrs. Cornbury, I think a turn or two would do her good. Don't you?"

"I can't say I do. She says she would rather not, and of course you won't press her."

"I don't see it in that light,—I really don't. A gentleman has his rights you know, Mrs. Cornbury. Miss Ray won't deny——"

"Miss Ray will deny that she intends to stand up for this dance. And one of the rights of a gentleman is to take a lady at her word."

"Really, Mrs. Cornbury, you are down upon one so hard."

"Rachel," said she, "would you mind coming across the room with me? There are seats on the sofa on the other side." Then Mrs. Cornbury sailed across the floor, and Rachel crept after her more dismayed than ever. Mr. Griggs the while stood transfixed to his place, stroking his mustaches with his hand, and showing plainly by his countenance that he didn't know what he ought to do next. "Well, that's cool," said he; "confounded cool!"

"Anything wrong, Griggs, my boy?" said a bank clerk, slapping him on the back.

"I call it very wrong; very wrong, indeed," said Griggs; "but people do give themselves such airs! Miss Cherry, may I have the honour of waltzing with you?"

"Certainly not," said Cherry, who was passing by. Then Mr. Griggs made his way back to the door.

Rachel felt that things were going wrong with her. It had so happened that she had parted on bad terms with three gen-

tlemen. She had offended Mr. Cornbury and Mr. Griggs, and
had done her best to make Mr. Rowan understand that he had
offended her! She conceived that all the room would know of it,
and that Mrs. Cornbury would become ashamed of her. That
Mrs. Tappitt was already very angry with her she was quite
sure. She wished she had not come to the ball, and began to
think that perhaps her sister might be right. It almost seemed
to herself that she had not known how to behave herself. For a
short time she had been happy,—very happy; but she feared
that she had in some way committed herself during the moments of her happiness. "I hope you are not angry with me,"
she said, "about Mr. Griggs?" appealing to her friend in a
plaintive voice.

"Angry!—oh dear, no. Why should I be angry with you? I
should be angry with that man, only I'm a person that never
gets angry with anybody. You were quite right not to dance
with him. Never be made to dance with any man you don't
like; and remember that a young lady should always have
her own way in a ball-room. She doesn't get much of it anywhere else; does she, my dear? And now I'll go whenever you
like it, but I'm not the least in a hurry. You're the young lady,
and you're to have your own way. If you're quite in earnest,
I'll get some one to order the carriage."—Rachel said that she
was quite in earnest, and then Walter was called. "So you're
going, are you?" said he. "Miss Ray has ill-treated me so dreadfully that I can't express my regret." "Ill-treated you, too, has
she? Upon my word, my dear, you've shown yourself quite
great upon the occasion. When I was a girl, there was nothing
I liked so much as offending all my partners." But Rachel was
red with dismay, and wretched that such an accusation should
be made against her. "Oh, Mrs. Cornbury, I didn't mean to offend him! I'll explain it all in the carriage. What will you think
of me?" "Think, my dear?—why, I shall think that you are going to turn all the young men's heads in Baslehurst. But I shall
hear all about it from Walter to-morrow. He tells me of all his
loves and all his disappointments."

While the carriage was being brought round, Rachel kept close to her chaperon; but every now and again her eyes, in spite of herself, would wander away to Mr. Rowan. Was he in any way affected by her leaving him, or was it all a joke to him? He was dancing now with Cherry Tappitt, and Rachel was sure that all of it was a joke. But it was a cruel joke,— cruel because it exposed her to so much ill-natured remark. With him she would quarrel,—quarrel really. She would let him know that he should not call her by her Christian name just when it suited him to do so, and then take himself off to play with others in the same way. She would tell Cherry, and make Cherry understand that all walks and visiting and friendly intercommunications must be abandoned because this young man would take advantage of her position to annoy her! He should be made to understand that she was not in his power! Then, as she thought of this, she caught his eye as he made a sudden stop in the dance close to her, and all her hard thoughts died away. Ah, dear, what was it that she wanted of him?

At that moment they got up to go away. Such a person as Mrs. Butler Cornbury could not, of course, escape without a parade of adieux. Mr. Tappitt was searched up from the little room in which the card-party held their meeting in order that he might hand the guest that had honoured him down to her carriage; and Mrs. Tappitt fluttered about, profuse in her acknowledgments for the favour done to them. "And we do so hope Mr. Cornbury will be successful," she said, as she bade her last farewell. This was spoken close to Mr. Tappitt's ear; and Mrs. Cornbury flattered herself that after that Mr. Tappitt's vote would be secure. Mr. Tappitt said nothing about his vote, but handed the lady down-stairs in solemn silence.

The Tappitt girls came and clustered about Rachel as she was going. "I can't conceive why you are off so early," said Martha. "No, indeed," said Mrs. Tappitt; "only of course it would be very wrong to keep Mrs. Cornbury waiting when she has been so excessively kind to you." "The naughty girl! It isn't that at all," said Cherry. "It's she that is hurrying Mrs. Cornbury away." "Good night," said Augusta very coldly. "And Rachel," said Cherry, "mind you come up to-morrow and talk it all over; we shall have so much to say." Then Rachel turned to go, and found Luke Rowan at her elbow waiting to take her down. She had no alternative;—she must take his arm; and thus they walked down-stairs into the hall together.

"You'll come up here to-morrow," said he.

"No, no; tell Cherry that I shall not come."

"Then I shall go to Bragg's End. Will your mother let me call?"

"No, don't come. Pray don't."

"I certainly shall;—certainly, certainly! What things have you got? Let me put your shawl on for you. If you do not come up to the girls, I shall certainly go down to you. Now, good night. Good night, Mrs. Cornbury." And Luke, getting hold of Rachel's reluctant hand, pressed it with all his warmth.

"I don't want to ask indiscreet questions," said Mrs. Cornbury; "but that young man seems rather smitten, I think."

"Oh, no," said Rachel, not knowing what to say.

"But I say,—oh, yes; a nice good-looking man he is too, and a gentleman, which is more than I can say for all of them there. What an escape you had of Mr. Griggs, my dear!"

"Yes, I had. But I was so sorry that you should have to speak to him."

"Of course I spoke to him. I was there to fight your battles for you. That's why married ladies go to balls. You were quite right not to dance with him. A girl should always avoid any intimacy with such men as that. It is not that he would have done you any harm; but they stand in the way of your satisfaction and contentment. Balls are given specially for young ladies; and it is my theory that they are to make themselves happy while they are there, and not sacrifice themselves to men whom they don't wish to know. You can't always refuse when you're asked, but you can always get out of an engagement afterwards if you know what you're about. That was my way when I was a girl." And this was the daughter of Mr. Comfort, whose somewhat melancholy discourses against the world's pleasures and vanities had so often filled Rachel's bosom with awe!

Rachel sat silent, thinking of what had occurred at Mrs. Tappitt's; and thinking also that she ought to make some little speech to her friend, thanking her for all that she had done. Ought she not also to apologise in some way for her own conduct? "What was that between you and my cousin Walter?" Mrs. Cornbury asked, after a few moments.

"I hope I wasn't to blame," said Rachel. "But——"

"But what? Of course you weren't to blame;—unless it was in being run after by so many gentlemen at once."

"He was going to take me down to supper,—and it was so kind of him. And then while we were waiting because the room down-stairs was full, there was another quadrille, and I was engaged to Mr. Rowan."

"Ah, yes; I understand. And so Master Walter got thrown once. His wrath in such matters never lasts very long. Here we are at Bragg's End. I've been so glad to have you with me, and I hope I may take you again with me somewhere before long. Remember me kindly to your mother. There she is at the door waiting for you." Then Rachel jumped out of the carriage, and ran across the little gravel path into the house.

Mrs. Ray had been waiting up for her daughter, and had been listening eagerly for the wheels of the carriage. It was not yet two o'clock, and by ball-going people the hour of Rachel's return would have been considered early; but to Mrs. Ray anything after midnight was very late. She was not, however, angry, or even vexed, but simply pleased that her girl had at last come back to her. "Oh, mamma, I'm afraid it has been very hard upon you, waiting for me!" said Rachel; "but I did come away as soon as I could." Mrs. Ray declared that she had not found it all hard, and then,—with a laudable curiosity, seeing how little she had known about balls,—desired to have an immediate account of Rachel's doings.

"And did you get anybody to dance with you?" asked the

mother, feeling a mother's ambition that her daughter should have been "respectit like the lave."

"Oh, yes; plenty of people asked me to dance."

"And did you find it come easy?"

"Quite easy. I was frightened about the waltzing, at first."

"Do you mean that you waltzed, Rachel?"

"Yes, mamma. Everybody did it. Mrs. Cornbury said she always waltzed when she was a girl; and as the things turned out I could not help myself. I began with her cousin. I didn't mean to do it, but I got so ashamed of myself that I couldn't refuse."

Mrs. Ray still was not angry; but she was surprised, and perhaps a little dismayed. "And did you like it?"

"Yes, mamma."

"Were they all kind to you?"

"Yes, mamma."

"You seem to have very little to say about it; but I suppose you're tired."

"I am tired, but it isn't that. It seems that there is so much to think about. I'll tell you everything to-morrow, when I get quiet again. Not that there is much to tell."

"Then I'll wish you good night, dear."

"Good night, mamma. Mrs. Cornbury was so kind,—you can have no idea how good-natured she is."

"She always was a good creature."

"If I'd been her sister she couldn't have done more for me. I feel as though I were really quite fond of her. But she isn't a bit like what I expected. She chooses to have her own way; but then she is so good-humoured! And when I got into any little trouble she——"

"Well, what else did she do; and what trouble had you?"

"I can't quite describe what I mean. She seemed to make so much of me;—just as she might have done if I'd been some grand young lady down from London, or any, any—you know what I mean."

Mrs. Ray sat with her candle in her hand, receiving great

comfort from the knowledge that her daughter had been "respectit." She knew well what Rachel meant, and reflected, with perhaps a pardonable pride, that she herself had "come of decent people." The Tappitts were higher than her in the world, and so were the Griggses. But she knew that her forbears had been gentlefolk, when there were, so to speak, no Griggses and no Tappitts in existence. It was pleasant to her to think that her daughter had been treated as a lady.

"And she did do me such a kindness. That horrid Mr. Griggs was going to dance with me, and she wouldn't let him."

"I don't like that young man at all."

"Poor Cherry! you should hear her talk of him! And she would have stayed ever so much longer if I had not pressed her to go; and then she has such a nice way of saying things."

"She always had that, when she was quite a young girl."

"I declare I feel that I quite love her. And there was such a grand supper. Champagne!"

"No!"

"I got some cold turkey. Mr. Rowan took me down to supper." These last words were spoken very mildly, and Rachel, as she uttered them, did not dare to look into her mother's face.

"Did you dance with him?"

"Yes, mamma, three times. I should have stayed later only I was engaged to dance with him twice more; and I didn't choose to do so."

"Was he——? Did he——?"

"Oh, mamma; I can't tell you. I don't know how to tell you. I wish you knew it all without my saying anything. He says he shall come here to-morrow if I don't go up to the brewery; and I can't possibly go there now, after that."

"Did he say anything more than that, Rachel?"

"He calls me Rachel, and speaks—I can't tell you how he speaks. If you think it wrong, mamma, I won't ever see him again."

Mrs. Ray didn't know whether she ought to think it wrong

or not. She was inclined to wish that it was right and to believe that it was wrong. A few minutes ago Rachel was unable to open her mouth, and was anxious to escape to bed; but, now that the ice was broken between her and her mother, they sat up for more than an hour talking about Luke Rowan.

"I wonder whether he will really come?" Rachel said to herself, as she laid her head upon her pillow—"and why does he want to come?"

CHAPTER IX

Mr. Prong at Home

MRS. TAPPITT'S BALL was celebrated on a Tuesday, and on the preceding Monday Mrs. Prime moved herself off, bag and baggage, to Miss Pucker's lodgings. Miss Pucker had been elated with a dismal joy when the proposition was first made to her. "Oh, yes; it was very dreadful. She would do anything;—of course she would give up the front bedroom up-stairs to Mrs. Prime, and get a stretcher for herself in the little room behind, which looked out on the tiles of Griggs's sugar warehouse. She hadn't thought such a thing would have been possible; she really had not. A ball! Mrs. Prime couldn't help coming away; —of course not. And there would be plenty of room for all her boxes in the small room behind the shop. Mrs. Ray's daughter go to a ball!" And then some threatening words were said as to the destiny of wicked people, which shall not be repeated here.

That flitting had been a very dismal affair. An old man out of Baslehurst had come for Mrs. Prime's things with a donkey-cart, and the old man, assisted by the girl, had carried them out together. Rachel had remained secluded in her mother's room. The two sisters had met at the same table at breakfast, but had not spoken over their tea and bread and butter. As Rachel was taking the cloth away Mrs. Prime had asked her solemnly whether she still persisted in bringing perdition upon herself and her mother. "You have no right to ask me such a question," Rachel had answered, and taking herself up-stairs had secluded herself till the old man with the donkey, followed by Mrs. Prime, had taken himself away from Bragg's End. Mrs. Ray, as her eldest daughter was leaving her, stood at the door of her house with her handkerchief to her eyes. "It makes me very unhappy, Dorothea; so it does." "And it makes me very unhappy, too, mother. Perhaps my sorrow in the matter is deeper than yours. But I must do my duty." Then the two widows kissed each other with a cold unloving kiss, and Mrs. Prime had taken her departure from Bragg's End cottage. "It will make a great difference in the housekeeping," Mrs. Ray said to Rachel, and then she went to work at her little accounts.

It was Dorcas-day at Miss Pucker's, and as the work of the meeting began soon after Mrs. Prime had unpacked her boxes in the front bedroom and had made her little domestic arrangements with her friend, that first day passed by without much tedium. Mrs. Prime was used to Miss Pucker, and was not therefore grievously troubled by the ways and habits of that lady, much as they were unlike those to which she had been accustomed at Bragg's End; but on the next morning, as she was sitting with her companion after breakfast, an idea did come into her head that Miss Pucker would not be a pleasant companion for life. She would talk incessantly of the wickednesses of the cottage, and ask repeated questions about Rachel and the young man. Mrs. Prime was undoubtedly very angry with her mother, and much shocked at her sister, but she did not relish the outspoken sympathy of her confidential friend. "He'll never marry her, you know. He don't think of such a thing," said Miss Pucker over and over again. Mrs. Prime did not find this pleasant when spoken of her sister. "And the young men I'm told goes on anyhow, as they pleases at them dances," said Miss Pucker, who in the warmth of her intimacy forgot some of those little restrictions in speech with which she had burdened herself when first striving to acquire the friendship of Mrs. Prime. Before dinner was over Mrs. Prime had made up her mind that she must soon move her staff again, and establish herself somewhere in solitude.

After tea she took herself out for a walk, having managed to decline Miss Pucker's attendance, and as she walked she thought of Mr. Prong. Would it not be well for her to go to him and ask his further advice? He would tell her in what way she had better live. He would tell her also whether it was impossible that she should ever return to the cottage, for already her heart was becoming somewhat more soft than was its wont. And as she walked she met Mr. Prong himself, intent on his pastoral business. "I was thinking of coming to you to-morrow," she said, after their first salutation was over.

"Do," said he; "do; come early,—before the toil of the day's work commences. I also am specially anxious to see you. Will nine be too early,—or, if you have not concluded your morning meal by that time, half-past nine?"

Mrs. Prime assured him that her morning meal was always concluded before nine o'clock, and promised to be with him by that hour. Then as she slowly paced up the High Street to the Cawston bridge and back again, she wondered within herself as to the matter on which Mr. Prong could specially want to see her. He might probably desire to claim her services for some woman's work in his sheepfold. He should have them willingly, for she had begun to feel that she would sooner co-operate with Mr. Prong than with Miss Pucker. As she returned down the High Street, and came near to her own door, she saw the cause of all her family troubles standing at the entrance to Griggs's wine-store. He was talking to the shopman within, and as she passed she frowned grimly beneath her widow's bonnet. "Send them to the brewery at once," said Luke Rowan to the man. "They are wanted this evening."

"I understand," said the man.

"And tell your fellow to take them round to the back door."

"All right," said the man, winking with one eye. He understood very well that young Rowan was ordering the champagne for Mrs. Tappitt's supper, and that it was thought desirable that Mr. Tappitt shouldn't see the bottles going into the house.

Miss Pucker possessed at any rate the virtue of being early, so that Mrs. Prime had no difficulty in concluding her "morning meal," and being at Mr. Prong's house punctually at nine o'clock. Mr. Prong, it seemed, had not been quite so steadfast to his purpose, for his teapot was still upon the table, together with the debris of a large dish of shrimps, the eating of small shell-fish being an innocent enjoyment to which he was much addicted.

"Dear me; so it is; just nine. We'll have these things away in a minute. Mrs. Mudge; Mrs. Mudge!" Whereupon Mrs. Mudge came forth, and between the three the table was soon cleared. "I wish you hadn't caught me so late," said Mr. Prong; "it looks as though I hadn't been thinking of you." Then he picked up the stray shell of a shrimp, and in order that he might get rid of it, put it into his mouth. Mrs. Prime said she hoped she didn't trouble him, and that of course she didn't expect him to be thinking about her particularly. Then Mr. Prong looked at her in a way that was very particular out of the corner of his eyes, and assured her that he had been thinking of her all night. After that Mrs. Prime sat down on a horsehair-seated chair, and Mr. Prong sat on another opposite to her, leaning back, with his eyes nearly closed, and his hands folded upon his lap.

"I don't think Miss Pucker's will quite do for me," said Mrs. Prime, beginning her story first.

"I never thought it would, my friend," said Mr. Prong, with his eyes still nearly closed.

"She's a very good woman,—an excellent woman, and her heart is full of love and charity. But——"

"I quite understand it, my friend. She is not in all things the companion you desire."

"I am not quite sure that I shall want any companion."

"Ah!" sighed Mr. Prong shaking his head, but still keeping his eyes closed.

"I think I would rather be alone, if I do not return to them at the cottage. I would fain return if only they——"

"If only they would return too. Yes! That would be a glorious end to the struggle you have made, if you can bring them back with you from following after the Evil One! But you cannot return to them now, if you are to countenance by your presence dancings and love-makings in the open air,"—why worse in the open air than in a close little parlour in a back street, Mr. Prong did not say,—"and loud revellings, and the absence of all good works, and rebellion against the Spirit." Mr. Prong was becoming energetic in his language, and at one time had raised himself in his chair, and opened his eyes. But he closed them at once, and again fell back. "No, my friend," said he, "no. It must not be so. They must be rescued from the burning; but not so,—not so." After that for a minute or two they both sat still in silence.

"I think I shall get two small rooms for myself in one of the quiet streets, near the new church," said she.

"Ah, yes, perhaps so,—for a time."

"Till I may be able to go back to mother. It's a sad thing families being divided, Mr. Prong."

"Yes, it is sad;—unless it tends to the doing of the Lord's work."

"But I hope;—I do hope, that all this may be changed. Rachel I know is obstinate, but mother means well, Mr. Prong. She means to do her duty, if only she had good teaching near her."

"I hope she may, I hope she may. I trust that they may both be brought to see the true light. We will wrestle for them,—you and me. We will wrestle for them,—together. Mrs. Prime, my friend, if you are prepared to hear me with attention, I have a proposition to make which I think you will acknowledge to be one of importance." Then suddenly he sat bolt upright, opened his eyes wide, and dressed his mouth with all the solemn dignity of which he was the master. "Are you prepared to listen to me, Mrs. Prime?"

Mrs. Prime, who was somewhat astonished, said in a low voice that she was prepared to listen.

"Because I must beg you to hear me out. I shall fail altogether in reaching your intelligence,—whatever effect I might possibly have upon your heart,—unless you will hear me to the end."

"I will hear you certainly, Mr. Prong."

"Yes, my friend, for it will be necessary. If I could convey to your mind all that is now passing through my own, without any spoken word, how glad should I be! The words of men, when taken at the best, how weak they are! They often tell a tale quite different from that which the creature means who uses them. Every minister has felt that in addressing his flock from the pulpit. I feel it myself sadly, but I never felt it so sadly as I do now."

Mrs. Prime did not quite understand him, but she assured him again that she would give his words her best attention, and that she would endeavour to gather from them no other meaning than that which seemed to be his. "Ah,—seemed!" said he. "There is so much of seeming in this deceitful world. But you will believe this of me, that whatever I do, I do as tending to the strengthening of my hands in the ministry." Mrs. Prime said that she would believe so much; and then as she looked into her companion's face, she became aware that there was something of weakness displayed in that assuming mouth. She did not argue about it within her own mind, but the fact had in some way become revealed to her.

"My friend," said he,—and as he spoke he drew his chair across the rug, so as to bring it very near to that on which Mrs. Prime was sitting—"our destinies in this world, yours and mine, are in many things alike. We are both alone. We both of us have our hands full of work, and of work which in many respects is the same. We are devoted to the same cause: is it not so?" Mrs. Prime, who had been told that she was to listen and not to speak, did not at first make any answer. But she was pressed by a repetition of the question. "Is it not so, Mrs. Prime?"

"I can never make my work equal to that of a minister of the Gospel," said she.

"But you can share the work of such a minister. You understand me now. And let me assure you of this; that in making this proposition to you, I am not self-seeking. It is not my own worldly comfort and happiness to which I am chiefly looking."

"Ah," said Mrs. Prime, "I suppose not." Perhaps there was in her voice the slightest touch of soreness.

"No;—not chiefly to that. I want assistance, confidential intercourse, sympathy, a congenial mind, support when I am like to faint, counsel when I am pressing on, aid when the toil is too heavy for me, a kind word when the day's work is over. And you,—do you not desire the same? Are we not alike in that, and would it not be well that we should come together?" Mr. Prong as he spoke had put out his hand, and rested it on the table with the palm upwards, as though expecting that she would put hers within it; and he had tilted his chair so as to bring his body closer to hers, and had dropped from his face his assumed look of dignity. He was quite in earnest, and being so had fallen away into his natural dispositions of body.

"I do not quite understand you," said Mrs. Prime. She did however understand him perfectly, but thought it expedient that he should be required to speak a little further before she answered him. She wanted time also to arrange her reply. As yet she had not made up her mind whether she would say yes or no.

"Mrs. Prime, I am offering to make you my wife. I have said nothing of love, of that human affection which one of God's creatures entertains for another;—not, I can assure you, because I do not feel it, but because I think that you and I should be governed in our conduct by a sense of duty, rather than by the poor creature-longings of the heart."

"The heart is very deceitful," said Mrs. Prime.

"That is true,—very true; but my heart, in this matter, is not deceitful. I entertain for you all that deep love which a man should feel for her who is to be the wife of his bosom."

"But Mr. Prong——"

"Let me finish before you give me your answer. I have thought much of this, as you may believe; and by only one consideration have I been made to doubt the propriety of taking this step. People will say that I am marrying you for—for your money, in short. It is an insinuation which would give me much pain, but I have resolved within my own mind, that it is my duty to bear it. If my motives are pure,"—here he paused a moment for a word or two of encouragement, but received none,—"and if the thing itself be good, I ought not to be deterred by any fear of what the wicked may say. Do you not agree with me in that?"

Mrs. Prime still did not answer. She felt that any word of assent, though given by her to a minor proposition, might be taken as involving some amount of assent towards the major proposition. Mr. Prong had enjoyed the advantage of thinking over his matrimonial prospects in undisturbed solitude, but she had as yet possessed no such advantage. As the idea had never before presented itself to her, she did not feel inclined to commit herself hastily.

"And as regards money," he continued.

"Well," said Mrs. Prime, looking down demurely upon the ground, for Mr. Prong had not at once gone on to say what were his ideas about money.

"And as regards money,—need I hardly declare that my motives are pure and disinterested? I am aware that in worldly affairs you are at present better off than I am. My professional income from the pew-rents is about a hundred and thirty pounds a year."—It must be admitted that it was very hard work. By this time Mr. Prong had withdrawn his hand from the table, finding that attempt to be hopeless, and had resettled his chair upon its four feet. He had commenced by requesting Mrs. Prime to hear him patiently, but he had probably not calculated that she would have listened with a patience so cruel and unrelenting. She did not even speak a word when he communicated to her the amount of his income. "That is what I receive here," he continued, "and you are probably aware that I have no private means of my own."

"I didn't know," said Mrs. Prime.

"No; none. But what then?"

"Oh, dear no."

"Money is but dross. Who feels that more strongly than you do?"

Mr. Prong in all that he was saying intended to be honest, and in asserting that money was dross, he believed that he spoke his true mind. He thought also that he was passing a just eulogium on Mrs. Prime, in declaring that she was of the same opinion. But he was not quite correct in this, either as regarded himself, or as regarded her. He did not covet money, but he valued it very highly; and as for Mrs. Prime, she had an almost unbounded satisfaction in her own independence. She had, after all, but two hundred a year, out of which she gave very much in charity. But this giving in charity was her luxury. Fine raiment and dainty food tempted her not at all; but nevertheless she was not free from temptations, and did not perhaps always resist them. To be mistress of her money, and to superintend the gifts, not only of herself but of others; to be great among the poor, and esteemed as a personage in her district,— that was her ambition. When Mr. Prong told her that money in her sight was dross, she merely shook her head. Why was it that she wrote those terribly caustic notes to the agent in Exeter if her quarterly payments were ever late by a single week? "Defend me from a lone widow," the agent used to say, "and especially if she's evangelical." Mrs. Prime delighted in the sight of the bit of paper which conveyed to her the possession of her periodical wealth. To her money certainly was not dross, and I doubt if it was truly so regarded by Mr. Prong himself.

"Any arrangements that you choose as to settlements or the like of that, could of course be made." Mr. Prong when he began, or rather when he made up his mind to begin, had determined that he would use all his best power of language in pressing his suit; but the work had been so hard that his fine language had got itself lost in the struggle. I doubt whether this made much difference with Mrs. Prime; or it may be, that he had sustained the propriety of his words as long as such propriety was needful and salutary to his purpose. Had he spoken of the "like of that" at the opening of the negotiation, he might have shocked his hearer; but now she was too deeply engaged in solid serious considerations to care much for the words which were used. "A hundred and thirty from pew-rents," she said to herself, as he endeavoured, unsuccessfully, to look under her bonnet into her face.

"I think I have said it all now," he continued. "If you will trust yourself into my keeping I will endeavour, with God's assistance, to do my duty by you. I have said but little personally of myself or of my feelings, hoping that it might be unnecessary."

"Oh, quite so," said she.

"I have spoken rather of those duties which we should undertake together in sweet companionship, if you will consent to—to—to be Mrs. Prong, in short." Then he waited for an answer.

As she sat in her widow's weeds, there was not, to the eye, the promise in her of much sweet companionship. Her old crape bonnet had been lugged and battered about—not out of all shape, as hats and bonnets are sometimes battered by young ladies, in which guise, if the young ladies themselves be pretty, the battered hats and bonnets are often more becoming than ever they were in their proper shapes—but so as closely to fit her head, and almost hide her face. Her dress was so made, and so put on, as to give to her the appearance of almost greater age than her mother's. She had studied to divest herself of all outward show of sweet companionship; but perhaps she was not the less, on that account, gratified to find that she had not altogether succeeded.

"I have done with the world, and all the world's vanities and cares," she said, shaking her head.

"No one can have done with the world as long as there is work in it for him or her to do. The monks and nuns tried that, and you know what they came to."

"But I am a widow."

"Yes, my friend; and have shown yourself, as such, very willing to do your part. But do you not know that you could be more active and more useful as a clergyman's wife than you can be as a solitary woman?"

"But my heart is buried, Mr. Prong."

"No; not so. While the body remains in this vale of tears, the heart must remain with it." Mrs. Prime shook her head; but in an anatomical point of view, Mr. Prong was no doubt strictly correct. "Other hopes will arise,—and perhaps, too, other cares, but they will be sources of gentle happiness."

Mrs. Prime understood him as alluding to a small family, and again shook her head at the allusion.

"What I have said may probably have taken you by surprise."

"Yes, it has, Mr. Prong;—very much."

"And if so, it may be that you would wish time for consideration before you give me an answer."

"Perhaps that will be best, Mr. Prong."

"Let it be so. On what day shall we say? Will Friday suit you? If I come to you on Friday morning, perhaps Miss Pucker will be there."

"Yes, she will."

"And in the afternoon."

"We shall be at the Dorcas meeting."

"I don't like to trouble you to come here again."

Mrs. Prime herself felt that there was a difficulty. Hitherto she had entertained no objection to calling on Mr. Prong at his own house. His little sitting-room had been as holy ground to her,—almost as part of the church, and she had taken herself there without scruple. But things had now been put on a different footing. It might be that that room would become her own peculiar property, but she could never again regard it in a simply clerical light. It had become as it were a bower of love, and she could not take her steps thither with the express object of assenting to the proposition made to her,—or even with that of dissenting from it. "Perhaps," said she, "you could call at ten on Saturday. Miss Pucker will be out marketing." To this Mr. Prong agreed, and then Mrs. Prime got up and took her leave. How fearfully wicked would Rachel have been in her eyes, had Rachel made an appointment with a young man at some hour and some place in which she might be found alone! But then it is so easy to trust oneself, and so easy also to distrust others.

"Good morning," said Mrs. Prime; and as she went she gave her hand as a matter of course to her lover.

"Good-bye," said he; "and think well of this if you can do so. If you believe that you will be more useful as my wife than you can be in your present position,—then——"

"You think it would be my duty to——"

"Well, I will leave that for you to decide. I merely wish to put the matter before you. But, pray, understand this; money need be no hindrance." Then, having said that last word, he let her go.

She walked away very slowly, and did not return by the most direct road to Miss Pucker's rooms. There was much to be considered in the offer that had been made to her. Her lot in life would be very lonely if this separation from her mother and sister should become permanent. She had already made up her mind that a continued residence with Miss Pucker would not suit her; and although, on that very morning, she had felt that there would be much comfort in living by herself, now, as she looked forward to that loneliness, it had for her very little attraction. Might it not be true, also, that she could do more good as a clergyman's wife than could possibly come within her reach as a single woman? She had tried that life once already, but then she had been very young. As that memory came upon her, she looked back to her early life, and thought of the hopes which had been hers as she stood at the altar, now so many years ago. How different had been everything with her then! She remembered the sort of love she had felt in her heart, and told herself that there could be no repetition of such love on Mr. Prong's behalf. She had come round in her walk to that very churchyard stile at which she had seen Rachel standing with Luke Rowan, and as she remembered some passages in her own girlish days, she almost felt inclined to forgive her sister. But then, on a sudden, she drew herself up almost with a gasp, and went on quickly with her walk. Had she not herself in those days walked in darkness, and had it not since that been vouchsafed to her to see the light? In her few months of married happiness it had been given to her to do but little of that work which might now be possible to her. Then she had been married in the flesh; now she would be married in the spirit;— she would be married in the spirit, if it should, on final consideration, seem good to her to accept Mr. Prong's offer in that light. Then unconsciously, she began to reflect on the rights of a married woman with regard to money,—and also on the wrongs. She was not sure as to the law, and asked herself whether it would be possible for her to consult an attorney. Finally, she thought it would not be practicable to do so before giving her answer to Mr. Prong.

And she could not even ask her mother. As to that, too, she questioned herself, and resolved that she could not so far lower herself under existing circumstances. There was no one to whom she could go for advice. But we may say this of her,— let her have asked whom she would, she would have at least been guided by her own judgment. If only she could have obtained some slight amount of legal information, how useful it would have been!

CHAPTER X

Luke Rowan Declares His Plans
as to the Brewery

"THE TRUTH IS, T., there was some joking among the young people about the wine, and then Rowan went and ordered it." This was Mrs. Tappitt's explanation about the champagne, made to her husband on the night of the ball, before she was allowed to go to sleep. But this by no means satisfied him. He did not choose, as he declared, that any young man should order whatever he might think necessary for his house. Then Mrs. Tappitt made it worse. "To tell the truth, T., I think it was intended as a present to the girls. We are doing a great deal to make him comfortable, you know, and I fancy he thought it right to make them this little return." She should have known her husband better. It was true that he grudged the cost of the wine; but he would have preferred to endure that to the feeling that his table had been supplied by another man,—by a young man whom he wished to regard as subject to himself, but who would not be subject, and at whom he was beginning to look with very unfavourable eyes. "A present to the girls? I tell you I won't have such presents. And if it was so, I think he has been very impertinent,—very impertinent indeed. I shall tell him so,—and I shall insist on paying for the wine. And I must say, you ought not to have taken it."

"Oh, dear T., I have been working so hard all night; and I do think you ought to let me go to sleep now, instead of scolding me."

On the following morning the party was of course discussed in the Tappitt family under various circumstances. At the breakfast-table Mrs. Rowan, with her son and daughter, were present; and then a song of triumph was sung. Everything had gone off with honour and glory, and the brewery had been immortalized for years to come. Mrs. Butler Cornbury's praises were spoken,—with some little drawback of a sneer on them, because "she had made such a fuss with that girl Rachel Ray"; and then the girls had told of their partners, and Luke had declared it all to have been superb. But when the Rowans' backs were turned, and the Tappitts were alone together, others besides old Tappitt himself had words to say in dispraise of Luke. Mrs. Tappitt had been much inclined to make little of her husband's objections to the young man while she hoped that he might possibly become her son-in-law. He might have been a thorn in the brewery, among the vats, but he would have been a flourishing young bay-tree in the outer world of Baslehurst. She had, however, no wish to encourage the growth of a thorn within her own premises, in order that Rachel Ray, or such as she, might have the advantage of the bay-tree. Luke Rowan had behaved very badly at her party. Not only had he failed to distinguish either of her own girls, but he had, as Mrs. Tappitt said, made himself so conspicuous with that foolish girl, that all the world had been remarking it.

"Mrs. Butler Cornbury seemed to think it all right," said Cherry.

"Mrs. Butler Cornbury is not everybody," said Mrs. Tappitt. "I didn't think it right, I can assure you;—and what's more, your papa didn't think it right."

"And he was going on all the evening as though he were quite master in the house," said Augusta. "He was ordering the musicians to do this and that all the evening."

"He'll find that he's not master. Your papa is going to speak to him this very day."

"What!—about Rachel?" asked Cherry, in dismay.

"About things in general," said Mrs. Tappitt. Then Mary Rowan returned to the room, and they all went back upon the glories of the ball. "I think it was nice," said Mrs. Tappitt, simpering. "I'm sure there was no trouble spared,—nor yet expense." She knew that she ought not to have uttered that last word, and she would have refrained if it had been possible to her;—but it was not possible. The man who tells you how much his wine costs a dozen, knows that he is wrong while the words are in his mouth; but they are in his mouth, and he cannot restrain them.

Mr. Tappitt was not about to lecture Luke Rowan as to his conduct in regard to Rachel Ray. He found some difficulty in speaking to his would-be partner, even on matters of business, in a proper tone, and with becoming authority. As he was so much the senior, and Rowan so much the junior, some such tone of superiority was, as he thought, indispensable. But he had great difficulty in assuming it. Rowan had a way with him that was not exactly a way of submission, and Tappitt would certainly not have dared to encounter him on any such matter as his behaviour in a drawing-room. When the time came he had not even the courage to allude to those champagne bottles; and it may be as well explained that Rowan paid the little bill at Griggs's, without further reference to the matter. But the question of the brewery management was a matter vital to Tappitt. There, among the vats, he had reigned supreme since Bungall ceased to be king, and for continual mastery there it was worth his while to make a fight. That he was under difficulties even in that fight he had already begun to know. He could not talk Luke Rowan down, and make him go about his work in an orderly, every-day, business-like fashion. Luke Rowan would not be talked down, nor would he be orderly,—not according to Mr. Tappitt's orders. No doubt Mr. Tappitt, under these circumstances, could decline the partnership; and this he was disposed to do; but he had been consulting lawyers, consulting papers, and looking into old accounts, and he had reason to fear, that under Bungall's will, Luke Rowan would have the power of exacting from him much more than he was inclined to give.

"You'd better take him into the concern," the lawyer had said. "A young head is always useful."

"Not when the young head wants to be master," Tappitt had answered. "If I'm to do that the whole thing will go to the dogs." He did not exactly explain to the lawyer that Rowan had carried his infatuation so far as to be desirous of brewing good beer, but he did make it very clear that such a partner would, in his eyes, be anything but desirable.

"Then, upon my word, I think you'll have to give him the ten thousand pounds. I don't even know but what the demand is moderate."

This was very bad news to Tappitt. "But suppose I haven't got ten thousand pounds!" Now it was very well known that the property and the business were worth money, and the lawyer suggested that Rowan might take steps to have the whole concern sold. "Probably he might buy it himself and undertake to pay you so much a year," suggested the lawyer. But this view of the matter was not at all in accordance with Mr. Tappitt's ideas. He had been brewer in Baslehurst for nearly thirty years, and still wished to remain so. Mrs. Tappitt had been of opinion that all difficulties might be overcome if only Luke would fall in love with one of her girls. Mrs. Rowan had been invited to Baslehurst specially with a view to some such arrangement. But Luke Rowan, as it seemed to them both now, was an obstinate young man, who, in matters of beer as well as in matters of love, would not be guided by those who best knew how to guide him. Mrs. Tappitt had watched him closely at the ball, and had now given him up altogether. He had danced only once with Augusta, and then had left her the moment the dance was over. "I should offer him a hundred and fifty pounds a year out of the concern, and if he didn't like that let him lump it," said Mrs. Tappitt. "Lump it!" said Mr. Tappitt. "That means going to a London lawyer." He felt the difficulties of his position as he prepared to speak his mind to young Rowan on the morning after the party; but on that occasion his strongest feeling was in favour of expelling the intruder. Any lot in life would be preferable to working in the brewery with such a partner as Luke Rowan.

"I suppose your head's hardly cool enough for business," he said, as Luke came in and took a stool in his office. Tappitt was sitting in his customary chair, with his arm resting on a large old-fashioned leather-covered table, which was strewed with his papers, and which had never been reduced to cleanliness or order within the memory of any one connected with the establishment. He had turned his chair round from its accustomed place so as to face Rowan, who had perched himself on a stool which was commonly occupied by a boy whom Tappitt employed in his own office.

"My head not cool!" said Rowan. "It's as cool as a cucumber. I wasn't drinking last night."

"I thought you might be tired with the dancing." Then Tappitt's mind flew off to the champagne, and he determined that the young man before him was too disagreeable to be endured.

"Oh, dear, no. Those things never tire me. I was across here with the men before eight this morning. Do you know, I'm sure we could save a third of the fuel by altering the flues. I never saw such contrivances. They must have been put in by the coal-merchants, for the sake of wasting coal."

"If you please, we won't mind the flues at present."

"I only tell you; it's for your sake much more than my own. If you won't believe me, do you ask Newman to look at them the first time you see him in Baslehurst."

"I don't care a straw for Newman."

"He's got the best concerns in Devonshire, and knows what he's about better than any man in these parts."

"I dare say. But now, if you please, we won't mind him. The concerns, as I have managed them, have done very well for me for the last thirty years;—very well I may say also for your uncle, who understood what he was doing. I'm not very keen for so many changes. They cost a great deal of money, and as far as I can see don't often lead to much profit."

"If we don't go on with the world," said Rowan, "the world will leave us behind. Look at the new machinery they're introducing everywhere. People don't do it because they like to spend their money. It's competition; and there's competition in beer as well as in other things."

For a minute or two Mr. Tappitt sat in silence collecting his thoughts, and then he began his speech. "I'll tell you what it is, Rowan, I don't like these new-fangled ways. They're very well for you, I dare say. You are young, and perhaps you may see your way. I'm old, and I don't see mine among all these changes. It's clear to me that you and I could not go on together as partners in the same concern. I should expect to have my own way,—first because I've a deal of experience, and next because my share in the concern would be so much the greatest."

"Stop a moment, Mr. Tappitt; I'm not quite sure that it would be much the greatest. I don't want to say anything about that now; only if I were to let your remark pass without notice it would seem that I had assented."

"Ah; very well. I can only say that I hope you'll find yourself mistaken. I've been over thirty years in the concern, and it would be odd if I with my large family were to find myself only equal to you, who have never been in the business at all, and ain't even married yet."

"I don't see what being married has to do with it."

"Don't you? You'll find that's the way we look at these things in these parts. You're not in London here, Mr. Rowan."

"Certainly not; but I suppose the laws are the same. This is an affair of capital."

"Capital!" said Mr. Tappitt. "I don't know that you've brought in any capital."

"Bungall did, and I'm here as his representative. But you'd better let that pass by just at present. If we can agree as to the management of the business, you won't find me a hard man to deal with as to our relative shares." Hereupon Tappitt scratched his head, and tried to think. "But I don't see how we are to agree about the management," he continued. "You won't be led by anybody."

"I don't know about that. I certainly want to improve the concern."

"Ah, yes; and so ruin it. Whereas I've been making money

out of it these thirty years. You and I won't do together; that's the long of it and the short of it."

"It would be a putting of new wine into old bottles, you think?" suggested Rowan.

"I'm not saying anything about wine; but I do think that I ought to know something about beer."

"And I'm to understand," said Rowan, "that you have definitively determined not to carry on the old concern in conjunction with me as your partner."

"Yes; I think I have."

"But it will be as well to be sure. One can't allow one's self to depend upon thinking."

"Well, I am sure; I've made up my mind. I've no doubt you're a very clever young man, but I am quite sure we should not do together; and to tell you the truth, Rowan, I don't think you'll ever make your fortune by brewing."

"You think not?"

"No; never."

"I'm sorry for that."

"I don't know that you need be sorry. You'll have a nice income for a single man to begin the world with, and there's other businesses besides brewing,—and a deal better."

"Ah! But I've made up my mind to be a brewer. I like it. There's opportunity for chemical experiments, and room for philosophical inquiry, which gives the trade a charm in my eyes. I dare say it seems odd to you, but I like being a brewer."

Tappitt only scratched his head, and stared at him. "I do indeed," continued Rowan. "Now a man can't do anything to improve his own trade as a lawyer. A great deal will be done; but I've made up my mind that all that must come from the outside. All trades want improving; but I like a trade in which I can do the improvements myself,—from the inside. Do you understand me, Mr. Tappitt?" Mr. Tappitt did not understand him,—was very far indeed from understanding him.

"With such ideas as those I don't think Baslehurst is the ground for you," said Mr. Tappitt.

"The very ground!" said Rowan. "That's just it;—it's the very place I want. Brewing, as I take it, is at a lower ebb here than in any other part of England,"—this at any rate was not complimentary to the brewer of thirty years' standing—"than in any other part of England. The people swill themselves with the nasty juice of the apple because sound malt and hops have never been brought within their reach. I think Devonshire is the very county for a man who means to work hard, and who wishes to do good; and in all Devonshire I don't think there's a more fitting town than Baslehurst."

Mr. Tappitt was dumbfounded. Did this young man mean him to understand that it was his intention to open a rival establishment under his nose; to set up with Bungall's money another brewery in opposition to Bungall's brewery? Could such ingratitude as that be in the mind of any one? "Oh," said Tappitt; "I don't quite understand, but I don't doubt but what you say is all very fine."

"I don't think that it's fine at all, Mr. Tappitt, but I believe that it's true. I represent Mr. Bungall's interest here in Baslehurst, and I intend to carry on Mr. Bungall's business in the town in which he established it."

"This is Mr. Bungall's business;—this here, where I'm sitting, and it is in my hands."

"The use of these premises depends on you certainly."

"Yes; and the name of the firm, and the—the—the——. In point of fact, this is the old establishment. I never heard of such a thing in all my life."

"Quite true; it is the old establishment; and if I should set up another brewery here, as I think it probable I may, I shall not make use of Bungall's name. In the first place it would hardly be fair; and in the next place, by all accounts, he brewed such very bad beer that it would not be a credit to me. If you'll tell me what your plan is, then I'll tell you mine. You'll find that everything shall be above-board, Mr. Tappitt."

"My plan? I've got no plan. I mean to go on here as I've always done."

"But I suppose you intend to come to some arrangement with me. My claims are these: I will either come into this establishment on an equal footing with yourself, as regards share and management, or else I shall look to you to give me the sum of money to which my lawyers tell me I am entitled. In fact, you must either take me in or buy me out."

"I was thinking of a settled income."

"No; it wouldn't suit me. I have told you what are my intentions, and to carry them out I must either have a concern of my own, or a share in a concern. A settled income would do me no good."

"Two hundred a year," suggested Tappitt.

"Psha! Three per cent. would give me three hundred."

"Ten thousand pounds is out of the question, you know."

"Very well, Mr. Tappitt. I can't say anything fairer than I have done. It will suit my own views much the best to start alone, but I do not wish to oppose you if I can help it. Start alone I certainly will, if I cannot come in here on my own terms."

After that there was nothing more said. Tappitt turned round, pretending to read his letters, and Rowan descending from his seat walked out into the yard of the brewery. His intention had been, ever since he had looked around him in Baslehurst, to be master of that place, or if not of that, to be master of some other. "It would break my heart to be sending out such stuff as that all my life," he said to himself, as he watched the muddy stream run out of the shallow coolers. He had resolved that he would brew good beer. As to that ambition of putting down the consumption of cider, I myself am inclined to think that the habits of the country would be too strong for him. At the present moment he lighted a cigar and sauntered about the yard. He had now, for the first time, spoken openly of his purpose to Mr. Tappitt; but, having done so, he resolved that there should be no more delay. "I'll give him till Saturday for an answer," he said. "If he isn't ready with one by that time I'll manage it through the lawyers."

After that he turned his mind to Rachel Ray and the events of
the past evening. He had told Rachel that he would go out to
Bragg's End if she did not come into town, and he was quite
resolved that he would do so. He knew well that she would not
come in, understanding exactly those feelings of hers which
would prevent it. Therefore his walk to Bragg's End on that
afternoon was a settled thing with him. They were to dine at
the brewery at three, and he would go almost immediately
after dinner. But what would he say to her when he got there,
and what would he say to her mother? He had not even yet
made up his mind that he would positively ask her on that day
to be his wife, and yet he felt that if he found her at home he
would undoubtedly do so. "I'll arrange it all," said he, "as I'm
walking over." Then he threw away the end of his cigar, and
wandered about for the next half-hour among the vats and tubs
and furnaces.

Mr. Tappitt took himself into the house as soon as he found
himself able to do so without being seen by young Rowan. He
took himself into the house in order that he might consult with
his wife as to this unexpected revelation that had been made to
him; or rather that he might have an opportunity of saying to
some one all the hard things which were now crowding themselves upon his mind with reference to this outrageous young
man. Had anything ever been known, or heard, or told, equal
in enormity to this wickedness! He was to be called upon to
find capital for the establishment of a rival in his own town, or
else he was to bind himself in a partnership with a youth who
knew nothing of his business, but was nevertheless resolved to
constitute himself the chief manager of it! He who had been
so true to Bungall in his young days was now to be sacrificed
in his old age to Bungall's audacious representative! In the
first glow of his anger he declared to his wife that he would
pay no money and admit of no partnership. If Rowan did not
choose to take his income as old Mrs. Bungall had taken hers
he might seek what redress the law would give him. It was in
vain that Mrs. Tappitt suggested that they would all be ru-

ined. "Then we will be ruined," said Tappitt, hot with indignation; "but all Baslehurst,—all Devonshire shall know why."
Pernicious young man! He could not explain,—he could not
even quite understand in what the atrocity of Rowan's proposed scheme consisted, but he was possessed by a full conviction that it was atrocious. He had admitted this man into
his house; he was even now entertaining as his guests the man's
mother and sister; he had allowed him to have the run of the
brewery, so that he had seen both the nakedness and the fat of
the land; and this was to be his reward! "If I were to tell it at
the reading-room," said Tappitt, "he would never be able to
show himself again in the High Street."

Mrs. Tappitt, who was anxious but not enraged, did not see
the matter quite in the same light, but she was not able to oppose her husband in his indignation. When she suggested that
it might be well for them to raise money and pay off their enemy's claim, merely stipulating that a rival brewery should not
be established in Baslehurst, he swore an oath that he would
raise no money for such a purpose. He would have no dealings
with so foul a traitor except through his lawyer, Honyman.
"But Honyman thinks you'd better settle with him," pleaded
Mrs. T. "Then I'll go to another lawyer," said Tappitt. "If Honyman won't stand to me I'll go to Sharpit and Longfite. They
won't give way as long as there's a leg to stand on." For the
time Mrs. Tappitt let this pass. She knew how useless it would
be to tell her husband at the present moment that Sharpit and
Longfite would be the only winners in such a contest as that
of which he spoke. At the present moment Mr. Tappitt felt a
pride in his anger, and was almost happy in the fury of his
wrath; but Mrs. Tappitt was very wretched. If that nasty girl,
Rachel Ray, had not come in the way all might have been well.

"He shan't eat another meal in this house," said Tappitt. "I
don't care," he went on, when his wife pleaded that Luke
Rowan must be admitted to their table because of Mrs. Rowan
and Mary. "You can say what you like to them. They're welcome to stay if they like it, or welcome to go; but he shan't put

his feet under my mahogany again." On this point, however, he was brought to relent before the hour of dinner. Baslehurst, his wife told him, would be against him if he turned his guests away from his house hungry. If a fight was necessary for them, it would be everything to them that Baslehurst should be with them in the fight. It was therefore arranged that Mrs. Tappitt should have a conversation with Mrs. Rowan after dinner, while the young people were out in the evening. "He shan't sleep in this house to-morrow," said Tappitt, riveting his assertion with very strong language; and Mrs. Tappitt understood that her communications were to be carried on upon that basis.

At three o'clock the Tappitts and Rowans all sat down to dinner. Mr. Tappitt ate his meal in absolute silence; but the young people were full of the ball, and the elder ladies were very gracious to each other. At such entertainments Paterfamilias is simply required to find the provender and to carve it. If he does that satisfactorily, silence on his part is not regarded as a great evil. Mrs. Tappitt knew that her husband's mood was not happy, and Martha may have remarked that all was not right with her father. To the others I am inclined to think his ill humour was a matter of indifference.

C H A P T E R   X I

Luke Rowan Takes His Tea
Quite like a Steady Young Man

IT WAS THE CUSTOM of the Miss Tappitts, during these long midsummer days, to start upon their evening walk at about seven o'clock, the hour for the family gathering round the tea-table being fixed at six. But, in accordance with the same custom, dinner at the brewery was usually eaten at one. At this immediate time with which we are now dealing, dinner had been postponed till three, out of compliment to Mrs. Rowan, Mrs. Tappitt considering three o'clock more fashionable than one; and consequently the afternoon habits of the family were disarranged. Half-past seven, it was thought, would be a becoming hour for tea, and therefore the young ladies were driven to go out at five o'clock, while the sun was still hot in the heavens.

"No," said Luke, in answer to his sister's invitation; "I don't think I will mind walking to-day: you are all going so early." He was sitting at the moment after dinner with his glass of brewery port wine before him.

"The young ladies must be very unhappy that their hours can't be made to suit you," said Mrs. Tappitt, and the tone of her voice was sarcastic and acid.

"I think we can do without him," said Cherry, laughing.

"Of course we can," said Augusta, who was not laughing.

"But you might as well come all the same," said Mary.

"There's metal more attractive somewhere else," said Augusta.

"I cannot bear to see so much fuss made with the young men," said Mrs. Tappitt. "We never did it when I was young. Did we, Mrs. Rowan?"

"I don't think there's much change," said Mrs. Rowan; "we used to be very glad to get the young men when we could, and to do without them when we couldn't."

"And that's just the way with us," said Cherry.

"Speak for yourself," said Augusta.

During all this time Mr. Tappitt spoke never a word. He also sipped his glass of wine, and as he sipped it he brooded over his wrath. Who were these Rowans that they should have come about his house and premises, and forced everything out of its proper shape and position? The young man sat there as though he were lord of everything,—so Tappitt declared to himself; and his own wife was snubbed in her own parlour as soon as she opened her mouth. There was an uncomfortable atmosphere of discord in the room, which gradually pervaded

them all, and made even the girls feel that things were going
wrong.

Mrs. Tappitt rose from her chair, and made a stiff bow
across the table to her guest, understanding that that was the
proper way in which to effect a retreat into the drawing-room;
whereupon Luke opened the door, and the ladies went.
"Thank you, sir," said Mrs. Tappitt very solemnly as she passed
by him. Mrs. Rowan, going first, had given him a loving little
nod of recognition, and Mary had pinched his arm. Martha uttered a word of thanks, intended for conciliation; Augusta
passed him in silence with her nose in the air; and Cherry, as
she went by, turned upon him a look of dismay. He returned
Cherry's look with a shake of his head, and both of them understood that things were going wrong.

"I don't think I'll take any more wine, sir," said Rowan.

"Do as you like," said Tappitt. "It's there if you choose to
take it."

"It seems to me, Mr. Tappitt, that you want to quarrel with
me," said Luke.

"You can form your own opinion about that. I'm not bound
to tell my mind to everybody."

"Oh, no; certainly not. But it's very unpleasant going on in
that way in the same house. I'm thinking particularly of Mrs.
Tappitt and the girls."

"You needn't trouble yourself about them at all. You may
leave me to take care of them."

Luke had not sat down since the ladies left the room, and
now determined that he had better not do so. "I think I'll say
good afternoon," said Rowan.

"Good day to you," said Tappitt, with his face turned away,
and his eyes fixed upon one of the open windows.

"Well, Mr. Tappitt, if I have to say good-bye to you in that
way in your own house, of course it must be for the last time.
I have not meant to offend you, and I don't think I've given
you ground for offence."

"You don't, don't you?"

"Certainly not. If, unfortunately, there must be any dis-agreement between us about matters of business, I don't see why that should be brought into private life."

"Look here, young man," said Tappitt, turning upon him. "You lectured me in my counting-house this morning, and I don't intend that you shall lecture me here also. I'm drinking my own wine in my own parlour, and choose to drink it in peace and quietness."

"Very well, sir; I will not disturb you much longer. Perhaps you will make my apologies to Mrs. Tappitt, and tell her how much obliged I am by her hospitality, but that I will not tres-pass upon it any longer. I'll get a bed at the Dragon, and I'll write a line to my mother or sister." Then Luke left the room, took his hat up from the hall, and made his way out of the house.

He had much to occupy his mind at the present moment. He felt that he was being turned out of Mr. Tappitt's house, but would not much have regarded that if no one was con-cerned in it but Mr. Tappitt himself. He had, however, been on very intimate terms with all the ladies of the family; even for Mrs. Tappitt he had felt a friendship; and for the girls — especially for Cherry — he had learned to entertain an easy brotherly affection, which had not weighed much with him as it grew, but which it was not in his nature to throw off without annoyance. He had acknowledged to himself, as soon as he found himself among them, that the Tappitts did not possess, in their ways and habits of life, quite all that he should desire in his dearest and most intimate friends. I do not know that he had thought much of this; but he had felt it. Nevertheless he had determined that he would like them. He intended to make his way in life as a tradesman, and boldly resolved that he would not be above his trade. His mother sometimes reminded him, with perhaps not the truest pride, that he was a gentle-man. In answer to this he had once or twice begged her to de-fine the word, and then there had been some slight, very slight, disagreement between them. In the end the mother always gave way to the son; as to whom she believed that the sun shone with more special brilliancy for him than for any other of God's creatures. Now, as he left the brewery house, he remembered how intimate he had been with them all but a few hours since, arranging matters for their ball, and giving orders about the place as though he had belonged to the family. He had allowed himself to be at home with them, and to be one of them. He was by nature impulsive, and had thus fallen instantly into the intimacy which had been permitted to him. Now he was turned out of the house; and as he walked across the churchyard to bespeak a bed for himself at the inn, and write the necessary note to his sister, he was melancholy and almost unhappy. He felt sure that he was right in his views regarding the business, and could not accuse himself of any fault in his manner of making them known to Mr. Tappitt; but, nevertheless, he was ill at ease with himself in that he had given offence. And with all these thoughts were mingled other thoughts as to Rachel Ray. He did not in the least imagine that any of the anger felt towards him at the brewery had been caused by his open admiration of Rachel. It had never occurred to him that Mrs. Tappitt had regarded him as a possible son-in-law, or that, having so regarded him, she could hold him in displeasure because he had failed to fall into her views. He had never regarded himself as being of value as a possible future husband, or entertained the idea that he was a prize. He had taken hold in good faith of the Tappitt right hand which had been stretched out to him, and was now grieved that that hand should be suddenly withdrawn.

But as he was impulsive, so also was he lighthearted, and when he had chosen his bedroom and written the note to Mary, in which he desired her to pack up his belongings and send them to him, he was almost at ease as regarded that matter. Old Tappitt was, as he said to himself, an old ass, and if he chose to make that brewery business a cause of quarrel no one could help it. Mary was bidden in the note to say very civil things to Mrs. Tappitt; but, at the same time, to speak out the truth boldly. "Tell her," said he, "that I am constrained to leave the house because Mr. Tappitt and I cannot agree at the present moment about matters of business." When this was done he looked at his watch, and started off on his walk to Bragg's End.

It has been said that Rowan had not made up his mind to ask Rachel to be his wife,—that he had not made up his mind on this matter, although he was going to Bragg's End in a mood which would very probably bring him to such a conclusion. It will, I fear, be thought from this that he was light in purpose as well as light in heart; but I am not sure that he was open to any special animadversion of that nature. It is the way of men to carry on such affairs without any complete arrangement of their own plans or even wishes. He knew that he admired Rachel and liked her. I doubt whether he had ever yet declared to himself that he loved her. I doubt whether he had done so when he started on that walk,—thinking it probable, however, that he had persuaded himself of the fact before he reached the cottage door. He had already, as we know, said words to Rachel which he should not have said unless he intended to seek her as his wife;—he had spoken words and done things of that nature, being by no means perfect in all his ways. But he had so spoken and so acted without premeditation, and now was about to follow up those little words and little acts to their natural consequence,—also without much premeditation.

Rachel had told her mother, on her return from the ball, that Luke Rowan had promised to call; and had offered to take herself off from the cottage for the whole afternoon, if her mother thought it wrong that she should see him. Mrs. Ray had never felt herself to be in greater difficulty.

"I don't know that you ought to run away from him," said she: "and besides, where are you to go to?"

Rachel said at once that if her absence were desirable she would find whither to betake herself. "I'd stay upstairs in my bedroom, for the matter of that, mamma."

"He'd be sure to know it," said Mrs. Rowan, speaking of

the young man as though he were much to be feared;—as indeed he was much feared by her.

"If you don't think I ought to go, perhaps it would be best that I should stay," said Rachel, at last, speaking in a very low tone, but still with some firmness in her voice.

"I'm sure I don't know what I'm to say to him," said Mrs. Ray.

"That must depend upon what he says to you, mamma," said Rachel.

After that there was no further talk of running away; but the morning did not pass with them lightly or pleasantly. They made an effort to sit quietly at their work, and to talk over the doings at Mrs. Tappitt's ball; but this coming of the young man threw its shadow, more or less, over everything. They could not talk, or even look at each other, as they would have talked and looked had no such advent been expected. They dined at one, as was their custom, and after dinner I think it probable that each of them stood before her glass with more care than she would have done on ordinary days. It was no ordinary day, and Mrs. Ray certainly put on a clean cap.

"Will that collar do?" she said to Rachel.

"Oh, yes, mamma," said Rachel, almost angrily. She also had taken her little precautions, but she could not endure to have such precautions acknowledged, even by a word.

The afternoon was very tedious. I don't know why Luke should have been expected exactly at three; but Mrs. Ray had, I think, made up her mind that he might be looked for at that time with the greatest certainty. But at three he was sitting down to dinner, and even at half-past five had not as yet left his room at the Dragon.

"I suppose that we can't have tea till he's been," said Mrs. Ray, just at that hour; "that is, if he does come at all."

Rachel felt that her mother was vexed, because she suspected that Mr. Rowan was not about to keep his word.

"Don't let his coming make any difference, mamma," said Rachel. "I will go and get tea."

"Wait a few minutes longer, my dear," said Mrs. Ray.

It was all very well for Rachel to beg that it might make "no difference." It did make a very great deal of difference.

"I think I'll go over and see Mrs. Sturt for a few minutes," said Rachel, getting up.

"Pray don't, my dear,—pray don't; I should never know what to say to him if he should come while you were away."

So Rachel again sat down.

She had just, for the second time, declared her intention of getting tea, having now resolved that no weakness on her mother's part should hinder her, when Mrs. Ray, from her seat near the window, saw the young man coming over the green. He was walking very slowly, swinging a big stick as he came, and had taken himself altogether away from the road, almost to the verge of Mrs. Sturt's farmyard. "There he is," said Mrs. Ray, with a little start. Rachel, who was struggling hard to retain her composure, could not resist her impulse to jump up and look out upon the green from behind her mother's shoulder. But she did this from some little distance inside the room, so that no one might possibly see her from the green. "Yes; there he is, certainly," and, having thus identified their visitor, she immediately sat down again. "He's talking to Farmer Sturt's ploughboy," said Mrs. Ray. "He's asking where we live," said Rachel. "He's never been here before."

Rowan, having completed his conversation with the ploughboy, which by the way seemed to Mrs. Ray to have been longer than was necessary for its alleged purpose, came boldly across the green, and without pausing for a moment made his way through the cottage gate. Mrs. Ray caught her breath, and could not keep herself quite steady in her chair. Rachel, feeling that something must be done, got up from her seat and went quickly out into the passage. She knew that the front door was open, and she was prepared to meet Rowan in the hall.

"I told you I should call," said he. "I hope you'll let me come in."

"Mamma will be very glad to see you," she said. Then she brought him up and introduced him. Mrs. Ray rose from her chair and curtseyed, muttering something as to its being a long way for him to walk out there to the cottage.

"I said I should come, Mrs. Ray, if Miss Ray did not make her appearance at the brewery in the morning. We had such a nice party, and of course one wants to talk it over."

"I hope Mrs. Tappitt is quite well after it,—and the girls," said Rachel.

"Oh, yes. You know we kept it up two hours after you were gone. I can't say Mr. Tappitt is quite right this morning."

"Is he ill?" asked Mrs. Ray.

"Well, no; not ill, I think, but I fancy that the party put him out a little. Middle-aged gentlemen don't like to have all their things poked away anywhere. Ladies don't mind it, I fancy."

"Ladies know where to find them, as it is they who do the poking away," said Rachel. "But I'm sorry about Mr. Tappitt."

"I'm sorry, too, for he's a good-natured sort of a man when he's not put out. I say, Mrs. Ray, what a very pretty place you have got here."

"We think so because we're proud of our flowers."

"I do almost all the gardening myself," said Rachel.

"There's nothing I like so much as a garden, only I never can remember the names of the flowers. They've got such grand names down here. When I was a boy, in Warwickshire, they used to have nothing but roses and sweetwilliams. One could remember them."

"We haven't got anything very grand here," said Rachel. Soon after that they were sauntering out among the little paths and Rachel was picking flowers for him. She felt no difficulty in doing it, as her mother stood by her, though she would not for worlds have given him even a rose if they'd been alone.

"I wonder whether Mr. Rowan would come in and have some tea," said Mrs. Ray.

"Oh, wouldn't I," said Rowan, "if I were asked?"

Rachel was highly delighted with her mother, not so much on account of her courtesy to their guest, as that she had shown herself equal to the occasion, and had behaved, in an unabashed manner, as a mistress of a house should do. Mrs. Ray had been in such dread of the young man's coming, that Rachel had feared she would be speechless. Now the ice was broken, and she would do very well. The merit, however, did not belong to Mrs. Ray, but to Rowan. He had the gift of making himself at home with people, and had done much towards winning the widow's heart, when, after an interval of ten minutes, they two followed Rachel into the house. Rachel then had her hat on, and was about to go over the green to the farmer's house. "Mamma, I'll just run over to Mrs. Sturt's for some cream," said she.

"Mayn't I go with you?" said Rowan.

"Certainly not," said Rachel. "You'd frighten Mrs. Sturt out of all her composure, and we should never get the cream." Then Rachel went off, and Rowan was again left with her mother.

He had seated himself at her request in an arm-chair, and there for a minute or two he sat silent. Mrs. Ray was busy with the tea-things, but she suddenly felt that she was oppressed by the stranger's presence. While Rachel had been there, and even when they had been walking among the flower-beds, she had been quite comfortable; but now the knowledge that he was there, in the room with her, as he sat silent in the chair, was becoming alarming. Had she been right to ask him to stay for tea? He looked and spoke like a sheep; but then, was it not known to all the world that wolves dressed themselves often in that guise, so that they might carry out their wicked purposes? Had she not been imprudent? And then there was the immediate trouble of his silence. What was she to say to him to break it? That trouble, however, was soon brought to an end by Rowan himself. "Mrs. Ray," said he, "I think your daughter is the nicest girl I ever saw in my life."

Mrs. Ray instantly put down the tea-caddy which she had

in her hand, and started, with a slight gasp in her throat, as
though cold water had been thrown over her. At the instant she
said nothing. What was she to say in answer to so violent a
proposition?

"Upon my word I do," said Luke, who was too closely engaged with his own thoughts and his own feelings to pay much
immediate attention to Mrs. Ray. "It isn't only that she's good-
looking, but there's something,—I don't know what it is,—but
she's just the sort of person I like. I told her I should come to-
day, and I have come on purpose to say this to you. I hope you
won't be angry with me."

"Pray, sir, don't say anything to her to turn her head."

"If I understand her, Mrs. Ray, it wouldn't be very easy to
turn her head. But suppose she has turned mine?"

"Ah, no. Young gentlemen like you are in no danger of that
sort of thing. But for a poor girl——"

"I don't think you quite understand me, Mrs. Ray. I didn't
mean anything about danger. My danger would be that she
shouldn't care twopence for me; and I don't suppose she ever
will. But what I want to know is whether you would object to
my coming over here and seeing her. I don't doubt but she
might do much better."

"Oh dear no," said Mrs. Ray.

"But I should like to have my chance."

"You've not said anything to her yet, Mr. Rowan?"

"Well, no; I can't say I have. I meant to do so last night at
the party, but she wouldn't stay and hear me. I don't think she
cares very much about me, but I'll take my chance if you'll let
me."

"Here she is," said Mrs. Ray. Then she again went to work
with the tea-caddy, so that Rachel might be led to believe that
nothing special had occurred in her absence. Nevertheless, had
Rowan been away, every word would have been told to her.

"I hope you like clotted cream," said Rachel, taking off her
hat. Luke declared that it was the one thing in all the world
that he liked best, and that he had come into Devonshire with

the express object of feasting upon it all his life. "Other Devonshire dainties were not," he said, "so much to his taste. He
had another object in life. He intended to put down cider."

"I beg you won't do anything of the kind," said Mrs. Ray,
"for I always drink it at dinner." Then Rowan explained how
that he was a brewer, and that he looked upon it as his duty
to put down so poor a beverage as cider. The people of Devonshire, he averred, knew nothing of beer, and it was his ambition to teach them. Mrs. Ray grew eager in the defence of cider, and then they again became comfortable and happy. "I
never heard of such a thing in my life," said Mrs. Ray. "What
are the farmers to do with all their apple trees? It would be
the ruin of the whole country."

"I don't suppose it can be done all at once," said Luke.

"Not even by Mr. Rowan," said Rachel.

He sat there for an hour after their tea, and Mrs. Ray had
in truth become fond of him. When he spoke to Rachel he did
so with the utmost respect, and he seemed to be much more intimate with the mother than with the daughter. Mrs. Ray's mind
was laden with the burden of what he had said in Rachel's absence, and with the knowledge that she would have to discuss
it when Rowan was gone; but she felt herself to be happy while
he remained, and had begun to hope that he would not go
quite yet. Rachel also was perfectly happy. She said very little,
but thought much of her different meetings with him,—of the
arm in the clouds, of the promise of his friendship, of her first
dance, of the little fraud by which he had secured her company at supper, and then of those words he had spoken when
he detained her after supper in the hall. She knew that she
liked him well, but had feared that such liking might not be
encouraged. But what could be nicer than this,—to sit and listen to him in her mother's presence? Now she was not afraid
of him. Now she feared no one's eyes. Now she was disturbed
by no dread lest she might be sinning against rules of propriety. There was no Mrs. Tappitt by, to rebuke her with an angry look.

"Oh, Mr. Rowan, I'm sure you need not go yet," she said, when he got up and sought his hat.

"Mr. Rowan, my dear, has got other things to do besides talking to us."

"Oh no, he has not. He can't go and brew after eight o'clock."

"When my brewery is really going, I mean to brew all night; but just at present I'm the idlest man in Baslehurst. When I go away I shall sit upon Cawston bridge and smoke for an hour, till some of the Griggses of the town come and drive me away. But I won't trouble you any longer. Good night, Mrs. Ray."

"Good night, Mr. Rowan."

"And I may come and see you again?"

Mrs. Ray was silent. "I'm sure mamma will be very happy," said Rachel.

"I want to hear her say so herself," said Luke.

Poor woman! She felt that she was driven into a position from which any safe escape was quite impossible. She could not tell her guest that he would not be welcome. She could not even pretend to speak to him with cold words after having chatted with him so pleasantly, and with such cordial good humour; and yet, were she to tell him that he might come, she would be granting him permission to appear there as Rachel's lover. If Rachel had been away, she would have appealed to his mercy, and have thrown herself, in the spirit, on her knees before him. But she could not do this in Rachel's presence.

"I suppose business will prevent your coming so far out of town again very soon."

It was a foolish subterfuge; a vain, silly attempt.

"Oh dear no," said he; "I always walk somewhere every day, and you shall see me again before long." Then he turned to Rachel. "Shall you be at Mr. Tappitt's to-morrow?"

"I don't quite know," said Rachel.

"I suppose I might as well tell you the truth and have done with it," said Luke, laughing. "I hate secrets among friends.

The fact is Mr. Tappitt has turned me out of his house."

"Turned you out?" said Mrs. Ray.

"Oh, Mr. Rowan!" said Rachel.

"That's the truth," said Rowan. "It's about that horrid brewery. He means to be honest, and so do I. But in such matters it is so hard to know what the right of each party really is. I fear we shall have to go to law. But there's a lady coming in, so I'll tell you the rest of it to-morrow. I want you to know it all, Mrs. Ray, and to understand it too."

"A lady!" said Mrs. Ray, looking out through the open window. "Oh dear, if here isn't Dorothea!"

Then Rowan shook hands with them both, pressing Rachel's very warmly, close under her mother's eyes; and as he went out of the house into the garden, he passed Mrs. Prime on the walk, and took off his hat to her with great composure.

CHAPTER   XII

Rachel Ray Thinks "She Does Like Him"

LUKE ROWAN'S APPEARANCE at Mrs. Ray's tea-table, as described in the last chapter, took place on Wednesday evening, and it may be remembered that on the morning of that same day Mrs. Prime had been closeted with Mr. Prong in that gentleman's parlour. She had promised to give Mr. Prong an answer to his proposal on Saturday, and had consequently settled herself down steadily to think of all that was good and all that might be evil in such an arrangement as that suggested to her. She wished much for legal advice, but she made up her mind that that was beyond her reach, was beyond her reach as a preliminary assistance. She knew enough of the laws of her country to enable her to be sure that, though she might accept the offer, her own money could be so tied up on her behalf that her husband could not touch the principal of her wealth; but she did not know whether things could be so settled that she might have in her own hands the spending of her income. By three o'clock on that day she thought that she would accept Mr. Prong, if she could be satisfied on that head. Her position as a clergyman's wife,—a minister's wife she called it,—would be unexceptionable. The company of Miss Pucker was distasteful. Solitude was not charming to her. And then, could she not work harder as a married woman than in the position which she now held? and also, could she not so work with increased power and increased perseverance? At three o'clock she had almost made up her mind, but still she was sadly in need of counsel and information. Then it occurred to her that her mother might have some knowledge in this matter. In most respects her mother was not a woman of the world; but it was just possible that in this difficulty her mother might assist her. Her mother might at any rate ask of others, and there was no one else whom she could trust to seek such information for her. And if she did this thing she must tell her mother. It is true that she had quarrelled with them both at Bragg's End; but there are affairs in life which will ride over family quarrels and trample them out, unless they be deeper and of longer standing than that between Mrs. Prime and Mrs. Ray. Therefore it was that she appeared at the cottage at Bragg's End just as Luke Rowan was leaving it.

She had entered upon the green with something of the olive-branch in her spirit, and before she reached the gate had determined that, as far as was within her power, all unkindness should be buried on the present occasion; but when she saw Luke Rowan coming out of her mother's door, she was startled out of all her good feeling. She had taught herself to look on Rowan as the personification of mischief, as the very mischief itself in regard to Rachel. She had lifted up her voice against him. She had left her home and torn herself from her family because it was not compatible with the rigour of her principles that any one known to her should be known to him also! But she had hardly left her mother's house when this most pernicious cause of war was admitted to all the freedom of family intercourse! It almost seemed to her that her mother must be a hypocrite. It was but the other day that Mrs. Ray could not hear Luke Rowan's name mentioned without wholesome horror. But where was that wholesome horror now? On Monday, Mrs. Prime had left the cottage; on Tuesday, Rachel had gone to a ball, expressly to meet the young man! and on Wednesday the young man was drinking tea at Bragg's End cottage! Mrs. Prime would have gone away without speaking a word to her mother or sister, had such retreat been possible.

Stately and solemn was the recognition which she accorded to Luke's salutation, and then she walked on into the house.

"Oh, Dorothea!" said her mother, and there was a tone almost of shame in Mrs. Ray's voice.

"We're so glad to see you, Dolly," said Rachel, and in Rachel's voice there was no tone of shame. It was all just as it should not be!

"I did not mean to disturb you, mother, while you were entertaining company."

Mrs. Ray said nothing,—nothing at the moment; but Rachel took upon herself to answer her sister. "You wouldn't have disturbed us at all, even if you had come a little sooner. But you are not too late for tea, if you'll have some."

"I've taken tea, thank you, two hours ago"; and she spoke as though there were much virtue in the distance of time at which she had eaten and drunk, as compared with the existing rakish and dissipated appearance of her mother's tea-table. Tea-things about at eight o'clock! It was all of a piece together.

"We are very glad to see you, at any rate," said Mrs. Ray; "I was afraid you would not have come out to us at all."

"Perhaps it would have been better if I had not come."

"I don't see that," said Rachel. "I think it's much better. I hate quarrelling, and I hope you're going to stay now you are here."

"No, Rachel, I'm not going to stay. Mother, it is impossible I should see that young man walking out of your house in that way without speaking of it; although I'm well aware that my voice here goes for nothing now."

"That was Mr. Luke Rowan," said Mrs. Ray.

"I know very well who it was," said Mrs. Prime, shaking her head. "Rachel will remember that I've seen him before."

"And you'll be likely to see him again if you stay here, Dolly," said Rachel. This she said out of pure mischief,—that sort of mischief which her sister's rebuke was sure to engender.

"I dare say," said Mrs. Prime; "whenever he pleases, no doubt. But I shall not see him. If you approve of it, mother, of course I can say nothing further,—nothing further than this, that I don't approve of such things."

"But what ails him that he shouldn't be a very good young man?" says Mrs. Ray. "And if it was so that he was growing fond of Rachel, why shouldn't he? And if Rachel was to like him, I don't see why she shouldn't like somebody some day as well as other girls." Mrs. Ray had been a little put beside herself or she would hardly have said so much in Rachel's presence. She had forgotten, probably, that Rachel had not as yet been made acquainted with the nature of Rowan's proposal.

"Mamma, don't talk in that way. There's nothing of that kind," said Rachel.

"I don't believe there is," said Mrs. Prime.

"I say there is then," said Mrs. Ray; "and it's very ill-natured in you, Dorothea, to speak and think in that way of your sister."

"Oh, very well. I see that I had better go back to Baslehurst at once."

"So it is very ill-natured. I can't bear to have these sort of quarrels; but I must speak out for her. I believe he's a very good young man, with nothing bad about him at all, and he is welcome to come here whenever he pleases. And as for Rachel, I believe she knows how to mind herself as well as you did when you were her age; only poor Mr. Prime was come and gone at that time. And as for his not intending, he came out here just because he did intend, and only to ask my permis-

sion. I didn't at first tell him he might because Rachel was over
at the farm getting the cream, and I thought she ought to be
consulted first; and if that's not straightforward and proper,
I'm sure I don't know what is; and he having a business of his
own, too, and able to maintain a wife to-morrow! And if a
young man isn't to be allowed to ask leave to see a young
woman when he thinks he likes her, I for one don't know how
young people are to get married at all." Then Mrs. Ray sat
down, put her apron up to her eyes, and had a great cry.

It was a most eloquent speech, and I cannot say which of
her daughters was the most surprised by it. As to Rachel, it
must be remembered that very much was communicated to her
of which she had hitherto known nothing. Very much indeed,
we may say, so much that it was of a nature to alter the whole
tone and tenor of her life. This young man of whom she had
thought so much, and of whom she had been so much in dread,
—fearing that her many thoughts of him were becoming dangerous,—this young man who had interested her so warmly,
had come out to Bragg's End simply to get her mother's leave
to pay his court to her. And he had done this without saying a
word to herself! There was something in this infinitely sweeter
to her than would have been any number of pretty speeches
from himself. She had hitherto been angry with him, though
liking him well; she had been angry with though almost loving him. She had not known why it was so, but the cause had
been this,—that he had seemed in their intercourse together,
to have been deficient in that respect which she had a right to
claim. But now all that sin was washed away by such a deed
as this. As the meaning of her mother's words sank into her
heart, and as she came to understand her mother's declaration
that Luke Rowan should be welcome to the cottage as her
lover, her eyes became full of tears, and the spirit of her animosity against her sister was quenched by the waters of her
happiness.

And Mrs. Prime was almost equally surprised, but was by
no means equally delighted. Had the whole thing fallen out in

a different way, she would probably have looked on a marriage
with Luke Rowan as good and salutary for her sister. At any
rate, seeing that the world is as it is, and that all men cannot
be hard-working ministers of the Gospel, nor all women the
wives of such or their assistants in godly ministrations, she
would not have taken upon herself to oppose such a marriage.
But as it was, she had resolved that Luke Rowan was a black
sheep; that he was pitch, not to be touched without defilement;
that he was, in short, a man to be regarded by religious people
as anathema,—a thing accursed; and of that idea she was not
able to divest herself suddenly. Why had the young man
walked about under the churchyard elms at night? Why, if he
were not wicked and abandoned, did he wear that jaunty look,
—that look which was so worldly? And, moreover, he went to
balls, and tempted others to do the like! In a word, he was a
young man manifestly of that class which was esteemed by
Mrs. Prime more dangerous than roaring lions. It was not possible that she should give up her opinion merely because this
roaring lion had come out to her mother with a plausible story.
Upon her at that moment fell the necessity of forming a judgment to which it would be necessary that she should hereafter
abide. She must either at once give in her adherence to the
Rowan alliance; or else, if she opposed it, she must be prepared to cling to that opposition. She was aware that some such
decision was now required, and paused for a moment before
she declared herself. But that moment only strengthened her
verdict against Rachel's lover. Could any serious young man
have taken off his hat with the flippancy which had marked
that action on his part? Would not any serious young man,
properly intent on matrimonial prospects, have been subdued
at such a moment to a more solemn deportment? Mrs. Prime's
verdict was still against him, and that verdict she proceeded to
pronounce.

"Oh, very well; then of course I shall interfere no further.
I shouldn't have thought that Rachel's seeing him twice, in
such a way as that, too—hiding under the churchyard trees!"

"I wasn't hiding," said Rachel, "and you've no business to say so." Her tears, however, prevented her from fighting her own battle manfully, or with her usual courage.

"It looked very much like it, Rachel, at any rate. I should have thought that mother would have wished you to have known a great deal more about any young man before she encouraged you to regard him in that way, than you can possibly know of Mr. Rowan."

"But how are they to know each other, Dorothea, if they mustn't see one another?" said Mrs. Ray.

"I have no doubt he knows how to dance very cleverly. As Rachel is being taught to live now, that may perhaps be the chief thing necessary."

This blow did reach poor Mrs. Ray, who a week or two since would certainly have agreed with her elder daughter in thinking that dancing was sinful. Into this difficulty, however, she had been brought by Mr. Comfort's advice. "But what else can she know of him?" continued Mrs. Prime. "He is able to maintain a wife you say,—and is that all that is necessary to consider in the choice of a husband, or is that the chief thing? Oh, mother, you should think of your responsibility at such a time as this. It may be very pleasant for Rachel to have this young man as her lover, very pleasant while it lasts. But what —what—what?" Then Mrs. Prime was so much oppressed by the black weight of her own thoughts, that she was unable further to express them.

"I do think about it," said Mrs. Ray. "I think about it more than anything else."

"And have you concluded that in this way you can best secure Rachel's welfare? Oh, mother!"

"He always goes to church on Sundays," said Rachel. "I don't know why you are to make him out so bad." This she said with her eyes fixed upon her mother, for it seemed to her that her mother was almost about to yield.

A good deal might be said in excuse for Mrs. Prime. She was not only acting for the best in accordance with her own lights, but the doctrine which she now preached was the doctrine which had been held by the inhabitants of the cottage at Bragg's End. The fault, if fault there was, had been in the teaching under which had lived both Mrs. Prime and her mother. In their desire to live in accordance with that teaching, they had agreed to regard all the outer world, that is all the world except their world, as wicked and dangerous. They had never conceived that in forming this judgment they were deficient in charity; nor, indeed, were they conscious that they had formed any such judgment. In works of charity they had striven to be abundant, but had taken simply the Dorcas view of that virtue. The younger and more energetic woman had become sour in her temper under the *régime* of this life, while the elder and weaker had retained her own sweetness partly because of her weakness. But who can say that either of them were other than good women,—good according to such lights as had been lit for their guidance? But now the younger was stanch to her old lessons while the elder was leaving them. The elder was leaving them, not by force of her own reason, but under the necessity of coming in contact with the world which was brought upon her by the vitality and instincts of her younger child. This difficulty she had sought to master, once and for ever, by a reference to her clergyman. What had been the result of that reference the reader already knows.

"Mother," said Mrs. Prime, very solemnly, "is this young man such a one as you would have chosen for Rachel's husband six months ago?"

"I never wished to choose any man for her husband," said Mrs. Ray. "I don't think you ought to talk to me in that way, Dorothea."

"I don't know in what other way to talk to you. I cannot be indifferent on such a subject as this. When you tell me, and that before Rachel herself, that you have given this young man leave to come and see her whenever he pleases."

"I never said anything of the kind, Dorothea."

"Did you not, mother? I am sure I understood you so."

"I said he had come to ask leave, and that I should be glad to see him when he did come, but I didn't say anything of having told him so. I didn't tell him anything of the kind; did I, Rachel? But I know he will come, and I don't see why he shouldn't. And if he does, I can't turn him out. He took his tea here quite like a steady young man. He drank three large cups; and if, as Rachel says, he always goes to church regularly, I don't know why we are to judge him and say that he's anything out of the way."

"I have not judged him, mother."

Then Rachel spoke out, and we may say that it was needful that she should do so. This offering of her heart had been discussed in her presence in a manner that had been very painful to her, though the persons discussing it had been her own mother and her own sister. But in truth she had been so much affected by what had been said, there had been so much in it that was first joyful and then painful to her, that she had not hitherto been able to repress her emotions so as to acquire the power of much speech. But she had struggled, and now so far succeeded as to be able to come to her mother's support.

"I don't know, mamma, why anybody should judge him yet; and as to what he has said to me, I'm sure no one has a right to judge him unkindly. Dolly has been very angry with me because she saw me speaking to him in the churchyard, and has said that I was—hiding."

"I meant that he was hiding."

"Neither of us were hiding, and it was an unkind word, not like a sister. I have never had to hide from anybody. And as for—for—for liking Mr. Rowan after such words as that, I will not say anything about it to anybody, except to mamma. If he were to ask me to be—his wife, I don't know what answer I should make,—not yet. But I shall never listen to any one while mamma lives, if she wishes me not." Then she turned to her mother, and Mrs. Ray, who had before been driven to doubt by Mrs. Prime's words, now again became strong in her resolution to cherish Rachel's lover.

"I don't believe she'll ever do anything to make me think that I oughtn't to have trusted her," said Mrs. Ray, embracing Rachel and speaking with her own eyes full of tears.

It now seemed to Mrs. Prime that there was nothing left for her but to go. In her eagerness about her sister's affairs, she had for a while forgotten her own; and now, as she again remembered the cause that had brought her on the present occasion to Bragg's End, she felt that she must return without accomplishing her object. After having said so much in reprobation of her sister's love-affair, it was hardly possible that she should tell the tale of her own. And yet her need was urgent. She had pledged herself to give Mr. Prong an answer on Friday, and she could hardly bring herself to accept that gentleman's offer without first communicating with her mother on the subject. Any such communication at the present moment was quite out of the question.

"Perhaps it would be better that I should go and leave you," she said. "If I can do no good, I certainly don't want to do any harm. I wish that Rachel would have taken to what I think a better course of life."

"Why, what have I done?" said Rachel, turning round sharply.

"I mean about the Dorcas meetings."

"I don't like the women there;—that's why I haven't gone."

"I believe them to be good, praiseworthy, godly women. But it is useless to talk about that now. Good night, Rachel," and she gave her hand coldly to her sister. "Good night, mother; I wish I could see you alone to-morrow."

"Come here for your dinner," said Mrs. Ray.

"No;—but if you would come to me in the morning I should take it kindly." This Mrs. Ray promised to do, and then Mrs. Prime walked back to Baslehurst.

Rachel, when her sister was gone, felt that there was much to be said between her and her mother. Mrs. Ray herself was so inconsequent in her mental workings, so shandy-pated if I may say so, that it did not occur to her that an entirely new view of Luke Rowan's purposes had been exposed to Rachel during this visit of Mrs. Prime's, or that anything had been said which made a further explanation necessary. She had, as it were, authorized Rachel to regard Rowan as her lover, and yet was not aware that she had done so. But Rachel had remembered every word. She had resolved that she would permit herself to form no special intimacy with Luke Rowan without her mother's leave; but she was also beginning to resolve that with her mother's leave, such intimacy would be very pleasant. Of this she was quite sure within her own heart,—that it should not be abandoned at her sister's instigation.

"Mamma," she said, "I did not know that he had spoken to you in that way."

"In what way, Rachel?" Mrs. Ray's voice was not quite pleasant. Now that Mrs. Prime was gone, she would have been glad to have had the dangerous subject abandoned for a while.

"That he had asked you to let him come here, and that he had said that about me."

"He did then,—while you were away at Mrs. Sturt's."

"And what answer did you give him?"

"I didn't give him any answer. You came back, and I'm sure I was very glad that you did, for I shouldn't have known what to say to him."

"But what was it that he did say, mamma?—that is, if you don't think it wrong to tell me."

"I hardly know; but I don't suppose it can be wrong, for no young man could have spoken nicer; and it made me happy to hear him,—so it did, for the moment."

"Oh, mamma, do tell me!" and Rachel kneeled down before her.

"Well;—he said you were the nicest girl he had ever seen."

"Did he, mamma?" And the girl clung closer to her mother as she heard the pleasant words.

"But I oughtn't to tell you such nonsense as that; and then he said that he wanted to come out here and see you, and—

and—and—; it is simply this, that he meant to ask you to be his sweetheart, if I would let him."

"And what did you say, mamma?"

"I couldn't say anything because you came back."

"But you told Dolly that you would be glad to see him whenever he might choose to come here."

"Did I?"

"Yes; you said he was welcome to come whenever he pleased, and that you believed him to be a very good young man."

"And so I do. Why should he be anything else?"

"I don't say that he's anything else; but, mamma——"

"Well, my dear."

"What shall I say to him if he does ask me that question? He has called me by my name two or three times, and spoken to me as though he wanted me to like him. If he does say anything to me like that, what shall I answer?"

"If you think you don't like him well enough, you must tell him so, of course."

"Yes, of course I must." Then Rachel was silent for a minute or two. She had not as yet received the full answer which she desired. In such an alternative as that which her mother had suggested, we may say that she would have known how to frame her answer to the young man without any advice from her mother. But there was another alternative as to which she thought it well that she should have her mother's judgment and opinion. "But, mamma, I think I do like him," said Rachel, burying her face.

"I'm sure I don't wonder at it," said Mrs. Ray, "for I like him very much. He has a way with him so much nicer than most of the young men now; and then, he's very well off, which, after all, must count for something. A young woman should never fall in love with a man who can't earn his bread, not if he was ever so religious or steady. And he's very good-looking, too. Good looks are only skin deep I know, and they won't bring much comfort when sorrow comes; but I do own I love to look on a young fellow with a sonsy face and a quick lively step. Mr. Comfort seemed to think it would do very well if there was to be any such thing; and if he's not able to tell, I'm sure I don't know who ought to be. And nothing could be fairer than his coming out here and telling me first. There's so many of them are sly; but there was nothing sly about that."

In this way, with many more rambling words, with many kisses also, and with some tears, Rachel Ray received from her mother permission to regard Luke Rowan as her lover.

CHAPTER XIII

Mr. Tappitt in His Counting-house

LUKE ROWAN, when he left the cottage, walked quickly back across the green towards Baslehurst. He had sauntered out slowly on his road from the brewery to Bragg's End, being in doubt as to what he would do when he reached his destination; but there was no longer room for doubt now; he had said that to Rachel's mother which made any further doubt impossible, and he was resolved that he would ask Rachel to be his wife. He had spoken to Mrs. Ray of his intention in that respect as though he thought that such an offer on his part might probably be rejected, and in so speaking had at the time spoken the truth; but he was eager, sanguine, and self-confident by nature, and though he was by no means disposed to regard himself as a conquering hero by whom any young lady would only be too happy to find herself beloved, he did not at the present moment look forward to his future fate with despair. He walked quickly home along the dusty road, picturing to himself a happy prosperous future in Baslehurst, with Rachel as his wife, and the Tappitts living in some neighbouring villa on an income paid to old Tappitt by him out of the proceeds of

the brewery. That was his present solution of the brewery difficulty. Tappitt was growing old, and it might be quite as well
not only for himself, but for the cause of humanity in Devonshire, that he should pass the remainder of his life in that dignity which comfortable retirement from business affords. He
did not desire Tappitt for a partner any more than Tappitt desired him. Nevertheless he was determined to brew beer, and
was anxious to do so if possible on the spot where his great-
uncle Bungall had commenced operations in that line.

It may be well to explain here that Rowan was not without
good standing-ground in his dispute with Tappitt. Old Bungall's will had somewhat confused matters, as it is in the nature
of wills to do; but it had been Bungall's desire that his full
share in the brewery should go to his nephew after his widow's
death, should he on dying leave a widow. Now it had happened that he had left a widow, and that the widow had contrived to live longer than the nephew. She had drawn an income of five hundred a year from the concern, by agreement
between her and her lawyer and Tappitt and his lawyer; and
Tappitt, when the elder Rowan, Bungall's nephew, died, had
taught himself to believe that all the affairs of the brewery
must now remain for ever in his own hands, unless he himself
might choose to make other provision. He knew that some
property in the concern would pass away from him when the
old lady died, but he had not acknowledged to himself that
young Rowan would inherit from his father all the rights which
old Rowan would have possessed had he lived. Luke's father
had gone into other walks of life, and had lived prosperously,
leaving behind him money for his widow, and money also for
his children; and Tappitt, when he found that there was a
young man with a claim to a partnership in his business, had
been not only much annoyed, but surprised also. He had been,
as we have seen, persuaded to hold out the right hand of
friendship, and the left hand of the partnership to the young
man. He had thought that he might manage a young man from
London who knew nothing of beer; and his wife had thought

that the young man might probably like to take a wife as well as an income out of the concern; but, as we have seen, they had both been wrong in their hopes. Luke chose to manage the brewery instead of being managed; and had foolishly fallen in love with Rachel Ray instead of taking Augusta Tappitt to himself as he should have done.

There was much certainly of harshness and cruelty in that idea of an opposition brewery in Baslehurst to be established in enmity to Bungall and Tappitt, and to be so established with Bungall's money, and by Bungall's heir. But Luke, as he walked back to Baslehurst, thinking now of his beer and now of his love, declared to himself that he wanted only his own. Let Tappitt deal justly with him in that matter of the partnership, and he would deal even generously with Tappitt. The concern gave an income of some fifteen hundred pounds, out of which Mrs. Bungall, as taking no share of the responsibility or work, had been allowed to have a third. He was informed by his lawyer that he was entitled to claim one-half of the whole concern. If Tappitt would give in his adhesion to that villa arrangement, he should still have his thousand a year for life, and Mrs. Tappitt afterwards should have due provision, and the girls should have all that could fairly be claimed for them. Or, if the villa scheme could not be carried out quite at present, he, Rowan, would do two shares of the work, and allow Tappitt to take two shares of the pay; but then, in that case, he must be allowed scope for his improvements. Good beer should be brewed for the people of Baslehurst, and the eyes of Devonshire should be opened. Pondering over all this, and resolving that he would speak out his mind openly to Rachel on the morrow, Luke Rowan reached his inn.

"There's a lady, sir, up-stairs, as wishes to speak to you," said the waiter.

"A lady?"

"Quite elderly, sir," said the waiter, intending to put an end to any excitement on Rowan's part.

"It's the gentleman's own mother," said the chambermaid,

in a tone of reproof, "and she's in number two sitting-room, private." So Luke went to number two sitting-room, private, and there he found his mother waiting for him.

"This is very sad," she said, when their first greetings were over.

"About old Tappitt? yes, it is; but what could I do, mother? He's a stupid old man, and pigheaded. He would quarrel with me, so that I was obliged to leave the house. If you and Mary like to come into lodgings while you stay here, I can get rooms for you."

But Mrs. Rowan explained that she herself did not wish to come to any absolute or immediate rupture with Mrs. Tappitt. Of course their visit would be shortened, but Mrs. Tappitt was disposed to be very civil, as were the girls. Then Mrs. Rowan suggested whether there might not be a reconciliation between Luke and the brewery family.

"But, mother, I have not quarrelled with the family."

"It comes to the same thing, Luke; does it not? Don't you think you could say something civil to Mr. Tappitt, so as to— to bring him round again? He's older than you are, you know, Luke."

Rowan perceived at once that his mother was ranging herself on the Tappitt side in the contest, and was therefore ready to fight with so much the more vigour. He was accustomed to yield to his mother in all little things, Mrs. Rowan being a woman who liked such yieldings; but for some time past he had held his own against her in all greater matters. Now and again, for an hour or so, she would show that she was vexed; but her admiration for him was so genuine, and her love so strong, that this vexation never endured, and Luke had been taught to think that his judgment was to be held supreme in all their joint concerns. "Yes, mother, he is older than I am; but I do not know that I can say anything particularly civil to him,—that is, more civil than what I have said. The civility which he wants is the surrender of my rights. I can't be so civil as that."

"No, Luke, I should be the last to ask you to surrender any of your rights; you must be sure of that. But—oh, Luke, if what I hear is true I shall be so unhappy!"

"And what have you heard, mother?"

"I am afraid all this is not about the brewery altogether."

"But it is about the brewery altogether;—about that and about nothing else to any smallest extent. I don't at all know what you mean."

"Luke, is there no young lady in the case?"

"Young lady! in what case;—in the case of my quarrel with old Tappitt;—whether he and I have had a difference about a young lady?"

"No, Luke; you know I don't mean that."

"But what do you mean, mother?"

"I'm afraid that you know too well. Is there not a young lady whom you've met at Mrs. Tappitt's, and whom you—you pretend to admire?"

"And suppose there is,—for the sake of the argument,— what has that to do with my difference with Mr. Tappitt?" As Rowan asked this question some slight conception of the truth flashed across his mind; some faint idea came home to him of the connecting link between his admiration for Rachel Ray and Mr. Tappitt's animosity.

"But is it so, Luke?" asked the anxious mother. "I care much more about that than I do about all the brewery put together. Nothing would make me so wretched as to see you make a marriage that was beneath you."

"I don't think I shall ever make you wretched in that way."

"And you tell me that there is nothing in this that I have heard;—nothing at all."

"No, by heavens!—I tell you no such thing. I do not know what you may have heard. That you have heard falsehood and calumny I guess by your speaking of a marriage that would be beneath me. But, as you think it right to ask me, I will not deceive you by any subterfuge. It is my purpose to ask a girl here in Baslehurst to be my wife."

"Then you have not asked her yet."

"You are cross-examining me very closely, mother. If I have not asked her I am bound to do so; not that any binding is necessary,—for without being bound I certainly should do so."

"And it is Miss Ray?"

"Yes, it is Miss Ray."

"Oh, Luke, then indeed I shall be very wretched."

"Why so, mother? Have you heard anything against her?"

"Against her! well; I will not say that, for I do not wish to say anything against any young woman. But do you know who she is, Luke; and who her mother is? They are quite poor people."

"And is that against them?"

"Not against their moral character certainly, but it is against them in considering the expediency of a connection with them. You would hardly wish to marry out of your own station. I am told that the mother lives in a little cottage, quite in a humble sphere, and that the sister——"

"I intend to marry neither the mother nor the sister; but Rachel Ray I do intend to marry,—if she will have me. If I had been left to myself I should not have told you of this till I had found myself to be successful; as you have asked me I have not liked to deceive you. But, mother, do not speak against her if you can say nothing worse of her than that she is poor."

"You misunderstand me, Luke."

"I hope so. I do not like to think that that objection should be made by you."

"Of course it is an objection, but it is not the one which I meant to make. There may be many a young lady whom it would be quite fitting that you should wish to marry even though she had not got a shilling. It would be much pleasanter of course that the lady should have something, though I should never think of making any serious objection about that. But what I should chiefly look to would be the young lady herself, and her position in life."

"The young lady herself would certainly be the main thing," said Luke.

"That's what I say;—the young lady herself and her position in life. Have you made any inquiries?"

"Yes, I have;—and am almost ashamed of myself for doing so."

"I have no doubt Mrs. Ray is very respectable, but the sort of people who are her friends are not your friends. Their most particular friends are the farmer's family that lives near them."

"How was it then that Mrs. Cornbury took her to the party?"

"Ah, yes; I can explain that. And Mrs. Tappitt has told me how sorry she is that people should have been deceived by what has occurred." Luke Rowan's brow grew black as Mrs. Tappitt's name was mentioned, but he said nothing and his mother continued her speech. "Her girls have been very kind to Miss Ray, inviting her to walk with them and all that sort of thing, because of her being so much alone without any companions of her own."

"Oh, that has been it, has it? I thought she had the farmer's family out near where she lived."

"If you choose to listen to me, Luke, I shall be obliged to you, but if you take me up at every word in that way, of course I must leave you." Then she paused, but as Luke said nothing she went on with her discourse. "It was in that way that she came to know the Miss Tappitts, and then one of them, the youngest I think, asked her to come to the party. It was very indiscreet; but Mrs. Tappitt did not like to go back from her daughter's word, and so the girl was allowed to come."

"And to make the blunder pass off easily, Mrs. Cornbury was induced to take her?"

"Mrs. Cornbury happened to be staying with her father, in whose parish they had lived for many years, and it certainly was very kind of her. But it has been an unfortunate mistake altogether. The poor girl has for a moment been lifted out of her proper sphere, and,—as you must have seen yourself,—

hardly knew how to behave herself. It made Mrs. Tappitt very unhappy."

This was more than Luke Rowan was able to bear. His anger was not against his own mother, but against the mistress of the brewery. It was manifest that she had been maligning Rachel, and instigating his mother to take up the cudgels against her. And he was vexed also that his mother had not perceived that Rachel held, or was entitled to hold, among women a much higher position than could be fairly accorded to Mrs. Tappitt. "I do not care one straw for Mrs. Tappitt's unhappiness," he said; "and as to Miss Ray's conduct at her house, I do not think that there was anything in it that did not become her. I do not know what you mean, the least in the world; and I think you would have no such idea yourself, if Mrs. Tappitt had not put it into your head."

"You should not speak in that way to your mother, Luke."

"I must speak strongly when I am defending my wife,—as I hope she will be. I never heard of anything in my life so little as this woman's conduct! It is mean, paltry jealousy, and nothing else. You, as my mother, may think it better that I should not marry."

"But, my dear, I want you to marry."

"Then I will do as you want. Or you may think that I should find some one with money, or with grand friends, or with a better connection. It is natural that you should think like this. But why should she want to belittle a young girl like Rachel Ray,—a girl that her own daughters call their friend? I'll tell you why, mother. Because Rachel Ray was admired and they were not."

"Is there anybody in Baslehurst that will say that she is your equal?"

"I am not disposed to ask any one in Baslehurst just at present; and I would not advise any one in Baslehurst to volunteer an opinion to me on the subject. I intend that she shall be my equal,—my equal in every respect, if I can make her so. I shall certainly ask her to be my wife; and, mother, as my mind is positively made up on that point,—as nothing on earth will alter me,—I hope you will teach yourself to think kindly of her. I should be very unhappy if my house could not be your home when you may choose to make it so."

But Mrs. Rowan, much as she was accustomed to yield to her son, could not bring herself to yield in this matter,—or, at least, not to yield with grace. She felt that the truth and wisdom all lay on her side in the argument, though she knew that she had lacked words in which to carry it on. She declared to herself that she was not at all inclined to despise anybody for living in a small cottage, or for being poor. She would have been delighted to be very civil to Mrs. Ray herself, and could have patronized Rachel quite as kindly, though perhaps not so graciously, as Mrs. Cornbury had done. But it was a different thing when her son came to think of making this young woman his wife! Old Mrs. Cornbury would have been very sorry to see either of her sons make such an alliance. When anything so serious as marriage was to be considered, it was only proper to remember that Mrs. Ray lived in a cottage, and that farmer Sturt was her friend and neighbour. But to all this prudence and wisdom Luke would not listen at all, and at last Mrs. Rowan left him in dudgeon. Foolish and hasty as she was, he could, as she felt, talk better than she could; and therefore she retreated, feeling that she had been worsted. "I have done my duty," said she, going away. "I have warned you. Of course you are your own master and can do as you please." Then she left him, refusing his escort, and in the last fading light of the long summer evening, made her way back to the brewery.

Luke's first impulse was to start off instantly to the cottage, and settle the matter out of hand; but before he had taken up his hat for this purpose he remembered that he could not very well call at Bragg's End on such a mission at eleven o'clock at night; so he threw himself back on the hotel sofa, and gave vent to his feelings against the Tappitt family. He would make them understand that they were not going to master him. He had come down there disposed to do them all manner of kind-

ness,—to the extent even of greatly improving their fortunes by
improving the brewing business,—and they had taken upon
themselves to treat him as though he were a dependent. He
did not tell himself that a plot had been made to catch him for
one of the girls; but he accused them of jealousy, meanness,
selfishness, and all those sins and abominations by which such
a plot would be engendered. When, about an hour afterwards,
he took himself off to bed, he was full of wrath, and determined to display his wrath early on the morrow. As he prayed
for forgiveness on condition that he forgave others, his conscience troubled him; but he gulped it down, and went on
with his angry feelings till sleep came upon him.

But in the morning some of this bitterness had worn away.
His last resolve overnight had been to go to the brewery before breakfast, at which period of the day Mr. Tappitt was always to be found for half an hour in his counting-house, and
curtly tell the brewer that all further negotiations between
them must be made by their respective lawyers; but as he was
dressing, he reflected that Mr. Tappitt's position was certainly
one of difficulty, that amicable arrangements would still be best
if amicable arrangements were possible, and that something
was due to the man who had for so many years been his uncle's partner. Mr. Tappitt, moreover, was not responsible for
any of those evil things which had been said about Rachel by
Mrs. Tappitt. Therefore, priding himself somewhat on his charity, he entered Mr. Tappitt's office without the display of any
anger on his face.

The brewer was standing with his back to the empty fireplace, with his hands behind the tails of his coat, and his eyes
fixed upon a letter which he had just read, and which lay open
upon his desk. Rowan advanced with his hand out, and Tappitt, hesitating a little as he obeyed the summons, put out his
own and just touched that of his visitor; then hastily he resumed his position, with his arm behind his coat-tail.

"I have come down," said Rowan, "because I thought it
might be well to have a little chat with you before breakfast."

The letter which lay open on the desk was from Rowan's lawyer in London, and contained that offer on Rowan's part of a thousand a year and retirement, to which Luke still looked as the most comfortable termination of all their difficulties. Luke had almost forgotten that he had, ten days since, absolutely instructed his lawyer to make the offer; but there was the offer made, and lying on Tappitt's table. Tappitt had been considering it for the last five minutes, and every additional moment had added to the enmity which he felt against Rowan. Rowan, at twenty-five, no doubt regarded Tappitt, who was nearer sixty than fifty, as a very old man; but men of fifty-five do not like to be so regarded, and are not anxious to be laid upon shelves by their juniors. And, moreover, where was Tappitt to find his security for the thousand a year,—as he had not failed to remark to himself on his first glance over the lawyer's letter. Buy him out, indeed, and lay him on one side! He hated Rowan with all his heart;—and his hatred was much more bitter in its nature than that which Rowan was capable of feeling for him. He remembered the champagne; he remembered the young man's busy calling for things in his own house; he remembered the sneers against the beer, and the want of respect with which his experience in the craft had been treated. Buy him out! No; not as long as he had a five-pound note to spend, or a leg to stand upon. He was strong in his resolution now, and capable of strength, for Mrs. Tappitt was also on his side. Mrs. Rowan had not quite kept her secret as to what had transpired at the inn, and Mrs. Tappitt was certain that Rachel Ray had succeeded. When Tappitt declared that morning that he would fight it out to the last, Mrs. T. applauded his courage.

"Oh! a little chat, is it?" said Tappitt. "About this letter that I've just got, I suppose"; and he gave a contemptuous poke to the epistle with one of his hands.

"What letter?" asked Rowan.

"Come now, young man, don't let us have any humbug and trickery, whatever we may do. If there's anything I do hate, it's deceit."

All Rowan's wrath returned upon him instantly, redoubled and trebled in its energy. "What do you mean, sir?" said he. "Who is trying to deceive anybody? How dare you speak to me in such language as that?"

"Now, look here, Mr. Rowan. This letter comes from your man in Craven Street, as of course you know very well. You have chosen to put our business in the hands of the lawyers, and in the hands of the lawyers it shall remain. I have been very wrong in attempting to have any dealings with you. I should have known what sort of a man you were before I let you put your foot in the concern. But I know enough of you now, and, if you please, you'll keep yourself on the other side of those gates for the future. D'ye hear me? Unless you wish to be turned out by the men, don't you put your feet inside the brewery premises any more." And Tappitt's face as he uttered these words was a face very unpleasant to behold.

Luke was so astounded that he could not bethink himself at the moment of the most becoming words in which to answer his enemy. His first idea had prompted him to repudiate all present knowledge of the lawyer's letter, seeing that the lawyer's letter had been the ground of that charge against him of deceit. But having been thus kicked out,—kicked out as far as words could kick him, and threatened with personal violence should those words not be obeyed, he found himself unable to go back to the lawyer's letter. "I should like to see any one of your men dare to touch me," said he.

"You shall see it very soon if you don't take yourself off," said Tappitt. Luckily the men were gone to breakfast, and opportunity for violence was wanting.

Luke looked round, and then remembered that he and Tappitt were probably alone in the place. "Mr. Tappitt," said he, "you're a very foolish man."

"I dare say," said Tappitt; "very foolish not to give up my own bread, and my wife's and children's bread, to an adventurer like you."

"I have endeavoured to treat you with kindness and also

with honesty, and because you differ from me, as of course you have a right to do, you think it best to insult me with all the Billingsgate you can muster."

"If you don't go out of my counting-house, young man, I'll see if I can't put you out myself"; and Tappitt, in spite of his fifty-five years, absolutely put his hand down upon the poker.

There is no personal encounter in which a young man is so sure to come by the worst as in that with a much older man. This is so surely the case that it ought to be considered cowardly in an old man to attack a young one. If an old man hit a young man over the head with a walking-stick, what can the young man do, except run away to avoid a second blow? Then the old man, if he be a wicked old man, as so many are, tells all his friends that he has licked the young man. Tappitt would certainly have acted in this way if the weapon in his hand had been a stick instead of a poker. But Tappitt, when he saw his own poker in his own hand, was afraid of it. If a woman attack a man with a knife, the man will be held to have fought fairly, though he shall have knocked her down in the encounter. And so also with an old man, if he take a poker instead of a stick, the world will refuse to him the advantage of his gray hairs. Some such an idea as this came upon Tappitt—by instinct, and thus, though he still held the poker, he refrained his hand.

"The man must be mad this morning," said Rowan, standing firmly before him, with his two hands fixed upon his hips.

"Am I to send for the police?" said Tappitt.

"For a mad-doctor, I should think," said Rowan. Then Tappitt turned round and rang a bell very violently. But as the bell was intended to summon some brewery servant who was now away at his breakfast, it produced no result.

"But I have no intention of staying here against your wish, Mr. Tappitt, whether you're mad or only foolish. This matter must of course be settled by the lawyers now, and I shall not again come on to these premises unless I acquire a legal right to do so as the owner of them." And then, having so spoken, Luke Rowan walked off.

Growling inwardly Tappitt deposited the poker within the upright fender, and thrusting his hands into his trousers pockets stood scowling at the door through which his enemy had gone. He knew that he had been wrong; he knew that he had been very foolish. He was a man who had made his way upwards through the world with fair success, and had walked his way not without prudence. He had not been a man of violence, or prone to an illicit use of pokers. He had never been in difficulty for an assault; and had on his conscience not even the blood of a bloody nose, or the crime of a blackened eye. He was hard-working and peaceable; had been churchwarden three times, and mayor of Baslehurst once. He was poor-law guardian and way-warden, and filled customarily the various offices of a steady good citizen. What had he to do with pokers, unless it were to extract heat from his coals? He was ashamed of himself as he stood scowling at the door. One fault he perhaps had; and of that fault he had been ruthlessly told by lips that should have been sealed for ever on such a subject. He brewed bad beer; and by whom had this been thrown in his teeth? By Bungall's nephew,—by Bungall's heir,—by him who claimed to stand in Bungall's shoes within that establishment! Who had taught him to brew beer—bad or good? Had it not been Bungall? And now, because in his old age he would not change these things, and ruin himself in a vain attempt to make some beverage that should look bright to the eye, he was to be turned out of his place by this chip from the Bungall block, this stave out of one of Bungall's vats! "*Ruat cœlum, fiat justitia,*" he said, as he walked forth to his own breakfast. He spoke to himself in other language, indeed, though the Roman's sentiment was his own. "I'll stand on my rights, though I have to go into the poor-house."

CHAPTER XIV

Luke Rowan Pays a Second Visit
to Bragg's End

EARLY AFTER BREAKFAST on that morning,—that morning on which Tappitt had for a moment thought of braining Luke Rowan with the poker,—Mrs. Ray started from the cottage on her mission into Baslehurst. She was going to see her daughter, Mrs. Prime, at Miss Pucker's lodgings, and felt sure that the object of her visit was to be a further discourse on the danger of admitting that wolf Rowan into the sheepfold at Bragg's End. She would willingly have avoided the conference had she been able to do so, knowing well that Mrs. Prime would get the better of her in words when called upon to talk without having Rachel at her back. And indeed she was not happy in her mind. It had been conceded at the cottage as an understood thing that Rachel was to have this man as her lover; but what, if after all, the man didn't mean to be a lover in the proper sense; and what, if so meaning, he should still turn out to be a lover of a bad sort,—a worldy, good-for-nothing, rakish lover? "I wonder," says the wicked man in the play, "I wonder any man alive, would ever rear a daughter!" Mrs. Ray knew nothing of the play, and had she done so, she would not have repeated such a line. But the hardness of the task which Providence had allotted to her struck her very forcibly on this morning. Rachel was dearer to her than aught else in the world. For Rachel's happiness she would have made any sacrifice. In Rachel's pres-ence, and sweet smile, and winning caresses was the chief de-light of her excellence. Nevertheless, in these days the posses-sion of Rachel was hardly a blessing to her. The responsibility was so great; and, worse than that as regarded her own com-fort, the doubts were so numerous; and then, they recurred over and over again, as often as they were settled!

"I'm sure I don't know what she can have to say to me."

Mrs. Ray, as she spoke, was tying on her bonnet, and Rachel was standing close to her with her light summer shawl.

"It will be the old story, mamma, I'm afraid; my terrible iniquity and backslidings, because I went to the ball, and because I won't go to Miss Pucker's. She'll want you to say that I shall go, or else be sent to bed without my supper."

"That's nonsense, Rachel. Dorothea knows very well that I can't make you go." Mrs. Ray was wont to become mildly petulant when things went against her.

"But, mamma, you don't want me to go?"

"I don't suppose it's about Miss Pucker at all. It's about that other thing."

"You mean Mr. Rowan?"

"Yes, my dear. I'm sure I don't know what's for the best. When she gets me to herself she does say such terrible things to me that it quite puts me in a heat to have to go to her. I don't think anybody ought to say those sort of things to me except a clergyman, or a person's parents, or a schoolmaster, or masters and mistresses, or such like." Rachel thought so too,— thought that at any rate a daughter should not so speak to such a mother as was her mother; but on that subject she said nothing.

"And I don't like going to that Miss Pucker's house," continued Mrs. Ray. "I'm sure I don't want her to come here. I wouldn't go, only I said that I would."

"I would go now, if I were you, mamma."

"Of course I shall go; haven't I got myself ready?"

"But I would not let her go on in that way."

"That's very easy said, Rachel; but how am I to help it? I can't tell her to hold her tongue; and if I did, she wouldn't. If I am to go I might as well start. I suppose there's cold lamb enough for dinner?"

"Plenty, I should think."

"And if I find poultry cheap, I can bring a chicken home in my basket, can't I?" And so saying, with her mind full of various cares, Mrs. Ray walked off to Baslehurst.

"I wonder when he'll come." Rachel, as she said or thought
these words, stood at the open door of the cottage looking after
her mother as she made her way across the green. It was a delicious midsummer day, warm with the heat of the morning
sun, but not yet oppressed with the full blaze of its noonday
rays. The air was alive with the notes of birds, and the flowers
were in their brightest beauty. "I wonder when he'll come."
None of those doubts which so harassed her mother troubled
her mind. Other doubts there were. Could it be possible that
he would like her well enough to wish to make her his own?
Could it be that any one so bright, so prosperous in the world,
so clever, so much above herself in all worldly advantages,
should come and seek her as his wife,—take her from their little cottage and lowly ways of life? When he had first said that
he would come to Bragg's End, she declared to herself that it
would be well that he should see in how humble a way they
lived. He would not call her Rachel after that, she said to herself; or, if he did, he should learn from her that she knew how
to rebuke a man who dared to take advantage of the humility
of her position. He had come, and he had not called her Rachel.
He had come, and taking advantage of her momentary absence, had spoken of her behind her back as a lover speaks,
and had told his love honestly to her mother. In Rachel's view
of the matter no lover could have carried himself with better
decorum or with a sweeter grace; but because he had so done,
she would not hold him to be bound to her. He had been carried away by his feelings too rapidly, and had not as yet known
how poor and lowly they were. He should still have opened to
him a clear path backwards. Then if the path backwards were
not to his mind, then in that case—— I am not sure that Rachel
ever declared to herself in plain terms what in such case would
happen; but she stood at the door as though she was minded
to stand there till he should appear upon the green.

"I wonder when he'll come." She had watched her mother's
figure disappear along the lane, and had plucked a flower or
two to pieces before she returned within the house. He will

not come till the evening, she determined,—till the evening,
when his day's work in the brewery would be over. Then she
thought of the quarrel between him and Tappitt, and wondered what it might be. She was quite sure that Tappitt was
wrong, and thought of him at once as an obstinate, foolish, pigheaded old man. Yes; he would come to her, and she would
take care to be provided in that article of cream which he pretended to love so well. She would not have to run away again.
But how lucky on that previous evening had been that necessity, seeing that it had given opportunity for that great display
of a lover's excellence on Rowan's part. Having settled all this
in her mind, she went into the house, and was beginning to
think of her household work, when she heard a man's steps in
the passage. She went at once out from the sitting-room, and
encountered Luke Rowan at the door.

"How d'ye do?" said he. "Is Mrs. Ray at home?"

"Mamma?—no. You must have met her on the road if
you've come from Baslehurst."

"But I could not meet her on the road, because I've come
across the fields."

"Oh!—that accounts for it."

"And she's away in Baslehurst, is she?"

"She's gone in to see my sister, Mrs. Prime." Rachel, still
standing at the door of the sitting-room, made no attempt of
asking Rowan into the parlour.

"And mayn't I come in?" he said. Rachel was absolutely ignorant whether, under such circumstances, she ought to allow
him to enter. But there he was, in the house, and at any rate
she could not turn him out.

"I'm afraid you'll have to wait a long time if you wait for
mamma," she said, slightly making way, so that he obtained
admittance. Was she not a hypocrite? Did she not know that
Mrs. Ray's absence would be esteemed by him as a great gain,
and not a loss? Why did she thus falsely talk of his waiting a
long time? Dogs fight with their teeth, and horses with their
heels; swans with their wings, and cats with their claws;—so

also do women use such weapons as nature has provided for them.

"I came specially to see you," said he; "not but what I should be very glad to see your mother, too, if she comes back before I am gone. But I don't suppose she will, for you won't let me stay so long as that."

"Well, now you mention it, I don't think I shall, for I have got ever so many things to do;—the dinner to get ready, and the house to look after." This she did by way of making him acquainted with her mode of life,—according to the plan which she had arranged for her own guidance.

He had come into the room, had put down his hat, and had got himself up to the window, so that his back was turned to her. "Rachel," he said, turning round quickly, and speaking almost suddenly. Now he had called her Rachel again, but she could find at the moment no better way of answering him than by the same plaintive objection which she had made before. "You shouldn't call me by my name in that way, Mr. Rowan; you know you shouldn't."

"Did your mother tell you what I said to her yesterday?" he asked.

"What you said yesterday?"

"Yes, when you were away across the green."

"What you said to mamma?"

"Yes; I know she told you. I see it in your face. And I am glad she did so. May I not call you Rachel now?"

As they were placed the table was still between them, so that he was debarred from making any outward sign of his presence as a lover. He could not take her hand and press it. She stood perfectly silent, looking down upon the table on which she leaned, and gave no answer to his question. "May I not call you Rachel now?" he said, repeating the question.

I hope it will be understood that Rachel was quite a novice at this piece of work which she now had in hand. It must be the case that very many girls are not novices. A young lady who has rejected the first half-dozen suitors who have asked for her love, must probably feel herself mistress of the occasion when she rejects the seventh, and will not be quite astray when she accepts the eighth. There are, moreover, young ladies who, though they may have rejected and accepted none, have had so wide an advantage in society as to be able, when the moment comes, to have their wits about them. But Rachel had known nothing of what is called society, and had never before known either the trouble or the joy of being loved. So when the question was pressed upon her, she trembled, and felt that her breath was failing her. She had filled herself full of resolutions as to what she would do when this moment came,—as to how she would behave and what words she would utter. But all that was gone from her now. She could only stand still and tremble. Of course he might call her Rachel;—might call her what he pleased. To him, with his wider experience, that now became manifest enough.

"You must give me leave for more than that, Rachel, if you would not send me away wretched. You must let me call you my own." Then he moved round the table towards her; and as he moved, though she retreated from him, she did not retreat with a step as rapid as his own. "Rachel,"—and he put out his hand to her—"I want you to be my wife." She allowed the tips of her fingers to turn themselves toward him, as though unable altogether to refuse the greeting which he offered her, but as she did so she turned away from him, and bent down her head. She had heard all she wanted to hear. Why did he not go away, and leave her to think of it? He had named to her the word so sacred between man and woman. He had said that he sought her for his wife. What need was there that he should stay longer?

He got her hand in his, and then passed his arm round her waist. "Say, love; say, Rachel;—shall it be so? Nay, but I will have an answer from you. You shall look it to me, if you will not speak it"; and he got his head round over her shoulder, as though to look into her eyes.

"Oh, Mr. Rowan; pray don't;—pray don't pull me."

"But, dearest, say a word to me. You must say some word. Can you learn to love me, Rachel?"

Learn to love him! The lesson had come to her very easily. How was it possible, she had once thought, not to love him.

"Say a word to me," said Rowan, still struggling to look into her face; "one word, and then I will let you go."

"What word?"

"Say to me, 'Dear Luke, I will be your wife.'"

She remained for a moment quite passive in his hands, trying to say it, but the words would not come. Of course she would be his wife. Why need he trouble her further?

"Nay, but, Rachel, you shall speak, or I will stay with you here till your mother comes, and she shall answer for you. If you had disliked me I think you would have said so."

"I don't dislike you," she whispered.

"And do you love me?" She slightly bowed her head. "And you will be my wife?" Again she went through the same little piece of acting. "And I may call you Rachel now?" In answer to this question she shook herself free from his slackened grasp, and escaped away across the room.

"You cannot forbid me now. Come and sit down by me, for of course I have got much to say to you. Come and sit down, and indeed I will not trouble you again."

Then she went to him very slowly, and sat with him, leaving her hand in his, listening to his words, and feeling in her heart the full delight of having such a lover. Of the words that were then spoken, but very few came from her lips; he told her all his story of the brewery quarrel, and was very eloquent and droll in describing Tappitt as he brandished the poker.

"And was he going to hit you with it?" said Rachel, with all her eyes open.

"Well, he didn't hit me," said Luke; "but to look at him he seemed mad enough to do anything." Then he told her how at the present moment he was living at the inn, and how it became necessary, from this unfortunate quarrel, that he should go at once to London. "But under no circumstances would I have gone," said he, pressing her hand very closely, "without an answer from you."

"But you ought not to think of anything like that when you are in such trouble."

"Ought I not? Well, but I do, you see." Then he explained to her that part of his project consisted in his marrying her out of hand,—at once. He would go up to London for a week or two, and then, coming back, be married in the course of the next month.

"Oh, Mr. Rowan, that would be impossible."

"You must not call me Mr. Rowan, or I shall call you Miss Ray."

"But indeed it would be impossible."

"Why impossible?"

"Indeed it would. You can ask mamma;—or rather, you had better give over thinking of it. I haven't had time yet even to make up my mind what you are like."

"But you say that you love me."

"So I do, but I suppose I ought not; for I'm sure I don't know what you are like yet. It seems to me that you're very fond of having your own way, sir;—and so you ought," she added; "but really you can't have your own way in that. Nobody ever heard of such a thing. Everybody would think we were mad."

"I shouldn't care one straw for that."

"Ah, but I should,—a great many straws."

He sat there for two hours, telling her of all things appertaining to himself. He explained to her that, irrespective of the brewery, he had an income sufficient to support a wife,— "though not enough to make her a fine lady like Mrs. Cornbury," he said.

"If you can give me bread and cheese, it's as much as I have a right to expect," said Rachel.

"I have over four hundred a year," said he: and Rachel, hearing it, thought that he could indeed support a wife. Why should a man with four hundred a year want to brew beer?

"But I have got nothing," said Rachel; "not a farthing."

"Of course not," said Rowan; "it is my theory that unmarried girls never ought to have anything. If they have, they ought to be considered as provided for, and then they shouldn't have husbands. And I rather think it would be better if men didn't have anything either, so that they might be forced to earn their bread. Only they would want capital."

Rachel listened to it all with the greatest content, and most unalloyed happiness. She did not quite understand him, but she gathered from his words that her own poverty was not a reproach in his eyes, and that he under no circumstances would have looked for a wife with a fortune. Her happiness was unalloyed at all she heard from him, till at last he spoke of his mother.

"And does she dislike me?" asked Rachel, with dismay.

"It isn't that she dislikes you, but she's staying with that Mrs. Tappitt, who is furious against me because,—I suppose it's because of this brewery row. But indeed I can't understand it. A week ago I was at home there; now I daren't show my nose in the house, and have been turned out of the brewery this morning with a poker."

"I hope it's nothing about me," said Rachel.

"How can it be about you?"

"Because I thought Mrs. Tappitt looked at the ball as though—— But I suppose it didn't mean anything."

"It ought to be a matter of perfect indifference whether it meant anything or not."

"But how can it be so about your mother? If this is ever to lead to anything——"

"Lead to anything! What it will lead to is quite settled."

"You know what I mean. But how could I become your wife if your mother did not wish it?"

"Look here, Rachel; that's all very proper for a girl, I dare say. If your mother thought I was not fit to be your husband, I won't say but what you ought to take her word in such a mat-

ter. But it isn't so with a man. It will make me very unhappy if
my mother cannot be friends with my wife; but no threats of
hers to that effect would prevent me from marrying, nor should
they have any effect upon you. I'm my own master, and from
the nature of things I must look out for myself."

This was all very grand and masterful on Rowan's part,
and might in theory be true; but there was that in it which
made Rachel uneasy, and gave to her love its first shade of
trouble. She could not be quite happy as Luke's promised
bride, if she knew that she would not be welcomed to that
place by Luke's mother. And then what right had she to think
it probable that Luke's mother would give her such a welcome?
At that first meeting, however, she said but little herself on the
subject. She had pledged to him her troth, and she would not
attempt to go back from her pledge at the first appearance of
a difficulty. She would talk to her own mother, and perhaps his
mother might relent. But throughout it all there ran a feeling
of dismay at the idea of marrying a man whose mother would
not willingly receive her as a daughter!

"But you must go," said she at last. "Indeed you must. I
have things to do, if you have nothing."

"I'm the idlest man in the world at the present moment. If
you turn me out I can only go and sit at the inn."

"Then you must go and sit at the inn. If you stay any
longer mamma won't have any dinner."

"If that's so, of course I'll go. But I shall come back to tea."

As Rachel gave no positive refusal to this proposition,
Rowan took his departure on the understanding that he might
return.

"Good-bye," said he. "When I come this evening I shall
expect you to walk with me."

"Oh, I don't know," said she.

"Yes, you will; and we will see the sun set again, and you
will not run from me this evening as though I were an ogre."
As he spoke he took her in his arms and held her, and kissed

her before she had time to escape from him. "You're mine altogether now," said he, "and nothing can sever us. God bless
you, Rachel!"

"Good-bye, Luke," and then they parted.

She had told him to go, alleging her household duties as
her ground for dismissing him; but when he was gone she did
not at once betake herself to her work. She sat on the seat
which he had shared with her, thinking of the thing which she
had done. She was now betrothed to this man as his wife, the
only man towards whom her fancy had ever turned with the
slightest preference. So far love for her had run very smoothly.
From her first meetings with him, on those evenings in which
she had hardly spoken to him, his form had filled her eye, and
his words had filled her mind. She had learned to love to see
him before she understood what her heart was doing for her.
Gradually, but very quickly, all her vacant thoughts had been
given to him, and he had become the hero of her life. Now, almost before she had had time to question herself on the matter, he was her affianced husband. It had all been so quick and
so very gracious that she seemed to tremble at her own good
fortune. There was that one little cloud in the sky,—that frown
on his mother's brow; but now, in the first glow of her happiness, she could not bring herself to believe that this cloud
would bring a storm. So she sat there dreaming of her happiness, and longing for her mother's return that she might tell it
all;—that it might be talked of hour after hour, and that Luke's
merits might receive their fitting mention. Her mother was not
a woman who on such an occasion would stint the measure of
her praise, or refuse her child the happiness of her sympathy.

But Rachel knew that she must not let the whole morning
pass by in idle dreams, happy as those dreams were, and
closely as they were allied to her waking life. After a while
she jumped up with a start. "I declare there will be nothing
done. Mamma will want her dinner though I'm ever so much
going to be married."

But she had not been long on foot, or done much in prepa-

ration of the cold lamb which it was intended they should eat
that day, before she heard her mother's footsteps on the gravel
path. She ran out to the front door full of her own news, though
hardly knowing as yet in what words she would tell it; but of
her mother's news, of any tidings which there might be to tell
as to that interview which had just taken place in Baslehurst,
Rachel did not think much. Nothing that Dorothea could say
would now be of moment. So at least Rachel flattered herself.
And as for Dorothea and all her growlings, had they not chiefly
ended in this;—that the young man did not intend to present
himself as a husband? But he had now done so in a manner
which Rachel felt to be so satisfactory that even Dorothea's
criticism must be disarmed. So Rachel, as she met her mother,
thought only of the tale which she had to tell, and nothing of
that which she was to hear.

But Mrs. Ray was so full of her tale, was so conscious of
the fact that her tidings were entitled to the immediate and
undivided attention of her daughter, and from their first greeting on the gravel path was so ready with her words, that Rachel, with all the story of her happiness, was for a while
obliterated.

"Oh, my dear," said Mrs. Ray, "I have such news for you!"

"So have I, mamma, news for you," said Rachel, putting out
her hand to her mother.

"I never was so warm in my life. Do let me get in; oh dear,
oh dear! It's no good looking in the basket, for when I came
away from Dorothea I was too full of what I had just heard to
think of buying anything."

"What have you heard, mamma?"

"I'm sure I hope she'll be happy; I'm sure I do. But it's a
great venture, a terribly great venture."

"What is it, mamma?" And Rachel, though she could not
yet think that her mother's budget could be equal in importance to her own, felt that there was that which it was necessary that she should hear.

"Your sister is going to be married to Mr. Prong."

"Dolly?"

"Yes, my dear. It's a great venture; but if any woman can live happy with such a man, she can do so. She's troubled about her money;—that's all."

"Marry Mr. Prong! I suppose she may if she likes. Oh dear! I can't think I shall ever like him."

"I never spoke to him yet, so perhaps I oughtn't to say; but he doesn't look a nice man to my eyes. But what are looks, my dear? They're only skin deep; we ought all of us to remember that always, Rachel; they're only skin deep; and if, as she says, she only wants to work in the vineyard, she won't mind his being so short. I dare say he's honest;—at least I'm sure I hope he is."

"I should think he's honest, at any rate, or he wouldn't be what he is."

"There's some of them are so very fond of money;—that is, if all that we hear is true. Perhaps he mayn't care about it; let us hope that he doesn't; but if so he's a great exception. However, she means to have it tied up as close as possible, and I think she's right. Where would she be if he was to go away some fine morning and leave her? You see, he's got nobody belonging to him. I own I do like people who have got people belonging to them; you feel sure, in a sort of way, that they'll go on living in their own houses."

Rachel immediately reflected that Luke Rowan had people belonging to him,—very nice people,—and that everybody knew who he was and from whence he came.

"But she has quite made up her mind about it," continued Mrs. Ray; "and when I saw that I didn't say very much against it. What was the use? It isn't as though he wasn't quite respectable. He is a clergyman, you know, my dear, though he never was at any of the regular colleges; and he might be a bishop, just as much as if he had been; so they tell me. And I really don't think that she would ever come back to the cottage, —not unless you had promised to have been ruled by her in everything."

"I certainly shouldn't have done that"; and Rachel, as she made this assurance with some little obstinacy in her voice, told herself that for the future she meant to be ruled by a very different person indeed.

"No, I suppose not; and I'm sure I shouldn't have asked you, because I think it isn't the thing, dragging people away out of their own parishes, here and there, to anybody's church. And I told her that though I would of course go and hear Mr. Prong now and then if she married him, I wouldn't leave Mr. Comfort, not as a regular thing. But she didn't seem to mind that now, much as she used always to be saying about it."

"And when is it to be, mamma?"

"On Friday; that is, to-morrow."

"To-morrow!"

"That is, she's to go and tell him to-morrow that she means to take him,—or he's to come to her at Miss Pucker's lodgings. It's not to be wondered at when one sees Miss Pucker, really; and I'm not sure I'd not have done the same if I'd been living with her too; only I don't think I ever should have begun. I think it's living with Miss Pucker has made her do it; I do indeed, my dear. Well, now that I have told you, I suppose I may as well go and get ready for dinner."

"I'll come with you, mamma. The potatoes are strained, and Kitty can put the things on the table. Mamma"—and now they were on the stairs,—"I've got something to tell also."

We'll leave Mrs. Ray to eat her dinner, and Rachel to tell her story, merely adding a word to say that the mother did not stint the measure of her praise, or refuse her child the happiness of her sympathy. That evening was probably the happiest of Rachel's existence, although its full proportions of joy were marred by an unforeseen occurrence. At four o'clock a note came from Rowan to his "Dearest Rachel," saying that he had been called away by telegraph to London about that "horrid brewery business." He would write from there. But Rachel was almost as happy without him, talking about him, as she would have been in his presence, listening to him.

CHAPTER XV

Maternal Eloquence

ON THE FRIDAY MORNING there was a solemn conference at the brewery between Mrs. Tappitt and Mrs. Rowan. Mrs. Rowan found herself to be in some difficulty as to the line of action which she ought to take, and the alliances which she ought to form. She was passionately attached to her son, and for Mrs. Tappitt she had no strong liking. But then she was very averse to this proposed marriage with Rachel Ray, and was willing for a while to make a treaty with Mrs. Tappitt, offensive and defensive, as against her own son, if by doing so she could put a stop to so outrageous a proceeding on his part. He had seen her before he started for London, and had told her both the occurrences of the day. He had described to her how Tappitt had turned him out of the brewery, poker in hand, and how, in consequence of Tappitt's "pigheaded obstinacy," it was now necessary that their joint affairs should be set right by the hand of the law. He had then told her also that there was no longer any room for doubt or argument between them as regarding Rachel. He had gone out to Bragg's End that morning, had made his offer, and had been accepted. His mother therefore would see,—so he surmised,—that, as any opposition on her part must now be futile, she might as well take Rachel to her heart at once. He went so far as to propose to her that she should go over to Rachel in his absence,—"it would be very gracious if you could do it to-morrow, mother," he said,—and go through that little process of taking her future daughter-in-law to her heart. But in answer to this Mrs. Rowan said very little. She said very little, but she looked much. "My dear, I cannot move so quick as you do; I am older. I am afraid, how-ever, that you have been rash." He said something, as on such occasions young men do, as to his privilege of choosing for himself, as to his knowing what wife would suit him, as to his contempt for money, and as to the fact,—"the undoubted fact," as he declared it,—and in that declaration I am prepared to go hand-in-hand with him,—that Rachel Ray was a lady. But he was clear-headed enough to perceive that his mother did not intend to agree with him. "When we are married she will come round," he said to himself, and then he took himself off by the night mail train to London.

Under these circumstances Mrs. Rowan felt that her only chance of carrying on the battle would be by means of a treaty with Mrs. Tappitt. Had the affair of the brewery stood alone, Mrs. Rowan would have ranged herself loyally on the side of her son. She would have resented the uplifting of that poker, and shown her resentment by an immediate withdrawal from the brewery. She would have said a word or two,—a stately word or two,—as to the justice of her son's cause, and have carried herself and her daughter off to the inn. As things were now, her visit to the brewery must no doubt be curtailed in its duration; but in the mean time might not a blow be struck against that foolish matrimonial project,—an opportune blow, and by the aid of Mrs. Tappitt? Therefore on that Friday morning, when Mr. Prong was listening with enraptured ears to Mrs. Prime's acceptance of his suit,—under certain pecuniary conditions,—Mrs. Rowan and Mrs. Tappitt were sitting in conference at the brewery.

They agreed together at that meeting that Rachel Ray was the head and front of the whole offence, the source of all the evil done and to be done, and the one great sinner in the matter. It was clear to Mrs. Rowan that Rachel could have no just pretensions to look for such a lover or such a husband as her son; and it was equally clear to Mrs. Tappitt that she could have had no right to seek a lover or a husband out of the brewery. If Rachel Ray had not been there all might have gone smoothly for both of them. Mrs. Tappitt did not, perhaps, argue very logically as to the brewery business, or attempt to show either to herself or to her ally that Luke Rowan would have made himself an agreeable partner if he had kept himself free from all love vagaries; but she was filled with an indefinite woman's idea that the mischief, which she felt, had been done by Rachel Ray, and that against Rachel and Rachel's pretensions her hand should be turned.

They resolved therefore that they would go out together and call at the cottage. Mrs. Tappitt knew, from long neighbourhood, of what stuff Mrs. Ray was made. "A very good sort of woman," she said to Mrs. Rowan, "and not at all headstrong and perverse like her daughter. If we find the young lady there we must ask her mamma to see us alone." To this proposition Mrs. Rowan assented, not eagerly, but with a slow, measured, dignified assent, feeling that she was derogating somewhat from her own position in allowing herself to be led by such a one as Mrs. Tappitt. It was needful that on this occasion she should act with Mrs. Tappitt and connect herself with the Tappitt interests; but all this she did with an air that distinctly claimed for herself a personal superiority. If Mrs. Tappitt did not perceive and understand this, it was her fault, and not Mrs. Rowan's.

At two o'clock they stepped into a fly at the brewery door and had themselves driven out to Bragg's End.

"Mamma, there's a carriage," said Rachel.

"It can't be coming here," said Mrs. Ray.

"But it is; it's the fly from the Dragon. I know it by the man's white hat. And, oh dear, there's Mrs. Rowan and Mrs. Tappitt! Mamma, I shall go away." And Rachel, without another word, escaped out into the garden. She escaped, utterly heedless of her mother's little weak prayer that she would remain. She went away quickly, so that not a skirt of her dress might be visible. She felt instantly, by instinct, that these two women had come out there especially as her enemies, as upsetters of her happiness, as opponents of her one great hope in life; and she knew that she could not fight her battle with them face to face. She could not herself maintain her love stoutly and declare her intention of keeping her lover to his word; and yet she did intend to maintain her love, not doubting that he would be true to his word without any effort on her part. Her mother would make a very poor fight,—of that she was quite well aware. It would have been well if her mother could have run away also. But, as that could not be, her mother must be left to succumb, and the fight must be carried on afterwards as best it might. The two ladies remained at the cottage for about an hour, and during that time Rachel was sequestered in the garden, hardening her heart against all enemies to her love. If Luke would only stand by her, she would certainly stand by him.

There was a good deal of ceremony between the three ladies when they first found themselves together in Mrs. Ray's parlour. Mrs. Rowan and Mrs. Tappitt were large and stiff in their draperies, and did not fit themselves easily in among Mrs. Ray's small belongings; and they were stately in their demeanour, conscious that they were visiting an inferior, and conscious also that they were there on no friendly mission. But the interview was commenced with a show of much civility. Mrs. Tappitt introduced Mrs. Rowan in due form, and Mrs. Rowan made her little bow, if with some self-asserting supremacy, still with fitting courtesy. Mrs. Ray hoped that Mrs. Tappitt and the young ladies were quite well, and then there was a short silence, very oppressive to Mrs. Ray, but refreshing rather than otherwise to Mrs. Rowan. It gave a proper business aspect to the visit, and paved the way for serious words.

"Miss Rachel is out, I suppose," said Mrs. Tappitt.

"Yes, she is out," said Mrs. Ray. "But she's about the place somewhere, if you want to see her." This she added in her weakness, not knowing how she was to sustain the weight of such an interview alone.

"Perhaps it is as well that she should be away just at present," said Mrs. Rowan, firmly but mildly.

"Quite as well," said Mrs. Tappitt, as firmly, but less mildly.

"Because we wish to say a few words to you, Mrs. Ray," said Mrs. Rowan.

"That is what has brought us out so early," said Mrs. Tappitt. It was only half-past two now, and company visiting was never done at Baslehurst till after three. "We want to say a few words to you, Mrs. Ray, about a very serious matter. I'm sure you know how glad I've always been to see Rachel with my girls, and I had her at our party the other night, you know. It isn't likely therefore that I should be disposed to say anything unkind about her."

"At any rate not to me, I hope," said Mrs. Ray.

"Not to anybody. Indeed I'm not given to say unkind things about people. No one in Baslehurst would give me that character. But the fact is, Mrs. Ray——"

"Perhaps, Mrs. Tappitt, you'll allow me," said Mrs. Rowan. "He's my son."

"Oh, yes, certainly;—that is, if you wish it," said Mrs. Tappitt, drawing herself up in her chair; "but I thought that perhaps, as I knew Miss Ray so well——"

"If you don't mind, Mrs. Tappitt—" and Mrs. Rowan, as she again took the words out of her friend's mouth, smiled upon her with a smile of great efficacy.

"Oh, dear, certainly not," said Mrs. Tappitt, acknowledging by her concession the superiority of Mrs. Rowan's nature.

"I believe you are aware, Mrs. Ray," said Mrs. Rowan, "that Mr. Luke Rowan is my son."

"Yes, I'm aware of that."

"And I'm afraid you must be aware also that there have been some—some—some talkings as it were, between him and your daughter."

"Oh, yes. The truth is, ma'am, that he has offered himself to my girl, and that she has accepted him. Whether it's for good or for bad, the open truth is the best, Mrs. Tappitt."

"Truth is truth," said Mrs. Tappitt; "and deception is not truth."

"I didn't think it had gone anything so far as that," said Mrs. Rowan,—who at the moment, perhaps, forgot that deception is not truth; "and in saying that he has actually offered

himself, you may perhaps,—without meaning it, of course,—
be attributing a more positive significance to his word than he
has intended."

"God forbid!" said Mrs. Ray very solemnly. "That would be
a very sad thing for my poor girl. But I think, Mrs. Rowan, you
had better ask him. If he says he didn't intend it, of course
there will be an end of it, as far as Rachel is concerned."

"I can't ask him just at present," said Mrs. Rowan, "because
he has gone up to London. He went away yesterday afternoon,
and there's no saying when he may be in Baslehurst again."

"If ever—," said Mrs. Tappitt, very solemnly. "Perhaps he
has not told you, Mrs. Ray, that that partnership between him
and Mr. T. is all over."

"He did tell us that there had been words between him and
Mr. Tappitt."

"Words indeed!" said Mrs. Tappitt.

"And therefore it isn't so easy to ask him," said Mrs. Rowan,
ignoring Mrs. Tappitt and the partnership. "But of course,
Mrs. Ray, our object in this matter must be the same. We both
wish to see our children happy and respectable." Mrs. Rowan,
as she said this, put great emphasis on the last word.

"As to my girl, I've no fear whatever but what she'll be respectable," said Mrs. Ray, with more heat than Mrs. Tappitt
had thought her to possess.

"No doubt; no doubt. But what I'm coming to is this, Mrs.
Ray; here has this boy of mine been behaving foolishly to your
daughter, as young men will do. It may be that he has really
said something to her of the kind you suppose——"

"Said something to her! Why, ma'am, he came out here and
asked my permission to pay his addresses to her, which I didn't
answer because just at that moment Rachel came in from
Farmer Sturt's opposite——"

"Farmer Sturt's!" said Mrs. Tappitt to Mrs. Rowan, in an
under voice and nodding her head. Whereupon Mrs. Rowan
nodded her head also. One of the great accusations made
against Mrs. Ray had been that she lived on the Farmer Sturt

level, and not on the Tappitt level;—much less on the Rowan level.

"Yes,—from Farmer Sturt's," continued Mrs. Ray, not at all understanding this by-play. "So I didn't give him any answer at all."

"You wouldn't encourage him," said Mrs. Rowan.

"I don't know about that; but at any rate he encouraged himself, for he came again the next morning when I was in Baslehurst."

"I hope Miss Rachel didn't know he was coming in your absence," said Mrs. Rowan.

"It would look so sly;—wouldn't it?" said Mrs. Tappitt.

"No, she didn't, and she isn't sly at all. If she had known anything she would have told me. I know what my girl is, Mrs. Rowan, and I can depend on her." Mrs. Ray's courage was up, and she was inclined to fight bravely, but she was sadly impeded by tears, which she now found it impossible to control.

"I'm sure it isn't my wish to distress you," said Mrs. Rowan.

"It does distress me very much, then, for anybody to say that Rachel is sly."

"I said I hoped she wasn't sly," said Mrs. Tappitt.

"I heard what you said," continued Mrs. Ray; "and I don't see why you should be speaking against Rachel in that way. The young man isn't your son."

"No," said Mrs. Tappitt, "indeed he's not;—nor yet he ain't Mr. Tappitt's partner."

"Nor wishes to be," said Mrs. Rowan, with a toss of her head. It was a thousand pities that Mrs. Ray had not her wits enough about her to have fanned into a fire of battle the embers which glowed hot between her two enemies. Had she done so they might probably have been made to consume each other,—to her great comfort. "Nor wishes to be!" Then Mrs. Rowan paused a moment, and Mrs. Tappitt assumed a smile which was intended to indicate incredulity. "But Mrs. Ray," continued Mrs. Rowan, "that is neither here nor there. Luke Rowan is my son, and I certainly have a right to speak. Such a marriage as this would be very imprudent on his part, and very disagreeable to me. From the way in which things have turned out it's not likely that he'll settle himself at Baslehurst."

"The most unlikely thing in the world," said Mrs. Tappitt. "I don't suppose he'll ever show himself in Baslehurst again."

"As for showing himself, Mrs. Tappitt, my son will never be ashamed of showing himself anywhere."

"But he won't have any call to come to Baslehurst, Mrs. Rowan. That's what I mean."

"If he's a gentleman of his word, as I take him to be," said Mrs. Ray, "he'll have a great call to show himself. He never can have intended to come out here, and speak to her in that way, and ask her to marry him, and then never to come back and see her any more! I wouldn't believe it of him, not though his own mother said it!"

"I don't say anything," said Mrs. Rowan, who felt that her position was one of some difficulty. "But we all do know that in affairs of that kind young men do allow themselves to go great lengths. And the greater lengths they go, Mrs. Ray, the more particular the young ladies ought to be."

"But what's a young lady to do? How's she to know whether a young man is in earnest, or whether he's only going lengths as you call it?" Mrs. Ray's eyes were still moist with tears; and I grieve to say that though, as far as immediate words are concerned, she was fighting Rachel's battle not badly, still the blows of the enemy were taking effect upon her. She was beginning to wish that Luke Rowan had never been seen, or his name heard, at Bragg's End.

"I think it's quite understood in the world," said Mrs. Rowan, "that a young lady is not to take a gentleman at his first word."

"Oh, quite," said Mrs. Tappitt.

"We've all of us daughters," said Mrs. Rowan.

"Yes, all of us," said Mrs. Tappitt. "That's what makes it so fitting that we should discuss this matter together in a friendly feeling."

"My son is a very good young man,—a very good young man indeed."

"But a little hasty, perhaps," said Mrs. Tappitt.

"If you'll allow me, Mrs. Tappitt."

"Oh, certainly, Mrs. Rowan."

"A very good young man indeed; and I don't think it at all probable that in such a matter as this he will act in opposition to his mother's wishes. He has his way to make in the world."

"Which will never be in the brewery line," said Mrs. Tappitt.

"He has his way to make in the world," continued Mrs. Rowan, with much severity; "and if he marries in four or five years' time, that will be quite as soon as he ought to think of doing. I'm sure you will agree with me, Mrs. Ray, that long engagements are very bad, particularly for the lady."

"He wanted to be married next month," said Mrs. Ray.

"Ah, yes; that shows that the whole thing couldn't come to much. If there was an engagement at all, it must be a very long one. Years must roll by." From the artistic manner in which Mrs. Rowan allowed her voice to dwell upon the words which signified duration of space, any hope of a marriage between Luke and Rachel seemed to be put off at any rate to some future century. "Years must roll by, and we all know what that means. The lady dies of a broken heart, while the gentleman lives in a bachelor's rooms, and dines always at his club. Nobody can wish such a state of things as that, Mrs. Ray."

"I knew a girl who was engaged for seven years," said Mrs. Tappitt, "and she wore herself to a thread-paper,—so she did. And then he married his housekeeper after all."

"I'd sooner see my girl make up her mind to be an old maid than let her have a long engagement," said Mrs. Rowan.

"And so would I, my girls, all three. If anybody comes, I say to them, 'Let your papa see them. He'll know what's the meaning of it.' It don't do for young girls to manage those things all themselves. Not but what I think my girls have almost as much wit about them as I have. I won't mention any names, but there's a young man about here as well-to-do as any young man in the South Hams, but Cherry won't as much as look at him." Mrs. Rowan again tossed her head. She felt her misfortune in being burthened with such a colleague as Mrs. Tappitt.

"What is it you want me to do, Mrs. Rowan?" asked Mrs. Ray.

"I want you and your daughter, who I am sure is a very nice young lady, and good-looking too,——"

"Oh, quite so," said Mrs. Tappitt.

"I want you both to understand that this little thing should be allowed to drop. If my boy has done anything foolish I'm here to apologize for him. He isn't the first that has been foolish, and I'm afraid he won't be the last. But it can't be believed, Mrs. Ray, that marriages should be run up in this thoughtless sort of way. In the first place the young people don't know anything of each other; absolutely nothing at all. And then,—but I'm sure I don't want to insist on any differences that there may be in their positions in life. Only you must be aware of this, Mrs. Ray, that such a marriage as that would be very injurious to a young man like my son Luke."

"My child wouldn't wish to injure anybody."

"And therefore, of course, she won't think any more about it. All I want from you is that you should promise me that."

"If Rachel will only just say that," said Mrs. Tappitt, "my daughters will be as happy to see her out walking with them as ever."

"Rachel has had quite enough of such walking, Mrs. Tappitt; quite enough."

"If harm has come of it, it hasn't been the fault of my girls," said Mrs. Tappitt.

Then there was a pause among the three ladies, and it appeared that Mrs. Rowan was waiting for Mrs. Ray's answer. But Mrs. Ray did not know what answer she should make. She was already disposed to regard the coming of Luke Rowan to Baslehurst as a curse rather than a blessing. She felt all but convinced that Fate would be against her and hers in that matter. She had ever been afraid of young men, believing them to be dangerous, bringers of trouble into families, roaring lions sometimes, and often wolves in sheep's clothing. Since she had first heard of Luke Rowan in connection with her daughter she had been trembling. If she could have acted in accordance with her own feelings at this moment, she would have begged that Luke Rowan's name might never again be mentioned in her presence. It would be better for them, she thought, to bear what had already come upon them, than to run further risk. But she could not give any answer to Mrs. Rowan without consulting Rachel;—she could not at least give any such answer as that contemplated without doing so. She had sanctioned Rachel's love, and could not now undertake to oppose it. Rachel had probably been deceived, and must bear her misfortune. But, as the question stood at present between her and her daughter, she could not at once accede to Mrs. Rowan's views in the matter. "I will talk to Rachel," she said.

"Give her my kindest respects," said Mrs. Rowan; "and pray make her understand that I wouldn't interfere if I didn't think it was for both their advantages. Good-bye, Mrs. Ray." And Mrs. Rowan got up.

"Good-bye, Mrs. Ray," said Mrs. Tappitt, putting out her hand. "Give my love to Rachel. I hope that we shall be good friends yet, for all that has come and gone."

But Mrs. Ray would not accept Mrs. Tappitt's hand, nor would she vouchsafe any answer to Mrs. Tappitt's amenities. "Good-bye, ma'am," she said to Mrs. Rowan. "I suppose you mean to do the best you can by your own child."

"And by yours too," said Mrs. Rowan.

"If so, I can only say that you must think very badly of your own son. Good-bye, ma'am." Then Mrs. Ray curtseyed them out,—not without a certain amount of dignity, although her eyes were red with tears, and her whole body trembling with dismay.

Very little was said in the fly between the two ladies on their way back to the brewery, nor did Mrs. Rowan remain very long as a visitor at Mrs. Tappitt's house. She had found herself compelled by circumstances to take a part inimical to Mrs. Ray, but she felt in her heart a much stronger animosity to Mrs. Tappitt. With Mrs. Ray she could have been very friendly, only for that disastrous love-affair; but with Mrs. Tappitt she could not again put herself into pleasant relations. I must point out how sadly unfortunate it was that Mrs. Ray had not known how to fan that flame of anger to her own and her daughter's advantage.

"Well, mamma," said Rachel, returning to the room as soon as she heard the wheels of the fly in motion upon the road across the green. She found her mother in tears,—hardly able to speak because of her sobs. "Never mind it, mamma: of course I know the kind of things they have been saying. It was what I expected. Never mind it."

"But, my dear, you will be broken-hearted."

"Broken-hearted! Why?"

"I know you will. Now that you have learned to love him, you'll never bear to lose him."

"And must I lose him?"

"She says so. She says that he doesn't mean it, and that it's all nonsense."

"I don't believe her. Nothing shall make me believe that, mamma."

"She says it would be ruinous to all his prospects, especially just now when he has quarrelled about this brewery."

"Ruinous to him!"

"His mother says so."

"I will never wish him to do anything that shall be ruinous to himself; never;—not though I were broken-hearted, as you call it."

"Ah, that is it, Rachel, my darling; I wish he had not come here."

Rachel went away across the room and looked out of the window upon the green. There she stood in silence for a few minutes while her mother was wiping her eyes and suppressing her sobs. Tears also had run down Rachel's cheeks; but they were silent tears, few in number and very salt. "I cannot bring myself to wish that yet," said she.

"But he has gone away, and what can you do if he does not come again?"

"Do! Oh, I can do nothing. I could do nothing, even though he were here in Baslehurst every day of his life. If I once thought that he didn't wish me—to—be—his wife, I should not want to do anything. But, mamma, I can't believe it of him. It was only yesterday that he was here."

"They say that young men don't care what they say in that way now-a-days."

"I don't believe it of him, mamma; his manner is so steadfast, and his voice sounds so true."

"But then she is so terribly against it."

Then again they were silent for a while, after which Rachel ended the conversation. "It is clear, at any rate, that you and I can do nothing, mamma. If she expects me to say that I will give him up, she is mistaken. Give him up! I couldn't give him up, without being false to him. I don't think I'll ever be false to him. If he's false to me, then—then I must bear it. Mamma, don't say anything to Dolly about this just at present." In answer to which request Mrs. Ray promised that she would not at present say anything to Mrs. Prime about Mrs. Rowan's visit.

The following day and the Sunday were not passed in much happiness by the two ladies at Bragg's End. Tidings reached them that Mrs. Rowan and her daughter were going to London on the Monday, but no letter came to them from Luke. By the Monday morning Mrs. Ray had quite made up her mind that Luke Rowan was lost to them for ever, and Rachel had already become worn with care. During that Saturday and Sunday nothing was seen of Mrs. Prime at Bragg's End.

CHAPTER XVI

Rachel Ray's First Love-letter

ON THE MONDAY EVENING, after tea, Mrs. Prime came out to the cottage. It was that Monday on which Mrs. Rowan and her daughter had left Baslehurst and had followed Luke up to London. She came out and sat with her mother and sister for about an hour, restraining herself with much discretion from the saying of disagreeable things about her sister's lover. She had heard that the Rowans had gone away, and she had also heard that it was probable that they would be no more seen in Baslehurst. Mr. Prong had given it as his opinion that Luke would not trouble them again by his personal appearance among them. Under these circumstances Mrs. Prime had thought that she might spare her sister. Nor had she said much about her own love-affairs. She had never mentioned Mr. Prong's offer in Rachel's presence; nor did she do so now. As long as Rachel remained in the room the conversation was very innocent and very uninteresting. For a few minutes the two widows were alone together, and then Mrs. Prime gave her mother to understand that things were not yet quite arranged between herself and Mr. Prong.

"You see, mother," said Mrs. Prime, "as this money has been committed to my charge, I do not think it can be right to let it go altogether out of my own hands."

In answer to this Mrs. Ray had uttered a word or two agreeing with her daughter. She was afraid to say much against Mr. Prong;—was afraid, indeed, to express any very strong opinion about this proposed marriage; but in her heart she would have been delighted to hear that the Prong alliance was to be abandoned. There was nothing in Mr. Prong to recommend him to Mrs. Ray.

"And is she going to marry him?" Rachel asked, as soon as her sister was gone.

"There's nothing settled as yet. Dorothea wants to keep her money in her own hands."

"I don't think that can be right. If a woman is married the money should belong to the husband."

"I suppose that's what Mr. Prong thinks;—at any rate, there's nothing settled. It seems to me that we know so little about him. He might go away any day to Australia, you know."

"And did she say anything about—Mr. Rowan?"

"Not a word, my dear."

And that was all that was then said about Luke even between Rachel and her mother. How could they speak about him? Mrs. Ray also believed that he would be no more seen in Baslehurst; and Rachel was well aware that such was her mother's belief, although it had never been expressed. What could be said between them now,—or ever afterwards,—unless, indeed, Rowan should take some steps to make it necessary that his doings should be discussed?

The Tuesday passed and the Wednesday, without any sign from the young man; and during these two sad days nothing was said at the cottage. On that Wednesday his name was absolutely not mentioned between them, although each of them was thinking of him throughout the day. Mrs. Ray had now become almost sure that he had obeyed his mother's behests, and had resolved not to trouble himself about Rachel any further; and Rachel herself had become frightened if not despondent. Could it be that all this should have passed over her and that it should mean nothing?—that the man should have been standing there, only three or four days since, in that very room, with his arm round her waist, begging for her love, and calling her his wife;—and that all of it should have no meaning? Nothing amazed her so much as her mother's firm belief in such an ending to such an affair. What must be her mother's thoughts about men and women in general if she could expect such conduct from Luke Rowan,—and yet not think of him as one whose falsehood was marvellous in its falseness!

But on the Thursday morning there came a letter from Luke addressed to Rachel. On that morning Mrs. Ray was up when the postman passed by the cottage, and though Rachel took the letter from the man's hand herself, she did not open it till she had shown it to her mother.

"Of course it's from him," said Rachel.

"I suppose so," said Mrs. Ray, taking the unopened letter in her hand and looking at it. She spoke almost in a whisper, as though there were something terrible in the coming of the letter.

"Is it not odd," said Rachel, "but I never saw his handwriting before? I shall know it now for ever and ever." She also spoke in a whisper, and still held the letter as though she dreaded to open it.

"Well, my dear," said Mrs. Ray.

"If you think you ought to read it first, mamma, you may."

"No, Rachel. It is your letter. I do not wish you to imagine that I distrust you."

Then Rachel sat herself down, and with extreme care opened the envelope. The letter, which she read to herself very slowly, was as follows:—

MY OWN DEAREST RACHEL,

It seems so nice having to write to you, though it would be much nicer if I could see you and be sitting with you at this moment at the churchyard stile. That is the spot in all Basle-hurst that I like the best. I ought to have written sooner, I know, and you will have been very angry with me; but I have had to go down into Northamptonshire to settle some affairs as to my father's property, so that I have been almost living in railway carriages ever since I saw you. I am resolved about the brewery business more firmly than ever, and as it seems that "T." [Mrs. Tappitt would occasionally so designate her lord, and her doing so had been a joke between Luke and Rachel], *will not come to reason without a lawsuit, I must scrape to-gether all the capital I have, or I shall be fifty years old before*

I can begin. He is a pigheaded old fool, and I shall be driven to ruin him and all his family. I would have done,—and still would do,—anything for him in kindness; but if he drives me to go to law to get what is as much my own as his share is his own, I will build another brewery just under his nose. All this will require money, and therefore I have to run about and get my affairs settled.

But this is a nice love-letter,—is it not? However, you must take me as I am. Just now I have beer in my very soul. The grand object of my ambition is to stand and be fumigated by the smoke of my own vats. It is a fat, prosperous, money-making business, and one in which there is a clear line between right and wrong. No man brews bad beer without knowing it, —or sells short measure. Whether the fatness and the honesty can go together;—that is the problem I want to solve.

You see I write to you exactly as if you were a man friend, and not my own dear sweet girl. But I am a very bad hand at love-making. I considered that that was all done when you nodded your head over my arm in token that you consented to be my wife. It was a very little nod, but it binds you as fast as a score of oaths. And now I think I have a right to talk to you about all my affairs, and expect you at once to get up the price of malt and hops in Devonshire. I told you, you remember, that you should be my friend, and now I mean to have my own way.

You must tell me exactly what my mother has been doing and saying at the cottage. I cannot quite make it out from what she says, but I fear that she has been interfering where she had no business, and making a goose of herself. She has got an idea into her head that I ought to make a good bargain in matrimony, and sell myself at the highest price going in the market;—that I ought to get money, or if not money, family connection. I'm very fond of money,—as is everybody, only people are such liars,—but then I like it to be my own; and as to what people call connection, I have no words to tell you how I despise it. If I know myself I should never have chosen a woman as my companion for life who was not a lady; but I

have not the remotest wish to become second cousin by mar-
riage to a baronet's grandmother. I have told my mother all
this, and that you and I have settled the matter together; but I
see that she trusts to something that she has said or done her-
self to upset our settling. Of course, what she has said can have
no effect on you. She has a right to speak to me, but she has
none to speak to you;—not as yet. But she is the best woman in
the world, and as soon as ever we are married you will find that
she will receive you with open arms.

You know I spoke of our being married in August. I wish it
could have been so. If we could have settled it when I was at
Bragg's End, it might have been done. I don't, however, mean
to scold you, though it was your fault. But as it is, it must now
be put off till after Christmas. I won't name a day yet for see-
ing you, because I couldn't well go to Baslehurst without put-
ting myself into Tappitt's way. My lawyer says I had better not
go to Baslehurst just at present. Of course you will write to me
constantly,—to my address here; say, twice a week at least.
And I shall expect you to tell me everything that goes on. Give
my kind love to your mother.

> Yours, dearest Rachel,
> Most affectionately,
> Luke Rowan.

The letter was not quite what Rachel had expected, but, nevertheless, she thought it very nice. She had never received a love-letter before, and probably had never read one,—even in print; so that she was in possession of no strong preconceived notions as to the nature or requisite contents of such a document. She was a little shocked when Luke called his mother a goose;—she was a little startled when he said that people were "liars," having an idea that the word was one not to be lightly used;—she was amused by the allusion to the baronet's grandmother, feeling, however, that the manner and language of his letter was less pretty and love-laden than she had expected;—and she was frightened when he so confidently

called upon her to write to him twice a week. But, nevertheless, the letter was a genial one, joyous, and, upon the whole,
comforting. She read it very slowly, going back over much of
it twice and thrice, so that her mother became impatient before the perusal was finished.

"It seems to be very long," said Mrs. Ray.

"Yes, mamma, it is long. It's nearly four sides."

"What can he have to say so much?"

"There's a good deal of it is about his own private affairs."

"I suppose, then, I mustn't see it."

"Oh yes, mamma!" And Rachel handed her the letter. "I
shouldn't think of having a letter from him and not showing it
to you;—not as things are now." Then Mrs. Ray took the letter
and spent quite as much time in reading it as Rachel had done.
"He writes as though he meant to have everything quite his
own way," said Mrs. Ray.

"That's what he does mean. I think he will do that always.
He's what people call imperious; but that isn't bad in a man,
is it?"

Mrs. Ray did not quite know whether it was bad in a man
or no. But she mistrusted the letter, not construing it closely so
as to discover what might really be its full meaning, but perceiving that the young man took, or intended to take, very
much into his own hands; that he demanded that everything
should be surrendered to his will and pleasure, without any
guarantee on his part that such surrendering should be properly acknowledged. Mrs. Ray was disposed to doubt people
and things that were at a distance from her. Some check could
be kept over a lover at Baslehurst; or, if perchance the lover
had removed himself only to Exeter, with which city Mrs. Ray
was personally acquainted, she could have believed in his return. He would not, in that case, have gone utterly beyond her
ken. But she could put no confidence in a lover up in London.
Who could say that he might not marry some one else to-
morrow;—that he might not be promising to marry half a
dozen? It was with her the same sort of feeling which made

her think it possible that Mr. Prong might go to Australia. She
would have liked as a lover for her daughter a young man
fixed in business,—if not at Baslehurst, then at Totnes, Dart-
mouth, or Brixham,—under her own eye as it were;—a young
man so fixed that all the world of South Devonshire would
know of all his doings. Such a young man, when he asked a girl
to marry him, must mean what he said. If he did not there
would be no escape for him from the punishment of his neighbours' eyes and tongues. But a young man up in London,—a
young man who had quarrelled with his natural friends in
Baslehurst,—a young man who was confessedly masterful and
impetuous,—a young man who called his own mother a goose,
and all the rest of the world liars, in his first letter to his lady-
love;—was that a young man in whom Mrs. Ray could place
confidence as a lover for her pet lamb? She read the letter
very slowly, and then, as she gave it back to Rachel, she
groaned.

For nearly half an hour after that nothing was said in the
cottage about the letter. Rachel had perceived that it had not
been thought satisfactory by her mother; but then she was inclined to believe that her mother would have regarded no letter as satisfactory until arguments had been used to prove to
her that it was so. This, at any rate, was clear,—must be clear
to Mrs. Ray as it was clear to Rachel,—that Luke had no intention of shirking the fulfilment of his engagement. And after all,
was not that the one thing as to which it was essentially necessary that they should be confident? Had she not accepted
Luke, telling him that she loved him? and was it not acknowledged by all around her that such a marriage would be good
for her? The danger which they feared was the expectation of
such a marriage without its accomplishment. Even the forebodings of Mrs. Prime had shown that this was the evil to
which they pointed. Under these circumstances what better
could be wished for than a ready, quick, warm assurance on
Luke's part, that he did intend all that he had said?

With Rachel now, as with all girls under such circum-

stances, the chief immediate consideration was as to the answer which should be given. Was she to write to him, to write
what she pleased; and might she write at once? She felt that
she longed to have the pen in her hand, and that yet, when
holding it, she would have to think for hours before writing the
first word. "Mamma," she said at last, "don't you think it's a
good letter?"

"I don't know what to think, my dear. I doubt whether any
letters of that sort are good for much."

"Of what sort, mamma?"

"Letters from men who call themselves lovers to young
girls. It would be safer, I think, that there shouldn't be any;—
very much safer."

"But if he hadn't written we should have thought that he
had forgotten all about us. That would not have been good.
You said yourself that if he did not write soon, there would be
an end of everything."

"A hundred years ago there wasn't all this writing between
young people, and these things were managed better then
than they are now, as far as I can understand."

"People couldn't write so much then," said Rachel, "because
there were no railways and no postage stamps. I suppose I
must answer it, mamma?" To this proposition Mrs. Ray made
no immediate answer. "Don't you think I ought to answer it,
mamma?"

"You can't want to write at once."

"In the afternoon would do."

"In the afternoon! Why should you be in so much hurry,
Rachel? It took him four or five days to write to you."

"Yes; but he was down in Northamptonshire on business.
Besides he hadn't any letter from me to answer. I shouldn't
like him to think——"

"To think what, Rachel?"

"That I had forgotten him."

"Psha!"

"Or that I didn't treat his letter with respect."

"He won't think that. But I must turn it over in my mind; and I believe I ought to ask somebody."

"Not Dolly," said Rachel, eagerly.

"No; not your sister. I will not ask her. But if you don't mind, my dear, I'll take the young man's letter out to Mr. Comfort, and consult him. I never felt myself so much in need of somebody to advise me. Mr. Comfort is an old man, and you won't mind his seeing the letter."

Rachel did mind it very much, but she had no means of saving herself from her fate. She did not like the idea of having her love-letter submitted to the clergyman of the parish. I do not know any young lady who would have liked it. But bad as that was, it was preferable to having the letter submitted to Mrs. Prime. And then she remembered that Mr. Comfort had advised that she might go to the ball, and that he was father to her friend Mrs. Butler Cornbury.

CHAPTER XVII

Electioneering

AND NOW, in these days,—the days immediately following the departure of Luke Rowan from Baslehurst,—the Tappitt family were constrained to work very hard at the task of defaming the young man who had lately been living with them in their house. They were constrained to do this by the necessities of their position; and in doing so by no means showed themselves to be such monsters of iniquity as the readers of the story will feel themselves inclined to call them. As for Tappitt himself, he certainly believed that Rowan was so base a scoundrel that no evil words against him could be considered as malicious or even unnecessary. Is it not good to denounce a scoundrel? And if the rascality of any rascal be specially directed against one-self and one's own wife and children, is it not a duty to de-nounce that rascal, so that his rascality may be known and thus

made of no effect? When Tappitt declared in the reading-room
at the Dragon, and afterwards in the little room inside the bar
at the King's Head, and again to a circle of respectable farmers and tradesmen in the Corn Market, that young Rowan had
come down to the brewery and made his way into the brewery
house with a ready prepared plan for ruining him—him, the
head of the firm,—he thought that he was telling the truth.
And again, when he spoke with horror of Rowan's intention of
setting up an opposition brewery, his horror was conscientious.
He believed that it would be very wicked in a man to oppose
the Bungall establishment with money left by Bungall,—that
it would be a wickedness than which no commercial rascality
could be more iniquitous. His very soul was struck with awe
at the idea. That anything was due in the matter to the con-
sumer of beer, never occurred to him. And it may also be said
in Tappitt's favour that his opinion,—as a general opinion,—
was backed by those around him. His neighbours could not be
made to hate Rowan as he hated him. They would not declare the young man to be the very Mischief, as he did. But
that idea of a rival brewery was distasteful to them all. Most
of them knew that the beer was almost too bad to be swallowed; but they thought that Tappitt had a vested interest in
the manufacture of bad beer;—that as a manufacturer of bad
beer he was a fairly honest and useful man;—and they looked
upon any change as the work, or rather the suggestion, of a
charlatan.

"This isn't Staffordshire," they said. "If you want beer like
that you can buy it in bottles at Griggs's."

"He'll soon find where he'll be if he tries to undersell me,"
said young Griggs. "All the same, I hope he'll come back, because he has left a little bill at our place."

And then to other evil reports was added that special evil
report,—that Rowan had gone away without paying his debts.
I am inclined to think that Mr. Tappitt can be almost justified
in his evil thoughts and his evil words.

I cannot make out quite so good a case for Mrs. Tappitt

and her two elder daughters;—for even Martha, Martha the just, shook her head in these days when Rowan's name was mentioned;—but something may be said even for them. It must not be supposed that Mrs. Tappitt's single grievance was her disappointment as regarded Augusta. Had there been no Augusta on whose behalf a hope had been possible, the predilection of the young moneyed stranger for such a girl as Rachel Ray would have been a grievance to such a woman as Mrs. Tappitt. Had she not been looking down on Rachel Ray and despising her for the last ten years? Had she not been wondering among her friends, with charitable volubility, as to what that poor woman at Bragg's End was to do with her daughter? Had she not been regretting that the young girl should be growing up so big, and promising to look so coarse? Was it not natural that she should be miserable when she saw her taken in hand by Mrs. Butler Cornbury, and made the heroine at her own party, to the detriment of her own daughters, by the fashionable lady in catching whom she had displayed so much unfortunate ingenuity? Under such circumstances how could she do other than hate Luke Rowan,—than believe him to be the very Mischief,—than prophesying all manner of bad things for Rachel,—and assist her husband tooth and nail in his animosity against the sinner?

Augusta was less strong in her feelings than her parents, but of course she disliked the man who could admire Rachel Ray. As regards Martha, her dislike to him,—or rather her judicial disapproval,—was founded on his social and commercial improprieties. She understood that he had threatened her father about the business,—and she had been scandalized in that matter of the champagne. Cherry was very brave, and still stood up for him before her mother and sisters;—but even Cherry did not dare to say a word in his favour before her father. Mr. Tappitt had been driven to forget himself, and to take a poker in his hand as a weapon of violence! After that let no one speak a word on the offender's behalf in Tappitt's house and within Tappitt's hearing!

In that affair of the champagne Rowan was most bitterly injured. He had ordered it, if not at the request, at least at the instigation of Mrs. Tappitt;—and he had paid for it. When he left Baslehurst he owed no shilling to any man in it; and, indeed, he was a man by no means given to owing money to any one. He was of a spirit masterful, self-confident, and perhaps self-glorious;—but he was at the same time honest and independent. That wine had been ordered in some unusual way,—not at the regular counter, and in the same way the bill for it had been paid. Griggs, when he made his assertion in the barroom at the King's Head, had stated what he believed to be the truth. The next morning he chanced to hear that the account had been settled, but not, at the moment, duly marked off the books. As far as Griggs went that was the end of it. He did not again say that Rowan owed money to him; but he never contradicted his former assertion, and allowed the general report to go on,—that report which had been founded on his own first statement. Thus before Rowan had been a week out of the place it was believed all over the town that he had left unpaid bills behind him.

"I am told that young man is dreadfully in debt," said Mr. Prong to Mrs. Prime. At this time Mr. Prong and Mrs. Prime saw each other daily, and were affectionate in their intercourse, —with a serious, solemn affection; but affairs were by no means settled between them. That affection was, however, strong enough to induce Mr. Prong to take a decided part in opposing the Rowan alliance. "They say he owes money all over the town."

"So Miss Pucker tells me," said Mrs. Prime.

"Does your mother know it?"

"Mother never knows anything that other people know. But he has gone now, and I don't suppose we shall hear of him or see him again."

"He has not written to her, Dorothea?"

"Not that I know of."

"You should find out. You should not leave them in this danger. Your mother is weak, and you should give her the aid of your strength. The girl is your sister, and you should not leave her to grope in darkness. You should remember, Dorothea, that you have a duty in this matter."

Dorothea did not like being told of her duty in so pastoral a manner, and resolved to be more than ever particular in the protection of her own pecuniary rights before she submitted herself to Mr. Prong's marital authority once and for ever. By Miss Pucker she was at any rate treated with great respect, and was allowed perhaps some display of pastoral manner on her own part. It began to be with her a matter of doubt whether she might not be of more use in that free vineyard which she was about to leave, than in that vineyard with closed doors and a pastoral overseer, which she was preparing herself to enter. At any rate she would be careful about the money. But, in the mean time, she did agree with Mr. Prong that Rowan's proper character should be made known to her mother, and with this view she went out to the cottage and whispered into Mrs. Ray's astonished ears the fact that Luke was terribly in debt.

"You don't say so!"

"But I do say so, mother. Everybody in Baslehurst is talking about it. And they all say that he has treated Mr. Tappitt shamefully. Has anything come from him since he went?"

Then Mrs. Ray told her elder daughter of the letter, and told her also that she intended to consult Mr. Comfort. "Oh, Mr. Comfort!" said Mrs. Prime, signifying her opinion that her mother was going to a very poor counsellor. "And what sort of a letter was it?" said Mrs. Prime, with a not unnatural desire to see it.

"It was an honest letter enough,—very honest to my thinking; and speaking as though everything between them was quite settled."

"That's nonsense, mother."

"Perhaps it may be nonsense, Dorothea; but I am only telling you what the letter said. He called his mother a goose; that was the worst thing in it."

"You can't expect that such a one as he should honour his parents."

"But his mother thinks him the finest young man in the world. And I must say this for him, that he has always spoken of her as though he loved her very dearly; and I believe he has been a most excellent son. He shouldn't have said goose;—at any rate in a letter;—not to my way of thinking. But perhaps they don't mind those things up in London."

"I never knew a young man so badly spoken of at a place he'd left as he is in Balsehurst. I think it right to tell you; but if you have made up your mind to ask Mr. Comfort——"

"Yes; I have made up my mind to ask Mr. Comfort. He has sent to say he will call the day after to-morrow." Then Mrs. Prime went back home, having seen neither the letter nor her sister.

It may be remembered that an election was impending over the town of Baslehurst, the coming necessities of which had induced Mrs. Butler Cornbury to grace Mrs. Tappitt's ball. It was now nearly the end of July, and the election was to be made early in September. Both candidates were already in the field, and the politicians of the neighbourhood already knew to a nicety how the affair would go. Mr. Hart the great clothier from Houndsditch and Regent Street,—Messrs. Hart and Jacobs of from 110 to 136 Houndsditch, and about as many more numbers in Regent Street,—would come in at the top of the poll with 173 votes, and Butler Cornbury, whose forefathers had lived in the neighbourhood for the last four hundred years and been returned for various places in Devonshire to dozens of parliaments, would be left in the lurch with 171 votes. A petition might probably unseat the Jew clothier; but then, as was well known, the Cornbury estate could not bear the expenditure of the necessary five thousand pounds for the petition, in addition to the twelve hundred which the election itself was computed to cost. It was all known and thoroughly understood; and men in Baslehurst talked about the result as though the matter were past a doubt. Nevertheless there were those who were ready to bet on the Cornbury side of the question.

But though the thing was thus accurately settled, and though its termination was foreseen by so many and with so perfect a certainty, still the canvassing went on. In fact there were votes that had not even yet been asked, much less promised,—and again, much less purchased. The Hart people were striving to frighten the Cornbury people out of the field by the fear of the probable expenditure; and had it not been for the good courage of Mrs. Butler Cornbury would probably have succeeded in doing so. The old squire was very fidgety about the money, and the young squire declared himself unwilling to lean too heavily upon his father. But the lady of the household declared her conviction that there was more smoke than fire, and more threats of bribery than intention of bribing. She would go on, she declared; and as her word passed for much at Cornbury Grange, the battle was still to be fought.

Among the votes which certainly had not as yet been promised was that of Mr. Tappitt. Mr. Hart in person had called upon him, but had not been quite satisfied with his reception. Mr. Tappitt was a man who thought much of his local influence and local privileges, and was by no means disposed to make a promise of his vote on easy terms, at a moment when his vote was becoming of so much importance. He was no doubt a Liberal as was also Mr. Hart; but in small towns politics become split, and a man is not always bound to vote for a Liberal candidate because he is a Liberal himself. Mr. Hart had been confident in his tone, and had not sufficiently freed himself from all outer taint of his ancient race to please Mr. Tappitt's taste. "He's an impudent low Jew," he had said to his wife. "As for Butler Cornbury he gives himself airs, and is too grand even to come and ask. I don't think I shall vote at all." His wife had reminded him how civil to them Mrs. Cornbury had been;—this was before the morning of the poker·—but Tappitt had only sneered, and declared he was not going to send a man to Parliament because his wife had come to a dance.

But we, who know Tappitt best, may declare now that his vote was to have been had by any one who would have joined him energetically in abuse of Luke Rowan. His mind was full of his grievance. His heart was laden with hatred of his enemy. His very soul was heavy with that sorrow. Honyman, whom he had not yet dared to desert, had again recommended submission to him, submission to one of the three terms proposed. Let him take the thousand a year and go out from the brewery. That was Honyman's first advice. If not that, then let him admit his enemy to a full partnership. If that were too distasteful to be possible, then let him raise ten thousand pounds on a mortgage on the whole property, and buy Rowan out. Honyman thought that the money might be raised if Tappitt were willing to throw into the lump the moderate savings of his past life. But in answer to either proposal Tappitt only raved. Had Mr. Hart known all about this, he might doubtless have secured Tappitt's vote.

Butler Cornbury refused to call at the brewery. "The man's a Liberal," he said to his wife, "and what's the use? Besides he's just the man I can't stand. We've always hated each other."

Whereupon Mrs. B. Cornbury determined to call on Mrs. Tappitt, and to see Tappitt himself if it were possible. She had heard something of the Rowan troubles, but not all. She had heard, too, of Rowan's liking for Rachel Ray, having also seen something of it, as we know. But, unfortunately for her husband's parliamentary interests, she had not learned that the two things were connected together. And, very unfortunately also for the same interests, she had taken it into her head that Rachel should be married to young Rowan. She had conceived a liking for Rachel; and being by nature busy, fond of employment, and apt at managing other people's affairs, she had put her finger on that match as one which she would task herself to further. This, I say, was unfortunate as regards her husband's present views. Her work, now in hand, was to secure

Tappitt's vote; and to have carried her point in that quarter, her surest method would have been to have entered the brewery open-mouthed against Luke Rowan and Rachel Ray.

But the conversation, almost at once, led to a word in praise of Rachel, and to following words in praise of Luke. Martha only was in the room with her mother. Mrs. Cornbury did not at once begin about the vote, but made, as was natural, certain complimentary speeches about the ball. Really she didn't remember when she had seen anything better done; and the young ladies looked so nice. She had indeed gone away early; but she had done so by no means on her own account, but because Rachel Ray had been tired. Then she said a nice good-natured genial word or two about Rachel Ray and her performance on that occasion. "It seemed to me," she added, "that a certain young gentleman was quite smitten."

Then Mrs. Tappitt's brow became black as thunder, and Mrs. Cornbury knew at once that she had trodden on unsafe ground,—on ground which she should specially have avoided.

"We are all aware," Mrs. Tappitt said, "that the certain young gentleman behaved very badly,—disgracefully, I may say;—but it wasn't our fault, Mrs. Cornbury."

"Upon my word, Mrs. Tappitt, I didn't see anything amiss."

"I'm afraid everybody saw it. Indeed, everybody has been talking of it ever since. As regards him, what he did then was only of a piece with his general conduct, which it doesn't become me to name in the language which it deserves. His behaviour to Mr. T. has been shameful;—quite shameful."

"I had heard something, but I did not know there was anything like that. I'm so sorry I mentioned his name."

"He has disagreed with papa about the brewery business," said Martha.

"It's more than that, Martha, as you know very well," continued Mrs. Tappitt, still speaking in her great heat. "He has shown himself bad in every way,—giving himself airs all over the town, and then going away without paying his debts."

"I don't think we know that, mamma."

"Everybody says so. Your own father heard Sam Griggs say with his own ears that there was a shop bill left there of I don't know how long. But that's nothing to us. He came here under false pretences, and now he's been turned out, and we don't want to have any more to do with him. But, Mrs. Cornbury, I am sorry about that poor foolish girl."

"I didn't think her poor or foolish at all," said Mrs. Cornbury, who had quite heart enough to forget the vote her husband wanted in her warmth for her young friend.

"I must say, then, I did;—I thought her very foolish, and I didn't at all like the way she went on in my house and before my girls. And as for him, he doesn't think of her any more than he thinks of me. In the first place, he's engaged to another girl."

"We are not quite sure that he's engaged, mamma," said Martha.

"I don't know what you call being sure, my dear. I can't say I've ever heard it sworn to, on oath. But his sister Mary told your sister Augusta that he was. I think that's pretty good evidence. But, Mrs. Cornbury, he's one of those that will be engaged to twenty, if he can find twenty foolish enough to listen to him. And for her, who never was at a dance before, to go on with him like that;—I must say that I thought it disgraceful!"

"Well, Mrs. Tappitt," said Mrs. Cornbury, speaking with much authority in her voice, "I can only say that I didn't see it. She was under my charge, and if it was as you say I must be very much to blame,—very much indeed."

"I'm sure I didn't mean that," said Mrs. Tappitt, frightened.

"I don't suppose you did,—but I mean it. As for the young gentleman, I know very little about him. He may be everything that is bad."

"You'll find that he is, Mrs. Cornbury."

"But as to Miss Ray, whom I've known all my life, and whose mother my father has known for all her life, I cannot allow anything of the kind to be said. She was under my charge;

and when young ladies are under my charge I keep a close eye
upon them,—for their own comfort's sake. I know how to manage for them, and I always look after them. On the night of
your party I saw nothing in Miss Ray's conduct that was not
nice, ladylike, and well-behaved. I must say so; and if I hear
a whisper to the contrary in any quarter, you may be sure that
I shall say so openmouthed. How d'you do, Mr. Tappitt? I'm
so glad you've come in, as I specially wanted to see you." Then
she shook hands with Mr. Tappitt, who entered the room at
the moment, and the look and manner of her face was altered.

Mrs. Tappitt was cowed. If her husband had not come in
at that moment she might have said a word or two in her own
defence, being driven to do so by the absence of any other
mode of retreating. But as he came in so opportunely, she allowed his coming to cover her defeat. Strong as was her feeling on the subject, she did not dare to continue her attack upon
Rachel in opposition to the defiant bravery which came full
upon her from Mrs. Cornbury's eyes. The words had been bad,
but the determined fire of those eyes had been worse. Mrs.
Tappitt was cowed, and allowed Rachel's name to pass away
without further remark.

Mrs. Cornbury saw it all at a glance;—saw it all and understood it. The vote was probably lost; but it would certainly be
lost if Tappitt and his wife discussed the matter before he had
pledged himself. The vote would probably be lost, even
though Tappitt should, in his ignorance of what had just
passed, pledge himself to give it. All that Mrs. Cornbury perceived, and knew that she could lose nothing by an immediate
request.

"Mr. Tappitt," said she, "I have come canvassing. The fact
is this: Mr. Cornbury says you are a Liberal, and that therefore he has not the face to ask you. I tell him that I think you
would rather support a neighbour from the county, even
though there may be a shade of difference in politics between
you, than a stranger, whose trade and religion cannot possibly
recommend him, and whose politics, if you really knew them,

would probably be quite as much unlike your own as are my husband's."

The little speech had been prepared beforehand, but was brought out quite as naturally as though Mrs. Cornbury had been accustomed to speak on her legs for a quarter of a century.

Mr. Tappitt grunted. The attack came upon him so much by surprise that he knew not what else to do but to grunt. If Mr. Cornbury had come with the same speech in his mouth, and could then have sided off into some general abuse of Luke Rowan, the vote would have been won.

"I'm sure Mrs. Tappitt will agree with me," said Mrs. Cornbury, smiling very sweetly upon the foe she had so lately vanquished.

"Women don't know anything about it," said Tappitt, meaning to snub no one but his own wife, and forgetting that Mrs. Cornbury was a woman. He blushed fiery red when the thought flashed upon him, and wished that his own drawing-room floor would open and receive him; nevertheless he was often afterwards heard to boast how he had put down the politician in petticoats when she came electioneering to the brewery.

"Well, that is severe," said Mrs. Cornbury, laughing.

"Oh, T.! you shouldn't have said that before Mrs. Cornbury!"

"I only meant my own wife, ma'am; I didn't indeed."

"I'll forgive your satire if you'll give me your vote," said Mrs. Cornbury, with her sweetest smile. "He owes it me now; doesn't he, Mrs. Tappitt?"

"Well,—I really think he do." Mrs. Tappitt, in her double trouble,—in her own defeat and her shame on behalf of her husband's rudeness,—was driven back, out of all her latter-day conventionalities, into the thoughts and even into the language of old days. She was becoming afraid of Mrs. Cornbury, and submissive, as of old, to the rank and station of Cornbury Grange. In her terror she was becoming a little forgetful of niceties learned somewhat late in life. "I really think he do," said Mrs. Tappitt.

Tappitt grunted again.

"It's a very serious thing," he said.

"So it is," said Mrs. Cornbury, interrupting him. She knew that her chance was gone if the man were allowed to get himself mentally upon his legs. "It is very serious; but the fact that you are still in doubt shows that you have been thinking of it. We all know how good a churchman you are, and that you would not willingly send a Jew to Parliament."

"I don't know," said Tappitt. "I'm not for persecuting even the Jews;—not when they pay their way and push themselves honourably in commerce."

"Oh, yes; commerce! There is nobody who has shown himself more devoted to the commercial interests than Mr. Cornbury. We buy everything in Baslehurst. Unfortunately our people won't drink beer because of the cider."

"Tappitt doesn't think a bit about that, Mrs. Cornbury."

"I'm afraid I shall be called upon in honour to support my party," said Tappitt.

"Exactly; but which is your party? Isn't the Protestant religion of your country your party? These people are creeping down into all parts of the kingdom, and where shall we be if leading men like you think more of shades of difference between Liberal and Conservative than of the fundamental truths of the Church of England? Would you depute a Jew to get up and speak your own opinions in your own vestry-room?"

"That you wouldn't, T.," said Mrs. Tappitt, who was rather carried away by Mrs. Cornbury's eloquence.

"Not in a vestry, because it's joined on to a church," said Tappitt.

"Or would you like a Jew to be mayor in Baslehurst;—a Jew in the chair where you yourself were sitting only three years ago?"

"That wouldn't be seemly, because our mayor is expected to attend in church on Roundabout Sunday." Roundabout Sunday, so called for certain local reasons which it would be long to explain, followed immediately on the day of the mayor's inauguration.

"Would you like to have a Jew partner in your own business?"

Mrs. Butler Cornbury should have said nothing to Mr. Tappitt as to any partner in the brewery, Jew or Christian.

"I don't want any partner, and what's more, I don't mean to have any."

"Mrs. Cornbury is in favour of Luke Rowan; she takes his side," said Mrs. Tappitt, some portion of her courage returning to her as this opportunity opened upon her. Mr. Tappitt turned his head full round and looked upon Mrs. Cornbury with an evil eye. That lady knew that the vote was lost, lost unless she would denounce the man whom Rachel loved; and she determined at once that she would not denounce him. There are many things which such a woman will do to gain such an object. She could smile when Tappitt was offensive; she could smile again when Mrs. Tappitt talked like a kitchenmaid. She could flatter them both, and pretend to talk seriously with them about Jews and her own Church feelings. She could have given up to them Luke Rowan,—if he had stood alone. But she could not give up the girl she had chaperoned, and upon whom, during that chaperoning, her good-will and kindly feelings had fallen. Rachel had pleased her eye, and gratified her sense of feminine nicety. She felt that a word said against Rowan would be a word said also against Rachel; and therefore, throwing her husband over for the nonce, she resolved to sacrifice the vote and stand up for her friend. "Well, yes; I do," said she, meeting Tappitt's eye steadily. She was not going to be looked out of countenance by Mr. Tappitt.

"She thinks he'll come back to marry that young woman at Bragg's End," said Mrs. Tappitt; "but I say that he'll never dare to show his face in Baslehurst again."

"That young woman is making a great fool of herself," said Tappitt, "if she trusts to a swindler like him."

"Perhaps, Mrs. Tappitt," said Mrs. Cornbury, "we needn't mind discussing Miss Ray. It's not good to talk about a young lady in that way, and I'm sure I never said that I thought she was engaged to Mr. Rowan. Had I done so I should have been very wrong, for I know nothing about it. What little I saw of the gentleman I liked"; and as she used the word "gentleman" she looked Tappitt full in the face; "and for Miss Ray, I've a great regard for her, and think very highly of her. Independently of her acknowledged beauty and pleasant, ladylike manners, she's a very charming girl. About the vote, Mr. Tappitt—; at any rate you'll think of it."

But had he not been defied in his own house? And as for her, the mother of those three finely educated girls, had not every word said in Rachel's favour been a dagger planted in her own maternal bosom? Whose courage would not have risen under such provocation?

Mrs. Cornbury had got up to go, but the indignant, injured Tappitts resolved mutually, though without concert, that she should be answered.

"I'm an honest man, Mrs. Cornbury," said the brewer, "and I like to speak out my mind openly. Mr. Hart is a Liberal, and I mean to support my party. Will you tell Mr. Cornbury so with my compliments? It's all nonsense about Jews not being in Parliament. It's not the same as being mayors or church-wardens, or anything like that. I shall vote for Mr. Hart; and, what's more, we shall put him in."

"And Mrs. Cornbury, if you have so much regard for Miss Rachel, you'd better advise her to think no more of that young man. He's no good; he's not indeed. If you ask, you'll find he's in debt everywhere."

"Swindler!" said Tappitt.

"I don't suppose it can be very bad with Miss Rachel yet, for she only saw him about three times,—though she was so intimate with him at our party."

Mrs. Butler Cornbury curtseyed and smiled, and got herself out of the room. Mrs. Tappitt, as soon as she remembered herself, rang the bell, and Mr. Tappitt, following her down to the hall door, went through the pretence of putting her into her carriage.

"She's a nasty meddlesome woman," said Tappitt, as soon as he got back to his wife.

"And how ever she can stand up and say all those things for that girl, passes me!" said Mrs. Tappitt, holding up both her hands. "She was flighty herself, when young; she was, no doubt; and now I suppose she likes others to be the same. If that's what she calls manners, I shouldn't like her to take my girls about."

"And him a gentleman!" said Tappitt. "If those are to be our gentlemen I'd sooner have all the Jews out of Jerusalem. But they'll find out their gentleman; they'll find him out! He'll rob that old mother of his before he's done; you mark my words else." Comforting himself with this hope he took himself back to his counting-house.

Mrs. Cornbury had smiled as she went, and had carried herself through the whole interview without any sign of temper. Even when declaring that she intended to take Rachel's part openmouthed, she had spoken in a half-drolling way which had divested her words of any tone of offence. But when she got into her carriage, she was in truth very angry. "I don't believe a word of it," she said to herself; "not a word of it." That in which she professed to herself her own disbelief was the general assertion that Rowan was a swindler, supported by the particular assertion that he had left Baslehurst over head and ears in debt. "I don't believe it." And she resolved that it should be her business to find out whether the accusation were true or false. She knew the ins and outs of Baslehurst life and Baslehurst doings with tolerable accuracy, and was at any rate capable of unravelling such a mystery as that. If the Tappitts in their jealousy were striving to rob Rachel Ray of her husband by spreading false reports, she would encourage Rachel Ray in her love by spreading the truth;—if, as she believed, the truth should speak in Rowan's favour. She would have considerable pleasure in countermining Mr. and Mrs. Tappitt.

As to Mr. Tappitt's vote for the election;—-that was gone!

C H A P T E R   X V I I I

Dr. Harford

THE CURRENT OF EVENTS forced upon Rachel a delay of three or four days in answering her letter, or rather forced upon her that delay in learning whether or no she might answer it; and this was felt by her to be a grievous evil. It had been arranged that she should not write until such writing should have received what might almost be called a parochial sanction, and no idea of acting in opposition to that arrangement ever occurred to her; but the more she thought of it the more she was vexed; and the more she thought of it the more she learned to doubt whether or no her mother was placing her in safe tutelage. During these few weeks a great change came upon the girl's character. When first Mrs. Prime had brought home tidings that Miss Pucker had seen her walking and talking with the young man from the brewery, angry as she had been with her sister, and disgusted as she had been with Miss Pucker, she had acknowledged to herself that such talking and walking were very dangerous, if not very improper, and she had half resolved that there should be no more of them. And when Mrs. Prime had seen her standing at the stile, and had brought home that second report, Rachel, knowing what had occurred at that stile, had then felt sure that she was in danger. At that time, though she had thought much of Luke Rowan, she had not thought of him as a man who could possibly be her husband. She had thought of him as having no right to call her Rachel, because he could not possibly become so. There had been great danger;—there had been conduct which she believed to be improper though she could not tell herself that she had been guilty. In her outlook into the world nothing so beautiful had promised itself to her as having such a man to love her as Luke Rowan. Though her mother was not herself ascetic,— liking tea and buttered toast dearly, and liking also little soft laughter with her child,—she had preached ascetisms till Rachel had learned to think that the world was all either ascetic or reprobate. The Dorcas meetings had become distasteful to her because the women were vulgar; but yet she had half believed herself to be wrong in avoiding the work and the vulgarity together. Idle she had never been. Since a needle had come easy to her hand, and the economies of a household had been made intelligible to her, she had earned her bread and assisted in works of charity. She had read no love stories, and been taught to expect no lover. She was not prepared to deny, —did not deny even to herself,—that it was wrong that she should even like to talk to Luke Rowan.

Then came the ball; or, rather, first came the little evening party, which afterwards grew to be a ball. She had been very desirous of going, not for the sake of any pleasure that she promised herself; not for the sake of such pleasure as girls do promise themselves at such gatherings; but because her female pride told her that it was well for her to claim the right of meeting this young man,—well for her to declare that nothing had passed between them which should make her afraid to meet him. That some other hopes had crept in as the evening had come nigh at hand,—hopes of which she had been made aware only by her efforts in repressing them,—may not be denied. She had been accused because of him; and she would show that no such accusation had daunted her. But would he, —would he give occasion for further accusation? She believed he would not; nay, she was sure; at any rate she hoped he would not. She told herself that such was her hopes; but had he not noticed her she would have been wretched.

We know now in what manner he had noticed her, and we know also whether she had been wretched. She had certainly

fled from him. When she left the brewery house, inducing Mrs.
Cornbury to bring her away, she did so in order that she might
escape from him. But she ran from him as one runs from some
great joy in order that the mind may revel over it in peace.
Then, little as she knew it, her love had been given. Her
heart was his. She had placed him upon her pinnacle, and
was prepared to worship him. She was ready to dress herself
in his eyes, to believe that to be good which he thought good,
and to repudiate that which he repudiated. When she bowed
her head over his breast a day or two afterwards, she could
have spoken to him with the full words of passionate love had
not maiden fear repressed her.

But she had not even bowed her head for him, she had not
acknowledged to herself that such love was possible to her, till
her mother had consented. That her mother's consent had been
wavering, doubtful, expressed without intention of such expression,—so expressed that Mrs. Ray hardly knew that she had
expressed it,—was not understood by Rachel. Her mother had
consented, and, that consent having been given, Rachel was
not now disposed to allow of any steps backwards. She seemed
to have learned her rights, or to have assumed that she had
rights. Hitherto her obedience to her mother had been pure
and simple, although, from the greater force of her character,
she had in many things been her mother's leader. But now,
though she was ill inclined to rebel, though in this matter of
the letter she had obeyed, she was beginning to feel that obedience might become a hardship. She did not say to herself,
"They have let me love him, and now they must not put out
their hands to hold back my love"; but the current of her feelings ran as though such unspoken words had passed across her
mind. She had her rights; and though she did not presume that
she could insist on them in opposition to her mother or her
mother's advisers, she knew that she would be wronged if those
rights were withheld from her. The chief of those rights was
the possession of her lover. If he was taken from her she would
be as one imprisoned unjustly,—as one robbed by those who

should have been his friends,—as one injured, wounded,
stricken in the dark, and treacherously mutilated by hands that
should have protected him. During these days she was silent,
and sat with that look upon her brow which her mother feared.

"I could not make Mr. Comfort come any sooner, Rachel,"
said Mrs. Ray.

"No, mamma."

"I can see how impatient you are."

"I don't know that I'm impatient. I'm sure that I haven't
said anything."

"If you said anything I shouldn't mind it so much; but I
can't bear to see you with that unhappy look. I'm sure I only
wish to do what's best. You can't think it right that you should
be writing letters to a gentleman without being sure that it is
proper."

"Oh, mamma, don't talk about it!"

"You don't like me to ask your sister; and I'm sure it's natural I should want to ask somebody. He's nearly seventy years
old, and he has known you ever since you were born. And then
he's a clergyman, and therefore he'll be sure to know what's
right. Not that I should have liked to have said a word about
it to Mr. Prong, because there's a difference when they come
from one doesn't know where."

"Pray, mamma, don't. I haven't made any objection to Mr.
Comfort. It isn't nice to be talked over in that way by anybody,
that's all."

"But what was I to do? I'm sure I liked the young man very
much. I never knew a young man who took his tea so pleasant.
And as for his manners and his way of talking, I had it in my
heart to fall in love with him myself. I had indeed. As far as
that goes, he's just the young man that I could make a son of."

"Dear mamma! my own dearest mamma!" and Rachel,
jumping up, threw herself upon her mother's neck. "Stop there.
You shan't say another word."

"I'm sure I didn't mean to say anything unpleasant."

"No, you did not; and I won't be impatient."

"Only I can't bear that look. And you know what his mother said,—and Mrs. Tappitt. Not that I care about Mrs. Tappitt; only a person's mother is his mother, and he shouldn't have called her a goose."

It must be acknowledged that Rachel's position was not comfortable; and it certainly would not have been improved had she known how many people in Baslehurst were talking about her and Rowan. That Rowan was gone everybody knew; that he had made love to Rachel everybody said; that he never meant to come back any more most professed to believe. Tappitt's tongue was loud in proclaiming his iniquities; and her follies and injuries Mrs. Tappitt whispered into the ears of all her female acquaintances.

"I'm sorry for her," Miss Harford said, mildly. Mrs. Tappitt was calling at the rectory, and had made her way in. Mr. Tappitt was an upholder of the old rector, and there was a fellow-townsman's friendship between them.

"Oh yes;—very sorry for her," said Mrs. Tappitt.

"Very sorry indeed," said Augusta, who was with her mother.

"She always seemed to me a pretty, quiet, well-behaved girl," said Miss Harford.

"Still waters run deepest, you know, Miss Harford," said Mrs. Tappitt. "I should never have imagined it of her;—never. But she certainly met him half-way."

"But we all thought he was respectable, you know," said Miss Harford.

Miss Harford was thoroughly good-natured; and though she had never gone half-way herself, and had perhaps lost her chance from having been unable to go any part of the way, she was not disposed to condemn a girl for having been willing to be admired by such a one as Luke Rowan.

"Well;—yes; at first we did. He had the name of money, you know, and that goes so far with some girls. We were on our guard,"—and she looked proudly round on Augusta,—"till we should hear what the young man really was. He has thrown off his sheep's clothing now with a vengeance. Mr. Tappitt feels quite ashamed that he should have introduced him to any of the people here; he does indeed."

"That may be her misfortune, and not her fault," said Miss Harford, who in defending Rachel was well enough inclined to give up Luke. Indeed, Baslehurst was beginning to have a settled mind that Luke was a wolf.

"Oh, quite so," said Mrs. Tappitt. "The poor girl has been very unfortunate no doubt."

After that she took her leave of the rectory.

On that evening Mr. Comfort dined with Dr. Harford, as did also Butler Cornbury and his wife, and one or two others. The chances of the election formed, of course, the chief subject of conversation both in the drawing-room and at the dinner-table; but in talking of the election they came to talk of Mr. Tappitt, and in talking of Tappitt they came to talk of Luke Rowan.

It has already been said that Dr. Harford had been rector of Baslehurst for many years at the period to which this story refers. He had nearly completed half a century of work in that capacity, and had certainly been neither an idle nor an inefficient clergyman. But, now in his old age, he was discontented and disgusted by the changes which had come upon him; and though some bodily strength for further service still remained to him, he had no longer any aptitude for useful work. A man cannot change as men change. Individual men are like the separate links of a rotatory chain. The chain goes on with continuous easy motion as though every part of it were capable of adapting itself to a curve, but not the less is each link as stiff and sturdy as any other piece of wrought iron. Dr. Harford had in his time been an active, popular man,—a man possessing even some Liberal tendencies in politics, though a country rector of nearly half a century's standing. In his parish he had been more than a clergyman. He had been a magistrate, and a moving man in municipal affairs. He had been a politician, and though now for many years he had supported the Conserva-

tive candidate, he had been loudly in favour of the Reform Bill
when Baslehurst was a close borough in the possession of a
great duke, who held property hard by. But Liberal politics
had gone on and had left Dr. Harford high and dry on the
standing-ground which he had chosen for himself in the early
days of his manhood. And then had come that pestilent act of
the legislature under which his parish had been divided. Not
that the Act of Parliament itself had been violently condemned
by the doctor on its becoming law. I doubt whether he had
then thought much of it.

But when men calling themselves Commissioners came actually upon him and his, and separated off from him a district
of his own town, taking it away altogether from his authority,
and giving it over to such inexperienced hands as chance
might send thither,—then Dr. Harford became a violent Tory.
And my readers must not conceive that this was a question
touching his pocket. One might presume that his pocket would
be in some degree benefited, seeing that he was saved from
the necessity of supplying the spiritual wants of a certain portion of his parish. No shilling was taken from his own income,
which, indeed, was by no means excessive. His whole parish
gave him barely six hundred a year, out of which he had kept
always one, and latterly two curates. It was no question of
money in any degree. Sooner than be invaded and mutilated
he would have submitted to an order calling upon him to find
a third curate,—could any power have given such order. His
parish had been invaded and his clerical authority mutilated.
He was no longer *totus teres atque rotundus.* The beauty of his
life was over, and the contentment of his mind was gone. He
knew that it was only left for him to die, spending such days
as remained to him in vague prophecies of evil against his devoted country,—a country which had allowed its ancient parochial landmarks to be moved, and its ecclesiastical fastnesses
to be invaded!

But perhaps hatred of Mr. Prong was the strongest passion
of Dr. Harford's heart at the present moment. He had ever

hated the dissenting ministers by whom he was surrounded. In Devonshire dissent has waxed strong for many years, and the pastors of the dissenting flocks have been thorns in the side of the Church of England clergymen. Dr. Harford had undergone his full share of suffering from such thorns. But they had caused him no more than a pleasant irritation in comparison with what he endured from the presence of Mr. Prong in Baslehurst. He would sooner have entertained all the dissenting ministers of the South Hams together than have put his legs under the same mahogany with Mr. Prong. Mr. Prong was to him the evil thing! Anathema! He believed all bad things of Mr. Prong with an absolute faith, but without any ground on which such faith should have been formed. He thought that Mr. Prong drank spirits; that he robbed his parishioners;—Dr. Harford would sooner have lost his tongue than have used such a word with reference to those who attended Mr. Prong's chapel;—that he had left a deserted wife on some parish; that he was probably not in truth ordained. There was nothing which Dr. Harford could not believe of Mr. Prong. Now all this was, to say the least of it, a pity, for it disfigured the close of a useful and conscientious life.

Dr. Harford of course intended to vote for Mr. Cornbury, but he would not join loudly in condemnation of Mr. Tappitt. Tappitt had stood stanchly by him in all parochial contests regarding the new district. Tappitt opposed the Prong faction at all points. Tappitt as churchwarden had been submissive to the doctor. Church of England principles had always been held at the brewery, and Bungall had been ever in favour with Dr. Harford's predecessor.

"He calls himself a Liberal, and always has done," said the doctor. "You can't expect that he should desert his own party."

"But a Jew!" said old Mr. Comfort.

"Well; why not a Jew?" said the doctor. Whereupon Mr. Comfort, and Butler Cornbury, and Dr. Harford's own curate, young Mr. Calclough, and Captain Byng, an old bachelor, who lived in Baslehurst, all stared at him; as Dr. Harford had intended that they should. "Upon my word," said he, "I don't see the use for caring for that kind of thing any longer; I don't indeed. In the way we are going on now, and for the sort of thing we do, I don't see why Jews shouldn't serve us as well in Parliament as Christians. If I am to have my brains knocked out, I'd sooner have it done by a declared enemy than by one who calls himself my friend."

"But our brains are not knocked out yet," said Butler Cornbury.

"I don't know anything about yours, but mine are."

"I don't think the world's coming to an end yet," said the captain.

"Nor do I. I said nothing about the world coming to an end. But if you saw a part of your ship put under the command of a landlubber, who didn't know one side of the vessel from the other, you'd think the world had better come to an end than be carried on in that way."

"It's not the same thing, you know," said the captain. "You couldn't divide a ship."

"Oh, well; you'll see."

"I don't think any Christian should vote for a Jew," said the curate. "A verdict has gone out against them, and what is man that he should reverse it?"

"Are you quite sure that you are reversing it by putting them into Parliament?" said Dr. Harford. "May not that be a carrying on of the curse?"

"There's consolation in that idea for Butler if he loses his election," said Mr. Comfort.

"Parliament isn't what it was," said the doctor. "There's no doubt about that."

"And who is to blame?" said Mr. Comfort, who had never supported the Reform Bill as his neighbour had done.

"I say nothing about blame. It's natural that things should get worse as they grow older."

"Dr. Harford thinks Parliament is worn out," said Butler Cornbury.

"And what if I do think so? Have not other things as great fallen and gone into decay? Did not the Roman senate wear out, as you call it? And as for these Jews, of whom you are speaking, what was the curse upon them but the wearing out of their grace and wisdom? I am inclined to think that we are wearing out; only I wish the garment could have lasted my time without showing so many thin places."

"Now I believe just the contrary," said the captain. "I don't think we have come to our full growth yet."

"Could we lick the French as we did at Trafalgar and Waterloo?" said the doctor.

The captain thought a while before he answered, and then spoke with much solemnity. "Yes," said he, "I think we could. And I hope the time will soon come when we may."

"We shan't do it if we send Jews to Parliament," said Mr. Comfort.

"I must say I think Tappitt wrong," said young Cornbury. "Of course, near as the thing is going, I'm sorry to lose his vote; but I'm not speaking because of that. He has always pretended to hold on to the Church party here, and the Church party has held on to him. His beer is none of the best, and I think he'd have been wise to stick to his old friends."

"I don't see the argument about the beer," said the doctor.

"He shouldn't provoke his neighbours to look at his faults."

"But the Jew's friends would find out that the beer is bad as well as yours."

"The truth is," said Cornbury, "that Tappitt thinks he has a personal grievance against me. He's as cross as a bear with a sore head at the present moment, because this young fellow who was to have been his partner has turned against him. There's some love-affair, and my wife has been there and made a mess of it. It's hard upon me, for I don't know that I ever saw the young man in my life."

"I believe that fellow is a scamp," said the doctor.

"I hope not," said Mr. Comfort, thinking of Rachel and her hopes.

"We all hope he isn't, of course," said the doctor. "But we can't prevent men being scamps by hoping. There are other scamps in this town in whom, if my hoping would do any good, a very great change would be made."—Everybody present knew that the doctor alluded especially to Mr. Prong, whose condition, however, if the doctor's hopes could have been carried out, would not have been enviable.—"But I fear this fellow Rowan is a scamp, and I think he has treated Tappitt badly. Tappitt told me all about it only this morning."

"Audi alteram partem," said Mr. Comfort.

"The scamp's party you mean," said the doctor. "I haven't the means of doing that. If in this world we suspend our judgment till we've heard all that can be said on both sides of every question, we should never come to any judgment at all. I hear that he's in debt; I believe he behaved very badly to Tappitt himself, so that Tappitt was forced to use personal violence to defend himself; and he has certainly threatened to open a new brewery here. Now that's bad, as coming from a young man related to the old firm."

"I think he should leave the brewery alone," said Mr. Comfort.

"Of course he should," said the doctor. "And I hear, moreover, that he is playing a wicked game with a girl in your parish."

"I don't know about a wicked game," said the other. "It won't be a wicked game if he marries her."

Then Rachel's chances of matrimonial success were discussed with a degree of vigour which must have been felt by her to be highly complimentary, had she been aware of it. But I grieve to say that public opinion, as expressed in Dr. Harford's dining-room, went against Luke Rowan. Mr. Tappitt was not a great man, either as a citizen or as a brewer: he was not one to whom Baslehurst would even rejoice to raise a monument; but such as he was he had been known for many years. No one in that room loved or felt for him anything like real friendship; but the old familiarity of the place was in his favour, and his form was known of old upon the High Street. He was not a drunkard, he lived becomingly with his wife, he had paid his way, and was a fellow-townsman. What was it to Dr. Harford, or even to Mr. Comfort, that he brewed bad beer? No man was compelled to drink it. Why should not a man employ himself, openly and legitimately, in the brewing of bad beer, if the demand for bad beer were so great as to enable him to live by the occupation? On the other hand, Luke Rowan was personally known to none of them; and they were jealous that a change should come among them with any view of teaching them a lesson or improving their condition. They believed, or thought they believed, that Mr. Tappitt had been ill-treated in his counting-house. It was grievous to them that a man with a wife and three daughters should have been threatened by a young unmarried man,—by a man whose shoulders were laden with no family burden. Whether Rowan's propositions had been in truth good or evil, just or unjust, they had not inquired, and would not probably have ascertained had they done so. But they judged the man and condemned him. Mr. Comfort was brought round to condemn him as thoroughly as did Dr. Harford,—not reflecting, as he did so, how fatal his condemnation might be to the happiness of poor Rachel Ray.

"The fact is, Butler," said the doctor, when Mr. Comfort had left them, and gone to the drawing-room;—"the fact is, your wife has not played her cards at the brewery as well as she usually does play them. She has been taking this young fellow's part; and after that I don't know how she was to expect that Tappitt would stand by you."

"No general can succeed always," said Cornbury, laughing.

"Well; some generals do. But I must confess your wife is generally very successful. Come; we'll go up-stairs; and don't you tell her that I've been finding fault. She's as good as gold, and I can't afford to quarrel with her; but I think she has tripped here."

When the old doctor and Butler Cornbury reached the

drawing-room the names of Rowan and Tappitt had not been as yet banished from the conversation; but to them had been added some others. Rachel's name had been again mentioned, as had also that of Rachel's sister.

"Papa, who do you think is going to be married?" said Miss Harford.

"Not you, my dear, is it?" said the doctor.

"Mr. Prong is going to be married to Mrs. Prime," said Miss Harford, showing by the solemnity of her voice that she regarded the subject as one which should by its nature repress any further joke.

Nor was Dr. Harford inclined to joke when he heard such tidings as these. "Mr. Prong!" said he. "Nonsense; who told you?"

"Well, it was Baker told me." Mrs. Baker was the housekeeper at the Baslehurst rectory, and had been so for the last thirty years. "She learned it at Drabbit's in the High Street, where Mrs. Prime had been living since she left her mother's cottage."

"If that's true, Comfort," said the doctor, "I congratulate you on your parishioner."

"Mrs. Prime is no parishioner of mine," said the vicar of Cawston. "If it's true, I'm very sorry for her mother,—very sorry."

"I don't believe a word of it," said Mrs. Cornbury.

"Poor, wretched, unfortunate woman!" said the doctor. "Her little bit of money is all in her own hands; is it not?"

"I believe it is," said Mr. Comfort.

"Ah, yes; I dare say it's true," said the vicar. "She's been running after him ever since he's been here. I don't doubt it's true. Poor creature!—poor creature! Poor thing!" And the doctor absolutely sighed as he thought of the misery in store for Mr. Prong's future bride. "It's an ill wind that blows nobody any good," he said after a while. "He'll go off, no doubt, when he has got the money in his hand, and we shall be rid of him. Poor thing;—poor thing!"

Before the evening was over Mrs. Cornbury and her father had again discussed the question of Rachel's possible engagement with Luke Rowan. Mr. Comfort had declared his conviction that it would be dangerous to encourage any such hopes; whereas his daughter protested that she would not see Rachel thrown over if she could help it. "Don't condemn him yet, papa," she said.

"I don't condemn him at all, my dear; but I hardly think we shall see him back at Baslehurst. And he shouldn't have gone away without paying his debts, Patty!"

CHAPTER XIX

Mr. Comfort Calls at the Cottage

MRS. RAY, in her trouble occasioned by Luke's letter, had walked up to Mr. Comfort's house, but had not found him at home. Therefore she had written to him, in his own study, a few very simple words, telling the matter on which she wanted his advice. Almost any other woman would have half hidden her real meaning under a cloud of ambiguous words; but with her there was no question of hiding anything from her clergyman. "Rachel has had a letter from young Mr. Rowan," she said, "and I have begged her not to answer it till I have shown it to you." So Mr. Comfort sent word down to Bragg's End that he would call at the cottage, and fixed an hour for his coming. This task was to be accomplished by him on the morning after Dr. Harford's dinner; and he had thought much of the coming conference between himself and Rachel's mother while Rowan's character was being discussed at Dr. Harford's house: but on that occasion he had said nothing to any one, not even to his daughter, of the application which had been made to him by Mrs. Ray. At eleven o'clock he presented himself at the cottage door, and, of course, found Mrs. Ray alone. Rachel had taken herself over to Mrs. Sturt, and greatly amazed that kind-hearted person by her silence and confusion. "Why, my dear," said Mrs. Sturt, "you hain't got a word to-day to throw at a dog." Rachel acknowledged that she had not; and then Mrs. Sturt allowed her to remain in her silence.

"Oh, Mr. Comfort, this is so good of you!" Mrs. Ray began as soon as her friend was inside the parlour. "When I went up to the parsonage I didn't think of bringing you down here all the way;—I didn't indeed." Mr. Comfort assured her that he thought nothing of the trouble, declared that he owed her a visit, and then asked after Rachel.

"To tell you the truth, then, she's just stept across the green to Mrs. Sturt's, so as to be out of the way. It's a trying time to her, Mr. Comfort,—very; and whatever way it goes, she's a good girl,—a very good girl."

"You needn't tell me that, Mrs. Ray."

"Oh! but I must. There's her sister thinks she's encouraged this young man too freely, but——"

"By-the-by, Mrs. Ray, I've been told that Mrs. Prime is engaged to be married herself."

"Have you, now?"

"Well, yes; I heard it in Baslehurst yesterday;—to Mr. Prong."

"She's kept it so close, Mr. Comfort, I didn't think anybody had heard it."

"It is true, then?"

"I can't say she has accepted him yet. He has offered to her; —there's no doubt about that, Mr. Comfort,—and she hasn't said him no."

"Do let her look sharp after her money," said Mr. Comfort.

"Well, that's just it. She's not a bit inclined to give it up to him, I can tell you."

"I can't say, Mrs. Ray, that the connection is one that I like very much, in any way. There's no reason at all why your eldest daughter should not marry again, but——"

"What can I do, Mr. Comfort? Of course I know he's not just what he should be,—that is, for a clergyman. When I knew he hadn't come from any of the colleges, I never had any fancy for going to hear him myself. But of course I should never have left your church, Mr. Comfort,—not if anybody had come there. And if I could have had my way with Dorothy, she would never have gone near him,—never. But what could I do, Mr. Comfort? Of course she can go where she likes."

"Mr. Prime was a gentleman and a Christian," said the vicar.

"That he was, Mr. Comfort; and a husband for a young woman to be proud of. But he was soon taken away from her —very soon! and she hasn't thought much of this world since."

"I don't know what she's thinking of now."

"It isn't of herself, Mr. Comfort; not a bit. Dorothy is very stern; but, to give her her due, it's not herself she's thinking of."

"Why does she want to marry him, then?"

"Because he's lonely without someone to do for him."

"Lonely!—and he should be lonely for me, Mrs. Ray."

"And because she says she can work in the vineyard better as a clergyman's wife."

"Pshaw! work in the vineyard, indeed! But it's no business of mine; and, as you say, I suppose you can't help it."

"Indeed I can't. She'd never think of asking me."

"I hope she'll look after her money, that's all. And what's all this about my friend Rachel? I'd a great deal sooner hear that she was going to be married,—if I knew that the man was worthy of her."

Then Mrs. Ray put her hand into her pocket, and taking out Rowan's letter, gave it to the vicar to read. As she did so, she looked into his face with eyes full of the most intense anxiety. She was herself greatly frightened by the magnitude of this marriage question. She feared the enmity of Mrs. Rowan; and she doubted the firmness of Luke. She could not keep herself from reflecting that a young man from London was very dangerous; that he might probably be a wolf; that she could not be safe in trusting her one lamb into such custody. But, nevertheless, she most earnestly hoped that Mr. Comfort's verdict

might be in the young man's favour. If he would only say that
the young man was not a wolf,—if he would only take upon
his own clerical shoulders the responsibility of trusting the
young man,—Mrs. Ray would become for the moment one of
the happiest women in Devonshire. With what a beaming face,
—with what a true joy,—with what smiles through her tears,
would she then have welcomed Rachel back from the farm-
house! How she would have watched her as she came across
the green, beckoning to her eagerly, and telling all her happy
tale beforehand by the signs of her joy! But there was to be
no such happy tale as that told on this morning. She watched
the vicar's face as he read the letter, and soon perceived that
the verdict was to be given against the writer of it. I do not
know that Mrs. Ray was particularly quick at reading the
countenances of men, but, in this instance, she did read
the countenance of Mr. Comfort. We, all of us, read more in the
faces of those with whom we hold converse, than we are aware
of doing. Of the truth, or want of truth in every word spoken
to us, we judge, in great part, by the face of the speaker. By
the face of every man and woman seen by us, whether they
speak or are silent, we form a judgment,—and in nine cases out
of ten our judgment is true. It is because our tenth judgment,
—that judgment which has been wrong,—comes back upon us
always with the effects of its error, that we teach ourselves to
say that appearances cannot be trusted. If we did not trust
them we should be walking ever in doubt, in darkness, and in
ignorance. As Mr. Comfort read the letter, Mrs. Ray knew that
it would not be allowed to her to speak words of happiness to
Rachel on that day. She knew that the young man was to be
set down as dangerous; but she was by no means aware that
she was reading the vicar's face with precise accuracy. Mr.
Comfort had been slow in his perusal, weighing the words of
the letter; and when he had finished it he slowly refolded the
paper and put it back into its envelope. "He means what he
says," said he, as he gave the letter back to Mrs. Ray.

"Yes; I think he means what he says."

"But we cannot tell how long he may mean it; nor can we tell as yet whether such a connection would be good for Rachel, even if he should remain steadfast in such meaning. If you ask me, Mrs. Ray——"

"I do ask you, Mr. Comfort."

"Then I think we should all of us know more about him, before we allow Rachel to give him encouragement;—I do indeed."

Mrs. Ray could not quite repress in her heart a slight feeling of anger against the vicar. She remembered the words,—so different not only in their meaning, but in the tone in which they were spoken,—in which he had sanctioned Rachel's going to the ball: "Young people get to think of each other," he had then said, speaking with good-humoured, cheery voice, as though such thinking were worthy of all encouragement. He had spoken then of marriage being the happiest condition for both men and women, and had inquired as to Rowan's means. Every word that had then fallen from him had expressed his opinion that Luke Rowan was an eligible lover. But now he was named as though he were undoubtedly a wolf. Why had not Mr. Comfort said then, at that former interview, when no harm had as yet been done, that it would be desirable to know more of the young man before any encouragement was given to him? Mrs. Ray felt that she was injured; but, nevertheless, her trust in her counsellor was not on that account the less.

"I suppose it must be answered," said Mrs. Ray.

"Oh, yes; of course it should be answered."

"And who should write it, Mr. Comfort?"

"Let Rachel write it herself. Let her tell him that she is not prepared to correspond with him as yet, any further that is, you understand, than the writing of that letter."

"And about—about—about what he says as to loving her, you know? There has been a sort of promise between them, Mr. Comfort, and no young man could have spoken more honestly than he did."

"And he meant honestly, no doubt; but you see, Mrs. Ray,

it is necessary to be so careful in these matters! It is quite evident his mother doesn't wish this marriage."

"And he shouldn't have called her a goose; should he?"

"I don't think much about that."

"Don't you, now?"

"It was all meant in good humour. But she thinks it a bad marriage for him as regards money, and money considerations always go so far, you know. And then he's away, and you've got no hold upon him."

"That's quite true, Mr. Comfort."

"He has quarrelled with the people here. And upon my word I'm inclined to think he has not behaved very well to Mr. Tappitt."

"Hasn't he, now?"

"I'm afraid not, Mrs. Ray. They were talking about him last night in Baslehurst, and I'm afraid he has behaved badly at the brewery. There were words between him and Mr. Tappitt, —very serious words."

"Yes; I know that. He told Rachel as much as that. I think he said he was going to law with Mr. Tappitt."

"And if so, the chances are that he may never be seen here again. It's ill coming to a place where one is quarrelling with people. And as to the lawsuit, it seems to me, from what I hear, that he would certainly lose it. No doubt he has a considerable property in the brewery; but he wants to be master of everything, and that can't be reasonable, you know. And then, Mrs. Ray, there's worse than that behind."

"Worse than that!" said Mrs. Ray, in whose heart every gleam of comfort was quickly being extinguished by darkening shadows.

"They tell me that he has gone away without paying his debts. If that is so, it shows that his means cannot be very good." Then why had Mr. Comfort taken upon himself expressly to say that they were good at that interview before Mrs. Tappitt's party? That was the thought in the widow's mind at the present moment. Mr. Comfort, however, went on with his caution. "And then, when the happiness of such a girl as Rachel is concerned, it is impossible to be too careful. Where should we all be if we found that we had given her to a scamp?"

"Oh dear, oh dear! I don't think he can be a scamp;—he did take his tea so nicely."

"I don't say he is;—I don't judge him. But then we should be careful. Why didn't he pay his debts before he went away? A young man should always pay his debts."

"Perhaps he's sent it down in a money-order," said Mrs. Ray. "They are so very convenient,—that is if you've got the money."

"If he hasn't I hope he will, for I can assure you I don't want to think badly of him. Maybe he will turn out all right. And you may be sure of this, Mrs. Ray, that if he is really attached to Rachel he won't give her up, because she doesn't throw herself into his arms at his first word. There's nothing becomes a young woman like a little caution, or makes a young man think more of her. If Rachel fancies that she likes him let her hold back a while and find out what sort of stuff he's made of. If I were her I should just tell him that I thought it better to wait a little before I made any positive engagement."

"But, Mr. Comfort, how is she to begin it? You see he calls her Dearest Rachel."

"Let her say Dear Mr. Rowan. There can't be any harm in that."

"She mustn't call him Luke, I suppose."

"I think she'd better not. Young men think so much of those things."

"And she's not to say 'Yours affectionately' at the end?"

"She'll understand all that when she comes to write the letter better than we can tell her. Give her my love; and tell her from me I'm quite sure she's a dear, good girl, and that it must be a great comfort to you to know that you can trust her so thoroughly." Then, having spoken these last words, Mr. Comfort took himself away.

Rachel, sitting in the window of Mrs. Sturt's large front kitchen on the other side of the green, could see Mr. Comfort come forth from the cottage and get into his low four-wheeled carriage, which, with his boy in livery, had been standing at the garden gate during the interview. Mrs. Sturt was away among the milk-pans, scalding cream or preparing butter, and did not watch either Rachel or the visitor at the cottage. But she knew with tolerable accuracy what was going on, and with all her heart wished that her young friend might have luck with her lover. Rachel waited for a minute or two till the little carriage was out of sight, till the sound of the wheels could be no longer heard, and then she prepared to move. She slowly got herself up from her chair as though she were afraid to show herself upon the green, and paused still a few moments longer before she left the kitchen.

"So, thou's off," said Mrs. Sturt, coming in from the back regions of her territory, with the sleeves of her gown tucked up, enveloped in a large roundabout apron which covered almost all her dress. Mrs. Sturt would no more have thought of doing her work in the front kitchen than I should think of doing mine in the drawing-room. "So thou's off home again, my lass," said Mrs. Sturt.

"Yes, Mrs. Sturt. Mr. Comfort has been with mamma,— about business; and as I didn't want to be in the way I just came over to you."

"Thou art welcome, as flowers in May, morning or evening; but thee knowest that, girl. As for Mr. Comfort,—it's cold comfort he is, I always say. It's little I think of what clergymen says, unless it be out of the pulpit or the like of that. What does they know about lads and lasses?"

"He's a very old friend of mamma's."

"Old friends is always best, I'll not deny that. But, look thee here, my girl; my man's an old friend too. He's know'd thee since he lifted thee in his arms to pull the plums off that bough yonder; and he's seen thee these ten years a deal oftener than Mr. Comfort. If they say anything wrong of thy joe there, tell

me, and Sturt'll find out whether it be true or no. Don't let ere
a parson in Devonshire rob thee of thy sweetheart. It's passing
sweet, when true hearts meet. But it breaks the heart, when
true hearts part." With the salutary advice contained in these
ancient local lines Mrs. Sturt put her arms round Rachel, and
having kissed her, bade her go.

With slow step she made her way across the green, hardly
daring to look to the door of the cottage. But there was no figure standing at the door; and let her have looked with all her
eyes, there was nothing there to have told her anything. She
walked very slowly, thinking as she went of Mrs. Sturt's words
—"Don't let ere a parson in Devonshire rob thee of thy sweetheart." Was it not hard upon her that she should be subjected
to the misery of such discussion, seeing that she had given no
hope, either to her lover or to herself, till she had received full
warranty for doing so? She would do what her mother should
bid her, let it be what it might; but she would be wronged,—
she felt that she would be wronged and injured, grievously injured, if her mother should now bid her think of Rowan as one
thinks of those that are gone.

She entered the cottage slowly, and turning into the parlour, found her mother seated there on the old sofa, opposite
to the fireplace. She was seated there in stiff composure, waiting the work which she had to do. It was no customary place
of hers, and she was a woman who, in the ordinary occupa-
tions of her life, never deserted her customary places. She had
an old easy chair near the fireplace, and another smaller chair
close to the window, and in one of these she might always be
found, unless when, on special occasions like the present,
some great thing had occurred to throw her out of the grooves
of her life.

"Well, mamma?" said Rachel, coming in and standing before her mother. Mrs. Ray, before she spoke, looked up into her
child's face, and was afraid. "Well, mamma, what has Mr. Comfort said?"

Was it not hard for Mrs. Ray that at such a moment she

should have had no sort of husband on whom to lean? Does the reader remember that in the opening words of this story Mrs. Ray was described as a woman who specially needed some standing-corner, some post, some strong prop to bear her weight,—some marital authority by which she might be guided? Such prop and such guiding she had never needed more sorely than she needed them now. She looked up into Rachel's face before she spoke, and was afraid. "He has been here, my dear," she said, "and has gone away."

"Yes, mamma, I knew that," said Rachel. "I saw his phaeton drive off; that's why I came over from Mrs. Sturt's."

Rachel's voice was hard, and there was no comfort in it. It was so hard that Mrs. Ray felt it to be unkind. No doubt Rachel suffered; but did not she suffer also? Would not she have given blood from her breast, like the maternal pelican, to have secured from that clerical counsellor a verdict that might have been comforting to her child? Would she not have made any sacrifice of self for such a verdict, even though the effecting of it must have been that she herself would have been left alone and deserted in the world? Why, then, should Rachel be stern to her? If misery was to fall on both of them, it was not of her doing.

"I know you will think it's my fault, Rachel; but I cannot help it, even though you should say so. Of course I was obliged to ask some one; and who else was there that would be able to tell me so well as Mr. Comfort? You would not have liked it at all if I had gone to Dorothea; and as for Mr. Prong——"

"Oh! mamma, mamma, don't! I haven't said anything. I haven't complained of Mr. Comfort. What has he said now? You forget that you have not told me."

"No, my dear, I don't forget; I wish I could. He says that Mr. Rowan has behaved badly to Mr. Tappitt, and that he hasn't paid his debts, and that the lawsuit will be sure to go against him, and that he will never show his face in Baslehurst again; and he says, too, that it would be very wrong for you to correspond with him,—very; because a young girl like you must be so careful about such things; and he says he'll be much more likely to respect you if you don't—don't—don't just throw yourself into his arms like. Those were his very words; and then he says that if he really cares for you, he'll be sure to come back again, and so you're to answer the letter, and you must call him Dear Mr. Rowan. Don't call him Luke, because young men think so much about those things. And you are to tell him that there isn't to be any engagement, or any letter-writing, or anything of that sort at all. But you can just say something friendly,—about hoping he's quite well, or something of that kind. And then when you come to the end, you had better sign yourself 'Yours truly.' It won't do to say anything about affection, because one never knows how it may turn out. And,—let me see; there was only one thing more. Mr. Comfort says that you are a good girl, and that he is sure you have done nothing wrong,—not even in a word or a thought; and I say so too. You are my own beautiful child; and, Rachel,—I do so wish I could make it all right between you."

Nobody can deny that Mrs. Ray had given, with very fair accuracy, an epitome of Mr. Comfort's words; but they did not leave upon Rachel's mind a very clear idea of what she was expected to do. "Go away in debt!" she said; "who says so?"

"Mr. Comfort told me so just now. But perhaps he'll send the money in a money-order, you know."

"I don't think he would go away in debt. And why should the lawsuit go against him if he's got right on his side? He does not wish to do any harm to Mr. Tappitt."

"I don't know about that, my dear; but at any rate they've quarrelled."

"But why shouldn't that be Mr. Tappitt's fault as much as his? And as for not showing his face in Baslehurst——! Oh, mamma! don't you know him well enough to be sure that he will never be ashamed of showing his face anywhere? He not show his face! Mamma, I don't believe a word of it all,—not a word."

"Mr. Comfort said so; he did indeed." Then Mrs. Sturt's words came back upon Rachel. "Don't let ere a parson in Devonshire rob thee of thy sweetheart." This lover of hers was her only possession,—the only thing of her own winning that she had ever valued. He was her great triumph, the rich upshot of her own prowess,—and now she felt that this parson was indeed robbing her. Had he been then present, she would have risen up and spoken at him, as she had never spoken before. The spirit of rebellion against all the world was strong within her;—against all the world except that one weak woman who now sat before her on the sofa. Her eyes were full of anger, and Mrs. Ray saw that it was so; but still she was minded to obey her mother.

"It's no good talking," said Rachel; "but when they say that he's afraid to show himself in Baslehurst, I don't believe them. Does he look like a man afraid to show himself?"

"Looks are so deceitful, Rachel."

"And as for debts,—people, if they're called away by telegraph in a minute, can't pay all that they owe. There are plenty of people in Baslehurst that owe a deal more than he does, I'm sure. And he's got his share in the brewery, so that nobody need be afraid."

"Mr. Comfort didn't say that you were to quarrel with him altogether."

"Mr. Comfort! What's Mr. Comfort to me, mamma?" This was said in such a tone that Mrs. Ray absolutely started up from her seat.

"But, Rachel, he is my oldest friend. He was your father's friend."

"Why did he not say it before, then? Why—why—why—? Mamma, I can't throw him off now. Didn't I tell him that—that—that I would—love him? Didn't you say that it might be so,—you yourself? How am I to show my face, if I go back now? Mamma, I do love him, with all my heart and all my strength, and nothing that anybody can say can make any difference. If he owed ever so much money I should love him the same. If he had killed Mr. Tappitt it wouldn't make any difference."

"Oh, Rachel!"

"No more it would. If Mr. Tappitt began it first, it wasn't his fault."

"But Rachel, my darling,—what can we do? If he has gone away we cannot make him come back again."

"But he wrote almost immediately."

"And you are going to answer it;—are you not?"

"Yes;—but what sort of an answer, mamma? How can I expect that he will ever want to see me again when I have written to him in that way? I won't say anything about hoping that he's very well. If I may not tell him that he's my own, own, own Luke, and that I love him with all my heart, I'll bid him stay away and not trouble himself any further. I wonder what he'll think of me when I write in that way!"

"If he's constant-hearted he'll wait a while and then he'll come back again."

"Why should he come back when I've treated him in that way? What have I got to give him? Mamma, you may write the letter yourself, and put in it what you please."

"Mr. Comfort said that you had better write it."

"Mr. Comfort! I don't know why I'm to do all that Mr. Comfort tells me," and then those other words of Mrs. Sturt's recurred to her, "It's little I think of what a clergyman says unless it be out of a pulpit." After that there was nothing further said for some minutes. Mrs. Ray still sat on the sofa, and as she gazed upon the table which stood in the middle of the room, she wiped her eyes with her handkerchief. Rachel was now seated in a chair with her back almost turned to her mother, and was beating with her impatient fingers on the table. She was very angry,—angry even with her mother; and she was half broken-hearted, truly believing that such a letter as that which she was desired to write would estrange her lover from her for ever. So they sat, and for a few minutes no word was spoken between them.

"Rachel," said Mrs. Ray at last, "if wrong has been done, is it not better that it should be undone?"

"What wrong have I done?" said Rachel, jumping up.

"It is I that have done it,—not you."

"No, mamma; you have done no wrong."

"I should have known more before I let him come here and encouraged you to think of him. It has been my fault. My dear, will you not forgive me?"

"Mamma, there has been no fault. There is nothing to forgive."

"I have made you unhappy, my child," and then Mrs. Ray burst out into open tears.

"No, mamma, I won't be unhappy;—or if I am I will bear it." Then she got up and threw her arms round her mother's neck, and embraced her. "I will write the letter, but I will not write it now. You shall see it before it goes."

CHAPTER XX

Showing What Rachel Ray Thought When She Sat on the Stile, and How She Wrote Her Letter Afterwards

RACHEL, as soon as she had made her mother the promise that she would write the letter, left the parlour and went up to her own room. She had many thoughts to adjust in her mind which could not be adjusted satisfactorily otherwise than in solitude, and it was clearly necessary that they should be adjusted before she could write her letter. It must be remembered, not only that she had never before written a letter to a lover, but that she had never before written a letter of importance to any one. She had threatened at one moment that she would leave the writing of it to her mother; but there came upon her a feeling, of which she was hardly conscious, that she herself might probably compose the letter in a strain of higher dignity than her mother would be likely to adopt. That her lover would be gone from her for ever she felt almost assured; but still it would be much to her that, on going, he should so leave her that his respect might remain, though his love would be a thing of the past. In her estimation he was a noble being, to have been loved by whom even for a few days was more honour than she had ever hoped to win. For a few days she had been allowed to think that her great fortune intended him to be her husband. But Fate had interposed, and now she feared that all her joy was at an end. But her joy should be so relinquished that she herself should not be disgraced in the giving of it up. She sat there alone for an hour, and was stronger, when that hour was over, than she had been when she left her mother. Her pride had supported her, and had been sufficient for her support in that first hour of her sorrow. It is ever so with us in our misery. In the first flush of our wretchedness, let the out-ward signs of our grief be what they may, we promise to our-selves the support of some inner strength which shall suffice to us at any rate as against the eyes of the outer world. But anon, and that inner staff fails us; our pride yields to our tears; our dignity is crushed beneath the load with which we have bur-dened it, and then with loud wailings we own ourselves to be the wretches which we are. But now Rachel was in the hour of her pride, and as she came down from her room she resolved that her sorrow should be buried in her own bosom. She had known what it was to love,—had known it, perhaps, for one whole week,—and now that knowledge was never to avail her again. Among them all she had been robbed of her sweetheart. She had been bidden to give her heart to this man,—her heart and hand; and now, when she had given all her heart, she was bidden to refuse her hand. She had not ventured to love till her love had been sanctioned. It had been sanctioned, and she had loved; and now that sanction was withdrawn! She knew that she was injured,—deeply, cruelly injured, but she would bear it, showing nothing, and saying nothing. With this resolve she came down from her room, and began to employ herself on her household work.

Mrs. Ray watched her carefully, and Rachel knew that she was watched; but she took no outward notice of it, going on with her work, and saying a soft, gentle word now and again, sometimes to her mother, and sometimes to the little maiden who attended them. "Will you come to dinner, mamma?" she said with a smile, taking her mother by the hand.

"I shouldn't mind if I never sat down to dinner again," said Mrs. Ray.

"Oh, mamma! don't say that; just when you are going to thank God for the good things he gives you."

Then Mrs. Ray, in a low voice, as though rebuked, said the grace, and they sat down together to their meal.

The afternoon went with them very slowly and almost in silence. Neither of them would now speak about Luke Rowan; and to neither of them was it as yet possible to speak about aught else. One word on the subject was said during those hours. "You won't have time for your letter after tea," Mrs. Ray said.

"I shall not write it till to-morrow," Rachel answered; "another day will do no harm now."

At tea Mrs. Ray asked her whether she did not think that a walk would do her good, and offered to accompany her; but Rachel, acceding to the proposition of the walk, declared that she would go alone. "It's very bad of me to say so, isn't it, when you're so good as to offer to go with me?" But Mrs. Ray kissed her; saying, with many words, that she was satisfied that it should be so. "You want to think of things, I know," said the mother. Rachel acknowledged, by a slight motion of her head, that she did want to think of things, and soon after that she started.

"I believe I'll call on Dolly," she said. "It would be bad to quarrel with her; and perhaps now she'll come back here to live with us;—only I forgot about Mr. Prong." It was agreed, however, that she should call on her sister, and ask her to dine at the cottage on the following day.

She walked along the road straight into Baslehurst, and went at once to her sister's lodgings. She had another place to visit before she returned home, but it was a place for which a later hour in the evening would suit her better. Mrs. Prime was at home; and Rachel, on being shown up into the sitting-room, —a room in which every piece of furniture had become known to her during those Dorcas meetings,—found not only her sister sitting there, but also Miss Pucker and Mr. Prong. Rachel had not seen that gentleman since she had learned that he was to become her brother-in-law, and hardly knew in what way to greet him; but it soon became apparent to her that no outward show of regard was expected from her at that moment.

"I think you know my sister, Mr. Prong," said Dorothea. Whereupon Mr. Prong rose from his chair, took Rachel's hand, pressing it between his own, and then sat down again. Rachel, judging from his countenance, thought that some cloud had passed also across the sunlight of his love. She made her little speech, giving her mother's love, and adding her own assurance that she hoped her sister would come out and dine at the cottage.

"I really don't know," said Mrs. Prime. "Such goings about do cut up one's time so much. I shouldn't be here again till——"

"Of course you'd stay for tea with us," said Rachel.

"And lose the whole afternoon!" said Mrs. Prime.

"Oh do!" said Miss Pucker. "You have been working so hard; hasn't she now, Mr. Prong? At this time of the year a sniff of fresh air among the flowers does do a body so much good." And Miss Pucker looked and spoke as though she also would like the sniff of fresh air.

"I'm very well in health, and am thankful for it. I can't say that it's needed in that way," said Mrs. Prime.

"But mamma will be so glad to see you," said Rachel.

"I think you ought to go, Dorothea," said Mr. Prong; and even Rachel could perceive that there was some slight touch of authority in his voice. It was the slightest possible intonation of a command; but, nevertheless, it struck Rachel's ears.

Mrs. Prime merely shook her head and sniffed. It was not for a supply of air that she used her nostrils on this occasion, but that she might indicate some grain of contempt for the authority which Mr. Prong had attempted to exercise. "I think I'd rather not, Rachel, thank you;—not to dinner, that is. Perhaps I'll walk out in the evening after tea, when the work of the day is over. If I come then, perhaps my friend, Miss Pucker, may come with me."

"And if your esteemed mamma will allow me to pay my respects," said Mr. Prong, "I shall be most happy to accompany the ladies."

It will be acknowledged that Rachel had no alternative left to her. She said that her mother would be happy to see Mr. Prong, and happy to see Miss Pucker also. As to herself, she made no such assertion, being in her present mood too full of her own thoughts to care much for the ordinary courtesies of life.

"I'm very sorry you won't come to dinner, Dolly," she said; but she abstained from any word of asking the others to tea.

"If it had only been Mr. Prong," she said to her mother afterwards, "I should have asked him; for I suppose he'll have to come to the house sooner or later. But I wouldn't tell that horrid, squinting woman that you wanted to see her, for I'm sure you don't."

"But we must give them some cake and a glass of sweet wine," said Mrs. Ray.

"She won't have to take her bonnet off for that as she would for tea, and it isn't so much like making herself at home here. I couldn't bear to have to ask her up to my room."

On leaving the house in the High Street, which she did about eight o'clock, she took her way towards the churchyard, —not passing down Brewery Lane, by Mr. Tappitt's house, but taking the main street which led from the High Street to the church. But at the corner, just as she was about to leave the

High Street, she was arrested by a voice that was familiar to her, and, turning round, she saw Mrs. Cornbury seated in a low carriage, and driving a pair of ponies. "How are you, Rachel?" said Mrs. Cornbury, shaking hands with her friend, for Rachel had gone out into the street up to the side of the carriage, when she found that Mrs. Cornbury had stopped. "I'm going by the cottage,—to papa's. I see you are turning the other way; but if you've not much delay, I'll stay for you and take you home."

But Rachel had before her that other visit to make, and she was not minded either to omit or postpone it. "I should like it so much," said Rachel, "only——"

"Ah! well; I see. You've got other fish to fry. But, Rachel, look here, dear." And Mrs. Cornbury almost whispered into her ear across the side of the pony carriage. "Don't you believe quite all you hear. I'll find out the truth, and you shall know. Good-bye."

"Good-bye, Mrs. Cornbury," said Rachel, pressing her friend's hand as she parted from her. This allusion to her lover had called a blush up over her whole face, so that Mrs. Cornbury well knew that she had been understood. "I'll see to it," she said, driving away her ponies.

See to it! How could she see to it when that letter should have been written? And Rachel was well aware that another day must not pass without the writing of it.

She went down across the churchyard, leaving the path to the brewery on her left, and that leading out under the elm trees to her right, and went on straight to the stile at which she had stood with Luke Rowan, watching the reflection of the setting sun among the clouds. This was the spot which she had determined to visit; and she had come hither hoping that she might again see some form in the heavens which might remind her of that which he had shown her. The stile, at any rate, was the same, and there were the trees beneath which they had stood. There were the rich fields, lying beneath her, over which they two had gazed together at the fading lights of the evening.

There was no arm in the clouds now, and the perverse sun was
retiring to his rest without any of that royal pageantry and illumination with which the heavens are wont to deck themselves when their king goes to his couch. But Rachel, though
she had come thither to look for these things and had not
found them, hardly marked their absence. Her mind became
so full of him and of his words, that she required no outward
signs to refresh her memory. She thought so much of his look
on that evening, of the tones of his voice, and of every motion
of his body, that she soon forgot to watch the clouds. She sat
herself down upon the stile with her face turned away from the
fields, telling herself that she would listen for the footsteps of
strangers, so that she might move away if any came near her;
but she soon forgot also to listen, and sat there thinking of him
alone. The words that had been spoken between them on that
occasion had been but trifling,—very few and of small moment;
but now they seemed to her to have contained all her destiny.
It was there that love for him had first come upon her—had
come over her with broad outspread wings like an angel; but
whether as an angel of darkness or of light, her heart had then
been unable to perceive. How well she remembered it all; how
he had taken her by the hand, claiming the right of doing so as
an ordinary farewell greeting; and how he had held her, looking into her face, till she had been forced to speak some word
of rebuke to him! "I did not think you would behave like that,"
she had said. But yet at that very moment her heart was going
from her. The warm friendliness of his touch, the firm, clear
brightness of his eye, and the eager tone of his voice, were even
then subduing her coy unwillingness to part with her maiden
love. She had declared to herself then that she was angry with
him; but, since that, she had declared to herself that nothing
could have been better, finer, sweeter than all that he had said
and done on that evening. It had been his right to hold her, if
he intended afterwards to claim her as his own. "I like you so
very much," he had said; "why should we not be friends?" She
had gone away from him then, fleeing along the path, bewil-

dered, ignorant as to her own feelings, conscious almost of a sin in having listened to him; but still filled with a wondrous delight that any one so good, so beautiful, so powerful as he, should have cared to ask for her friendship in such pressing words. During all her walk home she had been full of fear and wonder and mysterious delight. Then had come the ball, which in itself had hardly been so pleasant to her, because the eyes of many had watched her there. But she thought of the moment when he had first come to her in Mrs. Tappitt's drawing-room, just as she was resolving that he did not intend to notice her further. She thought of those repeated dances which had been so dear to her, but which, in their repetition, had frightened her so grievously. She thought of the supper, during which he had insisted on sitting by her; and of that meeting in the hall, during which he had, as it were, forced her to remain and listen to him,—forced her to stay with him till, in her agony of fear, she had escaped away to her friend and begged that she might be taken home! As she sat by Mrs. Cornbury in the carriage, and afterwards as she had thought of it all while lying in her bed, she had declared to herself that he had been very wrong;—but since that, during those few days of her permitted love, she had sworn to herself as often that he had been very right.

And he had been right. She said so to herself now again, though the words which he had spoken and the things which he had done had brought upon her all this sorrow. He had been right. If he loved her it was only manly and proper in him to tell his love. And for herself,—seeing that she had loved, had it not been proper and womanly in her to declare her love? What had she done; when, at what point, had she gone astray, that she should be brought to such a pass as this? At the beginning, when he had held her hand on the spot where she was now sitting, and again when he had kept her prisoner in Mr. Tappitt's hall, she had been half conscious of some sin, half ashamed of her own conduct; but that undecided fear of sin and shame had been washed out, and everything had been made white as snow, as pure as running water, as bright as sunlight, by the permission to love this man which had been accorded to her. What had she since done that she should be brought to such a pass as that in which she now found herself?

As she thought of this she was bitter against all the world except him;—almost bitter against her own mother. She had said that she would obey in this matter of the letter, and she knew well that she would in truth do as her mother bade her. But, sitting there, on the churchyard stile, she hatched within her mind plans of disobedience,—dreadful plans! She would not submit to this usage. She would go away from Baslehurst without knowledge of any one, and would seek him out in his London home. It would be unmaidenly;—but what cared she now for that;—unless, indeed, he should care? All her virgin modesty and young maiden fears,—was it not for him that she would guard them, for his delight and his pride? And if she were to see him no more, if she were to be forced to bid him go from her, of what avail would it be now to her to cherish and maintain the unsullied brightness of her woman's armour? If he were lost to her, everything was lost. She would go to him, and throwing herself at his feet would swear to him that life without his love was no longer possible for her. If he would then take her as his wife she would strive to bless him with all that the tenderness of a wife could give. If he should refuse her,—then she would go away and die. In such case what to her would be the judgment of any man or any woman? What to her would be her sister's scorn and the malignant virtue of such as Miss Pucker and Mr. Prong? What the upturned hands and amazement of Mr. Comfort? It would have been they who had driven her to this.

But how about her mother when she should have thus thrown herself overboard from the ship and cast herself away from the pilotage which had hitherto been the guide of her conduct? Why—why—why had her mother deserted her in her need? As she thought of her mother she knew that her plan of rebellion was nothing; but why—why had her mother deserted her?

As for him, and these new tidings which had come to the cottage respecting him, she would have cared for them not a jot. Mrs. Cornbury had cautioned her not to believe all that she heard; but she had already declined,—had altogether declined to believe any of it. It was to her, whether believed or disbelieved, matter altogether irrelevant. A wife does not cease to love her husband because he gets into trouble. She does not turn against him because others have quarrelled with him. She does not separate her lot from his because he is in debt! Those are the times when a wife, a true wife, sticks closest to her husband, and strives the hardest to lighten the weight of his cares by the tenderness of her love! And had she not been permitted to place herself in that position with regard to him when she had been permitted to love him? In all her thoughts she recognized the right of her mother to have debarred her from the privilege of loving this man, if such embargo had been placed on her before her love had been declared. She had never, even within her own bosom, assumed to herself the right of such privilege without authority expressed. But her very soul revolted against this withdrawal of the sanction that had been given to her. The spirit within her rebelled, though she knew that she would not carry on that rebellion by word or deed. But she had been injured;—injured almost to death; injured even to death itself as regarded all that life could give her worth her taking! As she thought of this injury that fierce look of which I have spoken came across her brow! She would obey her pastors and masters. Yes; she would obey them. But she could never again be soft and pliable within their hands. Obedience in this matter was a necessity to her. In spite of that wild thought of throwing off her maiden bonds and allowing her female armour to be splashed and sullied in the gutter, she knew that there was that which would hinder her from the execution of such scheme. She was bound by her woman's lot to maintain her womanly purity. Let her suffer as she might there was nothing for her but obedience. She could not go forth as though she were a man, and claim her right to stand or fall by her love. She had been injured in being brought to such plight as this, but she would bear her injury as best might be within her power.

She was still thinking of all this, and still sitting with her eyes turned towards the tower of the church, when she was touched on the back by a light hand. She turned round quickly, startled by the touch,—for she had heard no footstep,—and saw Martha Tappitt and Cherry. It was Cherry who had come close upon her, and it was Cherry's voice that she first heard. "A penny for your thoughts," said Cherry.

"Oh, you have so startled me!" said Rachel.

"Then I suppose your thoughts were worth more than a penny. Perhaps you were thinking of an absent knight." And then Cherry began to sing—"Away, away, away. He loves and he rides away."

Poor Rachel blushed and was unable to speak. "Don't be so foolish," said Martha to her sister. "It's ever so long since we've seen you, Rachel. Why don't you come and walk with us?"

"Yes, indeed,—why don't you?" said Cherry, whose good nature was quite as conspicuous as her bad taste. She knew now that she had vexed Rachel, and was thoroughly sorry that she had done so. If any other girl had quizzed her about her lover it would not have annoyed her, and she had not understood at first that Rachel Ray might be different from herself. "I declare we have hardly seen you since the night of the party, and we think it very ill-natured in you not to come to us. Do come and walk to-morrow."

"Oh, thank you;—not to-morrow, because my sister is coming out from Baslehurst, to spend the evening with us."

"Well;—on Saturday, then," said Cherry, persistingly.

But Rachel would make no promise to walk with them on any day. She felt that she must henceforth be divided from the

Tappitts. Had not he quarrelled with Mr. Tappitt; and could
it be fitting that she should keep up any friendship with the
family that was hostile to him? She was also aware that Mrs.
Tappitt was among those who were desirous of robbing her of
her lover. Mrs. Tappitt was her enemy as Mr. Tappitt was his.
She asked herself no question as to that duty of forgiving them
the injuries they had done her, but she felt that she was divided from them,—from Mr. and Mrs. Tappitt, and also from
the girls. And, moreover, in her present strait she wanted no
friend. She could not talk to any friend about her lover, and
she could not bring herself even to think on any other subject.

"It's late," she said, "and I must go home, as mamma will be
expecting me."

Cherry had almost replied that she had not been in so great
a hurry once before, when she had stood in the churchyard
with another companion; but she thought of Rachel's reproach-
ful face when her last little joke had been uttered, and she
refrained.

"She's over head and ears in love," said Cherry to her sister, when Rachel was gone.

"I'm afraid she has been very foolish," said Martha, seriously.

"I don't see that she has been foolish at all. He's a very nice
fellow, and as far as I can see he's just as fond of her as she is
of him."

"But we know what that means with young men," said
Martha, who was sufficiently serious in her way of thinking to
hold by that doctrine as to wolves in sheep's clothing in which
Mrs. Ray had been educated.

"But young men do marry,—sometimes," said Cherry.

"But not merely for the sake of a pretty face or a good figure. I believe mamma is right in that, and I don't think he'll
come back again."

"If he were my lover I'd have him back," said Cherry,
stoutly;—and so they went away to the brewery.

Rachel on her way home determined that she would write

her letter that night. Her mother was to read it when it was written; that was understood to be the agreement between them; but there would be no reason why she should not be alone when she wrote it. She could word it very differently, she thought, if she sat alone over it in her own bedroom, than she could do immediately under her mother's eye. She could not pause and think and perhaps weep over it, sitting at the parlour table, with her mother in her arm-chair, close by, watching her. It needed that she should write it with tears, with many struggles, with many baffled attempts to find the words that would be wanted,—with her very heart's blood. It must not be tender. No; she was prepared to omit all tenderness. And it must probably be short;—but if so its very shortness would be another difficulty. As she walked along she could not tell herself with what words she would write it; but she thought that the words would perhaps come to her if she waited long enough for them in the solitude of her own chamber.

She reached home by nine o'clock and sat with her mother for an hour, reading out loud some book on which they were then engaged.

"I think I'll go to bed now, mamma," she said.

"You always want to go to bed so soon," said Mrs. Ray. "I think you are getting tired of reading out loud. That will be very sad for me with my eyes."

"No, I'm not, mamma, and I'll go on again for half an hour, if you please; but I thought you liked going to bed at ten."

The watch was consulted, and as it was not quite ten Rachel did go on for another half-hour, and then she went up to her bedroom.

She sat herself down at her open window and looked out for a while upon the heavens. The summer moon was at its full, so that the green before the cottage was as clear before her as in the day, and she could see over into the gloom of Mr. Sturt's farmyard across it. She had once watched Rowan as he came over the turf towards the cottage swinging his stick in his hand,

and now she gazed on the spot where the Baslehurst road came in as though she expected that his figure might again appear. She looked and looked, thinking of this, till she would hardly have been surprised had that figure really come forth upon the road. But no figure was to be seen, and after a while she withdrew from the window and sat herself down at the little table. It was very late when she undressed herself and went to her bed, and later still when her eyes, red with many tears, were closed in sleep;—but the letter had been written and was ready for her mother's inspection. This was the letter as it stood after many struggles in the writing of it,—

> *Bragg's End,*
> *Thursday, 186—.*

My DEAR MR. ROWAN,

>   *I am much obliged to you for having written the letter which I received from you the other day, and I should have answered it sooner, only mamma thought it best to see Mr. Comfort first, as he is our clergyman here, and to ask his advice. I hope you will not be annoyed because I showed your letter to mamma, but I could not receive any letter from you without doing so, and I may as well tell you that she will read this before it goes.*
>   *And now that I have begun I hardly know how to write what I have to say. Mr. Comfort and mamma have determined that there must be nothing fixed as an engagement between us, and that for the present, at least, I may not correspond with you. This will be my first and last letter. As that will be so, of course I shall not expect you to write any more, and I know that you will be very angry. But if you understood all my feelings I think that perhaps you would not be very, very angry. I know it is true that when you asked me that question, I nodded my head as you say in your letter. If I had sworn the twenty oaths of which you speak they would not, as you say, have bound me tighter. But neither could bind me to anything against mamma's will. I thought that you were very generous*

to come to me as you did;—oh, so generous! I don't know why you should have looked to such a one as me to be your wife. But I would have done my best to make you happy, had I been able to do as I suppose you then wished me. But you well know that a man is very different from a girl, and of course I must do as mamma wishes.

They say that as the business here about the brewery is so very unsettled they think it probable that you will not have to come back to Baslehurst any more; and that as our acquaintance has been so very short, it is not reasonable to suppose that you will care much about me after a little while. Perhaps it is not reasonable, and after this I shall have no right to be angry with you if you forget me. I don't think you will quite forget me; but I shall never expect or even hope to see you again. [Twice in writing her letter Rachel cut out this latter assertion, but at last, sobbing in despair, she restored the words. What right would she have to hope that he would come to her, after she had taken upon herself to break that promise which had been conveyed to him, when she bent her head over his arm?] I shall not forget you, and I will always be your friend, as you said I should be. Being friends is very different to anything else, and nobody can say that I may not do that.

I will always remember what you showed me in the clouds; and, indeed, I went there this very evening to see if I could see another arm. But there was nothing there, and I have taken that as an omen that you will not come back to Baslehurst. ["To me," had been the words as she had first written them; but there was tenderness in those words, and she found it necessary to alter them.] I will now say good-bye to you, for I have told you all that I have to tell. Mamma desires that I will remember her to you kindly.

May God bless you and protect you always!

Believe me to be
Your sincere friend,
Rachel Ray.

In the morning she took down the letter in her hand and gave it to her mother. Mrs. Ray read it very slowly and demurred over it at sundry places. She especially demurred at that word about the omen, and even declared that it ought to be expunged. But Rachel was very stern and held her ground. She had put into the letter, she said, all that she had been bidden to say. Such a word from herself to one who had been so dear to her must be allowed to her.

The letter was not altered and was taken away by the postman that evening.

CHAPTER XXI

Mrs. Ray Goes to Exeter,
and Meets a Friend

SIX WEEKS PASSED over them at Bragg's End, and nothing was heard of Luke Rowan. Rachel's letter, a copy of which was given in our last chapter, was duly sent away by the postman, but no answer to it came to Bragg's End. It must, however, be acknowledged that it not only required no answer, but that it even refused to be answered. Rachel had told her lover that he was not to correspond with her, and that she certainly would not write to him again. Having so said, she had no right to expect an answer; and she protested over and over again that she did expect none. But still she would watch, as she thought unseen, for the postman's coming; and her heart would sink within her as the man would pass the gate without calling. "He has taken me at my word," she said to herself very bitterly. "I deserve nothing else from him; but—but—but——" In those days she was ever silent and stern. She did all that her mother bade her, but she did little or nothing from love. There were no more banquets, with clotted cream brought over from Mrs. Sturt's. She would speak a word or two now and then to

Mrs. Sturt, who understood the whole case perfectly; but such words were spoken on chance occasions, for Rachel now never went over to the farm. Farmer Sturt's assistance had been offered to her; but what could the farmer do for her in such trouble as hers?

During the whole of these six weeks she did her household duties; but gradually she became slower in them and still more slow, and her mother knew that her disappointment was becoming the source of permanent misery. Rachel never said that she was ill; nor, indeed, of any special malady did she show signs: but gradually she became thin and wan, her cheeks assumed a haggard look, and that aspect of the brow which her mother feared had become habitual to her. Mrs. Ray observed her closely in all that she did. She knew well of those watchings for the postman. She was always thinking of her child, and, after a while, longing that Luke Rowan might come back to them, with a heart almost as sore with longing as was that of Rachel herself. But what could she do? She could not bring him back. In all that she had done,—in giving her sanction to this lover, and again in withdrawing it, she had been guided by the advice of her clergyman. Should she go again to him and beg him to restore that young man to them? Ah! no; great as was her trust in her clergyman she knew that even he could not do that for her.

During all these weeks hardly a word was spoken openly between the mother and daughter about the matter that chiefly occupied the thoughts of them both. Luke Rowan's name was hardly mentioned between them. Once or twice some allusion was made to the subject of the brewery, for it was becoming generally known that the lawyers were already at work on behalf of Rowan's claim; but even on such occasions as these Mrs. Ray found that her speech was stopped by the expression of Rachel's eyes, and by those two lines which on such occasions would mark her forehead. In those days Mrs. Ray became afraid of her younger daughter,—almost more so than she had ever been afraid of the elder one. Rachel, indeed, never spoke as Mrs. Prime would sometimes speak. No word of scolding ever passed her mouth; and in all that she did she was gentle and observant. But there was ever on her countenance that look of reproach which by degrees was becoming almost unendurable. And then her words during the day were so few! She was so anxious to sit alone in her own room! She would still read to her mother for some hours in the evening; but this reading was to her so manifestly a task, difficult and distasteful!

It may be remembered that Mrs. Prime, with her lover, Mr. Prong, and her friend Miss Pucker, had promised to call at Bragg's End on the evening after Rachel's walk into Baslehurst. They did come as they had promised, about half an hour after Rachel's letter to Luke had been carried away by the postman. They had come, and had remained at Bragg's End for an hour, eating cake and drinking currant wine, but not having, on the whole, what our American friends call a good time of it. That visit had been terrible to Mrs. Ray. Rachel had sat there cold, hard, and speechless. Not only had she not asked Miss Pucker to take off her bonnet, but she had absolutely declined to speak to that lady. It was wonderful to her mother that she should thus, in so short a time, have become wilful, masterful, and resolved in following out her own purposes. Not one word on that occasion did she speak to Miss Pucker; and Mrs. Prime, observing this, had grown black and still blacker, till the horror of the visit had become terrible to Mrs. Ray. Miss Pucker had grinned and smiled, and striven gallantly, poor woman, to make the best of it. She had declared how glad she had been to see Miss Rachel on the previous evening, and how well Miss Rachel had looked, and had expressed quite voluminous hopes that Miss Rachel would come to their Dorcas meetings. But to all this Rachel answered not a syllable. Now and then she addressed a word or two to her sister. Now and then she spoke to her mother. When Mr. Prong specially turned himself to her, asking her some question, she would answer him with one or two monosyllables, always calling him Sir; but to Miss Pucker she never once opened her mouth. Mrs. Prime became very angry,—very black and very angry; and the time of the visit was a terrible time to Mrs. Ray.

But this visit is to be noticed in our story chiefly on account of a few words which Mr. Prong found an opportunity of saying to Mrs. Ray respecting his proposed marriage. Mrs. Ray knew that there were difficulties about the money, and was disposed to believe, and perhaps to hope, that the match would be broken off. But on this occasion Mr. Prong was very marked in his way of speaking to Mrs. Ray, as though everything were settled. Mrs. Ray was thoroughly convinced by this that it was so, and her former beliefs and possible hopes were all dispersed. But then Mrs. Ray was easily convinced by any assertion. In thus speaking to his future mother-in-law he had contrived to turn his back round upon the other three ladies, so as to throw them together for the time, and thus make their position the more painful. It must be acknowledged that Rachel was capable of something great, after her determined resistance to Miss Pucker's blandishments under such circumstances as these.

"Mrs. Ray," Mr. Prong had said,—and as he spoke his voice was soft with mingled love and sanctity,—"I cannot let this moment pass without expressing one word of what I feel at the prospect of connecting myself with your amiable family."

"I'm sure I'm much obliged," Mrs. Ray had answered.

"Of course I am aware that Dorothea has mentioned the matter to you."

"Oh yes; she has mentioned it, certainly."

"And therefore I should be remiss, both as regards duty and manners, if I did not take this opportunity of assuring you how much gratification I feel in becoming thus bound up in family affection with you and Miss Rachel. Family ties are sweet bonds of sanctified love; and as I have none of my own, —nearer, that is, than Geelong, the colony of Victoria, where my mother and brother and sisters have located themselves,— I shall feel the more pleasure in taking you and Miss Rachel to my heart."

This was complimentary to Mrs. Ray; but with her peculiar feelings as to the expediency of people having their own belongings, she almost thought that it would have been better for all parties if Mr. Prong had gone to Geelong with the rest of the Prong family: this opinion, however, she did not express. As to taking Mr. Prong to her heart, she felt some doubts of her own capacity for such a performance. It would be natural for her to love a son-in-law. She had loved Mr. Prime very dearly, and trusted him thoroughly. She would have been prepared to love Luke Rowan, had fate been propitious in that quarter. But she could not feel secure as to loving Mr. Prong. Such love, moreover, should come naturally, of its own growth, and not be demanded categorically as a right. It certainly was a pity that Mr. Prong had not made himself happy, with that happiness for which he sighed, in the bosom of his family at Geelong. "I'm sure you're very kind," Mrs. Ray had said.

"And when we are thus united in the bonds of this world," continued Mr. Prong, "I do hope that other bonds, more holy in their nature even than those of family, more needful even than them, may join us together. Dorothea has for some months past been a constant attendant at my church——"

"Oh, I couldn't leave Mr. Comfort; indeed I couldn't," said Mrs. Ray in alarm. "I couldn't go away from my own parish church was it ever so."

"No, no; not altogether, perhaps. I am not sure that it would be desirable. But will it not be sweet, Mrs. Ray, when we are bound together as one family, to pour forth our prayers in holy communion together?"

"I think so much of my own parish church, Mr. Prong," Mrs. Ray replied. After that Mr. Prong did not, on that occasion, press the matter further, and soon turned round his chair so as to relieve the three ladies behind him.

"I think we had better be going, Mr. Prong," said Mrs. Prime, rising from her seat with a display of anger in the very motion of her limbs. "Good evening, mother: good evening to you, Rachel. I'm afraid our visit has put you out. Had I guessed as much, we would not have come."

"You know, Dolly, that I am always glad to see you,—only you come to us so seldom," said Rachel. Then with a very cold bow to Miss Pucker, with a very warm pressure of the hand from Mr. Prong, and with a sisterly embrace for Dorothea, that was not cordial as it should have been, she bade them good-bye. It was felt by all of them that the visit had been a failure; —it was felt so, at least, by all the Ray family. Mr. Prong had achieved a certain object in discussing his marriage as a thing settled; and as regarded Miss Pucker, she also had achieved a certain object in eating cake and drinking wine in Mrs. Ray's parlour.

For some weeks after that but little had been seen of Mrs. Prime at the cottage; and nothing had been said of her matrimonial prospects. Rachel did not once go to her sister's lodgings; and, on the few occasions of their meeting, asked no questions as to Mr. Prong. Indeed, as the days and weeks went on, her heart became too heavy to admit of her asking any questions about the love-affairs of others. She still went about her work, as I have before said. She was not ill,—not ill so as to demand the care due to an invalid. But she moved about the house slowly, as though her limbs were too heavy for her. She spoke little, unless when her mother addressed her. She would sit for hours on the sofa doing nothing, reading nothing, and looking at nothing. But still, at the postman's morning hours, she would keep her eye upon the road over which he came, and that dull look of despair would come across her face when he passed on without calling at the cottage.

But on a certain morning towards the end of the six weeks the postman did call,—as indeed he had called on other days, though bringing with him no letter from Luke Rowan. Neither now, on this occasion, did he bring a letter from Luke Rowan. The letter was addressed to Mrs. Ray; and, as Rachel well knew from the handwriting, it was from the gentleman who

managed her mother's little money matters,—the gentleman
who had succeeded to the business left by Mr. Ray when he
died. So Rachel took the letter up to her mother and left it, saying that it was from Mr. Goodall.

Mrs. Ray's small income arose partly from certain cottages
in Baslehurst, which had been let in lump to a Baslehurst
tradesman, and partly from shares in a gas company at Exeter.
Now the gas company at Exeter was the better investment of
the two, and was considered to be subject to less uncertainty
than the cottages. The lease under which the cottages had been
let was out, and Mrs. Ray had been advised to sell the property. Building ground near the town was rising in value; and
she had been advised by Mr. Goodall to part with her little estate. Both Mrs. Ray and Rachel were aware that this business,
to them very important, was imminent; and now had come a
letter from Mr. Goodall, saying that Mrs. Ray must go to Exeter to conclude the sale. "We should only bungle matters,"
Mr. Goodall had said, "if I were to send the deeds down to
you; and as it is absolutely necessary that you should understand all about it, I think you had better come up on Tuesday;
you can get back to Baslehurst easily on the same day."

"My dear," said Mrs. Ray, coming into the parlour, "I must
go to Exeter."

"To-day, mamma?"

"No, not to-day, but on Tuesday. Mr. Goodall says I must
understand all about the sale. It is a dreadful trouble."

But, dreadful as the trouble was, it seemed that Mrs. Ray
was not made unhappy by the prospect of the little expedition.
She fussed and fretted as ladies do on such occasions, but—as
is also common with ladies,—the excitement of the journey
was, upon the whole, a gratification to her. She asked Rachel to
accompany her, and at first pressed her to do so strongly; but
such work at the present moment was not in accord with Rachel's mood, and at last she escaped from it under the plea of
expense.

"I think it would be foolish, mamma," she said. "Now that

Dolly has gone you will be run very close; and when Mr. Good-all first spoke of selling the cottages, he said that perhaps you might be without anything from them for a quarter."

"But he has sold them now, my dear; and there will be the money at once."

"I don't see why you should throw away ten and sixpence, mamma," said Rachel.

And as she spoke in that resolved and masterful tone, her mother, of course, gave up the point. So when the Tuesday morning came, she went with her mother only as far as the station.

"Don't mind meeting me, because I can't be sure about the train," said Mrs. Ray. "But I shall be back to-night, certainly."

"And I'll wait tea for you," said Rachel. Then, when her mother was gone, she walked back to the cottage by herself.

She walked back at once, but took a most devious course. She was determined to avoid the length of the High Street, and she was determined also to avoid Brewery Lane; but she was equally determined to pass through the churchyard. So she walked down from the railway station to the hamlet at the bottom of the hill below the church, and from thence went up by the field-path to the stile. In order to accomplish this she went fully two miles out of her way, and now the sun over her head was very hot. But what was the distance or the heat of the sun to her when her object was to stand for a few moments in that place? Her visit, however, to the spot which was so constantly in her thoughts did her no good. Why had she been so injured? Why had this sacrifice of herself been demanded from her? As she sat for a moment on the stile this was the mat-ter that filled her breast. She had been exalted to the heavens when she first heard her mother speak of Mr. Rowan as an ac-ceptable suitor. She had been filled with joy as though Para-dise had been opened to her, when she found herself to be the promised bride of Luke Rowan. Then had come her lover's letter, and the clergyman's counsel, and her own reply; and after that the gates of her Paradise had been closed against her! "I wonder whether it's the same thing to him," she said to herself. "But I suppose not. I don't think it can be the same thing or he would come. Wouldn't I go to him if I were free as he is!" She barely rested in the churchyard, and then walked on between the elms at a quick pace, with a heart sore,—sore almost to breaking. She would never have been brought to this condition had not her mother told her that she might love him! Thence came her vexation of spirit. There was the cruelty. All the world knew that this man had been her lover;—all her world knew it. Cherry Tappitt had sung her little witless song about it. Mrs. Tappitt had called at the cottage about it. Mr. Comfort had given his advice about it. Mrs. Cornbury had whispered to her about it out of her pony carriage. Mrs. Sturt had counselled her about it. Mr. Prong had thought it very wrong on her part to love the man. Mr. Sturt had thought it very right, and had offered his assistance. All this would have been as nothing had her lover remained to her. Cherry might have sung till her little throat was tired, and Mr. Prong might have expressed his awe with outspread hands, and have looked as though he expected the skies to fall. Had her Paradise not been closed to her, all this talking would have been a thing of course. But such talking,—such wide-spread knowledge of her condition, with the gates of her Paradise closed against her, was very hard to bear! And who had closed the gates? Her own hands had done it. He, her lover, had not deserted her. He had done for her all that truth and earnestness demanded, and per-haps as much as love required. Men were not so soft as girls, she argued within her own breast. Let a man be ever so true it could not be expected that he should stand by his love after he had been treated with such cold indifference as had been shown in her letter! She would have stood by her love, let his letter have been as cold as it might. But then she was a woman, and her love, once encouraged, had become a necessity to her. A man, she said to herself, would be more proud but less stanch. Of course she would hear no more from him. Of course the gates of her Paradise were shut. Such were her thoughts as she walked home, and such the thoughts over which she sat brooding alone throughout the entire day.

At half-past seven in the evening Mrs. Ray came back home, wearily trudging across the green. She was very weary, for she had now walked above two miles from the station. She had also been on her feet half the day, and, which was probably worse than all the rest had she known it, she had travelled nearly eighty miles by railway. She was very tired, and would under ordinary circumstances have been disposed to reckon up her grievances in the evening quite as accurately as Rachel had reckoned hers in the morning. But something had occurred in Exeter, the recollection of which still overcame the sense of weariness which Mrs. Ray felt;—overcame it, or rather over-topped it; so that when Rachel came out to her at the cottage door she did not speak at once of her own weariness, but looked lovingly into her daughter's face,—lovingly and anxiously, and said some little word intended to denote affection.

"You must be very tired," said Rachel, who, with many self-reproaches and much communing within her own bosom, had for the time vanquished her own hard humour.

"Yes, I am tired, my dear; very. I thought the train never would have got to the Baslehurst station. It stopped at all the little stations, and really I think I could have walked as fast." A dozen years had not as yet gone by since the velocity of these trains had been so terrible to Mrs. Ray that she had hardly dared to get into one of them!

"And whom have you seen?" said Rachel.

"Seen!" said Mrs. Ray. "Who told you that I had seen any-body?"

"I suppose you saw Mr. Goodall."

"Oh yes, I saw him of course. I saw him, and the cottages are all sold. We shall have seven pounds ten a year more than before. I'm sure it will be a very great comfort. Seven pounds ten will buy so many things."

"But ten pounds would buy more."

"Of course it would, my dear. And I told Mr. Goodall I

wished he could make it ten, as it would make it sound so much more regular like; but he said he couldn't do it because the gas has gone up so much. He could have done it if I had sixty pounds, but of course I hadn't."

"But, mamma, whom did you see except Mr. Goodall? I know you saw somebody, and you must tell me."

"That's nonsense, Rachel. You can't know that I saw anybody." It may, however, be well to explain at once the cause of Mrs. Ray's hesitation, and that this may be done in the proper course, we will go back to her journey to Exeter. All the incidents of her day may be told very shortly; but there was one incident in her day which filled her with so much anxiety, and almost dismay, that it must be narrated.

On arriving at Exeter she got into an omnibus which would have taken her direct to Mr. Goodall's office in the Close; but she was minded to call at a shop in the High Street, and had herself put down at the corner of one of those passages which lead from the High Street to the Close. She got down from the step of the vehicle, very carefully, as is the wont with middle-aged ladies from the country, and turned round to walk directly into the shop; but before her, on the pavement, she saw Luke Rowan. He was standing close to her, so that it was impossible that they should have pretended to miss seeing each other, even had they been so minded. Any such pretence would have been impossible to Mrs. Ray, and would have been altogether contrary to Luke Rowan's nature. He had been coming out of the shop, and had been arrested at once by Mrs. Ray's figure as he saw it emerging from the door of the omnibus.

"How d'you do?" said he, coming forward with outstretched hand, and speaking as though there was nothing between him and Mrs. Ray which required any peculiar word or tone.

"Oh, Mr. Rowan! is this you?" said she. "Dear, dear! I'm sure I didn't expect to see you in Exeter."

"I dare say not, Mrs. Ray; and I didn't expect to see you. But the odd thing is I've come here about the same business as you, though I didn't know anything about it till yesterday."

"What business, Mr. Rowan?"

"I've bought your cottages in Baslehurst."

"No!"

"But I have, and I've paid for them too, and you're going this very minute to Mr. Goodall to sign the deed of sale. Isn't that true? So you see I know all about it."

"Well, that is strange! Isn't it, now?"

"The fact is I must have a bit of land at Baslehurst for building. Tappitt will go on fighting; and as I don't mean to be beaten, I'll have a place of my own there."

"And you'll pull down the cottages?"

"If I don't pull him down first, so as to get the old brewery. I was obliged to buy your bit of ground now, as I might not have been able to get any just when I wanted it. You've sold it a deal too cheap. You tell Mr. Goodall I say so."

"But he says I'm to gain something by selling it."

"Does he? If it is so, I'm very glad of it. I only came down from London yesterday to finish this piece of business, and I'm going back to-day."

During all this time not a word had been said about Rachel. He had not even asked after her in the ordinary way in which men ask after their ordinary acquaintance. He had not looked as though he were in the least embarrassed in speaking to Rachel's mother, and now it seemed as though he were going away, as though all had been said between them that he cared to say. Mrs. Ray at the first moment had dreaded any special word; but now, as he was about to leave her, she felt disappointed that no special word had been spoken. But he was not as yet gone.

"I literally haven't a minute to spare," he said, offering her his hand for a second time; "for I've two or three people to see before I get to the train."

"Good-bye," said Mrs. Ray.

"Good-bye, Mrs. Ray. I don't think I've been very well treated among you. I don't indeed. But I won't say any more about that at present. Is she quite well?"

"Pretty well, thank you," said she, all of a tremble.

"I won't send her any message. As things are at present, no message would be of any service. Good-bye." And so saying he went from her.

Mrs. Ray at that moment had no time for making up her mind as to what she would do or say in consequence of this meeting,—or whether she would do or say anything. She looked forward to all the leisure time of her journey home for thinking of that; so she finished her shopping and hurried on to Mr. Goodall's office without resolving whether or no she would tell Rachel of the encounter. At Mr. Goodall's she remained some little time, dining at that gentleman's house as well as signing the deed, and asking questions about the gas company. He had grateful recollections of kindnesses received from Mr. Ray, and always exercised his hospitality on those rare occasions which brought Mrs. Ray up to Exeter. As they sat at table he asked questions about the young purchaser of the property which somewhat perplexed Mrs. Ray. Yes, she said, she did know him. She had just met him in the street and heard his news. Young Rowan, she told her friend, had been at the cottage more than once, but no mention had been made of his desire to buy these cottages. Was he well spoken of in Baslehurst? Well;—she was so little in Baslehurst that she hardly knew. She had heard that he had quarrelled with Mr. Tappitt, and she believed that many people had said that he was wrong in his quarrel. She knew nothing of his property; but certainly had heard somebody say that he had gone away without paying his debts. It may easily be conceived how miserable and ineffective she would be under this cross-examination, although it was made by Mr. Goodall without any allusion to Rachel.

"At any rate we have got our money," said Mr. Goodall; "and I suppose that's all we care about. But I should say he's rather a harum-scarum sort of fellow. Why he should leave his debts behind him I can't understand, as he seems to have plenty of money."

All this made Mrs. Ray's task the more difficult. During the last two or three weeks she had been wishing that she had not gone to Mr. Comfort,—wishing that she had allowed Rachel to answer Rowan's letter in any terms of warmest love that she might have chosen,—wishing, in fact, that she had permitted the engagement to go on. But now she began again to think that she had been right. If this man were in truth a harum-scarum fellow was it not well that Rachel should be quit of him,—even with any amount of present sorrow? Thinking of this on her way back to Baslehurst she again made up her mind that Rowan was a wolf. But she had not made up her mind as to what she would, or what she would not tell Rachel about the meeting, even when she reached her own door. "I will send her no message," he had said. "As things are at present no message would be of service." What had he meant by this? What purpose on his part did these words indicate? These questions Mrs. Ray had asked herself, but had failed to answer them.

But no resolution on Mrs. Ray's part to keep the meeting secret would have been of avail, even had she made such resolution. The fact would have fallen from her as easily as water falls from a sieve. Rachel would have extracted from her the information, had she been ever so determined not to impart it. As things had turned out she had at once given Rachel to understand that she had met some one in Exeter whom she had not expected to meet.

"But, mamma, whom did you see except Mr. Goodall?" Rachel asked. "I know you saw somebody, and you must tell me."

"That's nonsense, Rachel; you can't know that I saw anybody."

After that there was a pause for some moments, and then Rachel persisted in her inquiry. "But, mamma, I do know that you met somebody."—Then there was another pause.—"Mamma, was it Mr. Rowan?"

Mrs. Ray stood convicted at once. Had she not spoken a word, the form of her countenance when the question was asked would have answered it with sufficient clearness. But she did speak a word. "Well; yes, it was Mr. Rowan. He had come down to Exeter on business."

"And what did he say, mamma?"

"He didn't say anything,—at least, nothing particular. It is he that has bought the cottages, and he had come down from London about that. He told me that he wanted some ground near Baslehurst, because he couldn't get the brewery."

"And what else did he say, mamma?"

"I tell you that he said nothing else."

"He didn't—didn't mention me then?"

Mrs. Ray had been looking away from Rachel during this conversation,—had been purposely looking away from her. But now there was a tone of agony in her child's voice which forced her to glance round. Ah me! She beheld so piteous an expression of woe in Rachel's face that her whole heart was melted within her, and she began to wish instantly that they might have Rowan back again with all his faults.

"Tell me the truth, mamma; I may as well know it."

"Well, my dear, he didn't mention your name, but he did say a word about you."

"What word, mamma?"

"He said he would send no message because it would be no good."

"He said that, did he?"

"Yes, he said that. And so I suppose he meant it would be no good sending anything till he came himself."

"No, mamma; he didn't mean quite that. I understand what he meant. As it is to be so, he was quite right. No message could be of any use. It has been my own doing, and I have no right to blame him. Mamma, if you don't mind, I think I'll go to bed."

"My dear, you're wrong. I'm sure you're wrong. He didn't mean that."

"Didn't he, mamma?" And as she spoke a sad, weary, woebegone smile came over her face,—a smile so sad and piteous that it went to her mother's heart more keenly than would have done any sound of sorrow, any sobs, or wail of grief. "But I think he did mean that, mamma. It's no good doubting or fearing any longer. It's all over now."

"And it has been my fault!"

"No, dearest. It has not been your fault, nor do I think that it has been mine. I think we'd better not talk of faults. Ah dear; —I do wish he had never come here!"

"Perhaps it may be all well yet, Rachel."

"Perhaps it may,—in another world. It will never be well again for me in this. Good night, mamma. You must never think that I am angry with you."

Then she went up-stairs, leaving Mrs. Ray alone with her sorrow.

CHAPTER XXII

Domestic Politics at the Brewery

IN THE MEAN TIME things were not going on very pleasantly at the brewery, and Mr. Tappitt was making himself unpleasant in the bosom of his family. A lawsuit will sometimes make a man extremely pleasant company to his wife and children. Even a losing lawsuit will sometimes do so, if he be well backed up in his pugnacity by his lawyer, and if the matter of the battle be one in which he can take a delight to fight. "Ah," a man will say, "though I spend a thousand pounds over it, I'll stick to him like a burr. He shan't shake me off." And at such times he is almost sure to be in a good humour, and in a generous mood. Then let his wife ask him for money for a dinner-party, and his daughters for new dresses. He has taught himself for the moment to disregard money, and to think that he can sow five-pound notes broadcast without any inward pangs. But such was by no means the case with Mr. Tappitt. His lawyer Honyman was not backing him up; and as cool reflection

came upon him he was afraid of trusting his interests to those
other men, Sharpit and Longfite. And Mrs. Tappitt, when cool
reflection came on her, had begun to dread the ruin which it
seemed possible that terrible young man might inflict upon
them. She had learned already, though Mrs. Ray had not, how
false had been that report which had declared Luke Rowan
to be frivolous, idle, and in debt. To her it was very manifest
that Honyman was afraid of the young man; and Honyman,
though he might not be as keen as some others, was at any rate
honest. Honyman also thought that if the brewery were given
up to Rowan that thousand a year which had been promised
would be paid regularly; and to this solution of the difficulty
Mrs. Tappitt was gradually bending herself to submit as the
best which an untoward fate offered to them. Honyman himself had declared to her that Mr. Tappitt, if he were well advised, would admit Rowan in as a partner, on equal terms as
regarded power and ultimate possession, but with that lion's
share of the immediate concern for himself which Rowan offered. But this she knew that Tappitt would not endure; and
she knew, also, that if he were brought to endure it for a while,
it would ultimately lead to terrible sorrows. "They would be
knocking each other about with the pokers, Mr. Honyman,"
she had said; "and where would the custom be when that got
into the newspapers?" "If I were Mr. Tappitt, I would just let
him have his own way," Honyman had replied. "That shows
that you don't know Tappitt," had been Mrs. Tappitt's re-
joinder. No;—the thousand a year and dignified retirement in
a villa had recommended itself to Mrs. Tappitt's mind. She
would use all her influence to attain that position,—if only she
could bring herself to feel assured that the thousand a year
would be forthcoming.

As to Tappitt himself, he was by no means so anxious to
prolong the battle as he had been at the time of Rowan's departure. His courage for fighting was not maintained by good
backing. Had Honyman clapped him on the shoulder and
bade him put ready money in his purse, telling him that all

wouldn't be a bad place. You see it's out of the thoroughfare of the town, and yet, as one may say, within a stone's throw of the High Street."

I will not repeat Mr. Tappitt's exclamation as he listened to these suggestions of his lawyer, but it was of a nature to show that he had not heard the news with indifference.

"You see he's such a fellow that you don't know where to have him," continued Honyman. "It's not only that he don't mind ruining you, but he don't mind ruining himself either."

"I don't believe he's got anything to lose."

"Ah! that's where you're wrong. He has paid ready money for this bit of land to begin with, or Goodall would never have let him have it. Goodall knows what he's about as well as any man."

"And do you mean to tell me that he's going to put up buildings there at once?" And Tappitt's face as he asked the question would have softened the heart of any ordinary lawyer. But Honyman was one whom nothing could harden and nothing soften.

"I don't know what he's going to put up, Mr. Tappitt, and I don't know when. But I know this well enough; that when a man buys little bits of property about a place it shows that he means to do something there."

"If he had twenty thousand pounds, he'd lose it all."

"That's very likely; but the question is, how would you fare in the mean time? If he hadn't this claim upon you, of course you'd let him build what he liked, and only laugh at him." Then Mr. Tappitt uttered another exclamation, and pulling his hat tighter on to his head, walked out of the lawyer's office and returned to the brewery.

They dined at three o'clock at the brewery, and during dinner on this day the father of the family made himself very disagreeable. He scolded the maid-servant till the poor girl didn't know the spoons from the forks. He abused the cook's performances till that valuable old retainer declared that if "master got so rumpageous he might suit hisself, the sooner

would come out right eventually, and that Rowan would 1
crushed, he would have gone about Baslehurst boasting loudl
and would have been happy. Then Mrs. T. and the girls woul
have had a merry time of it; and the Tappitts would hav
come out of the contest with four or five hundred a year for
life instead of the thousand now offered to them, and nobody
would have blamed anybody for such a result. But Honyman
had not spirit for such backing. In his dull, slow, droning way
he had shaken his head and said that things were looking
badly. Then Tappitt had cursed and had sworn, and had half
resolved to go to Sharpit and Longfite. Sharpit and Longfite
would have clapped him on the back readily enough, and have
bade him put plenty of money in his purse. But we may suppose that Fate did not intend the ruin of Tappitt, seeing that
she did not make him mad enough to seek the counsels of
Sharpit and Longfite. Fate only made him very cross and unpleasant in the bosom of his family. Looking out himself for
some mode of escape from this terrible enemy that had come
upon him, he preferred the raising of the sum of money which
would be necessary to buy off Rowan altogether. Rowan had
demanded ten thousand pounds, but Tappitt still thought that
seven, or, at any rate, eight thousand would do it.

"I don't think he'll take less than ten," said Honyman, "because his share is really worth as much as that."

This was very provoking; and who can wonder that Tappitt was not pleasant company in his own house?

On the day after Mrs. Ray's visit to Exeter, Tappitt, as was
now his almost daily practice, made his way into Mr. Honyman's little back room, and sat there with his hat on, discussing his affairs.

"I find that Mr. Rowan has bought those cottages of the
widow Ray's," said Honyman.

"Nonsense!" shouted Tappitt, as though such a purchase on
Rowan's part was a new injury done to himself.

"Oh, but he has," said Honyman. "There's not a doubt in
life about it. If he does mean to build a new brewery, it

the better; she didn't care how soon; she'd cooked victuals for his betters and would again." He snarled at his daughters till they perked up their faces and came silently to a mutual agreement that they would not condescend to notice him further while he held on in his present mood. And he replied to his wife's questions,—questions intended to be soothing and kindly conjugal,—in such a tone that she determined to have it out with him before she allowed him to go to bed. "She knew her duty," she said to herself, "and she could stand a good deal. But there were some things she couldn't stand and some things that weren't her duty." After dinner Tappitt took himself out at once to his office in the brewery, and then, for the first time, saw the "Baslehurst Gazette and Totnes Chronicle" for that week. The "Baslehurst Gazette and Totnes Chronicle" was an enterprising weekly newspaper, which had been originally intended to convey on Sunday mornings to the inhabitants of South Devonshire the news of the past week, and the paper still bore the dates of successive Sundays. But it had gradually pushed itself out into the light of its own world before its own date, gaining first a night and then a day, till now, at the period of which I am speaking, it was published on the Friday morning.

"You ought just to look at this," a burly old foreman had said, handing him the paper in question, with his broad thumb placed upon a certain column. This foreman had known Bungall, and though he respected Tappitt, he did not fear him. "You should just look at this. Of course it don't amount to nothing; but it's as well to see what folks say." And he handed the paper to his master, almost making a hole in it by screwing his thumb on to the spot he wished to indicate.

Tappitt read the article, and his spirit was very bitter within him. It was a criticism on his own beer written in no friendly tone. "There is no reason," said the article, "why Baslehurst should be flooded with a liquor which no Christian ought to be asked to drink. Baslehurst is as capable of judging good beer from bad as any town in the British empire. Let Mr. Tappitt look to it, or some young rival will spring up beneath his feet and seize from his brow the hop-leaf wreath which Bungall won and wore." This attack was the more cruel because the paper had originally been established by Bungall's money, and had, in old days, been altogether devoted to the Bungall interest. That this paper should turn against him was very hard. But what else had he a right to expect? It was known that he had promised his vote to the Jew candidate, and the paper in question supported the Cornbury interest. A man that lives in a glass house should throw no stones. The brewer who brews bad beer should vote for nobody.

But Tappitt would not regard this attack upon him in its proper political light. Every evil at present falling upon him was supposed to come from his present enemy. "It's that dirty underhand blackguard," he said to the foreman.

"I don't think so, Mr. Tappitt," said the foreman. "I don't think so indeed."

"But I tell you it is," said Tappitt, "and I don't care what you think."

"Just as you please, Mr. Tappitt," said the foreman, who thereupon retired from the office, leaving his master to meditate over the newspaper in solitude.

It was a very bitter time for the poor brewer. He was one of those men whose spirit is not wanting to them while the noise and tumult of contest are around them, but who cannot hold on by their own convictions in the quiet hours. He could storm, and talk loud, and insist on his own way while men stood around him listening and perhaps admiring; but he was cowed when left by himself to think of things which seemed to be adverse. What could he do, if those around him, who had known him all his life as those newspaper people had known him,—what could he do if they turned against him, and talked of bad beer as Rowan had talked? He was not man enough to stand up and face this new enemy unless he were backed by his old friends. Honyman had told him that he would be beaten. How would it fare with him and his family if he were beaten? As he sat in his little office, with his hat low down over his eyes, balancing himself on the hind legs of his chair, he abused Honyman roundly. Had Honyman been possessed of wit, of skill, of professional craft,—had he been the master of any invention, all might have been well. But the attorney was a fool, an ass, a coward. Might it not be that he was a knave? But luckily for Honyman, and luckily also for Mr. Tappitt himself, this abuse did not pass beyond the precincts of Tappitt's own breast. We all know how delightful is the privilege of abusing our nearest friends after this fashion; but we generally satisfy ourselves with that limited audience to which Mr. Tappitt addressed himself on the present occasion.

In the mean time Mrs. Tappitt was sitting up-stairs in the brewery drawing-room with her daughters, and she also was not happy in her mind. She had been snubbed, and almost browbeaten, at dinner time, and she also had had a little conversation in private with Mr. Honyman. She had been snubbed, and, if she did not look well about her, she was going to be ruined. "You mustn't let him go on with this lawsuit," Mr. Honyman had said. "He'll certainly get the worst of it if he does, and then he'll have to pay double." She disliked Rowan quite as keenly as did her husband, but she was fully alive to the folly of spiting Rowan by doing an injury to her own face. She would speak to Tappitt that night very seriously, and in the mean time she turned the Rowan controversy over in her own mind, endeavouring to look at it from all sides. It had never been her custom to make critical remarks on their father's conduct to any of the girls except Martha; but on the present great occasion she waived that rule, and discussed the family affairs in full female family conclave. "I don't know what's come over your papa," she began by saying. "He seems quite beside himself to-day."

"I think he is troubled about Mr. Rowan and this lawsuit," said the sagacious Martha.

"Nasty man! I wish he'd never come near the place," said Augusta.

"I don't know that he's very nasty either," said Cherry. "We all liked him when he was staying here."

"But to be so false to papa!" said Augusta. "I call it swindling, downright swindling."

"One should know and understand all about it before one speaks in that way," said Martha, "I dare say it is very vexatious to papa; but after all perhaps Mr. Rowan may have some right on his side."

"I don't know about right," said Mrs. Tappitt. "I don't think he can have any right to come and set himself up here in opposition, as one may say, to the very ghost of his own uncle. I agree with Augusta, and think it is a very dirty thing to do."

"Quite shameful," said Augusta, indignantly.

"But if he has got the law on his side," continued Mrs. Tappitt, "it's no good your papa trying to go against that. Where should we be if we were to lose everything and be told to pay more money than your papa has got? It wouldn't be very pleasant to be turned out of the house."

"I don't think he'd ever do it," said Cherry.

"I declare, Cherry, I think you are in love with the man," said Augusta.

"If I ain't I know who was," said Cherry.

"As for love," said Mrs. Tappitt, "we all know who is in love with him,—nasty little sly minx! In the whole matter nothing makes me so angry as to think that she should have come here to our dance."

"That was Cherry's doing," said Augusta. This remark Cherry noticed only by a grimace addressed specially to her sister. A battle in Rachel's favour under present circumstances would have been so losing an affair that Cherry had not pluck enough to adventure it on her friend's behalf.

"But the question is,—what are we to do about the lawsuit?" said Mrs. Tappitt. "It is easy to see from your papa's manner that he is very much harassed. He won't admit him as a partner;—that's certain."

"Oh dear! I should hope not," said Augusta.

"That's all very well," said Martha; "but if the young man can prove his right, he must have it. Mamma, do you know what Mr. Honyman says about it?"

"Yes, my dear, I do." Mrs. Tappitt's manner became very solemn, and the girls listened with all their ears. "Yes, my dear, I do. Mr. Honyman thinks your father should give way."

"And take him in as a partner?" said Augusta. "Papa has got that spirit that he couldn't do it."

"It doesn't follow that your papa should take Mr. Rowan in as a partner because he gives up the lawsuit. He might pay him the money that he asks."

"But has he got it?" demanded Martha.

"Besides, it's such a deal; isn't it?" said Augusta.

"Or," continued Mrs. Tappitt, "your papa might accept his offer by retiring with a very handsome income for us all. Your papa has been in business for a great many years, working like a galley-slave. Nobody knows how he has toiled and moiled, except me. It isn't any joke being a brewer,—and having it all on himself as he has had. And if young Rowan ever begins it, I wish him joy of it."

"But would he pay the income?" Martha asked.

"Mr. Honyman says that he would; and if he did not, there would be the property to fall back upon."

"And where should we live?" said Cherry.

"That can't be settled quite yet. It must be somewhere near, so that your papa might keep an eye on the concern, and know that it was going all right. Perhaps Torquay would be the best place."

"Torquay would be delicious," said Cherry.

"And would that man come and live at the brewery?" said Augusta.

"Of course he would, if he pleased," said Martha.

"And bring Rachel Ray with him as his wife?" said Cherry.

"He'll never do that," said Mrs. Tappitt with energy.

"Never; never!" said Augusta,—with more energy.

In this way the large and influential feminine majority of

the family at the brewery was brought round to look at one of
the propositions made by Rowan without disfavour. It was not
that that young man's sins had been in any degree forgiven,
but that they all perceived, with female prudence, that it would
be injudicious to ruin themselves because they hated him. And
then to what lady living in a dingy brick house, close adjoin-
ing to the smoke and smells of beer-brewing, would not the
idea of a marine villa at Torquay be delicious? None of the
family, not even Mrs. Tappitt herself, had ever known what
annual profit had accrued to Mr. T. as the reward of his life's
work. But they had been required to live in a modest, homely
way,—as though that annual profit had not been great. Under
the altered circumstances, as now proposed, they would all
know that papa had a thousand a year to spend;—and what
might not be done at Torquay with a thousand a year? Before
Mr. Tappitt came home for the evening,—which he did not do
on that day till past ten, having been detained, by business, in
the bar of the Dragon Inn,—they had all resolved that the combined ease and dignity of a thousand a year should be accepted.

Mr. Tappitt was still perturbed in spirit when he took himself to the marital chamber. What had been the nature of the
business which had detained him at the bar of the Dragon he
did not condescend to say, but it seemed to have been of a nature not well adapted to smooth his temper. Mrs. Tappitt perhaps guessed what that business had been; but if so, she said
nothing of the subject in direct words. One little remark she
did make, which may perhaps have had allusion to that business.

"Bah!" she exclaimed, as Mr. Tappitt came near her; "if
you must smoke at all, I wish to goodness you'd smoke good
tobacco."

"So I do," said Tappitt, turning round at her sharply. "It's
best mixed bird's-eye. As if you could know the difference, indeed!"

"So I do, T. I know the difference very well. It's all poison
to me,—absolute poison,—as you're very well aware. But that

filthy strong stuff that you've taken to lately, is enough to kill anybody."

"I haven't taken to any filthy strong stuff," said Tappitt.

This was the beginning of that evening's conversation. I am inclined to think that Mrs. Tappitt had made her calculations, and had concluded that she could put forth her coming observations more efficaciously by having her husband in bad humour, than she could, if she succeeded in coaxing him into a good humour. I think that she made the above remarks, not solely because the fumes of tobacco were distasteful to her, but because the possession of a grievance might give her an opportunity of commencing the forthcoming debate with some better amount of justified indignation on her own side. It was not often that she begrudged Tappitt his pipe, or made ill-natured remarks about his gin and water.

"T.," she said, when Tappitt had torn off his coat in some anger at the allusion to "filthy strong stuff,"—"T., what do you mean to do about this lawsuit?"

"I don't mean to do anything."

"That's nonsense, T.; you must do something, you know. What does Mr. Honyman say?"

"Honyman is a fool."

"Nonsense, T.; he's not a fool. Or if he is, why have you let him manage your affairs so long? But I don't believe he's a fool at all. I believe he knows what he's talking about, quite as well as some others, who pretend to be so clever. As to your going to Sharpit and Longfite, it's quite out of the question."

"Who's talking of going to them?"

"You did talk of it."

"No I didn't. You heard me mention their names; but I never said that I should go to them at all. I almost wish I had."

"Now, T., don't talk in that way, or you'll really put me beside myself."

"I don't want to talk of it at all. I only want to go to bed."

"But we must talk of it, T. It's all very well for you to say you don't want to talk of things; but what is to become of me and my girls if everything goes astray at the brewery? You can't expect me to sit by quiet and see you ruined."

"Who talks about my being ruined?"

"Well, I believe all Baslehurst pretty well is talking about it. If a man will go on with a lawsuit when his own lawyer says he oughtn't, what else can come to him but ruin?"

"You don't know anything about it. I wish you'd hold your tongue, and let me go to bed."

"I do know something about it, Mr. Tappitt; and I won't hold my tongue. It's all very well for you to bid me hold my tongue; but am I to sit by and see you ruined, and the girls left without a bit to eat or a thing to wear? Goodness knows I've never thought much about myself. Nobody will ever say that of me. But it has come to this, T.; that something must be settled about Rowan's claim. If he hasn't got justice, he's got law on his side; and he seems to be one of those who don't care much as long as he's got that. If you ask me, T.——"

"But I didn't ask you," said Tappitt.

Tappitt never actually succumbed in these matrimonial encounters, and would always maintain courage for a sharp word, even to the last.

"No, I know you didn't;—and more shame to you, not to consult the wife of your bosom and the mother of your children, when such an affair as this has to be settled. But if you think I'm going to hold my tongue, you're mistaken. I know very well how things are going. You must either let this young man come in as a partner——"

"I'll be——"

Tappitt would not have disgraced himself by such an exclamation in his wife's bedroom as he then used if his business in the bar of the Dragon had been legitimate.

"Very well, sir. I say nothing about the coarseness of your language on the present occasion, though I might say a great deal if I pleased. But if you don't choose to have him for a partner,—why then you must do something else."

"Of course I must."

"Exactly;—and therefore the only thing is for you to take the offer of a thousand a year that he has made. Now, T., don't begin cursing and swearing again, because you know that can't do any good. Honyman says that he'll pay the income;—and if he don't,—if he gets into arrear with it, then you can come down upon him and turn him out. Think how you'd like that! You've only just to keep a little ready money by you, so that you'll have something for six months or so, if he should get into arrear."

"And I'm to give up everything myself?"

"No, T.; you would not give up anything; quite the other way. You would have every comfort found you that any man can possibly want. You can't go on at it always, toiling and moiling as you're doing now. It's quite dreadful for a man never to have a moment to himself at your time of life, and of course it must tell on any constitution if it's kept up too long. You're not the man you were, T.; and of course you couldn't expect it."

"Oh, bother!"

"That's all very well; but it's my duty to see these things, and to think of them, and to speak of them too. Where should I be, and the girls, if you was hurried into your grave by working too hard?" Mrs. Tappitt's voice, as this terrible suggestion fell from her, was almost poetic, through the depth of its solemnity. "Do you think I don't know what it is that takes you to the Dragon so late at night?"

"I don't go to the Dragon late at night."

"I'm not finding fault, T.; and you needn't answer me so sharp. It's only natural you should want something to sustain you after such slavery as you have to go through. I'm not unreasonable. I know very well what a man is, and what it is he can do, and what he can't. It would be all very well your going on if you had a partner you could trust."

"Nothing on earth shall induce me to carry on with that fellow."

"And therefore you ought to take him at his word and re-

tire. It would be the gentlemanlike thing to do. Of course you'd
have the power of going over and seeing that things was
straight. And if we was living comfortable at some genteel
place, such as Torquay or the like, of course you wouldn't want
to be going out to Dragons every evening then. I shouldn't
wonder if, in two or three years, you didn't find yourself as
strong as ever again."

Tappitt, beneath the clothes, insisted that he was strong;
and made some virile remark in answer to that further allusion
to the Dragon. He by no means gave way to his wife, or uttered any word of assent; but the lady's scheme had been made
known to him; the ice had been broken; and Mrs. Tappitt,
when she put out the candle, felt that she had done a good evening's work.

CHAPTER XXIII

Mrs. Ray's Penitence

ANOTHER FORTNIGHT WENT BY, and still nothing further was
heard at Bragg's End from Luke Rowan. Much was heard of
him in Baslehurst. It was soon known by everybody that he
had bought the cottages; and there was a widely-spread and
well-credited rumour that he was going to commence the necessary buildings for a new brewhouse at once. Nor were these
tidings received by Baslehurst with all that horror,—with that
loud clamour of indignation,—which Tappitt conceived to be
due to them. Baslehurst, I should say, as a whole, received the
tidings with applause. Why should not Bungall's nephew carry
on a brewery of his own? Especially why should he not, if he
were resolved to brew good beer? Very censorious remarks
about the Tappitt beer were to be heard in all bar-rooms, and
were re-echoed with vehemence in the kitchens of the Baslehurst aristocracy.

"It ain't beer," said Dr. Harford's cook, who had come from

the midland counties, and knew what good beer was. "It's a nasty muddle of stuff, not fit for any Christian who has to earn her victuals over a kitchen fire."

It came to pass speedily that Luke Rowan was expected to build a new brewery, and that the event of the first brick was looked for with anxious expectation. And that false report which had spread itself through Baslehurst respecting him and his debts had taken itself off. It had been banished by a contrary report; and there now existed in Baslehurst a very general belief that Rowan was a man of means,—of very considerable means,—a man of substantial capital, whom to have settled in the town would be very beneficial to the community. That false statement as to the bill at Griggs's had been sifted, and the truth made known,—and somewhat to the disgrace of the Tappitt faction. The only article supplied by Griggs to Rowan's order had been the champagne consumed at Tappitt's supper, and for this Rowan had paid ready money within a week of the transaction. It was Mrs. Cornbury who discovered all this, and who employed means for making the truth known in Baslehurst. This truth also became known at last to Mrs. Ray,—but of what avail was it then? She had desired her daughter to treat the young man as a wolf, and as a wolf he had been hounded off from her little sheep-cot. She heard now that he was expected back at Baslehurst;—that he was a weathy man; that he was thought well of in the town; that he was going to do great things. With what better possible husband could any young woman have been blessed? And yet she had turned him away from her cottage as though he had been a wolf!

It was from Mrs. Sturt that Mrs. Ray first learned the truth. Mr. Sturt was a tenant on the Cornbury estate, and Mrs. Sturt was of course well known to Mrs. Cornbury. That lady, when she had sifted to the bottom the story of Griggs's bill, and had assured herself that Rowan was by no means minded to surrender his interest in Baslehurst, determined that the truth should be made known to Mrs. Ray. But she was not willing to call on Mrs. Ray herself, nor did she wish to present herself before Rachel at the cottage, unless she could bring with her some more substantial comfort than could be afforded by simple evidence as to Rowan's good character. She therefore took herself to Mrs. Sturt, and discussed the matter with her.

"I suppose she does care about him," said Mrs. Cornbury, sitting in Mrs. Sturt's little parlour that opened out upon the kitchen garden. Mrs. Sturt was also seated, leaning on the corner of the table, with the sleeves of her gown tucked up, ready for work when the squire's lady should be gone, but very willing to postpone her work as long as the squire's lady would stay and gossip with her.

"Oh! that she do, Mrs. Butler,—in her heart of hearts. If I know anything of true love, she do love that young man."

"And he did offer to her? There can be no doubt about that, I suppose."

"Not a doubt on earth, Mrs. Butler. She never told me so outright,—nor yet didn't her mother;—but if he didn't, I'll give my head for a cream cheese. Laws love you, Mrs. Butler, I know what's what well enough. I know when a girl's wild and flighty, and thinks of things as she oughtn't;—and I know when she's proper behaved, and gives a young man encouragement only when it becomes her."

"Of course you do, Mrs. Sturt."

"It isn't for me, Mrs. Butler, to say anything against your papa. Nobody can have more respect for their clergyman than Sturt has and I; and before it was all settled like, Sturt never had a word with Mr. Comfort about tithes; but, Mrs. Butler, I think your papa was wrong here. As far as I can learn, it was he that told Mrs. Ray that this young man wasn't all that he should be."

"Papa meant it for the best. There were strange things said about him, you know."

"I never believes one word of what I hears, and never will. People are such liars; bean't they, Mrs. Butler? And I didn't

believe a word again him. He's as fine a young man as you'd
wish to see in a hundred years, and of course that goes a long
way with a young woman. Well, Mrs. Butler, I'll tell Mrs. Ray
what you say, but I'm afeard it's too late; I'm afeard it is. He's
of a stubborn sort, I think. He's one of them that says, 'If you
will not when you may, when you will you shall have nay.'"

Mrs. Cornbury still entertained hope that the stubbornness
of the stubborn man might be overcome; but as to that she said
nothing to Mrs. Sturt.

Mrs. Sturt, with what friendly tact she possessed, made her
communication to Mrs. Ray, but it may be doubted whether
more harm than good was not thus done. "And he didn't owe
a shilling then?" asked Mrs. Ray.

"Not a shilling," said Mrs. Sturt.

"And he is going to come back to Baslehurst about this
brewery business?"

"There's not a doubt in life about that," answered Mrs.
Sturt. If these tidings could have come in time they would have
been very salutary; but what was Mrs. Ray to do with them
now? She felt that she could not honestly withhold them from
Rachel; and yet she knew not how to tell them without adding
to Rachel's misery. It was very improbable that Rachel should
hear anything about Rowan from other lips than her own. It
was clear that Mrs. Sturt did not intend to speak to her, and
also clear that Mrs. Sturt expected that Mrs. Ray would do so.

Rachel's demeanour at this time was cause of great sorrow
to Mrs. Ray. She never smiled. She sought no amusement. She
read no books. She spoke but little, and when she did speak her
words were hard and cold, and confined almost entirely to
household affairs. Her mother knew that she was not ill, because she ate and drank and worked. Even Dorothea must
have been satisfied with the amount of needlework which she
produced in these days. But though not ill, she was thin and
pale, and unlike herself. But perhaps of all the signs which
her mother watched so carefully, the signs which tormented
her most were those ever-present lines on her daughter's fore-

head,—lines which Mrs. Ray had now learned to read correctly, and which indicated some settled inward purpose, and
an inward resolve that that purpose should become the subject
of no outward discussion. Rachel had formerly been everything to her mother;—her friend, her minister, her guide, her
great comfort;—the subject on which could be lavished all the
soft tenderness of her nature, the loving object to whom could
be addressed all the little innocent petulances of her life. But
now Mrs. Ray did not dare to be either tender with Rachel, or
petulant. She hardly dared to speak to her on subjects that
were not indifferent. On this matter of Luke Rowan she did
not dare to speak to her. Rachel never upbraided her with
words,—had never spoken one word of reproach. But every
moment of their passing life was an unspoken reproach, so severe and heavy that the poor mother hardly knew how to bear
the burden of her fault.

As Mrs. Ray became more afraid of her younger daughter
she became less afraid of the elder. This was occasioned partly,
no doubt, by the absence of Mrs. Prime from the cottage.
When there she only came as a visitor; and no visitor to a
house can hold such dominion there as may be held by a domestic tyrant, present at all meals, and claiming an ascendancy
in all conversations. But it arose in part also from the overwhelming solicitude which filled Mrs. Ray's heart from morning to night, as she watched poor Rachel in her misery. Her
bowels yearned towards her child, and she longed to give her
relief with an excessive longing. Had the man been a very wolf
indeed,—such were her feelings at present,—I think that she
would have welcomed him to the cottage. In ordering his repulse she had done a deed of which she had by no means anticipated the consequences, and now she repented in the sackcloth and ashes of a sorrow-stricken spirit. Ah me! what could
she do to relieve that oppressed one! So thoroughly did this desire override all others in her breast, that she would snub Mrs.
Prime without dreading or even thinking of the consequences.
Her only hopes and her only fears at the present moment had

reference to Rachel. Had Rachel proposed to her that they should both start off to London and there search for Luke Rowan, I doubt whether she would have had the heart to decline the journey.

In these days Mrs. Prime came to the cottage regularly twice a week,—on Wednesdays and Saturdays. On Wednesday she came after tea, and on Saturday she drank tea with her mother. On these occasions much was, of course, said as to the prospect of her marriage with Mr. Prong. Nothing was as yet settled, and Rachel had concluded, in her own mind, that there would be no such wedding. As to Mrs. Ray's opinion, she, of course, thought there would be a wedding or that there would not, in accordance with the last words spoken by Mrs. Prime to herself on the occasion of that special conversation.

"She'll never give up her money," Rachel had said, "and he'll never marry her unless she does."

Mrs. Prime at this period acknowledged to her mother that she was not happy.

"I want," said she, "to do what's right. But it's not always easy to find out what is right."

"That's very true," said Mrs. Ray, thinking that there were difficulties in the affairs of other people quite as embarrassing as those of which Mrs. Prime complained.

"He says," continued the younger widow, "that he wants nothing for himself, but that it is not fitting that a married woman should have a separate income."

"I think he's right there," said Mrs. Ray.

"I quite believe what he says about himself," said Mrs. Prime. "It is not that he wants my money for the money's sake, but that he chooses to dictate to me how I shall use it."

"So he ought if he's to be your husband," said Mrs. Ray.

These conversations usually took place in Rachel's absence. When Mrs. Prime came Rachel would remain long enough to say a word to her, and on the Saturdays would pour out the tea for her and would hand to her the bread and butter with the courtesy due to a visitor; but after that she would take herself to her own bedroom, and only come down when Mrs. Prime had prepared herself for going. At last, on one of these evenings, there came a proposition from Mrs. Prime that she should return to the cottage, and live again with her mother and sister. She had not said that she had absolutely rejected Mr. Prong, but she spoke of her return as though it had become expedient because the cause of her going away had been removed. Very little had been said between her and her mother about Rachel's love-affair, nor was Mrs. Prime inclined to say much about it now; but so much as that she did say. "No doubt it's all over now about that young man, and therefore, if you like it, I don't see why I shouldn't come back."

"I don't at all know about it's being all over," said Mrs. Ray, in a hurried quick tone, and as she spoke she blushed with emotion.

"But I suppose it is, mother. From all that I can hear he isn't thinking of her; and I don't suppose he ever did much."

"I don't know what he's thinking about, Dorothea; and I ain't sure that there's any good talking about it. Besides, if you're going to have Mr. Prong at last——"

"If I did, mother, it needn't prevent my coming here for a month or two first. It wouldn't be quite yet certainly,—if at all. And I thought that perhaps, if I am going to settle myself in that way, you'd be glad that we should be all together again for a little while."

"So I should, Dorothea,—of course. I have never wanted to be divided from my children. Your going away was your own doing, not mine. I'm sure it made me so wretched I didn't know what to do at the time. Only other things have come since, that have pretty nearly put all that out of my mind."

"But you can't think I was wrong to go when I felt it to be right."

"I don't know how that may be," said Mrs. Ray. "If you thought it right to go I suppose you were right to go; but perhaps you shouldn't have had such thoughts."

"Well, mother, we won't go back to that."

"No; we won't, if you please."

"This at any rate is certain, that Rachel, in departing from our usual ways of life, has brought great unhappiness upon herself. I'm afraid she is thinking of this young man now more than she ought to do."

"Of course she is thinking of him. Why should she not think of him?"

"Why, mother! Surely it cannot be good that any girl should think of a man who thinks nothing of her!"

Then Mrs. Ray spoke out,—as perhaps she had never spoken before.

"What right have you to say that he thinks nothing of her? Who can tell? He did think of her,—as honestly as any man ever thought of the woman he wished to mate with. He came to her fairly, and asked her to be his wife. What can any man do more by a girl than that? And she didn't say a word to him to encourage him till those she had a right to look to had encouraged him too. So she didn't. And I don't believe any woman ever had a child that behaved better, or truer, or more maidenly than she has done. And I was a fool, and worse than a fool, when I allowed any one to have an evil thought of her for a moment."

"Do you mean me, mother?"

"I don't mean anybody except myself; so I don't." Mrs. Ray as she spoke was weeping bitterly, and rubbing the tears from her red eyes with her apron. "I've behaved like a fool to her,—worse than a fool,—and I've broken her heart. Not think of him! How's a girl not to think of a man day and night when she loves him better than herself? Think of him! She'll think of him till she's in her grave. She'll think of him till she's past all other thinking. I hate such cruelty; and I hate myself for having been cruel. I shall never forgive myself, the longest day I have to live."

"You only did your duty, mother."

"No; I didn't do my duty at all. It can't be a mother's duty to break her child's heart and to be set against her by what

anybody else can say. She was ever and always the best child
that ever lived; and she came away from him, and strove to
banish him from her thoughts, and wouldn't own to herself
that she cared for him the least in the world, till he'd come
here and spoken out straight, like a man as he is. I tell you
what, Dorothea, I'd go to London, on my knees to him, if I
could bring him back to her! I would. And if he comes here, I
will go to him."

"Oh, mother!"

"I know he loves her. He's not one of your inconstant ones
that take up with a girl for a week or so and then forgets her.
But she has offended him, and he's stubborn. She has offended
him at my bidding, and it's my doing;—and I'd humble myself
in the dust to bring him back to her;—so I would. Never tell
me of her not thinking of him. I tell you, Dorothea, she'll think
of him always; not because she has loved him, but because she
has been brought to confess her love."

Mrs. Ray was so strong in her mingled passion and grief,
that Mrs. Prime made no attempt to rebuke her. The daughter
was indeed quelled by her mother's vehemence, and felt that
for the present the subject of Rachel's love and Rachel's lover
was not a fitting one for the exercise of her own talents as a
preacher. The tragedy had progressed beyond the reach of her
preaching. Mrs. Ray protested that Rachel had been right
throughout, and that she herself had been wrong only when
she had opposed Rachel's wishes. Such a view of the matter
was altogether at variance with that entertained by Mrs. Prime,
who was still of opinion that young people shouldn't be allowed to please themselves, and who feared the approach of
any lover who came with lute in hand, and with light, soft,
loving, worldly words. Men and women, according to her theory, were right to marry and have children; but she thought
that such marriages should be contracted not only in a solemn
spirit, but with a certain dinginess of solemnity, with a pains-
taking absence of mirth, that would divest love of its worldly
alloy. Rachel had gone about her business in a different spirit,

and it may almost be said that Mrs. Prime rejoiced that she had failed. She did not believe in broken hearts; she did believe in the efficacy of chastisement; and she thought that on the whole the present state of affairs would be beneficial to her sister. Had she been possessed of sufficient power she would now, on this occasion, have preached her sermon again as she had preached it before; but her mother's passion had overcome her, and she was unable to express her convictions.

"I hope that she will be better soon," she said.

"I hope she will," said Mrs. Ray.

At this moment Rachel came down from her own room and joined them in the parlour. She came in with that same look of sad composure on her face, as though she were determined to speak nothing of her thoughts to any one, and sat herself down near to her sister. In doing so, however, she caught a glimpse of her mother's face, and saw that she had been crying,—saw, indeed, that she was still crying at that moment.

"Mamma," she said, "what is the matter;—has anything happened?"

"No, dear, nothing;—nothing has happened."

"But you would not cry for nothing. What is it, Dolly?"

"We have been talking," said Dorothea. "Things in this world are not so pleasant in themselves that they can always be spoken of without tears,—either outward tears or inward. People are too apt to think that there is no true significance in their words when they say that this world is a vale of tears."

"All the same. I don't like to see mamma crying like that."

"Don't mind it, Rachel," said Mrs. Ray. "If you will not regard me I shall be better soon."

"I was saying that I thought I would come back to the cottage," said Mrs. Prime; "that is, if mother likes it."

"But that did not make mamma cry."

"There were other things arose out of my saying so." Then Rachel asked no further questions, but sat silent, waiting till her sister should go.

"Of course we shall be very glad to have you back again if

it suits you to come," said Mrs. Ray. "I don't think it at all nice
that a family should be divided,—that is, as long as they are the
same family." Having received so much encouragement with
reference to her proposed return, Mrs. Prime took her departure and walked back to Baslehurst.

For some minutes after they had been so left, neither Mrs.
Ray nor Rachel spoke. The mother sat rocking herself in her
chair, and the daughter remained motionless in the seat which
she had taken when she first came into the room. Their faces
were not turned to each other, but Rachel was so placed that
she could watch her mother without being observed. Every
now and again Mrs. Ray would put her hand up to her eyes to
squeeze away the tears, and a low gurgling sound would come
from her, as though she were striving without success to repress her sobs. She had thought that she would speak to Rachel
when Mrs. Prime was gone,—that she would confess her error
in having sent Rowan away, and implore her child to pardon
her and to love her once again. It was not, however, that she
doubted Rachel's love,—that she feared that Rachel was cast-
ing her out from her heart, or that she was learning to hate her.
She knew well enough that her child still loved her. It was this,
—that her life had become barren to her, cold, and altogether
tasteless without those thousand little signs of ever-present affection to which she had been accustomed. If it was to be always thus between them, what would the world be to her for
the remainder of her days? She could have borne to part with
Rachel, had Rachel married, as in parting with her she would
have looked forward to some future return of her girl's caresses; and in such case she would at least have felt that her
loss had come from no cessation of the sweet loving nature of
their mutual connection. She would have wept as she gave Rachel over to a husband, but her tears would have been sweet
as well as bitter. But there was nothing of sweetness in her
tears as she shed them now,—nothing of satisfaction in her sorrow. If she could get Rachel to talk with her freely on the matter, if she could find an opportunity for confessing herself to

have been wrong, might it not be that the soft caresses would be restored to her,—caresses that would be soft, though moistened with salt tears? But she feared to speak to her child. She knew that Rachel's face was still hard and stern, and that her voice was not the voice of other days. She knew that her daughter brooded over the injury that had been done to her,—though she knew also that no accusation was made, even in the girl's own bosom, against herself. She thoroughly understood the state of Rachel's mind, but she was unable to find the words that might serve to soften it.

"I suppose we may as well go to bed," she said at last, giving the matter up, at any rate for that evening.

"Mamma, why were you crying when I came into the room?" said Rachel.

"Was I crying, my dear?"

"You are crying still, mamma. Is it I that make you unhappy?"

Mrs. Ray was anxious to declare that the reverse of that was true,—that it was she who had made the other unhappy; but even now she could not find the words in which to say this. "No," she said; "it isn't you. It isn't anybody. I believe it's true what Mr. Comfort has told us so often when he's preaching. It's all vanity and vexation. There isn't anything to make anybody happy. I suppose I cry because I'm foolisher than other people. I don't know that anybody is happy. I'm sure Dorothea is not, and I'm sure you ain't."

"I don't want you to be unhappy about me, mamma."

"Of course you don't. I know that. But how can I help it when I see how things have gone? I tried to do for the best, and I have—" broken my child's heart, Mrs. Ray intended to say; but she failed altogether before she got as far as that, and bursting out into a flood of tears, hid her face in her apron.

Rachel still kept her seat, and her face was still hard and unmoved. Her mother did not see it; she did not dare to look upon it; but she knew that it was so; she knew her daughter would have been with her, close to her, embracing her, throwing her arms round her, had that face relented. But Rachel still kept her chair, and Mrs. Ray sobbed aloud.

"I wish I could be a comfort to you, mamma," Rachel said after another pause, "but I do not know how. I suppose in time we shall get over this, and things will be as they used to be."

"They'll never be to me as they used to be before he came to Baslehurst," said Mrs. Ray, through her tears.

"At any rate that is not his fault," said Rachel, almost angrily. "Whoever may have done wrong, no one has a right to say that he has done wrong."

"I'm sure I never said so. It is I that have done wrong," exclaimed Mrs. Ray. "I know it all now, and I wish I'd never asked anybody but just my own heart. I didn't mean to say anything against him, and I don't think it. I'm sure I liked him as I never liked any young man the first time of seeing him, that night he came out here to tea; and I know that what they said against him was all false. So I do."

"What was all false, mamma?"

"About his going away in debt, and being a ne'er-do-well, and about his going away from Baslehurst and not coming back any more. Everybody has a good word for him now."

"Have they, mamma?" said Rachel. And Mrs. Ray learned in a moment, from the tone of her daughter's voice, that a change had come over her feeling. She asked her little question with something of the softness of her old manner, with something of the longing loving wishfulness which used to make so many of her questions sweet to her mother's ears. "Have they, mamma?"

"Yes they have, and I believe it was those wicked people at the brewery who spread the reports about him. As for owing anybody money, I believe he's got plenty. Of course he has, or how could he have bought our cottages and paid for them all in a minute? And I believe he'll come back and live at Baslehurst; so I do; only——"

"Only what, mamma?"

"If he's not to come back to you I'd rather that he never showed his face here again."

"He won't come to me, mamma. Had he meant it, he would have sent me a message."

"Perhaps he meant that he wouldn't send the message till he came himself," said Mrs. Ray.

But she made the suggestion in a voice so full of conscious doubt that Rachel knew that she did not believe in it herself.

"I don't think he means that, mamma. If he did why should he keep me in doubt? He is very true and very honest, but I think he is very hard. When I wrote to him in that way after accepting the love he had offered me, he was angered, and felt that I was false to him. He is very honest, but I think he must be very hard."

"I can't think that if he loved you he would be so hard as that."

"Men are different from women, I suppose. I feel about him that whatever he might do I should forgive it. But then I feel, also, that he would never do anything for me to forgive."

"I'll never forgive him, never, if he doesn't come back again."

"Don't say that, mamma. You've no right even to be angry with him, because it was we who told him that there was to be no engagement,—after I had promised him."

"I didn't think he'd take you up so at the first word," said Mrs. Ray;—and then there was again silence for a few minutes.

"Mamma," said Rachel.

"Well, Rachel."

Mrs. Ray was still rocking her chair, and had hardly yet repressed that faint gurgling sound of half-controlled sobs.

"I am so glad to hear you say that you—respect him, and don't believe of him what people have said."

"I don't believe a word bad of him, except that he oughtn't to take huff in that way at one word that a girl says to him. He ought to have known that you couldn't write just what letter you liked, as he could."

"We won't say anything more about that. But as long as you don't think him bad——"

"I don't think him bad. I don't think him bad at all. I think him very good. I'd give all I have in the world to bring him back again. So I would."

"Dear mamma!"

And now Rachel moved away from her chair and came up to her mother.

"And I know it's been all my fault. Oh, my child, I am so unhappy! I don't get half an hour's sleep at night thinking of what I have done;—I, that would have given the very blood out of my veins to make you happy."

"No, mamma; it wasn't you."

"Yes, it was. I'd no business going away to other people after I had told him he might come here. You, who had always been so good too!"

"You mustn't say again that you wish he hadn't come here."

"Oh! but I do wish it, because then he would have been nothing to you. I do wish he hadn't ever come, but now I'd do anything to bring him back again. I believe I'll go to him and tell him that it was my doing."

"No, mamma, you won't do that."

"Why should I not? I don't care what people say. Isn't your happiness everything to me?"

"But I shouldn't take him if he came in that way. What! beg him to come and have compassion on me, as if I couldn't live without him! No, mother; that wouldn't do. I do love him. I do love him. I sometimes think I cannot live without his love. I sometimes feel as though stories about broken hearts might be true. But I wouldn't have him in that way. How could he love me afterwards, when I was his wife? But, mamma, we'll be friends again;—shall we not? I've been so unhappy that you should have thought ill of him!"

That night the mother and daughter shared the same bed

together, and Mrs. Ray was able to sleep. She would not confess to herself that her sorrow had been lightened, because nothing had been said or done to lessen that of her daughter; but on the morrow Rachel came and hovered round her again, and the bitterness of Mrs. Ray's grief was removed.

C H A P T E R   X X I V

The Election at Baslehurst

TOWARDS THE END of September the day of the election arrived, and with it arrived Luke Rowan at Baslehurst. The vacancy had been occasioned by the acceptance of the then sitting member of that situation under the crown which is called the stewardship of the manor of Helpholme. In other words an old gentleman who had done his life's work retired and made room for some one more young and active. The old member had kept his seat till the end of the session, just leaving time for the moving for a new writ, and now the election was about to be held, almost at the earliest day possible. It had been thought that a little reflection would induce the Baslehurst people to reject the smiles of the Jew tailor from London, and therefore as little time for reflection was given to them as possible. The wealth, the liberal politics, the generosity, and the successes of Mr. Hart were dinned into their ears by a succession of speeches, and by an overpowering flight of enormous posters; and then the Jewish hero, the tailor himself, came among them, and astonished their minds by the ease and volubility of his speeches. He did not pronounce his words with any of those soft slushy Judaic utterances by which they had been taught to believe he would disgrace himself. His nose was not hookey, with any especial hook, nor was it thicker at the bridge than was becoming. He was a dapper little man, with bright eyes, quick motion, ready tongue, and a very new hat. It seemed that he knew well how to canvass. He had a smile and a good word for all,—enemies as well as friends. The task of abusing the Cornbury party he left to his committee and backers. He spent a great deal of money,—throwing it away in every direction in which he could do so, without laying himself open to the watchful suspicion of the other side. He ate and drank like a Christian, and only laughed aloud when some true defender of the Protestant faith attempted to scare him away out of the streets by carrying a gammon of bacon up on high. Perhaps his strength as a popular candidate was best known by his drinking a pint of Tappitt's beer in the little parlour behind the bar at the Dragon.

"He beats me there," said Butler Cornbury, when he heard of that feat.

But the action was a wise one. The question as to Tappitt's brewery and Tappitt's beer was running high at Baslehurst, and in no stronger way could Mr. Hart have bound to him the Tappitt faction than by swallowing in public that pint of beer. "Let me have a small glass of brandy at once," said Mr. Hart to his servant, having retired to his room immediately after the performance of the feat. His constitution was good, and I may as well at once declare that before half an hour had passed over his head he was again himself, and at his work.

The question of Tappitt's beer and Tappitt's brewery was running high in Baslehurst, and had gotten itself involved in the mouths of the people of Baslehurst, not only with the loves and sorrows of poor Rachel Ray, but with the affairs of this election. We know how Tappitt had been driven to declare himself a stanch supporter of the Jew. He had become very stanch,—stanch beyond the promising of his own vote,—stanch even to a final sitting on the Jew's committee, and an active canvasser on the Jew's behalf. His wife, whose passions were less strong than his own and her prudence greater, had remonstrated with him on the matter. "You can vote against Cornbury, if you please," she had said, "but do it quietly. Keep your toe in your pump and say nothing. Just as we stand at present

about the business of Rowan's, it would almost be better that
you shouldn't vote at all." But Tappitt was an angry man, at
this moment uncontrollable by the laws of prudence, and he
went into these election matters heart and soul, to his wife's
great grief. Butler Cornbury, or Mrs. Butler Cornbury,—it was
all the same to him which,—had openly taken up Rowan's part
in the brewery controversy. A rumour had reached Tappitt that
the inmates of Cornbury Grange had loudly expressed a desire
for good beer! Under such circumstances it was not possible
for him not to rush to the fight. He did rush into the thick of it,
and boasted among his friends that the Jew was safe. I think
he was right,—right at any rate as regarded his own peace of
mind. Nothing gives a man such spirit for a fight, as the act of
fighting. During these election days he was almost regardless
of Rowan. He was to second the nomination of the Jew, and so
keen was he as to the speech that he would make, and as to the
success of what he was doing against Mr. Cornbury, that he
was able to talk down his wife, and browbeat Honyman in his
own office. Honyman was about to vote for Butler Cornbury,
was employed in the Cornbury interest, and knew well on
which side his bread was buttered. Sharpit and Longfite were
local attorneys for the Jew, and in this way Tappitt was thrown
into close intercourse with that eminent firm. "Of course we
wouldn't interfere," said Sharpit confidently to the brewer.
"We never do interfere with the clients of another firm. We
never did such a thing yet, and don't mean to begin. We find
people drop in to us quick enough without that. But in a
friendly way, Mr. Tappitt, let me caution you, not to let your
fine business be injured by that young sharper."

Mr. Tappitt found this to be very kind,—and very sensible
too. He gave no authority to Sharpit on that occasion to act
for him; but he thought of it, resolving that he would set his
shoulders firmly to that wheel as soon as he had carried through
this business of the election.

But even in the matter of the election everything did not
go well with Tappitt. He had appertaining to his establishment

a certain foreman of the name of Worts, a heavy, respectable, useful man, educated on the establishment by Bungall and bequeathed by Bungall to Tappitt,—a man by no means ambitious of good beer, but very ambitious of profits to the firm, a servant indeed almost invaluable in such a business. But Tappitt had ever found him deficient in this,—that he had a certain objectionable pride in having been Bungall's servant, and that as such he thought himself absolved from the necessity of subserviency to his latter master. Once a day indeed he did touch his cap, but when that was done he seemed to fancy that he was almost equal to Mr. Tappitt upon the premises. He never shook in his shoes if Tappitt were angry, nor affected to hasten his steps if Tappitt were in a hurry, nor would he even laugh at Tappitt's jokes, if,—as was too usual,—such jokes were not mirth-moving in their intrinsic nature. Clearly he was not at all points a good servant, and Tappitt in some hours of his prosperity had ventured to think that the brewery could go on without him. Now, since the day in which Rowan's treachery had first loomed upon Tappitt, he had felt much inclined to fraternize on easier terms with his foreman. Worts when he touched his cap had been received with a smile, and his advice had been asked in a flattering tone,—not demanded as belonging to the establishment by right. Then Tappitt began to talk of Rowan to his man, and to speak evil things of him, as was natural, expecting a reciprocity of malignity from Worts. But Worts on such occasions had been ominously silent. "H—m, I bean't so zure o' that," Worts had once said, thus differing from his master on some fundamental point of Tappitt strategy as opposed to Rowan strategy. "Ain't you?" said Tappitt, showing his teeth. "You'd better go now and look after those men at the carts." Worts had looked after the men at the carts, but he had done so with an idea in his head that perhaps he would not long look after Tappitt's men or Tappitt's carts. He had not himself been ambitious of good beer, but the idea had almost startled him into acquiescence by its brilliancy.

Now Worts had a vote in the borough, and it came to Tappitt's ears that his servant intended to give that vote to Mr. Cornbury. "Worts," said he, a day or two before the election, "of course you intend to vote for Mr. Hart?"

Worts touched his cap, for it was the commencement of the day.

"I don't jest know," said he. "I was thinking of woting for the young squoire. I've know'd him ever since he was born, and I ain't never know'd the Jew gentleman;—never at all."

"Look here, Worts; if you intend to remain in this establishment I shall expect you to support the Liberal interest, as I support it myself. The Liberal interest has always been supported in Baslehurst by Bungall and Tappitt ever since Bungall and Tappitt have existed."

"The old maister, he wouldn't a woted for ere a Jew in Christendom,—not agin the squoire. The old maister was allays for the Protestant religion."

"Very well, Worts; there can't be two ways of thinking here, that's all; especially not at such a time as this, when there's more reason than ever why those connected with the brewery should all stand shoulder to shoulder. You've had your bread out of this establishment, Worts, for a great many years."

"And I've 'arned it hard;—no man can't say otherwise. The sweat o' my body belongs to the brewery, but I didn't ever sell 'em my wote;—and I don't mean." Saying which words, with an emphasis that was by no means servile, Worts went out from the presence of his master.

"That man's turning against me," said Tappitt to his wife at breakfast time, in almost mute despair.

"What! Worts?" said Mrs. Tappitt.

"Yes;—the ungrateful hound. He's been about the place almost ever since he could speak, for more than forty years. He's had two pound a week for the last ten years;—and now he's turning against me."

"Is he going over to Rowan?"

"I don't know where the d— he's going. He's going to vote for Butler Cornbury, and that's enough for me."

"Oh, T., I wouldn't mind that; especially not just now. Only think what a help he'll be to that man!"

"I tell you he shall walk out of the brewery the week after this, if he votes for Cornbury. There isn't room for two opinions here, and I won't have it."

For a moment or two Mrs. Tappitt sat mute, almost in despair. Then she took courage and spoke out.

"T.," said she, "it won't do."

"What won't do?"

"All this won't do. We shall be ruined and left without a home. I don't mind myself; I never did; but think of the girls! What would they do if we was turned out of this?"

"Who's to turn you out?"

"I know. I see it. I am beginning to understand. T., that man would not go against you and the brewery if he didn't know which way the wind is blowing. Worts is wide awake,—quite wide; he always was. T., you must take the offer Rowan has made of a regular income and live retired. If you don't do it,—I shall!" And Mrs. Tappitt, as she spoke the audacious words, rose up from her chair, and stood with her arms leaning upon the table.

"What!" said Tappitt, sitting aghast with his mouth open.

"Yes, T.; if you don't think of your family I must. What I'm saying Mr. Honyman has said before; and indeed all Baslehurst is saying the same thing. There's an offer made to you that will put your family on a footing quite genteel,—no gentlefolks in the county more so; and you, too, that are getting past your work!"

"I ain't getting past my work."

"I shouldn't say so, T., if it weren't for your own good,—and if I'm not to know about that, who is? It's all very well going about electioneering; and indeed it's just what gentlefolks is fit for when they're past their regular work. And I'm sure I shan't begrudge it so long as it don't cost anything; but that's not work you know, T."

"Ain't I in the brewery every day for seven or eight hours, and often more?"

"Yes, T., you are; and what's like to come of it if you go on so? What would be my feelings if I saw you brought into the house struck down with apoplepsy and paralepsy because I let you go on in that way when you wasn't fit? No, T.; I know my duty and I mean to do it. You know Dr. Haustus said only last month that you were that bilious——"

"Pshaw! bilious! it's enough to make any man bilious!"

"Or any dog," he would have added, had he thought of it. Thereupon Tappitt rushed away from his wife, back into his little office, and from that soon made his way to the Jew's committee-room at the Dragon, at which he was detained till nearly eleven o'clock at night.

"It's a kind of work in which one has to do as much after dinner as before," he said to his wife when he got back.

"For the matter of that," said she, "I think the after-dinner work is the chief part of it."

On the day of the election Luke Rowan was to be seen standing in the High Street talking to Butler Cornbury the candidate. Rowan was not an elector, for the cottages had not been in his possession long enough to admit of his obtaining from them a qualification to vote; but he was a declared friend of the Cornbury party. Mrs. Butler Cornbury had sent a message to him saying that she hoped to see him soon after the election should be over: on the following day or on the next, and Butler Cornbury himself had come to him in the town. Though absent from Baslehurst Rowan had managed to declare his opinions before that time, and was suspected by many to have written those articles in the "Baslehurst Gazette" which advocated the right of any constituency to send a Jew to Parliament if it pleased, but which proved at the same time that any constituency must be wrong to send any Jew to Parliament, and that the constituency of Baslehurst would in the present instance be specially wrong to send Mr. Hart to Parliament. "We have always advocated," said one of these articles, "the right of absolute freedom of choice for every borough and every county in the land; but we trust that the day is far distant in which the electors of England shall cease to look to their nearest neighbours as their best representatives." There wasn't much in the argument, but it suited the occasion, and added strength to Rowan's own cause in the borough. All the stanch Protestants began to feel a want of good beer. Questions very ill-natured as toward Tappitt were asked in the newspapers. "Who owns the Spotted Dog at Busby-porcorum; and who compels the landlord to buy his liquor at Tappitt's brewery?" There were scores of questions of the same nature, all of which Tappitt attributed, wrongly, to Luke Rowan. Luke had written that article about freedom of election, but he had not condescended to notice the beer at the Spotted Dog.

And there was another quarrel taking place in Baslehurst, on the score of that election, between persons with whom we are connected in this story. Mr. Prong had a vote in the borough, and was disposed to make use of it; and Mrs. Prime, regarding her own position as Mr. Prong's affianced bride, considered herself at liberty to question Mr. Prong as to the use which he proposed to make of that vote. To Mrs. Prime it appeared that anything done in any direction for the benefit of a Jew was a sin not to be forgiven. To Mr. Prong it seemed to be as great a sin not to do anything in his power for the hindrance and vexation of those with whom Dr. Harford and Mr. Comfort were connected by ties of friendship. Mrs. Prime, who, of the two, was the more logical, would not disjoin her personal and her scriptural hatreds. She also hated Dr. Harford; but she hated the Jews more. She was not disposed to support a Jew in Baslehurst because Mr. Comfort, in his doctrines, had fallen away from the purity of his early promise. Her idea was that a just man and a good Christian could not vote for either of the Baslehurst candidates under the present unhappy local circumstances;—but that under no circumstances should a Christian vote for a Jew. All this she said, in a voice not so soft as should be the voice of woman to her betrothed.

"Dorothea," said Mr. Prong very solemnly;—they were sitting at the time in his own little front parlour, as to the due arrangement of the furniture in which Mrs. Prime had already ventured to make some slight alterations which had not been received favourably by Mr. Prong,—"Dorothea, in this matter you must allow me to be the best judge. Voting for Members of Parliament is a thing which ladies naturally are not called upon to understand."

"Ladies can understand as well as gentlemen," said Mrs. Prime, "that a curse has gone out from the Lord against that people; and gentlemen have no more right than ladies to go against the will of the Lord."

It was in vain that Mr. Prong endeavoured to explain to her that the curse attached to the people as a nation, and did not necessarily follow units of that people who had adopted other nationalities.

"Let the units become Christians before they go into Parliament," said Mrs. Prime.

"I wish they would," said Mr. Prong. "I heartily wish they would: and Mr. Hart, if he be returned, shall have my prayers."

But this did not at all suffice for Mrs. Prime, who, perhaps, in the matter of argument had the best of it. She told her betrothed to his face that he was going to commit a great sin, and that he was tempted to this sin by grievous worldly passions. When so informed Mr. Prong closed his eyes, crossed his hands meekly on his breast, and shook his head.

"Not from thee, Dorothea," said he, "not from thee should this have come."

"Who is to speak out to you if I am not?" said she.

But Mr. Prong sat in silence, and with closed eyes again shook his head.

"Perhaps we had better part," said Mrs. Prime, after an interval of five minutes. "Perhaps it will be better for both of us."

Mr. Prong, however, still shook his head in silence; and it

was difficult for a lady in Mrs. Prime's position to read accurately the meaning of such shakings under such circumstances. But Mrs. Prime was a woman sufficiently versed in the world's business to be able to resolve that she would have an answer to her question when she required an answer.

"Mr. Prong," she said, "I remarked just now that perhaps we had better part."

"I heard the words," said Mr. Prong,—"I heard the cruel words." But even then he did not open his eyes, or remove his hands from his breast. "I heard the words, and I heard those other words, still more cruel. You had better leave me now that I may humble myself in prayer."

"That's all very well, Mr. Prong, and I'm sure I hope you will; but situated as we are, of course I should choose to have an answer. It seems to me that you dislike that kind of interference which I regard as a wife's best privilege and sweetest duty. If this be so, it will be better for us to part,—as friends of course."

"You have accused me of a great sin," he said; "of a great sin;—of a great sin!"

"And so in my mind it would be."

"Judge not, lest ye be judged, Dorothea; remember that."

"That doesn't mean, Mr. Prong, that we are not to have our opinions, and that we are not to warn those that are near us when we see them walking in the wrong path. I might as well say the same to you, when you——"

"No, Dorothea; it is by bounden duty. It is my work. It is that to which I am appointed as a minister. If you cannot see the difference I have much mistaken your character,—have much mistaken your character."

"Do you mean to say that nobody but a clergyman is to know what's right and what's wrong? That must be nonsense, Mr. Prong. I'm sorry to say anything to grieve you,—" Mr. Prong was now shaking his head again, with his eyes most pertinaciously closed,—"but there are some things which really one can't bear."

But he only shook his head. His inward feelings were too many for him, so that he could not at the present moment bring himself to give a reply to the momentous proposition which his betrothed had made him. Nor, indeed, had he at this moment fixed his mind as to the step which Duty and Wisdom combined would call upon him to take in this matter. The temper of the lady was not certainly all that he had desired. As an admiring member of his flock she had taken all his ghostly counsels as infallible; but now it seemed to him as though most of his words and many of his thoughts and actions were made subject by her to a bitter criticism. But in this matter he was inclined to rely much upon his own strength. Should he marry the lady, as he was still minded to do for many reasons, he would be to her a loving, careful husband; but he would also be her lord and master,—as was intended when marriage was made a holy ordinance. In this respect he did not doubt himself or his own powers. Hard words he could bear, and, as he thought, after a time control. So thinking, he was not disposed to allow the lady to recede from her troth to him, simply because in her anger she expressed a wish to do so. Therefore he had wisely been silent, and had shaken his head in reproach. But unfortunately the terms of their compact had not been finally settled with reference to another heading. Mrs. Prime had promised to be his wife, but she had burdened her promise with certain pecuniary conditions which were distasteful to him,—which were much opposed to that absolute headship and perfect mastery, which, as he thought, should belong to the husband as husband. His views on this subject were very strong, and he was by no means inclined to abate one jot of his demand. Better remain single in his work than accept the name of husband without its privileges! But he had hoped that by mingled firmness and gentle words he might bring his Dorothea round to a more womanly way of thinking. He had flattered himself that there was a power of eloquence in him which would have prevailed over her. Once or twice he thought that he was on the brink of success. He knew well that there were many points in his favour. A woman who has spoken of herself, and been spoken of, as being on the point of marriage, does not like to recede; and his Dorothea, though not specially womanly among women, was still a woman. Moreover he had the law on his side,—the old law as coming from the Scriptures. He could say that such a pecuniary arrangement as that proposed by his Dorothea was sinful. He had said so,—as he had then thought not without effect; but now she retaliated upon him with accusation of another sin! It was manifestly in her power to break away from him on that money detail. It seemed now to be her wish to break away from him; but she preferred doing so on that other matter. He began to fear that he must lose his wife, seeing that he was resolved never to yield on the money question; but he did not choose to be entrapped into an instant resignation of his engagement by Dorothea's indignation on a point of abstruse Scripturo-political morality. His Dorothea had assumed her indignation as a cloak for her pecuniary obstinacy. It might be that he must yield; but he would not surrender thus at the sound of a false summons. So he closed his eyes very pertinaciously and shook his head.

"I think upon the whole," said she again, "that we had better make up our minds to part." Then she stood up, feeling that she should thus employ a greater power in forcing an answer from him. He must have seen her motion through some cranny of his pertinaciously closed eyes, for he noticed it by rising from his own chair, with both his hands firmly fixed upon the table; but still he did not open his eyes,—unless it might be to the extent of that small cranny.

"Good-bye, Mr. Prong," said she.

Then he altered the form of his hands, and taking them from the table he dashed them together before his face. "God bless you, Dorothea!" said he. "God bless you! God bless you!" And he put out his hands as though blessing her in his darkness. She, perceiving the inutility of endeavouring to shake hands with a man who wouldn't open his eyes, moved away from her chair towards the door, purposely raising a sound of

motion with her dress, so that he might know that she was going. In that I think she took an unnecessary precaution, for the
cranny at the corner of his eye was still at his disposal.

"Good-bye, Mr. Prong," she said again, as she opened the
door for herself.

"God bless you, Dorothea!" said he. "May God bless you!"

Then, without assistance at the front door she made her way
out into the street, and as she stepped along the pavement, she
formed a resolve,—which no eloquence from Mr. Prong could
ever overcome,—that she would remain a widow for the rest
of her days.

At twelve o'clock on the morning of the election Mr. Hart
was declared by his own committee to be nine ahead, and was
admitted to be six ahead by Mr. Cornbury's committee. But
the Cornbury folk asserted confidently that in this they saw
certain signs of success. Their supporters were not men who
could be whipped up to the poll early in the day, whereas
Hart's voters were all, more or less, under control, and had
been driven up hurriedly to the hustings so as to make this early
show of numbers. Mr. Hart was about everywhere speaking,
and so was Butler Cornbury; but in the matter of oratory I am
bound to acknowledge that the Jew had by much the mastery
over the Christian. There are a class of men,—or rather more
than a class, a section of mankind,—to whom a power of easy
expression by means of spoken words comes naturally. English
country gentlemen, highly educated as they are, undaunted as
they usually are, self-confident as they in truth are at the bottom, are clearly not in this section. Perhaps they are further removed from it, considering the advantages they have for such
speaking, than any other class of men in England,—or I might
almost say elsewhere. The fact, for it is a fact, that some of the
greatest orators whom the world has known have been found
in this class, does not in any degree affect the truth of my proposition. The best grapes in the world are perhaps grown in England, though England is not a land of grapes. And for the same
reason. The value of the thing depends upon its rarity, and its

value instigates the efforts for excellence. The power of vocal expression which seems naturally to belong to an American is to an ordinary Englishman very marvellous; but in America the talking man is but little esteemed. "Very wonderful power of delivery,—that of Mr. So-and-So," says the Englishman, speaking of an American.

"Guess we don't think much of that kind of thing here," says the Yankee. "Theres 'a deal too much of that coin in circulation."

English country gentlemen are not to be classed among that section of mankind which speaks easily in public, but Jews, I think, may be so classed. The men who speak thus easily and with natural fluency, are also they who learn languages easily. They are men who observe rather than think, who remember rather than create, who may not have great mental powers, but are ever ready with what they have, whose best word is at their command at a moment, and is then serviceable though perhaps incapable of more enduring service.

At any rate, as regarded oratory in Baslehurst the dark little man with the bright new hat from London was very much stronger than his opponent,—so much stronger that poor Butler Cornbury began to sicken of elections and to wish himself comfortably at home at Cornbury Grange. He knew that he was talking himself down while the Israelitish clothier was talking himself up. "It don't matter," Honyman said to him comfortably. "It's only done for the show of the thing and to fill up the day. If Gladstone were here he wouldn't talk a vote out of them one way or the other;—nor yet the devil himself." This consoled Butler Cornbury, but nevertheless he longed that the day might be over.

And Tappitt spoke too more than once,—as did also Luke Rowan, in spite of various noisy interruptions in which he was told that he was not an elector, and in spite also of an early greeting with a dead cat. Tappitt, in advocating the claims of Mr. Hart to be returned to Parliament as member for Baslehurst, was clever enough to introduce the subject of his own wrongs. And so important had this brewery question become that he was listened to with every sign of interest when he told the people for how many years Bungall and Tappitt had brewed beer for them, there in Baslehurst. Doubtless he was met by sundry interruptions from the Rowanites.

"What sort of tipple has it been, T.?" was demanded by one voice.

"Do you call that beer?" said a second.

"Where do you buy your hops?" asked a third.

But he went on manfully, and was buoyed up by a strong belief that he was fighting his own battle with success.

Nor was Rowan slow to answer him. He was proud to say that he was Bungall's heir, and as such he intended to continue Bungall's business. Whether he could improve the quality of the old tap he didn't know, but he would try. People had said a few weeks ago that he had been hounded out of Baslehurst, and did not mean to come back again. Here he was. He had bought property in Baslehurst. He meant to live in Balsehurst. He pledged himself to brew beer in Baslehurst. He already regarded himself as belonging to Baslehurst. And, being a bachelor, he hoped that he might live to marry a wife out of Baslehurst. This last assurance was received with unqualified applause from both factions, and went far in obtaining for Rowan that local popularity which was needful to him. Certainly the Rowan contest added much to the popular interest of that election.

At the close of the poll on that evening it was declared by the mayor that Mr. Butler Cornbury had been elected to serve the borough in Parliament by a majority of one vote.

CHAPTER XXV

The Baslehurst Gazette

BY ONE VOTE! Old Mr. Cornbury when he heard of it gasped with dismay, and in secret regretted that his son had not been beaten. What seat could be gained by one vote and not be contested, especially when the beaten candidate was a Jew clothier rolling in money? And what sums would not a petition and scrutiny cost? Butler Cornbury himself was dismayed, and could hardly participate in the exultation of his more enthusiastic wife. Mr. Hart of course declared that he would petition, and that he was as sure of the seat as though he already occupied it. But as it was known that every possible electioneering device had been put in practice on his behalf during the last two hours of the poll, the world at large in Baslehurst believed that young Cornbury's position was secure. Tappitt and some few others were of a different opinion. At the present moment Tappitt could not endure to acknowledge to himself that he had been beaten. Nothing but the prestige and inward support of immediate success could support him in that contest, so much more important to himself, in which he was now about to be engaged. That matter of the petition, however, can hardly be brought into the present story. The political world will understand that it would be carried on with great vigour.

The news of the election of Butler Cornbury reached the cottage at Bragg's End by the voice of Mr. Sturt on the same evening; and Mrs. Ray, in her quiet way, expressed much joy that Mr. Comfort's son-in-law should have been successful, and that Baslehurst should not have disgraced itself by any connection with a Jew. To her it had appeared monstrous that such a one should have been even permitted to show himself in the town as a candidate for its representation. To such she would have denied all civil rights, and almost all social rights. For a true spirit of persecution one should always go to a woman;

and the milder, the sweeter, the more loving, the more womanly the woman, the stronger will be that spirit within her. Strong love for the thing loved necessitates strong hatred for the thing hated, and thence comes the spirit of persecution. They in England who are now keenest against the Jews, who would again take from them rights that they have lately won, are certainly those who think most of the faith of a Christian. The most deadly enemies of the Roman Catholics are they who love best their religion as Protestants. When we look to individuals we always find it so, though it hardly suits us to admit as much when we discuss these subjects broadly. To Mrs. Ray it was wonderful that a Jew should have been entertained in Baslehurst as a future member for the borough, and that he should have been admitted to speak aloud within a few yards of the church tower!

On the day but one after the election Mrs. Sturt brought over to the cottage an extra sheet of the "Baslehurst Gazette," which had been published out of its course, and which was devoted to the circumstances of the election. I am not sure that Mrs. Sturt would have regarded this somewhat dull report of the election speeches as having any peculiar interest for Mrs. Ray and her daughter had it not been for one special passage. Luke Rowan's speech about Baslehurst was given at length, and in it was contained that public promise as to his matrimonial intentions. Mrs. Sturt came into the cottage parlour with the paper doubled into four, and with her finger on a particular spot. To her it had seemed that Rowan's promise must have been intended for Rachel, and it seemed also that nothing could be more manly, straightforward, or gallant than that assurance. It suited her idea of chivalry. But she was not quite sure that Rachel would enjoy the publicity of the declaration, and therefore she was prepared to point the passage out more particularly to Mrs. Ray. "I've brought 'ee the account of it all," said she, still holding the paper in her hand. "The gudeman,— he's done with t' paper, and you'll keep it for good and all. One young man that we know of has made t' finest speech of 'em all to my mind. Luik at that, Mrs. Ray." Then, with a knowing wink at the mother, and a poke at the special words with her finger, she left the sheet in Mrs. Ray's hand, and went her way.

Mrs. Ray, who had not quite understood the pantomime, and whose eye had not caught the words relating to marriage, saw however that the column indicated contained the report of a speech made by Luke Rowan, and she began it at the beginning and read it throughout. Luke had identified himself with the paper, and therefore received from it almost more than justice. His words were given at very full length, and for some ten minutes she was reading before she came to the words which Mrs. Sturt had hoped would be so delightful.

"What is it, mamma?" Rachel asked.

"A speech, my dear, made at the election."

"And who made it, mamma?"

Mrs. Ray hesitated for a moment before she answered, thereby letting Rachel know full well who made the speech before the word was spoken. But at last she did speak the word —"Mr. Rowan, my dear."

"Oh!" said Rachel; she longed to get hold of the newspaper, but she would utter no word expressive of such longing. Since that evening on which she had been bidden to look at the clouds she had regarded Luke as a special hero, cleverer than other men around her, as a man born to achieve things and make himself known. It was not astonishing to her that a speech of his should be reported at length in the newspaper. He was a man certain to rise, to make speeches, and to be reported. So she thought of him; and so thinking had almost wished that it were not so. Could she expect that such a one would stoop to her? or that if he did so that she could be fit for him? He had now perceived that himself, and therefore had taken her at her word, and had left her. Had he been more like other men around her;—more homely, less prone to rise, with less about him of fire and genius, she might have won him and kept him. The prize would not have been so precious; but still, she thought, it might have been sufficient for her heart. A young man who could find printers and publishers to report his words in that way, on the first moment of his coming among them, would he turn aside from his path to look after her? Would he not bring with him some grand lady down from London as his wife?

"Dear me!" said Mrs. Ray, quite startled. "Oh, dear! What do you think he says?"

"What does he say, mamma?"

"Well, I don't know. Perhaps he mayn't mean it. I don't think I ought to have spoken of it."

"If it's in the newspaper I suppose I should have heard of it, unless you sent it back without letting me see it."

"She said we were to keep it, and it's because of that, I'm sure. She was always the most good-natured woman in the world. I don't know what we should have done if we hadn't found such a neighbour as Mrs. Sturt."

"But what is it, mamma, that you are speaking of in the newspapers?"

"Mr. Rowan says—Oh, dear! I wish I'd let you come to it yourself. How very odd that he should get up and say that kind of thing in public before all the people. He says;—but any way I know he means it because he's so honest. And after all if he means it, it doesn't much matter where he says it. Handsome is that handsome does. There, my dear; I don't know how to tell it you, so you had better read it yourself."

Rachel with eager hands took the paper, and began the speech as her mother had done, and read it through. She read it through till she came to those words, and then she put the paper down beside her. "I understand what you mean, mamma, and what Mrs. Sturt meant; but Mr. Rowan did not mean that."

"What did he mean, my dear?"

"He meant them to understand that he intended to become a man of Baslehurst like one of themselves."

"But then why did he talk about finding a wife there?"

"He wouldn't have said that, mamma, if he had meant any-thing particular. If anything of that sort had been at all in his mind, it would have kept him from saying what he did say."

"But didn't he mean that he intended to marry a Baslehurst lady?"

"He meant it in that sort of way in which men do mean such things. It was his way to make them think well of him. But don't let us talk any more about it, mamma. It isn't nice."

"Well, I'm sure I can't understand it," said Mrs. Ray. But she became silent on the subject, and the reading of the news-paper was passed over to Rachel.

This had not been completed when a step was heard on the gravel walk outside, and Mrs. Ray, jumping up, declared it to be the step of her eldest daughter. It was so, and Mrs. Prime was very soon in the room. It was at this time about four o'clock in the afternoon, and therefore, as the hour for tea at the cottage was half-past five, it was naturally understood that Mrs. Prime had come there to join them at their evening meal. After their first greeting she had seated herself on the sofa, and there was that in her manner which showed both to her mother and sister that she was somewhat confused,—that she had something to say as to which there was some hesitation. "Do take off your bonnet, Dorothea," said her mother.

"Will you come up-stairs, Dolly," said her sister, "and put your hair straight after your walk?"

But Dolly did not care whether her hair was straight or tossed, as the Irish girls say when the smoothness of their locks has been disarranged. She took off her bonnet, however, and laid it on the sofa beside her. "Mother," she said, "I've got something particular that I want to say to you."

"I hope it's not anything serious the matter," said Mrs. Ray.

"Well, mother, it is serious. Things are serious mostly, I think,—or should be."

"Shall I go into the garden while you are speaking to mamma?" said Rachel.

"No, Rachel; not on my account. What I've got to say

should be said to you as well as to mother. It's all over between me and Mr. Prong."

"No!" said Mrs. Ray.

"I thought it would be," said Rachel.

"And why did you think so?" said Mrs. Prime, turning round upon her sister, almost angrily.

"I felt that he wouldn't suit you, Dolly; that's why I thought so. If it's all over now, I suppose there's no harm in saying that I didn't like him well enough to hope he'd be my brother-in-law."

"But that couldn't make you think it. However, it's all over between us. We agreed that it should be so this morning; and I thought it right to come out and let you know at once."

"I'm glad you've told us," said Mrs. Ray.

"Was there any quarrel?" asked Rachel.

"No, Rachel, there was no quarrel; not what you call a quarrel, I suppose. We found there were subjects of disagreement between us,—matters on which we had adverse opinions; and therefore it was better that we should part."

"It was about the money, perhaps?" said Mrs. Ray.

"Well, yes; it was in part about the money. Had I known then as much as I do now about the law in such matters, I should have told Mr. Prong from the first that it could not be. He is a good man, and I hope I have not disturbed his happiness."

"I used to be afraid that he would disturb yours," said Rachel, "and therefore I cannot pretend to regret it."

"That's not charitable, Rachel. But if you please we won't say anything more about it. It's over, and that is enough. And now, mother, I want to know if you will object to my returning here and living at the cottage again."

Mrs. Ray could not bethink herself at the moment what answer she might best make, and therefore for some moments she made none. For herself she would have been delighted that her eldest daughter should return to the cottage. Under no circumstances could she refuse her own child a home under

her own roof. But at the present moment she could not forget the circumstances under which Mrs. Prime had gone, and
it militated sorely against Mrs. Ray's sense of justice that the
return should be made to depend on other circumstances. Mrs.
Prime had gone away in loud disapproval of Rachel's conduct;
and now she proposed to return, on this breaking up of her
own matrimonial arrangements, as though she had left the cottage because of her proposed marriage. Mrs. Prime should be
welcomed back, but her return should be accompanied by a
withdrawal of her accusation against Rachel. Mrs. Ray did not
know how to put her demand into words, but her mind was
clear on the subject.

"Well, mother," said Mrs. Prime; "is there any objection?"

"No, my dear; no objection at all: of course not. I shall be
delighted to have you back, and so, I'm sure, will Rachel;
but——"

"But what? Is it about money?"

"Oh, dear, no! Nothing about money at all. If you do come
back,—and I'm sure I hope you will; and indeed it seems quite
unnatural that you should be staying in Baslehurst, while we
are living here. But I think you ought to say, my dear, that Rachel behaved just as she ought to behave in all that matter
about,—about Mr. Rowan, you know."

"Don't mind me, mamma," said Rachel,—who could, however, have smothered her mother with kisses, on hearing these
words.

"But I think we all ought to understand each other, Rachel.
You and your sister can't go on comfortably together, if there's
to be more black looks about that."

"I don't know that there have been any black looks," said
Mrs. Prime, looking very black as she spoke.

"At any rate we should understand each other," continued
Mrs. Ray, with admirable courage. "I've thought a great deal
about it since you've been away. Indeed I haven't thought
about much else. And I don't think I shall ever forgive myself
for having let a hard word be said to Rachel about it."

"Oh, mamma, don't,—don't," said Rachel. But those meditated embraces were continued in her imagination.

"I don't want to say any hard words," said Mrs. Prime.

"No; I'm sure you don't;—only they were said,—weren't they, now? Didn't we blame her about being out there in the churchyard that evening?"

"Mamma!" exclaimed Rachel.

"Well, my dear, I won't say any more;—only this. Your sister went away because she thought you weren't good enough for her to live with; and if she comes back again,—which I'm sure I hope she will,—I think she ought to say that she's been mistaken."

Mrs. Prime looked very black, and no word fell from her. She sat there silent and gloomy, while Mrs. Ray looked at the fireplace, lost in wonder at her own effort. Whether she would have given way or not, had she and Mrs. Prime been alone, I cannot say. That Mrs. Prime would have uttered no outspoken recantation I feel sure. It was Rachel at last who settled the matter.

"If Dolly comes back to live here, mamma," said she, "I shall take that as an acknowledgment on her part that she thinks I am good enough to live with."

"Well, my dear," said Mrs. Ray, "perhaps that'll do; only there should be an understanding, you know."

Mrs. Prime at the moment said nothing; but when next she spoke her words showed her intention of having her things brought back to the cottage on the next day. I think it must be felt that Rachel had won the victory. She felt it so herself, and was conscious that no further attempt would be made to carry her off to Dorcas meetings against her own will.

CHAPTER XXVI

Cornbury Grange

LUKE ROWAN had been told that Mrs. Butler Cornbury wished to see him when the election should be over; and on the evening of the election the victorious candidate, before he returned home, asked Luke to come to the Grange on the following Monday and stay till the next Wednesday. Now it must be understood that Rowan during this period of the election had become, in a public way, very intimate with Cornbury. They were both young men, the new member of Parliament not being over thirty, and for the time they were together employed on the same matter. Luke Rowan was one with whom such a man as Mr. Cornbury could not zealously co-operate without reaching a considerable extent of personal intimacy. He was pleasant-mannered, free in speech, with a bold eye, assuming though not asserting his equality with the best of those with whom he might be brought in contact. Had Cornbury chosen to consider himself by reason of his social station too high for Rowan's fellowship, he might of course have avoided him; but he could not have put himself into close contact with the man, without submitting himself to that temporary equality which Rowan assumed, and to that temporary familiarity which sprung from it. Butler Cornbury had thought little about it. He had found Rowan to be a pleasant associate and an able assistant, and had fallen into that mode of fellowship which the other man's ways and words had made natural to him. When his wife begged him to ask Rowan up to the Grange, he had been startled for a moment, but had at once assented.

"Well," said he; "he's an uncommon pleasant fellow. I don't see why he shouldn't come."

"I've a particular reason," said Mrs. Butler.

"All right," said the husband. "Do you explain it to my father." And so the invitation had been given.

But Rowan was a man more thoughtful than Cornbury, and was specially thoughtful as to his own position. He was a radical at heart if ever there was a radical. But in saying this I must beg my reader to understand that a radical is not necessarily a revolutionist or even a republican. He does not, by reason of his social or political radicalism, desire the ruin of thrones, the degradation of nobles, the spoliation of the rich, or even the downfall of the bench of bishops. Many a young man is frightened away from the just conclusions of his mind and the strong convictions of his heart by dread of being classed with those who are jealous of the favoured ones of fortune. A radical may be as ready as any aristocrat to support the crown with his blood, and the church with his faith. It is in this that he is a radical; that he desires, expects, works for, and believes in, the gradual progress of the people. No doctrine of equality is his. Liberty he must have, and such position, high or low, for himself and others, as each man's individual merits will achieve for him. The doctrine of outward equality he eschews as a barrier to all ambition, and to all improvement. The idea is as mean as the thing is impracticable. But within,—is it in his soul or in his heart?—within his breast there is a manhood that will own no inferiority to the manhood of another. He retires to a corner that an earl with his suite may pass proudly through the doorway, and he grudges the earl nothing of his pride. It is the earl's right. But he also has his right; and neither queen, nor earl, nor people shall invade it. That is the creed of a radical.

Rowan, as I have said, was a man thoughtful as to his own position. He had understood well the nature of the league between himself and Butler Cornbury. It was his intention to become a brewer in Baslehurst; and a brewer in Baslehurst would by no means be as the mighty brewers of great name, who marry lords' daughters, and give their daughters in marriage to mighty lords. He would simply be a tradesman in the town. It might well be that he should not find the society of the

Tappitts and the Griggses much to his taste, but such as it was he would make the best of it. At any rate he would make no attempt to force his way into other society. If others came to him let that be their look-out. Now, when Cornbury asked him thus to come to Cornbury Grange, as though they two were men living in the same class of life,—as though they were men who might be bound together socially in their homes as well as politically on the hustings, the red colour came to his face and he hesitated for a moment in his answer.

"You are very kind," said he.

"Oh! you must come," said Cornbury. "My wife particularly desires it."

"She is very kind," said he. "But if you ask all your supporters over to the Grange you'll get rather a mixed lot."

"I suppose I should; but I don't mean to do that. I shall be very glad, however, to see you;—very glad."

"And I shall be very happy to come," said Rowan, having again hesitated as he gave his answer.

"I wish I hadn't promised that I'd go there," he said to himself afterwards. This was on the Sunday, after evening church, —an hour or more after the people had all gone home, and he was sitting on that stile, looking to the west, and thinking, as he looked, of that sunset which he and another had seen as they stood there together. He did wish that he had not undertaken to go to Mr. Cornbury's house. What to him would be the society of such people as he should find there,—to him who had laid out for himself a career that would necessarily place his life among other associates? "I'll send and excuse myself," he said. "I'll be called away to Exeter. I have things to do there. I shall only get into a mess by knowing people who will drop me when this ferment of the election is over." And yet the idea of an intimacy at such a house as Cornbury Grange, —with such people as Mrs. Butler Cornbury, was very sweet to him; only this, that if he associated with them or such as them it must be on equal terms. He could acknowledge them to be people apart from him, as ice creams and sponge cakes are things apart from the shillingless schoolboy. But as the school-boy, if brought within the range of cakes and creams, must de-vour them with unchecked relish, as though his pocket were lined with coin; so must he, Rowan, carry himself with these curled darlings of society if he found himself placed among them. He liked cakes and creams, but had made up his mind that other viands were as wholesome and more comfortably within his reach. Was it worth his while to go to this banquet which would unsettle his taste, and at which perhaps if he sat there at his ease, he might not be wholly welcome? All his thoughts were not noble. He had declared to himself that a certain thing could not be his except at a cost which he would not pay, and yet he hankered for that thing. He had declared to himself that no social position in which he might ever find himself should make a change in him, on his inner self or on his outward manner; and now he feared to go among these people, lest he should find himself an inferior among superiors. It was not all noble; but there was beneath it a basis of nobil-ity. "I will go," he said at last, fearing that if he did not, there would have been some grain of cowardice in the motives of his action. "If they don't like me it's their fault for asking me."

Of course as he sat there he was thinking of Rachel. Of course he had thought of Rachel daily, almost hourly, since he had been with her at the cottage, when she had bent her head over his shoulder, and submitted to have his arm round her waist. But his thoughts of her were not as hers of him. Nor is it often that a man's love is like a woman's,—restless, fearful, un-comfortable, sleepless, timid, and all-pervading. Not the less may it be passionate, constant, and faithful. He had been an-gered by Rachel's letter to him,—greatly angered. Of a truth when Mrs. Ray met him in Exeter he had no message to send back to Cawston. He had done his part, and had been rejected; —had been rejected too clearly because on the summing up of his merits and demerits at the cottage, his demerits had been found to be the heavier. He did not suspect that the calcula-tion had been made by Rachel herself; and therefore he had never said to himself that all should be over between them. He had never determined that there should be a quarrel between them. But he was angered, and he would stand aloof from her. He would stand aloof from her, and would no longer acknowledge that he was in any way bound by the words he had spoken. All such bonds she had broken. Nevertheless I think he loved her with a surer love after receiving that letter than he had ever felt before.

He had been here, at this spot, every evening since his return to Baslehurst; and here had thought much of his future life, and something, too, of the days that were past. Looking to the left he could see the trees that stood in front of the old brewery, hiding the building from his eyes. That was the house in which old Bungall had lived, and there Tappitt had lived for the last twenty years. "I suppose," said he, speaking to himself, "it will be my destiny to live there too, with the vats and beer barrels under my nose. But what farmer ever throve who disliked the muck of his own farmyard?" Then he had thought of Tappitt and of the coming battle, and had laughed as he remembered the scene with the poker. At that moment his eye caught the bright colours of women's bonnets coming into the field beneath him, and he knew that the Tappitt girls were returning home from their walk. He had retired quickly round the chancel of the church, and had watched, thinking that Rachel would be with them. But Rachel, of course, was not there. He said to himself that they had thrown her off; and said also that the time should come when they should be glad to win from her a kind word and an encouraging smile. His love for Rachel was as true and more strong than ever; but it was of that nature that he was able to tell himself that it had for the present moment been set aside by her act, and that it became him to leave it for a while in abeyance.

"What on earth shall I do with myself all Tuesday?" he said again as he walked away from the churchyard on the Sunday evening. "I don't know what these people do with themselves when there's no hunting and shooting. It seems unnatural to me that a man shouldn't have his bread to earn,—or a woman either in some form." After that he went back to his inn.

On the Monday he went out to Cornbury Grange late in the afternoon. Butler Cornbury drove into Baslehurst with a pair of horses, and took him back in his phaeton.

"Give my fellow your portmanteau. That's all right. You never were at the Grange, were you? It's the prettiest five miles of a drive in Devonshire; but the walk along the river is the prettiest walk in England,—which is saying a great deal more."

"I know the walk well," said Rowan, "though I never was inside the park."

"It isn't much of a park. Indeed there isn't a semblance of a park about it. Grange is just the name for it, as it's an upper-class sort of homestead for a gentleman farmer. We've lived there since long before Adam, but we've never made much of a house of it."

"That's just the sort of place that I should like to have myself."

"If you had it you wouldn't be content. You'd want to pull down the house and build a bigger one. It's what I shall do some day, I suppose. But if I do it will never be so pretty again. I suppose that fellow will petition; won't he?"

"I should say he would—though he won't get anything by it."

"He knows his purse is longer than ours, and he'll think to frighten us;—and by George, he will frighten us too! My father is not a rich man by any means."

"You should stand to your guns now."

"I mean to do so, if I can. My wife's father is made of money."

"What! Mr. Comfort?"

"Yes. He's been blessed with the most surprising number of unmarried uncles and aunts that ever a man had. He's rather fond of me, and likes the idea of my being in Parliament. I think I shall hint to him that he must pay for the idea. Here we are. Will you come and take a turn round the place before dinner?"

Rowan was then taken into the house and introduced to the old squire, who received him with the stiff urbanity of former days.

"You are welcome to the Grange, Mr. Rowan. You'll find us very quiet here; which is more, I believe, than can have been said of Baslehurst these last two or three days. My daughter-in-law is somewhere with the children. She'll be here before dinner. Butler, has that tailor fellow gone back to London yet?"

Butler told his father that the tailor had at least gone away from Baslehurst; and then the two younger men went out and walked about the grounds till dinner time.

It was Mrs. Butler Cornbury who gave soul and spirit to daily life at Cornbury Grange,—who found the salt with which the bread was quickened, and the wine with which the heart was made glad. Marvellous is the power which can be exercised, almost unconsciously, over a company, or an individual, or even upon a crowd by one person gifted with good temper, good digestion, good intellects, and good looks. A woman so endowed charms not only by the exercise of her own gifts, but she endows those who are near her with a sudden conviction that it is they whose temper, health, talents, and appearance is doing so much for society. Mrs. Butler Cornbury was such a woman as this. The Grange was a popular house. The old squire was not found to be very dull. The young squire was thought to be rather clever. The air of the house was lively and bracing. Men and women did not find the days there to be over-long. And Mrs. Butler Cornbury did it all.

Rowan did not see her till he met her in the dining-room, just before dinner, when he found that two or three other ladies were also staying there. She came up to him when he entered the room, and greeted him as though he were an old friend. All conversation at that moment of course had reference to the election. Thanks were given and congratulations received; and when old Mr. Cornbury shook his head, his daughter-in-law assured him that there would be nothing to fear.

"I don't know what you call nothing to fear, my dear. I call two thousand pounds a great deal to fear."

"I shouldn't wonder if we don't hear another word about him," said she.

The old man uttered a long sigh. "It seems to me," said he, "that no gentleman ought to stand for a seat in Parliament since these people have been allowed to come up. Purity of election, indeed! It makes me sick. Come along, my dear." Then he gave his arm to one of the young ladies, and toddled into the dining-room.

Mrs. Butler Cornbury said nothing special to Luke Rowan on that evening, but she made the hours very pleasant to him. All those half-morbid ideas as to social difference between himself and his host's family soon vanished. The house was very comfortable, the girls were very pretty, Mrs. Cornbury was very kind, and everything went very well. On the following morning it was nearly ten when they sat down to breakfast, and half the morning before lunch had passed away in idle chat before the party bethought itself of what it should do for the day. At last it was agreed that they would all stroll out through the woods up to a special reach of the river which there ran through a ravine of rock, called Cornbury Cleeves. Many in those parts declared that Cornbury Cleeves was the prettiest spot in England. I am not prepared to bear my testimony to the truth of that very wide assertion. I can only say that I know no prettier spot. The river here was rapid and sparkling; not rapid because driven into small compass, for its breadth was greater and more regular in its passage through the Cleeves than it was either above or below, but rapid from the declivity of its course. On one side the rocks came sheer down to the water, but on the other there was a strip of meadow, or rather a grassy amphitheatre, for the wall of rocks at the back of it was semicircular, so as to enclose the field on every side. There might be four or five acres of green meadow here; but the whole was so interspersed with old stunted oak trees and thorns standing alone that the space looked larger than it was. The rocks on each side were covered here and there with the richest foliage; and the spot might be taken to be a valley from which, as from that of Rasselas, there was no escape. Down close upon the margin of the water a bathing-house had been built, from which a plunge could be taken into six or seven feet of the coolest, darkest, cleanest water that a bather could desire in his heart.

"I suppose you never were here before," said Mrs. Cornbury to Rowan.

"Indeed I have," said he. "I always think it such a grand thing that you landed magnates can't keep all your delights to yourself. I dare say I've been here oftener than you have during the last three months."

"That's very likely, seeing that it's my first visit this summer."

"And I've been here a dozen times. I suppose you'll think I'm a villainous trespasser when I tell you that I've bathed in that very house more than once."

"Then you've done more than I ever did; and yet we had it made thinking it would do for ladies. But the water looks so black."

"Ah! I like that, as long as it's a clear black."

"I like bathing where I can see the bright stones like jewels at the bottom. You can never do that in fresh water. It's only in some nook of the sea, where there is no sand, when the wind outside has died away, and when the tide is quiet and at its full. Then one can drop gently in and almost fancy that one belongs to the sea as the mermaids do. I wonder how the idea of mermaids first came?"

"Some one saw a crowd of young women bathing."

"But then how came they to have looking-glasses and fishes' tails?"

"The fishes' tails were taken as granted because they were

in the sea, and the looking-glasses because they were women,"
said Rowan.

"And the one with as much reason as the other. By-the-by,
Mr. Rowan, talking of women, and fishes' tails, and looking-
glasses, and all other feminine attractions, when did you see
Miss Ray last?"

Rowan paused before he answered her, and looking round
perceived that he had strayed with Mrs. Cornbury to the fur-
thest end of the meadow, away from their companions. It immediately came across his mind that this was the matter on
which Mrs. Cornbury wished to speak to him, and by some
combative process he almost resolved that he would not be
spoken to on that matter.

"When did I see Miss Ray?" said he, repeating her question. "Two or three days after Mrs. Tappitt's party. I have not
seen her since that."

"And why don't you go and see her?" said Mrs. Cornbury.

Now this was asked him in a tone which made it necessary
that he should either answer her question or tell her simply
that he would not answer it. The questioner's manner was so
firm, so eager, so incisive, that the question could not be
turned away.

"I am not sure that I am prepared to tell you," said he.

"Ah! but I want you to be prepared," said she; "or rather,
perhaps, to tell the truth, I want to drive you to an answer
without preparation. Is it not true that you made her an offer,
and that she accepted it?"

Rowan thought a moment, and then he answered her, "It
is true."

"I should not have asked the question if I had not positively
known that such was the case. I have never spoken a word to
her about it, and yet I knew it. Her mother told my father."

"Well?"

"And as that is so, why do you not go and see her? I am sure
you are not one of those who would play such a trick as that
upon such a girl with the mere purpose of amusing yourself."

"Upon no girl would I do so, Mrs. Cornbury."

"I feel sure of it. Therefore why do you not go to her?"
They walked along together for a few minutes under the rocks
in silence, and then Mrs. Cornbury again repeated her question, "Why do you not go to her?"

"Mrs. Cornbury," he said, "you must not be angry with me
if I say that that is a matter which at the present moment I am
not willing to discuss."

"Nor must you be angry with me if, as Rachel's friend, I say
something further about it. As you do not wish to answer me,
I will ask no other question; but at any rate you will be willing
to listen to me. Rachel has never spoken to me on this subject
—not a word; but I know from others who see her daily that
she is very unhappy."

"I am grieved that it should be so."

"Yes, I knew you would be grieved. But how could it be
otherwise? A girl, you know, Mr. Rowan, has not other things
to occupy her mind as a man has. I think of Rachel Ray that
she would have been as happy there at Bragg's End as the day
is long, if no offer of love had come in her way. She was not a
girl whose head had been filled with romance, and who looked
for such things. But for that very reason is she less able to bear
the loss of it when the offer has come in her way. I think, perhaps, you hardly know the depth of her character and the
strength of her love."

"I think I know that she is constant."

"Then why do you try her so hardly?"

Mrs. Cornbury had promised that she would ask no more
questions; but the asking of questions was her easiest mode of
saying that which she had to say. And Rowan, though he had
declared that he would answer no question, could hardly avoid
the necessity of doing so.

"It may be that the trial is the other way."

"I know;—I understand. They made her write a letter to
you. It was my father's doing. I will tell you the whole truth. It
was my father's doing, and therefore it is that I think myself

bound to speak to you. Her mother came to him for advice, and he had heard evil things spoken of you in Baslehurst. You will see that I am very frank with you. And I will take some credit to myself too. I believed such tidings to be altogether false, and I made inquiry which proved that I was right. But my father had given the advice which he thought best. I do not know what Rachel wrote to you, but a girl's letter under such circumstances can hardly do more than express the will of those who guide her. It was sad enough for her to be forced to write such a letter, but it will be sadder still if you cannot be brought to forgive it."

Then she paused, standing under the gray rock and looking up eagerly into his face. But he made her no answer, nor gave her any sign. His heart was very tender at that moment towards Rachel, but there was that in him of the stubbornness of manhood which would not let him make any sign of his tenderness.

"I will not press you to say anything, Mr. Rowan," she continued, "and I am much obliged to you for having listened to me. I've known Rachel Ray for many years, and that must be my excuse."

"No excuse is wanting," he said. "If I do not say anything it is not because I am offended. There are things on which a man should not allow himself to speak without considering them."

"Oh, certainly. Come; shall we go back to them at the bathing-house? They'll think we've lost ourselves."

Thus Mrs. Cornbury said the words which she had desired to speak on Rachel Ray's behalf.

When they reached the Grange there were still two hours left before the time of dressing for dinner should come, and during these hours Luke returned by himself to the Cleeves. He escaped from his host, and retraced his steps, and on reaching the river sat himself down on the margin, and looked into the cool dark running water. Had he been severe to Rachel? He would answer no such question when asked by Mrs. Cornbury, but he was very desirous of answering it to himself. The women at the cottage had doubted him,—Mrs. Ray and her daughter, with perhaps that other daughter of whom he had only heard; and he had resolved that they should see him no more and hear of him no more till there should be no further room for doubt. Then he would show himself again at the cottage, and again ask Rachel to be his wife. There was some manliness in this; but there was also a hardness in his pride which deserved the rebuke which Mrs. Cornbury's words had conveyed to him. He had been severe to Rachel. Lying there, with his full length stretched upon the grass, he acknowledged to himself that he had thought more of his own feelings than of hers. While Mrs. Cornbury had been speaking he could not bring himself to feel that this was the case. But now in his solitude he did acknowledge it. What amount of sin had she committed against him that she should be so punished by him who loved her? He took out her letter from his pocket, and found that her words were loving, though she had not been allowed to put into them that eager, pressing, speaking love which he had desired.

"Spoken ill of me, have they?" said he to himself, as he got up to walk back to the Grange. "Well, that was natural too. What an ass a man is to care for such things as that!"

On that evening and the next morning the Cornburys were very gracious to him; and then he returned to Baslehurst, on the whole well pleased with his visit.

CHAPTER XXVII

In Which the Question of the Brewery Is Settled

DURING THE DAY OR TWO immediately subsequent to the election, Mr. Tappitt found himself to be rather downhearted. The excitement of the contest was over. He was no longer buoyed

up by the consoling and almost triumphant assurances of success for himself against his enemy Rowan, which had been administered to him by those with whom he had been acting on
behalf of Mr. Hart. He was alone and thoughtful in his counting-house, or else subjected to the pressure of his wife's arguments in his private dwelling. He had never yet been won over
to say that he would agree to any proposition, but he knew that
he must now form some decision. Rowan would not even wait
till the lawsuit should be decided by legal means. If Mr. Tappitt would not consent to one of the three propositions made to
him, Rowan would at once commence the building of his new
brewery. "He is that sort of man," said Honyman, "that if he
puts a brick down nothing in the world will prevent him from
going on."

"Of course it won't," said Mrs. Tappitt. "Oh dear, oh dear,
T.! if you go on in this way we shall all be ruined; and then
people will say that it was my fault, and that I ought to have
had you inquired into about your senses."

Tappitt gnashed his teeth and rushed out of the dining-
room back into his brewery. Among all those who were around
him there was not one to befriend him. Even Worts had turned
against him, and had received notice to go with a stern satisfaction which Tappitt had perfectly understood.

Tappitt was in this frame of mind, and was seated on his
office stool, with his hat over his eyes, when he was informed
by one of the boys about the place that a deputation from the
town had come to wait upon him;—so he pulled off his hat, and
begged that the deputation might be shown into the counting-
house. The deputation consisted of three tradesmen who were
desirous of convening a meeting with the view of discussing
the petition against Mr. Cornbury's return to Parliament, and
they begged that Mr. Tappitt would take the chair. The meeting was to be held at the Dragon, and it was proposed that
after the meeting there should be a little dinner. Mr. Tappitt
would perhaps consent to take the chair at the dinner also. Mr.
Tappitt did consent to both propositions, and when the deputa-

tion withdrew, he felt himself to be himself once more. His courage had returned to him, and he would at once rebuke his wife for the impropriety of the words she had addressed to him. He would rebuke his wife, and would then proceed to meet Mr. Sharpit the attorney, at the Dragon, and to take the chair at the meeting. It could not be that a young adventurer such as Rowan could put down an old-established firm, such as his own, or banish from the scene of his labours a man of such standing in the town as himself! It was all the fault of Hony-man,—of Honyman, who never was firm on any matter. When the meeting should be over he would say a word or two to Sharpit, and see if he could not put the matter into better training.

With a heavy tread, a tread that was intended to mark his determination, he ascended to the drawing-room and from thence to the bedroom above in which Mrs. Tappitt was then seated. She understood the meaning of the footfall, and knew well that it indicated a purpose of marital authority. A woman must have much less of natural wit than had fallen to Mrs. Tappitt's share, who has not learned from the experience of thirty years the meaning of such marital signs and sounds. So she sat herself firmly in her seat, caught hold of the petticoat which she was mending with a stout grasp, and prepared her-self for the battle. "Margaret," said he, when he had carefully closed the door behind him, "I have come up to say that I do not intend to dine at home to-day."

"Oh, indeed," said she. "At the Dragon, I suppose then."

"Yes; at the Dragon. I've been asked to take the chair at a popular meeting which is to be held with reference to the late election."

"Take the chair!"

"Yes, my dear, take the chair at the meeting and at the dinner."

"Now, T., don't you make a fool of yourself."

"No, I won't; but Margaret, I must tell you once for all that that is not the way in which I like you to speak to me. Why you should have so much less confidence in my judgment than other people in Baslehurst, I cannot conceive; but——"

"Now, T., look here; as for your taking the chair as you call it, of course you can do it if you like it."

"Of course I can; and I do like it, and I mean to do it. But it isn't only about that I've come to speak to you. You said something to me to-day, before Honyman, that was very improper."

"What I say always is improper, I know."

"I don't suppose you could have intended to insinuate that you thought that I was a lunatic."

"I didn't say so."

"You said something like it."

"No, I didn't, T."

"Yes you did, Margaret."

"If you'll allow me for a moment, T., I'll tell you what I did say, and if you wish it, I'll say it again."

"No; I'd rather not hear it said again."

"But, T., I don't choose to be misunderstood, nor yet misrepresented."

"I haven't misrepresented you."

"But I say you have misrepresented me. If I ain't allowed to speak a word, of course it isn't any use for me to open my mouth. I hope I know what my duty is and I hope I've done it; both by you, T., and by the children. I know I'm bound to submit, and I hope I have submitted. Very hard it has been sometimes when I've seen things going as they have gone; but I've remembered my duty as a wife, and I've held my tongue when any other woman in England would have spoken out. But there are some things which a woman can't stand and shouldn't; and if I'm to see my girls ruined and left without a roof over their heads, or a bit to eat, or a thing to wear, it shan't be for want of a word from me."

"Didn't they always have plenty to eat?"

"But where is it to come from if you're going to rush open-mouthed into the lion's jaws in this way? I've done my duty by you, T., and no man nor yet no woman can say anything to the contrary. And if it was myself only I'd see myself on the brink of starvation before I'd say a word; but I can't see those poor girls brought to beggary without telling you what everybody in Baslehurst is talking about; and I can't see you, T., behaving in such a way and sit by and hold my tongue."

"Behave in what way? Haven't I worked like a horse? Do you mean to tell me that I am to give up my business, and my position, and everything I have in the world, and go away because a young scoundrel comes to Baslehurst and tells me that he wants to have my brewery? I tell you what, Margaret, if you think I'm that sort of man, you don't know me yet."

"I don't know about knowing you, T."

"No; you don't know me."

"If you come to that, I know very well that I have been deceived. I didn't want to speak of it, but now I must. I have been made to believe for these last twenty years that the brewery was all your own, whereas it now turns out that you've only got a share in it, and for aught I can see, by no means the best share. Why wasn't I told all that before?"

"Woman!" shouted Mr. Tappitt.

"Yes; woman indeed! I suppose I am a woman, and therefore I'm to have no voice in anything. Will you answer me one question, if you please? Are you going to that man, Sharpit?"

"Yes, I am."

"Then, Mr. Tappitt, I shall consult my brothers." Mrs. Tappitt's brothers were grocers in Plymouth; men whom Mr. Tappitt had never loved. "They mayn't hold their heads quite as high as you do,—or rather as you used to do when people thought that the establishment was all your own; but such as it is nobody can turn them out of their shop in the Market-place. If you are going to Sharpit, I shall consult them."

"You may consult the devil, if you like it."

"Oh, oh! very well, Mr. Tappitt. It's clear enough that you're not yourself any longer, and that somebody must take up your affairs and manage them for you. If you'll follow my advice you'll stay at home this evening and take a dose of physic and see Dr. Haustus quietly in the morning."

"I shall do nothing of the kind."

"Very well. Of course I can't make you. As yet you're your own master. If you choose to go to this silly meeting and then to drink gin and water and to smoke bad tobacco till all hours at the Dragon, and you in the dangerous state you are at present, I can't help it. I don't suppose that anything I could do now, that is quite immediately, would enable me to put you under fitting restraint."

"Put me where?" Then Mr. Tappitt looked at his wife with a look that was intended to annihilate her, for the time being, —seeing that no words that he could speak had any such effect, —and he hurried out of the room without staying to wash his hands or brush his hair before he went off to preside at the meeting.

Mrs. Tappitt remained where she was for about half an hour and then descended among her daughters.

"Isn't papa going to dine at home?" said Augusta.

"No, my dear; your papa is going to dine with some friends of Mr. Hart's, the candidate who was beaten."

"And has he settled anything about the brewery?" Cherry asked.

"No; not as yet. Your papa is very much troubled about it, and I fear he is not very well. I suppose he must go to this electioneering dinner. When gentlemen take up that sort of thing, they must go on with it. And as they wish your father to preside over the petition, I suppose he can't very well help himself."

"Is papa going to preside over the petition?" asked Augusta.

"Yes, my dear."

"I hope it won't cost him anything," said Martha. "People say that those petitions do cost a great deal of money."

"It's a very anxious time for me, girls; of course, you must all of you see that. I'm sure when we had our party I didn't

think things were going to be as anxious as this, or I wouldn't
have had a penny spent in such a way as that. If your papa
could bring himself to give up the brewery, everything would
be well."

"I do so wish he would," said Cherry, "and let us all go and
live at Torquay. I do so hate this nasty dirty old place."

"I shall never live in a house I like so well," said Martha.

"The house is well enough, my dears, and so is the brewery;
but it can't be expected that your father should go on working
for ever as he does at present. It's too much for his strength;—
a great deal too much. I can see it, though I don't suppose any
one else can. No one knows, only me, what your father has
gone through in that brewery."

"But why doesn't he take Mr. Rowan's offer?" said Cherry.

"Everybody seems to say now that Rowan is ever so rich,"
said Augusta.

"I suppose papa doesn't like the feeling of being turned
out," said Martha.

"He wouldn't be turned out, my dear; not the least in the
world," said Mrs. Tappitt. "I don't choose to interfere much
myself because, perhaps, I don't understand it; but certainly I
should like your papa to retire. I have told him so; but gentlemen sometimes don't like to be told of things."

Mrs. Tappitt could be very severe to her husband, could say
to him terrible words if her spirit were put up, as she herself
was wont to say. But she understood that it did not become her
to speak ill of their father before her girls. Nor would she willingly have been heard by the servants to scold their master.
And though she said terrible things she said them with a conviction that they would not have any terrible effect. Tappitt
would only take them for what they were worth, and would
measure them by the standard which his old experience had
taught him to adopt. When a man has been long consuming
red pepper, it takes much red pepper to stimulate his palate.
Had Mrs. Tappitt merely advised her husband, in proper conjugal phraseology, to relinquish his trade and to retire to Tor-

quay, her advice, she knew, would have had no weight. She was eager on the subject, feeling convinced that this plan of retirement was for the good of the family generally, and therefore she had advocated it with energy. There may be those who think that a wife goes too far in threatening a husband with a commission of lunacy, and frightening him with a prospect of various fatal diseases; but the dose must be adapted to the constitution, and the palate that is accustomed to large quantities of red pepper must have quantities larger than usual whenever some special culinary effect is to be achieved. On the present occasion Mrs. Tappitt went on talking to the girls of their father in language that was quite eulogistic. No threat against the absent brewer passed her mouth,—or theirs. But they all understood each other, and were agreed that everything was to be done to induce papa to accept Mr. Rowan's offer.

"Then," said Cherry, "he'll marry Rachel Ray, and she'll be mistress of the brewery house."

"Never!" said Mrs. Tappitt, very solemnly. "Never! He'll never be such a fool as that."

"Never!" said Augusta. "Never!"

In the mean time the meeting went on at the Dragon. I can't say that Mr. Tappitt was on this occasion called upon to preside over the petition. He was simply invited to take the chair at a meeting of a dozen men at Baslehurst who were brought together by Mr. Sharpit in order that they might be induced by him to recommend Mr. Hart to employ him, Mr. Sharpit, in getting up the petition in question; and in order that there might be some sufficient temptation to these twelve men to gather themselves together, the dinner at the Dragon was added to the meeting. Mr. Tappitt took the chair in the big, uncarpeted, fusty room upstairs, in which masonic meetings were held once a month, and in which the farmers of the neighbourhood dined once a week, on market days. He took the chair and some seven or eight of his townsmen clustered round him. The others had sent word that they would manage to come in time for the dinner. Mr. Sharpit, before he put the brewer in his place of authority, prompted him as to what he was to do, and in the course of a quarter of an hour two resolutions, already prepared by Mr. Sharpit, had been passed unanimously. Mr. Hart was to be told by the assembled people of Baslehurst that he would certainly be seated by a scrutiny, and he was to be advised to commence his proceedings at once. These resolutions were duly committed to paper by one of Mr. Sharpit's clerks, and Mr. Tappitt, before he sat down to dinner, signed a letter to Mr. Hart on behalf of the electors of Baslehurst. When the work of the meeting was completed it still wanted half an hour to dinner, during which the nine electors of Baslehurst sauntered about the yard of the inn, looked into the stables, talked to the landlady at the bar, indulged themselves with gin and bitters, and found the time very heavy on their hands. They were nine decent-looking, middle-aged men, dressed in black not of the newest, in swallow-tailed coats and black trousers, with chimney-pot hats, and red faces; and as they pottered about the premises of the Dragon they seemed to be very little at their ease.

"What's up, Jim?" said one of the postboys to the ostler.

"Sharpit's got 'em all here to get some more money out of that ere Jew gent;—that's about the ticket," said the ostler.

"He's a clever un," said the postboy.

At last the dinner was ready; and the total number of the party having now completed itself, the Liberal electors of Baslehurst prepared to enjoy themselves. No bargain had been made on the subject, but it was understood by them all that they would not be asked to pay for their dinner. Sharpit would see to that. He would probably know how to put it into his little bill; and if he failed in that the risk was his own.

But while the body of the Liberal electors was peeping into the stables and drinking gin and bitters, Mr. Sharpit and Mr. Tappitt were engaged in a private conference.

"If you come to me," said Sharpit, "of course I must take it up. The etiquette of the profession don't allow me to decline."

"But why should you wish to decline?" said Tappitt, not altogether pleased by Mr. Sharpit's manner.

"Oh, by no means; no. It's just the sort of work I like;—not much to be made by it, but there's injury to be redressed and justice to be done. Only you see poor Honyman hasn't got much of a practice left to him, and I don't want to take his bread out of his mouth."

"But I'm not to be ruined because of that!"

"As I said before, if you bring the business to me I must take it up. I can't help myself, if I would. And if I do take it up I'll see you through it. Everybody who knows me knows that of me."

"I suppose I shall find you at home about ten to-morrow?"

"Yes; I'll be in my office at ten;—only you should think it well over, you know, Mr. Tappitt. I've nothing to say against Mr. Honyman,—not a word. You'll remember that, if you please, if there should be anything about it afterwards. Ah! you're wanted for the chair, Mr. Tappitt. I'll come and sit alongside of you, if you'll allow me."

The dinner itself was decidedly bad, and the company undoubtedly dull. I am inclined to think that every individual there would have dined more comfortably at home. A horrid mess concocted of old gravy, catsup, and bad wine was distributed under the name of soup. Then there came upon the table half a huge hake,—the very worst fish that swims, a fish with which Devonshire is peculiarly invested. Some hard dark brown mysterious balls were handed round, which on being opened with a knife were found to contain sausage-meat, very greasy and by no means cooked through. Even the *dura ilia* of the Liberal electors of Baslehurst declined to make acquaintance with these dainties. After that came the dinner, consisting of a piece of roast beef very raw, and a leg of parboiled mutton, absolutely blue in its state of rawness. When the gory mess was seen which displayed itself on the first incision made into these lumps of meat, the vice-president and one or two of his friends spoke out aloud. That hard and greasy sausage-meat might have been all right for anything they knew to the contrary, and the soup they had swallowed without complaint. But they did know what should be the state of a joint of meat when brought to the table, and therefore they spoke out in their anger. Tappitt himself said nothing that was intended to be carried beyond the waiter, seeing that beer from his own brewery was consumed in the tap of the Dragon; but the vice-president was a hardware dealer with whom the Dragon had but small connection of trade, and he sent terrible messages down to the landlady, threatening her with the Blue Boar, the Mitre, and even with that nasty little pot-house the Chequers. "What is it they expects for their three and sixpence?" said the landlady, in her wrath; for it must be understood that Sharpit knew well that he was dealing with one who understood the value of money, and that he did not feel quite sure of passing the dinner in Mr. Hart's bill. Then came a pie with crust an inch thick, which nobody could eat, and a cabinet pudding, so called, full of lumps of suet. I venture to assert that each Liberal elector there would have got a better dinner at home, and would have been served with greater comfort; but a public dinner at an inn is the recognized relaxation of a middle-class Englishman in the provinces. Did he not attend such banquets his neighbours would conceive him to be constrained by domestic tyranny. Others go to them, and therefore he goes also. He is bored frightfully by every speech to which he listens. He is driven to the lowest depths of dismay by every speech which he is called upon to make. He is thoroughly disgusted when he is called on to make no speech. He has no point of sympathy with the neighbours between whom he sits. The wine is bad. The hot water is brought to him cold. His seat is hard and crowded. No attempt is made at the pleasures of conversation. He is continually called upon to stand up that he may pretend to drink a toast in honour of some person or institution for which he cares nothing; for the hero of the evening, as to whom he is probably indifferent; for the church, which perhaps he never enters; the army, which he regards as a hotbed

of aristocratic insolence; or for the Queen, whom he reveres
and loves by reason of his nature as an Englishman, but against
whose fulsome praises as repeated to him ad nauseam in the
chairman's speech his very soul unconsciously revolts. It is all
a bore, trouble, ennui, nastiness, and discomfort. But yet he
goes again and again,—because it is the relaxation natural to
an Englishman. The Frenchman who sits for three hours tilted
on the hind legs of a little chair with his back against the
window-sill of the café, with first a cup of coffee before him
and then a glass of sugar and water, is perhaps as much to be
pitied as regards his immediate misery; but the liquids which
he imbibes are not so injurious to him.

Mr. Tappitt with the eleven other Liberal electors of Baslehurst went through the ceremony of their dinner in the usual
way. They drank the health of the Queen, and of the volun-
teers of the county because there was present a podgy little
grocer who had enrolled himself in the corps and who was thus
enabled to make a speech; and then they drank the health of
Mr. Hart, whose ultimate return for the borough they pledged
themselves to effect. Having done so much for business, and
having thus brought to a conclusion the political work of the
evening, they adjourned their meeting to a cosy little parlour
near the bar, and then they began to be happy. Some few of
the number, including the angry vice-president, who sold hardware, took themselves home to their wives. "Mrs. Tongs keeps
him sharp enough by the ears," said Sharpit, winking to Tappitt. "Come along, old fellow, and we'll get a drop of something really hot." Tappitt winked back again and shook his
head with an affected laugh; but as he did so he thought of
Mrs. T. at home, and the terrible words she had spoken to
him;—and at the same moment an idea came across him that
Mr. Sharpit was a very dangerous companion.

About half a dozen entered the cosy little parlour, and
there they remained for a couple of hours. While sitting in that
cosy little parlour they really did enjoy themselves. About nine
o'clock they had a bit of the raw beef broiled, and in that

guise it was pleasant enough; and the water was hot, and the
tobacco was grateful and the stiffness of the evening was gone.
The men chatted together and made no more speeches, and
they talked of matters which bore a true interest to them.
Sharpit explained to them how each man might be assisted in
his own business if this rich London tailor could be brought in
for the borough. And by degrees they came round to the affairs of the brewery, and Tappitt, as the brandy warmed him,
spoke loudly against Rowan.

"By George!" said the podgy grocer, "if anybody would offer me a thousand a year to give up, I'd take it hopping."

"Then I wouldn't," said Tappitt, "and what's more, I won't.
But brewing ain't like other businesses;—there's more in it
than in most others."

"Of course there is," said Sharpit; "it isn't like any common
trade."

"That's true too," said the podgy grocer.

A man usually receives some compensation for having gone
through the penance of the chairman's duties. For the remainder of the evening he is entitled to the flattery of his companions, and generally receives it till they become tipsy and
insubordinate. Tappitt had not the character of an intemperate
man, but on this occasion he did exceed the bounds of a becoming moderation. The room was hot and the tobacco smoke
was thick. The wine had been bad and the brandy was strong.
Sharpit, too, urged him to new mixtures and stronger denunci-
ations against Rowan, till at last, at eleven o'clock, when he
took himself to the brewery, he was not in a condition proper
for the father of such daughters or for the husband of such a
wife.

"Shall I see him home?" said the podgy grocer to Mr.
Sharpit.

Tappitt, with the suspicious quickness of a drunken man,
turned sharply upon the podgy and abashed grocer, and abused
him for his insolence. He then made his way out of the inn-
yard, and along the High Street, and down Brewery Lane to

his own door, knowing the way as well as though he had been sober, and passing over it as quickly. Nor did he fall or even stumble, though now and again he reeled slightly. And as he went the idea came strongly upon him that Sharpit was a dangerous man, and that perhaps at this very moment he, Tappitt, was standing on the brink of a precipice. Then he remembered that his wife would surely be watching for him, and as he made his first attempt to insert the latch-key into the door his heart became forgetful of the brandy, and sank low within his breast.

How affairs went between him and Mrs. Tappitt on that night I will not attempt to describe. That she used her power with generosity I do not doubt. That she used it with discretion I am quite convinced. On the following morning at ten o'clock Tappitt was still in bed; but a note had been written by Mrs. T. to Messrs. Sharpit and Longfite, saying that the projected visit had, under altered circumstances, become unnecessary. That Tappitt's head was racked with pain, and his stomach disturbed with sickness, there can be no doubt, and as little that Mrs. T. used the consequent weakness of her husband for purposes of feminine dominion; but this she did with discretion and even with kindness. Only a word or two was said as to the state in which he had returned home,—a word or two with the simple object of putting that dominion on a firm basis. After that Mrs. Tappitt took his condition as an established fact, administered to him the comforts of her medicine-chest and teapot, excused his illness to the girls as having been produced by the fish, and never left his bedside till she had achieved her purpose. If ever a man got tipsy to his own advantage, Mr. Tappitt did so on that occasion. And if ever a man in that condition was treated with forbearing kindness by his wife, Mr. Tappitt was so treated then.

"Don't disturb yourself, T.," she said; "there's nothing wants doing in the brewery, and if it did what would it signify in comparison with your health? The brewery won't be much to you now, thank goodness; and I'm sure you've had enough of

it. Thirty years of such work as that would make any man sick
and weak. I'm sure I don't wonder at your being ill;—not the
least. The wonder is that you've ever stood up against it so
long as you have. If you'll take my advice you'll just turn
round and try to sleep for an hour or so."

Tappitt took her advice at any rate, so far that he turned
round and closed his eyes. Up to this time he had not given
way about the brewery. He had uttered no word of assent. But
he was gradually becoming aware that he would have to yield
before he would be allowed to put on his clothes. And now, in
the base and weak condition of his head and stomach, yielding did not seem to him to be so very bad a thing. After all, the
brewery was troublesome, the fight was harassing. Rowan was
young and strong, and Mr. Sharpit was very dangerous. Rowan,
too, had risen in his estimation as in that of others, and he
could not longer argue, even to himself, that the stipulated income would not be paid. He did not sleep, but got into that
half-drowsy state in which men think of their existing affairs,
but without any power of active thought. He knew that he
ought to be in his counting-house and at work. He half feared
that the world was falling away from him because he was not
there. He was ashamed of himself, and sometimes almost entertained a thought of rising up and shaking off his lethargy.
But his stomach was bad, and he could not bring himself to
move. His head was tormented, and his pillow was soft; and
therefore there he lay. He wondered what was the time of day,
but did not think of looking at his watch which was under his
head. He heard his wife's steps about the room as she shaded
some window from his eyes, or crept to the door to give some
household order to one of her girls outside; but he did not
speak to her, nor she to him. She did not speak to him as long
as he lay there motionless, and when he moved with a small
low groan she merely offered him some beef tea.

It was nearly six o' clock, and the hour of dinner at the
brewery was long passed, when Mrs. Tappitt sat herself down
by the bedside determined to reap the fruit of her victory. He

had just raised himself in his bed and announced his intention of getting up,—declaring, as he did so, that he would never again eat any of that accursed fish. The moment of his renovation had come upon him, and Mrs. Tappitt perceived that if he escaped from her now, there might even yet be more trouble.

"It wasn't only the fish, T.," she said, with somewhat of sternness in her eye.

"I hardly drank anything," said Tappitt.

"Of course I wasn't there to see what you took," said she; "but you were very bad when you came home last night;—very bad indeed. You couldn't have got in at the door only for me."

"That's nonsense."

"But it is quite true. It's a mercy, T., that neither of the girls saw you. Only think! But there'll be nothing more of that kind, I'm sure, when we are out of this horrid place; and it wouldn't have happened now, only for all this trouble."

To this Tappitt made no answer, but he grunted, and again said that he thought he would get up.

"Of course it's settled now, T., that we're to leave this place."

"I don't know that at all."

"Then, T., you ought to know it. Come now; just look at the common sense of the thing. If we don't give up the brewery what are we to do? There isn't a decent respectable person in the town in favour of our staying here, only that rascal Sharpit. You desired me this morning to write and tell him you'd have nothing more to do with him; and so I did." Tappitt had not seen his wife's letter to the lawyer,—had not asked to see it, and now became aware that his only possible supporter might probably have been driven away from him. Sharpit too, though dangerous as an enemy, was ten times more dangerous as a friend!

"Of course you'll take that young man's offer. Shall I sit down and write a line to Honyman, and tell him to come in the morning?"

Tappitt groaned again and again, said that he would get up, but Mrs. T. would not let him out of bed till he had assented to her proposition that Honyman should be again invited to the brewery. He knew well that the battle was gone from him,—had in truth known it through all those half-comatose hours of his bedridden day. But a man, or a nation, when yielding must still resist even in yielding. Tappitt fumed and fussed under the clothes, protesting that his sending for Honyman would be useless. But the letter was written in his name and sent with his knowledge; and it was perfectly understood that that invitation to Honyman signified an unconditional surrender on the part of Mr. Tappitt. One word Mrs. T. said as she allowed her husband to escape from his prison amidst the blankets, one word by which to mark that the thing was done, and one word only. "I suppose we needn't leave the house for about a month or so,—because it would be inconvenient about the furniture."

"Who's to turn you out if you stay for six months?" said Tappit.

The thing was marked enough then, and Mrs. Tappitt retired in muffled triumph,—retired when she had made all things easy for the simplest ceremony of dressing.

"Just sponge your face, my dear," she said, "and put on your dressing-gown, and come down for half an hour or so."

"I'm all right now," said Tappitt.

"Oh! quite so;—but I wouldn't go to the trouble of much dressing." Then she left him, descended the stairs, and entered the parlour among her daughters. When there she could not abstain from one blast of the trumpet of triumph. "Well, girls," she said, "it's all settled, and we shall be in Torquay now before the winter."

"No!" said Augusta.

"That'll be a great change," said Martha.

"In Torquay before the winter!" said Cherry. "Oh, mamma, how clever you have been!"

"And now your papa is coming down, and you should thank

him for what he's doing for you. It's all for your sake that he's doing it."

Mr. Tappitt crept into the room, and when he had taken his seat in his accustomed arm-chair, the girls went up to him and kissed him. Then they thanked him for his proposed kindness in taking them out of the brewery.

"Oh, papa, it is so jolly!" said Cherry.

Mr. Tappitt did not say much in answer to this;—but luckily there was no necessity that he should say anything. It was an occasion on which silence was understood as giving a perfect consent.

CHAPTER XXVIII

What Took Place at Bragg's End Farm

WHEN MRS. TAPPITT had settled within her own mind that the brewery should be abandoned to Rowan, she was by no means, therefore, ready to assent that Rachel Ray should become the mistress of the brewery house. "Never," she had exclaimed when Cherry had suggested such a result; "never!" And Augusta had echoed the protestation, "Never, never!" I will not say that she would have allowed her husband to remain in his business in order that she might thus exclude Rachel from such promotion, but she could not bring herself to believe that Luke Rowan would be so fatuous, so ignorant of his own interests, so deluded, as to marry that girl from Bragg's End! It is thus that the Mrs. Tappitts of the world regard other women's daughters when they have undergone any disappointment as to their own. She had no reason for wishing well to Rowan, and would not have cared if he had taken to his bosom a harpy in marriage; but she could not endure to hear of the success of the girl whose attractions had foiled her own little plan. "I don't believe that the man can ever be such a fool as that!" she

said again to Augusta, when on the evening of the day following Tappitt's abdication, a rumour reached the brewery that
Luke Rowan had been seen walking out upon the Cawston
road.

Mr. Honyman, in accordance with his instructions, called at
the brewery on that morning, and was received by Mr. Tappitt with a sullen and almost savage submission. Mrs. T. had
endeavoured to catch him first, but in that she had failed; she
did, however, manage to see the attorney as he came out from
her husband.

"It's all settled," said Honyman; "and I'll see Rowan myself
before half an hour is over."

"I'm sure it's a great blessing, Mr. Honyman," said the lady,
—not on that occasion assuming any of the glory to herself.

"It was the only thing for him," said Mr. Honyman;—"that
is if he didn't like to take the young man in as acting partner."

"That wouldn't have done at all," said Mrs. T. And then the
lawyer went his way.

In the mean time Tappitt sat sullen and wretched in the
counting-house. Such moments occur in the lives of most of us,
—moments in which the real work of life is brought to an end,
—and they cannot but be sad. It is very well to talk of ease and
dignity; but ease of spirit comes from action only, and the
world's dignity is given to those who do the world's work. Let
no man put his neck from out of the collar till in truth he can
no longer draw the weight attached to it. Tappitt had now got
rid of his collar, and he sat very wretched in his brewery
counting-house.

"Be I to go, sir?"

Tappitt in his meditation was interrupted by these words,
spoken not in a rough voice, and looking up he saw Worts
standing in the counting-house before him. Worts had voted
for Butler Cornbury, whereas, had he voted for Mr. Hart, Mr.
Hart would have been returned; and, upon that, Worts, as a
rebellious subject, had received notice to quit the premises.
Now his time was out, and he came to ask whether he was to

leave the scene of his forty years of work. But what would be the use of sending Worts away even if the wish to punish his contumacy still remained? In another week Worts would be brought back again in triumph, and would tread those brewery floors with the step almost of a master, while he, Tappitt, could tread them only as a stranger, if he were allowed to tread them at all.

"You can stay if you like," said Tappitt, hardly looking up at the man.

"I know you be a going, Mr. Tappitt," said the man; "and I hear you be a going very handsome like. Gentlefolk such as yeu needn't go on working allays like uz. If so be yeu be a going, Mr. Tappitt, I hope yeu and me'll part friendly. We've been together a sight o' years;—too great a sight for uz to part unfriendly."

Mr. Tappitt admitted the argument, shook hands with the man, and then of course took him into his immediate confidence with more warmth than he would have done had there been no quarrel between them. And I think he found some comfort in this. He walked about the premises with Worts, telling him much that was true, and some few things that were not strictly accurate. For instance, he said that he had made up his mind to leave the place, whereas that action of decisive resolution which we call making up our minds had perhaps been done by Mrs. Tappitt rather than by him. But Worts took all these assertions with an air of absolute belief which comforted the brewer. Worts was very wise in his discretion on that day, and threw much oil on the troubled waters; so that Tappitt when he left him bade God bless him, and expressed a hope that the old place might still thrive for his sake.

"And for your'n too, master," said Worts, "for yeu'll allays have the best egg still. The young master, he'll only be a working for yeu."

There was comfort in this thought; and Tappitt, when he went into his dinner, was able to carry himself like a man.

The tidings which had reached Mrs. Tappitt as to Rowan having been seen on that evening walking on the Cawston road with his face towards Bragg's End were true. On that morning Mr. Honyman had come to him, and his career in life was at once settled for him.

"Mr. Tappitt is quite in time, Mr. Honyman," he had said. "But he would not have been in time this day week unless he had consented to pay for what work had been already done; for I had determined to begin at once."

"The truth is, Mr. Rowan, you step into an uncommon good thing; but Mr. Tappitt is tired of the work, and glad to give it up."

Thus the matter was arranged between them, and before nightfall everybody in Baslehurst knew that Tappitt and Rowan had come to terms, and that Tappitt was to retire upon a pension. There was some little discrepancy as to the amount of Tappitt's annuity, the Liberal faction asserting that he was to receive two thousand a year, and those of the other side cutting him down to two hundred.

On the evening of that day—in the cool of the evening—Luke Rowan sauntered down the High Street of Baslehurst, and crossed over Cawston bridge. On the bridge he was all alone, and he stood there for a moment or two leaning upon the parapet looking down upon the little stream beneath the arch. During the day many things had occupied him, and he had hardly as yet made up his mind definitely as to what he would do and what he would say during the hours of the evening. From the moment in which Honyman had announced to him Tappitt's intended resignation he became aware that he certainly should go out to Bragg's End before that day was over. It had been with him a settled thing, a thing settled almost without thought ever since the receipt of Rachel's letter, that he would take this walk to Bragg's End when he should have put his affairs at Baslehurst on some stable footing; but that he would not take that walk before he had so done.

"They say," Rachel had written in her letter, "they say that as the business here about the brewery is so very unsettled, they think it probable that you will not have to come back to Baslehurst any more."

In that had been the offence. They had doubted his stability, and, beyond that, had almost doubted his honesty. He would punish them by taking them at their word till both should be put beyond all question. He knew well that the punishment would fall on Rachel, whereas none of the sin would have been Rachel's sin; but he would not allow himself to be deterred by that consideration.

"It is her letter," he said to himself, "and in that way will I answer her. When I do go there again they will all understand me better."

It had been, too, a matter of pride to him that Mr. Comfort and Mrs. Butler Cornbury should thus be made to understand him. He would say nothing of himself and his own purposes to any of them. He would speak neither of his own means nor his own stedfastness. But he would prove to them that he was stedfast, and that he had boasted of nothing which he did not possess. When Mrs. Butler Cornbury had spoken to him down by the Cleeves, asking him of his purpose, and struggling to do a kind thing by Rachel, he had resolved at once that he would tell her nothing. She should find him out. He liked her for loving Rachel; but neither to her, nor even to Rachel herself, would he say more till he could show them that the business about the brewery was no longer unsettled.

But up to this moment—this moment in which he was standing on the bridge, he had not determined what he would say to Rachel or to Rachel's mother. He had never relaxed in his purpose of making Rachel his wife since his first visit to the cottage. He was one who, having a fixed resolve, feels certain of their ultimate success in achieving it. He was now going to Bragg's End to claim that which he regarded as his own; but he had not as yet told himself in what terms he would put forward his claim. So he stood upon the bridge thinking.

He stood upon the bridge thinking, but his thoughts would

only go backwards, and would do nothing for him as to his future conduct. He remembered his first walk with her, and the churchyard elms with the setting sun, and the hot dances in Mrs. Tappitt's house; and he remembered them without much of the triumph of a successful lover. It had been very sweet, but very easy. In so saying to himself he by no means threw blame upon Rachel. Things were easy, he thought, and it was almost a pity that they should be so. As for Rachel, nothing could have been more honest or more to his taste, than her mode of learning to love him. A girl who, while intending to accept him, could yet have feigned indifference, would have disgusted him at once. Nevertheless he could not but wish that there had been some castles for him to storm in his career. Tappitt had made but poor pretence of fighting before he surrendered; and as to Rachel, it had not been in Rachel's nature to make any pretence. He passed from the bridge at last without determining what he would say when he reached the cottage, but he did not pass on till he had been seen by the scrutinizing eyes of Miss Pucker.

"If there ain't young Rowan going out to Bragg's End again!" she said to herself, comforting herself, I fear, or striving to comfort herself, with an inward assertion that he was not going there for any good. Striving to comfort herself, but not effectually; for though the assertion was made by herself to herself, yet it was not believed. Though she declared, with well-pronounced mental words, that Luke Rowan was going on that path for no good purpose, she felt a wretched conviction at her heart's core that Rachel Ray would be made to triumph over her and her early suspicions by a happy marriage. Nevertheless she carried the tidings up into Baslehurst, and as she repeated it to the grocers' daughters and the bakers' wives she shook her head with as much apparent satisfaction as though she really believed that Rachel oscillated between a ruined name and a broken heart.

He walked on very slowly towards Bragg's End, as though he almost dreaded the interview, swinging his stick as was his

custom, and keeping his feet on the grassy edges of the road till
he came to the turn which brought him on to the green. When
on the green he did not take the highway, but skirted along
under Farmer Sturt's hedge, so that he had to pass by the entrance of the farmyard before he crossed over to the cottage.
Here, just inside her own gate, he encountered Mrs. Sturt
standing alone. She had been intent on the cares of her poultry-
yard till she had espied Luke Rowan; but then she had forgotten chickens and ducks and all, and had given herself up to
thoughts of Rachel's happiness in having her lover back again.

"It's he as sure as eggs," she had said to herself when she
first saw him; "how mortal slow he do walk, to be sure! If he
was coming as joe to me I'd soon shake him into quicker steps
than them."

"Oh, Mrs. Sturt!" said he, "I hope you're quite well," and he
stopped short at her gate.

"Pretty bobbish, thankee, Mr. Rowan; and how's yourself?
Are you going over to the cottage this evening?"

"Who's at home there, Mrs. Sturt?"

"Well, they're all at home; Mrs. Ray, and Rachel, and Mrs.
Prime. I doubt whether you know the eldest daughter, Mr.
Rowan?"

Luke did not know Mrs. Prime, and by no means wished to
spend any of the hours of the present evening in making her
acquaintance.

"Is Mrs. Prime there?" he asked.

" 'Deed she is, Mr. Rowan. She's come back these last two
days."

Thereupon Rowan paused for a moment, having carefully
placed himself inside the gate-posts of the farmyard so that
he might not be seen by the inmates of the cottage, if haply he
had hitherto escaped their eyes.

"Mrs. Sturt," said he, "I wonder whether you'd do me a
great favour."

"That depends—" said Mrs. Sturt. "If it's to do any good to
any of them over there, I will."

"If I wanted to do harm to any of them I shouldn't come to you."

"Well, I should hope not. Is she and you going to be one, Mr. Rowan? That's about the whole of it."

"It shan't be my fault if we're not," said Rowan.

"That's spoken honest," said the lady; "and now I'll do anything in my power to bring you together. If you'll just go into my little parlor, I'll bring her to you in five seconds; I will indeed, Mr. Rowan. You won't mind going through the kitchen for once, will you?"

Luke did not mind going through the kitchen, and immediately found himself shut up in Mrs. Sturt's back parlour, looking out among the mingled roses and cabbages.

Mrs. Sturt walked quickly across the road to the cottage door, and went at once to the open window of the sitting-room. Mrs. Ray was there with a book in her hand,—a serious book, the perusal of which I fear was in some degree due to the presence of her elder daughter; and Mrs. Prime was there with another book, evidently very serious; and Rachel was there too, seated on the sofa, deeply buried in the manipulation of a dress belonging to her mother. Mrs. Sturt was sure at once that they had not seen Luke Rowan as he passed inside the farmyard gate, and that they did not suspect that he was near them.

"Oh, Mrs. Sturt, is that you?" said the widow, looking up. "You'll just come in for a minute, won't you?" and Mrs. Ray showed by a suppressed yawn that her attention had not been deeply fixed by that serious book. Rachel looked up, and bade the visitor welcome with a little nod; but it was not a cheery nod as it would have been in old days, before her sorrow had come upon her.

"I'll have the cherries back in her cheeks before the evening's over," said Mrs. Sturt to herself, as she looked at the pale-faced girl. Mrs. Prime also made some little salutation to their neighbour; but she did so with the very smallest expenditure of thoughts or moments. Mrs. Sturt was all very well, but

Mrs. Prime had greater work on hand than gossiping with Mrs. Sturt.

"I'll not just come in, thankee, Mrs. Ray; but if it ain't troubling you I want to speak a word to you outside; and a word to Rachel too, if she don't mind coming."

"A word to me!" said Rachel getting up and putting down her dress. Her thoughts now-a-days were always fixed on the same subject, and it seemed that any special word to her must have reference to that. Mrs. Ray also got up, leaving her mark in her book. Mrs. Prime went on reading, harder than ever. There was to be some conference of importance from which she could not but feel herself to be excluded in a very special way. Something wicked was surely to be proposed, or she would have been allowed to hear it. She said nothing, but her head was almost shaken by the vehemence with which she read the book in her lap.

Mrs. Sturt retired beyond the precincts of the widow's front garden before she said a word. Rachel had followed her first through the gate, and Mrs. Ray came after with her apron turned over her head. "What is it, Mrs. Sturt?" said Rachel. "Have you heard anything?"

"Heard anything? Well; I'm always a hearing of something. Do you slip across the green while I speak just one word to your mother. And Rachel, wait for me at the gate. Mrs. Ray, he's in my little parlour."

"Who? not Luke Rowan?"

"But he is though; that very young man! He's come over to make it up with her. He's told me so with his own mouth. You may be as sure of it as—as—as anything. You leave 'em to me, Mrs. Ray; I wouldn't bring them together if it wasn't for good. It's my belief our pet would a' died if he hadn't come back to her;—it is then." And Mrs. Sturt put her apron up to her eyes.

Rachel having paused for a moment, as she looked first at her mother and then at Mrs. Sturt, had done as she was bidden, and had walked quickly across the green. Mrs. Ray, when she heard her neighbour's tidings, stood fixed by dismay and dread, mingled with joy. She had longed for his coming back; but now that he was there, close upon them, intending to do all that she had wished him to do, she was half afraid of him! After all was he not a young man; and might he not, even yet, be a wolf? She was horrorstricken at the idea of sending Rachel over to see a lover, and looked back at the cottage window, towards Mrs. Prime, as though to see whether she was being watched in her iniquity. "Oh, Mrs. Sturt!" she said, "why didn't you give us time to think about it?"

"Give you time! How could I give you time, and he here on the spot? There's been too much time to my thinking. When young folk are agreeable and the old folk are agreeable too, there can't be too little time. Come along over and we'll talk of it in the kitchen while they talks in the parlour. He'd a' been in there among you all only for Mrs. Prime. She is so dour like for a young man to have to say anything before her, of the likes of that. That's why I took him into our place."

They overtook Rachel at the house door and they all went through together into the great kitchen. "Oh, Rachel!" said Mrs. Ray. "Oh, dear!"

"What is it, mamma?" said Rachel. Then looking into her mother's face, she guessed the truth. "Mamma," she said, "he's here! Mr. Rowan is here!" And she took hold of her mother's arm, as though to support herself.

"And that's just the truth," said Mrs. Sturt, triumphantly. "He's through there in the little parlour, and you must just go to him, my dear, and hear what he's got to say to you."

"Oh, mamma!" said Rachel.

"I suppose you must do what she tells you," said Mrs. Ray.

"Of course she must," said Mrs. Sturt.

"Mamma, you must go to him," said Rachel.

"That won't do at all," said Mrs. Sturt.

"And why has he come here?" said Rachel.

"Ah! I wonder why," said Mrs. Sturt. "I wonder why any young man should come on such an errand! But it won't do to leave him there standing in my parlour by himself, so do you come along with me."

So saying Mrs. Sturt took Rachel by the arm to lead her away. Mrs. Ray in this great emergency was perfectly helpless. She could simply look at her daughter with imploring, loving eyes, and stand quivering in doubt against the dresser. Mrs. Sturt had very decided views on the matter. She had put Luke Rowan into the parlour with a promise that she would bring Rachel to him there, and she was not going to break her word through any mock delicacy. The two young people liked one another, and they should have this opportunity of saying so in each other's hearing. So she took Rachel by the arm, and opening the door of the parlour led her into the room. "Mr. Rowan," she said, "when you and Miss Rachel have had your say out, you'll find me and her mamma in the kitchen." Then she closed the door and left them alone.

Rachel, when first summoned out of the cottage, had felt at once that Mrs. Sturt's visit must have reference to Luke Rowan. Indeed everything with her in her present moods had some reference to him,—some reference though it might be ever so remote. But now before she had time to form a thought, she was told that he was there in the same house with her, and that she was taken to him in order that she might hear his words and speak her own. It was very sudden; and for the space of a few moments she would have fled away from Mrs. Sturt's kitchen had such flight been possible. Since Rowan had gone from her there had been times in which she would have fled to him, in which she would have journeyed alone any distance so that she might tell him of her love, and ask whether she had got any right to hope for his. But all that seemed to be changed. Though her mother was there with her and her friend, she feared that this seeking of her lover was hardly maidenly. Should he not have come to her,—every foot of the way to her feet, and there have spoken if he had aught to say, before she had been called on to make any sign? Would he like her for thus going to him? But then she had no chance of escape. She found herself in Mrs. Sturt's kitchen under her mother's sanction, before she had been able to form any purpose; and then an idea did come to her, even at that moment, that poor Luke would have had a hard task of it in her sister's presence. When she was first told that he was there in the farmhouse parlour, her courage left her and she dreaded the encounter; but she was able to collect her thoughts as she passed out of the kitchen, and across the passage, and when she followed Mrs. Sturt into the room she had again acquired the power to carry herself as a woman having a soul of her own.

"Rachel!" Rowan said, stepping up to her and tendering his hand to her. "I have come to answer your letter in person."

"I knew," she said, "when I wrote it, that my letter did not deserve any answer. I did not expect an answer."

"But am I wrong now to bring you one in person? I have thought so much of seeing you again! Will you not say a word of welcome to me?"

"I am glad to see you, Mr. Rowan."

"Mr. Rowan! Nay; if it is to be Mr. Rowan I may as well go back to Baslehurst. It has come to that, that it must be Luke now, or there must be no naming of names between us. You chided me once when I called you Rachel."

"You called me so once, sir, when I should have chided you and did not. I remember it well. You were very wrong, and I was very foolish."

"But I may call you Rachel now?" Then, when she did not answer him at the moment, he asked the question again in that imperious way which was common with him. "May I not call you now as I please? If it be not so my coming here is useless. Come, Rachel, say one word to me boldly. Do you love me well enough to be my wife?"

She was standing at the open window, looking away from him, while he remained at a little distance from her as though he would not come close to her till he had exacted from her some positive assurance of her love as a penance for the fault committed by her letter. He certainly was not a soft lover, nor by any means inclined to abate his own privileges. He paused a moment as though he thought that his last question must elicit a plain reply. But no reply to it came. She still looked away from him through the window, as though resolved that she would not speak till his mood should have become more tender.

"You said something in your letter," he continued, "about my affairs here in Baslehurst being unsettled. I would not show myself here again till that matter was arranged."

"It was not I," she said, turning sharply round upon him. "It was not I who thought that."

"It was in your letter, Rachel."

"Do you know so little of a girl like me as to suppose that what was written there came from me, myself? Did I not tell you that I said what I was told to say? Did I not explain to you that mamma had gone to Mr. Comfort? Did you not know that all that had come from him?"

"I only know that I read it in your letter to me,—the only letter you had ever written to me."

"You are unfair to me, Mr. Rowan. You know that you are unfair."

"Call me Luke," he said. "Call me by my own name."

"Luke," she said, "you are unfair to me."

"Then by heavens it shall be for the last time. May things in this world and the next go well with me as I am fair to you for the future!" So saying he came up close to her, and took her at once in his arms.

"Luke, Luke; don't. You frighten me; indeed you do."

"You shall give me a fair open kiss, honestly, before I leave you,—in truth you shall. If you love me, and wish to be my wife, and intend me to understand that you and I are now pledged to each other beyond the power of any person to separate us by his advice, or any mother by her fears, give me a bold, honest kiss, and I will understand that it means all that."

Still she hesitated for a moment, turning her face away from him while he held her by the waist. She hesitated while she was weighing the meaning of his words, and taking them home to herself as her own. Then she turned her neck towards him, still holding back her head till her face was immediately under his own, and after another moment's pause she gave him her pledge as he had asked it. Mrs. Sturt's words had come true, and the cherries had returned to her cheek.

"My own Rachel! And now tell me one thing: are you happy?"

"So happy!"

"My own one!"

"But, Luke,—I have been wretched;—so wretched! I thought you would never come back to me."

"And did that make you wretched?"

"Ah!—did it? What do you think yourself? When I wrote that letter to you I knew I had no right to expect that you would think of me again."

"But how could I help thinking of you when I loved you?"

"And then when mamma saw you in Exeter, and you sent me no word of message!"

"I was determined to send none till this business was finished."

"Ah! that was cruel. But you did not understand. I suppose no man can understand. I couldn't have believed it myself till —till after you had gone away. It seemed as though all the sun had deserted us, and that everything was cold and dark."

They stood at the open window looking out upon the roses and cabbages till the patience of Mrs. Sturt and of Mrs. Ray was exhausted. What they said, beyond so much of their words as I have repeated, need not be told. But when a low half-abashed knock at the door interrupted them, Luke thought that they had hardly been there long enough to settle the preliminaries of the affair which had brought him to Bragg's End.

"May we come in?" said Mrs. Sturt very timidly.

"Oh, mamma, mamma!" said Rachel, and she hid her face upon her mother's shoulder.

CHAPTER XXIX

Mrs. Prime Reads Her Recantation

ABOVE AN HOUR had passed after the interruption mentioned at the end of the last chapter before Mrs. Ray and Rachel crossed back from the farmhouse to the cottage, and when they went they went alone. During that hour they had been sitting in Mrs. Sturt's parlour; and when at last they got up to go they did not press Luke Rowan to go with them. Mrs. Prime was at the cottage, and it was necessary that everything should be explained to her before she was asked to give her hand to her future brother-in-law. The farmer had come in and had joked his joke, and Mrs. Sturt had clacked over them as though they were a brood of chickens of her own hatching; and Mrs. Ray had smiled and cried, and sobbed and laughed till she had become almost hysterical. Then she had jumped up from her seat, saying, "Oh, dear, what will Dorothea think has become of us?" After that Rachel insisted upon going, and the mother and daughter returned across the green, leaving Luke at the farm-house, ready to take his departure as soon as Mrs. Ray and Rachel should have safely reached their home.

"I knew thee was minded stedfast to take her," said Mrs. Sturt, "when it came out upon the newspaper how thou hadst told them all in Baslehurst that thou wouldst wed none but a Baslehurst lass."

In answer to this Luke protested that he had not thought of Rachel when he was making that speech, and tried to explain that all that was "soft sawder" as he called it, for the election. But the words were too apposite to the event, and the sentiment too much in accordance with Mrs. Sturt's chivalric views to allow of her admitting the truth of any such assurance as this.

"I know," she said; "I know. And when I read them words

in the newspaper I said to the gudeman there, we shall have bridecake from the cottage now before Christmas."

"For the matter of that, so you shall," said Luke, shaking hands with her as he went, "or the fault will not be mine."

Rachel, as she followed her mother out from the farmyard gate, had not a word to say. Could it have been possible she would have wished to remain silent for the remainder of the evening and for the night, so that she might have time to think of this thing which she had done, and to enjoy the full measure of her happiness. Hitherto she had hardly had any joy in her love. The cup had been hardly given to her to drink before it had been again snatched away, and since then she had been left to think that the draught for which she longed would never again be offered to her lips. The whole affair had now been managed so suddenly, and the action had been so quick, that she had hardly found a moment for thought. Could it be that things were so fixed that there was no room for further disappointment? She had been scalded so cruelly that she still feared the hot water. Her heart was sore with the old hurt, as the head that has ached will be still sore when the actual malady has passed away. She longed for hours of absolute quiet, in which she might make herself sure that her malady had also passed away, and that the soreness which remained came only from the memory of former pain. But there was no such perfect rest within her reach as yet.

"Will you tell her or shall I?" said Mrs. Ray, pausing for a moment at the cottage gate.

"You had better tell her, mamma."

"I suppose she won't set herself against it; will she?"

"I hope not, mamma. I shall think her very ill-natured if she does. But it can't make any real difference now, you know."

"No; it can't make any difference. Only it will be so uncomfortable."

Then with half-frightened, muffled steps they entered their own house, and joined Mrs. Prime in the sitting-room.

Mrs. Prime was still reading the serious book; but I am bound to say that her mind had not been wholly intent upon it during the long absence of her mother and sister. She had struggled for a time to ignore the slight fact that her companions were away gossiping with the neighbouring farmer's wife; she had made a hard fight with her book, pinning her eyes down upon the page over and over again, as though in pinning down her eyes she could pin down her mind also. But by degrees the delay became so long that she was tantalized into surmises as to the subject of their conversation. If it were not wicked, why should not she have been allowed to share it? She did not imagine it to be wicked according to the world's ordinary wickedness;—but she feared that it was wicked according to that tone of morals to which she was desirous of tying her mother down as a bond slave. They were away talking about love and pleasure, and those heart-throbbings in which her sister had so unfortunately been allowed to indulge. She felt all but sure that some tidings of Luke Rowan had been brought in Mrs. Sturt's budget of news, and she had never been able to think well of Luke Rowan since the evening on which she had seen him standing with Rachel in the churchyard. She knew nothing against him; but she had then made up her mind that he was pernicious, and she could not bring herself to own that she had been wrong in that opinion. She had been loud and defiant in her denunciation when she had first suspected Rachel of having a lover. Since that she had undergone some troubles of her own by which the tone of her remonstrances had been necessarily moderated; but even now she could not forgive her sister such a lover as Luke Rowan. She would have been quite willing to see her sister married, but the lover should have been dingy, black-coated, lugubrious, having about him some true essence of the tears of the valley of tribulation. Alas, her sister's taste was quite of another kind!

"I'm afraid you will have been thinking that we were never coming back again," said Mrs. Ray, as she entered the room.

"No, mother, I didn't think that. But I thought you were staying late with Mrs. Sturt."

"So we were,—and really I didn't think we had been so long. But, Dorothea, there was some one else over there besides Mrs. Sturt, and he kept us."

"He! What he?" said Mrs. Prime. She had not even suspected that the lover had been over there in person.

"Mr. Rowan, my dear. He has been at the farm."

"What! the young man that was dismissed from Mr. Tappitt's?"

It was ill said of her,—very ill said, and so she was herself aware as soon as the words were out of her mouth. But she could not help it. She had taken a side against Luke Rowan, and could not restrain herself from ill-natured words. Rachel was still standing in the middle of the room when she heard her lover thus described; but she would not condescend to plead in answer to such a charge. The colour came to her cheeks, and she threw up her head with a gesture of angry pride, but at the moment she said nothing. Mrs. Ray spoke.

"It seems to me, Dorothea," she said, "that you are mistaken there. I think he has dismissed Mr. Tappitt."

"I don't know much about it," said Mrs. Prime; "I only know that they've quarrelled."

"But it would be well that you should learn, because I'm sure you will be glad to think as well of your brother-in-law as possible."

"Do you mean that he is engaged to marry Rachel?"

"Yes, Dorothea. I think we may say that it is all settled now; —mayn't we, Rachel? And a very excellent young man he is,— and as for being well off, a great deal better than what a child of mine could have expected. And a fine comely fellow he is, as a woman's eye would wish to rest on."

"Beauty is but skin deep," said Mrs. Prime, with no little indignation in her tone, that a thing so vile as personal comeliness should have been mentioned by her mother on such an occasion.

"When he came out here and drank tea with us that evening," continued Mrs. Ray, "I took a liking to him most unaccountable, unless it was that I had a foreshadowing that he was going to be so near and dear to me."

"Mother, there can have been nothing of the kind. You should not say such things. The Lord in his providence allows us no foreshadowing of that kind."

"At any rate I liked him very much; didn't I, Rachel?—from the first moment I set eyes on him. Only I don't think he'll ever do away with cider in Devonshire, because of the apple trees. But if people are to drink beer it stands to reason that good beer will be better than bad."

All this time Rachel had not spoken a word, nor had her sister uttered anything expressive of congratulation or good wishes. Now, as Mrs. Ray ceased, there came a silence in the room, and it was incumbent on the elder sister to break it.

"If this matter is settled, Rachel——"

"It is settled,—I think," said Rachel.

"If it is settled I hope that it may be for your lasting happiness and eternal welfare."

"I hope it will," said Rachel.

"Marriage is a most important step."

"That's quite true, my dear," said Mrs. Ray.

"A most important step, and one that requires the most exact circumspection,—especially on the part of the young woman. I hope you may have known Mr. Rowan long enough to justify your confidence in him."

It was still the voice of a raven! Mrs. Prime as she spoke thus knew that she was croaking, and would have divested herself of her croak and spoken joyously, had such mode of speech been possible to her. But it was not possible. Though she would permit no such foreshadowings as those at which her mother had hinted, she had committed herself to forebodings against this young man, to such extent that she could not wheel her thoughts round and suddenly think well of him. She could not do so as yet, but she would make the struggle.

"God bless you, Rachel!" she said, when they parted for the night. "You have my best wishes for your happiness. I hope you do not doubt my love because I think more of your welfare in another world than in this." Then she kissed her sister and they parted for the night.

Rachel now shared her mother's room; and from her mother, when they were alone together, she received abundance of that sympathy for which her heart was craving.

"You mustn't mind Dorothea," the widow said.

"No, mamma; I do not."

"I mean that you mustn't mind her seeming to be so hard. She means well through it all, and is as affectionate as any other woman."

"Why did she say that he had been dismissed when she knew that it wasn't true?"

"Ah, my dear! can't you understand? When she first heard of Mr. Rowan——"

"Call him Luke, mamma."

"When she first heard of him she was taught to believe that he was giddy, and that he didn't mean anything."

"Why should she think evil of people? Who taught her?"

"Miss Pucker, and Mr. Prong, and that set."

"Yes; and they are the people who talk most of Christian charity!"

"But, my dear, they don't mean to be uncharitable. They try to do good. If Dorothea really thought that this young man was a dangerous acquaintance what could she do but say so? And you can't expect her to turn round all in a minute. Think how she has been troubled herself about this affair of Mr. Prong's."

"But that's no reason she should say that Luke is dangerous. Dangerous! What makes me so angry is that she should think everybody is a fool except herself. Why should anybody be more dangerous to me than to anybody else?"

"Well, my dear, I think that perhaps she is not so wrong there. Of course everything is all right with you now, and I'm sure I'm the happiest woman in the world to feel that it is so. I don't know how to be thankful enough when I think how things have turned out;—but when I first heard of him I thought he was dangerous too."

"But you don't think he is dangerous now, mamma?"

"No, my dear; of course I don't. And I never did after he drank tea here that night; only Mr. Comfort told me it wouldn't be safe not to see how things went a little before you—you understand, dearest?"

"Yes, I understand. I ain't a bit obliged to Mr. Comfort, though I mean to forgive him because of Mrs. Cornbury. She has behaved best through it all,—next to you, mamma."

I am afraid it was late before Mrs. Ray went to sleep that night, and I almost doubt whether Rachel slept at all. It seemed to her that in the present condition of her life sleep could hardly be necessary. During the last month past she had envied those who slept while she was kept awake by her sorrow. She had often struggled to sleep as she sat in her chair, so that she might escape for a few moments from the torture of her waking thoughts. But why need she sleep now that every thought was a new pleasure? There was no moment that she had ever passed with him that had not to be recalled. There was no word of his that had not to be re-weighed. She remembered, or fancied that she remembered, her idea of the man when her eye first fell upon his outside form. She would have sworn that her first glance of him had conveyed to her far more than had ever come to her from many a day's casual looking at any other man. She could almost believe that he had been specially made and destined for her behoof. She blushed even while lying in bed as she remembered how the gait of the man, and the tone of his voice, had taken possession of her eyes and ears from the first day on which she had met him. When she had gone to Mrs. Tappitt's party, so consciously alive to the fact that he was to be there, she had told herself that she was sure she thought no more of him than of any other man that she might meet; but she now declared to herself that she had been a weak fool in thus attempting to deceive herself; that she had loved him from the first,—or at any rate from that evening when he had told her of the beauty of the clouds; and that from that day to the present hour there had been no other chance of happiness to her but that chance which had now been so wondrously decided in her favour. When she came down to breakfast on the next morning she was very quiet,—so quiet that her sister almost thought she was frightened at her future prospects; but I think that there was no such fear. She was so happy that she could afford to be tranquil in her happiness.

On that day Rowan came out to the cottage in the evening and was formally introduced to Mrs. Prime. Mrs. Ray, I fear, did not find the little tea-party so agreeable on that evening as she had done on the previous occasion. Mrs. Prime did make some effort at conversation; she did endeavour to receive the young man as her future brother-in-law; she was gracious to him with such graciousness as she possessed;—but the duration of their meal was terribly long, and even Mrs. Ray herself felt relieved when the two lovers went forth together for their evening walk. I think there must have been some triumph in Rachel's heart as she tied on her hat before she started. I think she must have remembered the evening on which her sister had been so urgent with her to go to the Dorcas meeting;— when she had so obstinately refused that invitation, and had instead gone out to meet the Tappitt girls, and had met with them the young man of whom her sister had before been speaking with so much horror. Now he was there on purpose to take her with him, and she went forth with him, leaning lovingly on his arm, while yet close under her sister's eyes. I think there must have been a gleam of triumph in her face as she put her hand with such confidence well round her lover's arm.

Girls do triumph in their lovers,—in their acknowledged and permitted lovers, as young men triumph in their loves which are not acknowledged or perhaps permitted. A man's triumph is for the most part over when he is once allowed to take his place at the family table, as a right, next to his be-

trothed. He begins to feel himself to be a sacrificial victim,—
done up very prettily with blue and white ribbons round his
horns, but still an ox prepared for sacrifice. But the girl feels
herself to be exalted for those few weeks as a conqueror, and
to be carried along in an ovation of which that bucolic victim,
tied round with blue ribbons on to his horns, is the chief grace
and ornament. In this mood, no doubt, both Rachel and Luke
Rowan went forth, leaving the two widows together in the
cottage.

"It is pretty to see her so happy, isn't it now?" said Mrs.
Ray.

The question for the moment made Mrs. Prime uncomfortable and almost wretched, but it gave her the opportunity which
in her heart she desired of recanting her error in regard to
Luke Rowan's character. She wished to give in her adhesion
to the marriage,—to be known to have acknowledged its fitness
so that she could, with some true word of sisterly love, wish
her sister well. In Rachel's presence she could not have first
made this recantation. Though Rachel spoke no triumph, there
was a triumph in her eye, which prevented almost the possi-
bility of such yielding on the part of Dorothea. But when the
thing should have been once done, when she should once have
owned that Rachel was not wrong, then gradually she could
bring herself round to the utterance of some kindly expression.

"Pretty," she said; "yes, it is pretty. I do not know that anybody ever doubted its prettiness."

"And isn't it nice too? Dear girl! It does make me so happy
to see her lighthearted again. She has had a sad time of it,
Dorothea, since we made her write that letter to him; a very
sad time of it."

"People here, mother, do mostly have what you call a sad
time of it. Are we not taught that it is better for us that it
should be so? Have not you and I, mother, had a sad time of
it? It would be all sad enough if this were to be the end of it."

"Yes, just so; of course we know that. But it can't be wrong
that she should be happy now, when things are so bright all

around her. You wouldn't have thought it better for her, or for him either, that they should be kept apart, seeing that they really love each other?"

"No; I don't say that. If they love one another of course it is right that they should marry. I only wish we had known him longer."

"I am not sure that these things always go much better because young people have known each other all their lives. It seems to be certain that he is an industrious, steady young man. Everybody seems to speak well of him now."

"Well, mother, I have nothing to say against him,—not a word. And if it will give Rachel any pleasure,—though I don't suppose it will, the least in the world; but if it would, she may know that I think she has done wisely to accept him."

"Indeed it will; the greatest pleasure."

"And I hope they will be happy together for very many years. I love Rachel dearly, though I fear she does not think so, and anything I have said, I have said in love, not in anger."

"I'm sure of that, Dorothea."

"Now that she is to be settled in life as a married woman, of course she must not look for counsel either to you or to me. She must obey him, and I hope that God may give him grace to direct her steps aright."

"Amen!" said Mrs. Ray, solemnly. It was thus that Mrs. Prime read her recantation, which was repeated on that evening to Rachel with some little softening touches. "You won't be living together in the same house after a bit," said Mrs. Ray, thinking, with some sadness, that those little evening festivities of buttered toast and thick cream were over for her now, —"but I do hope you will be friends."

"Of course we will, mamma. She has only to put out her hand the least little bit in the world, and I will go the rest of the way. As for her living, I don't know what will be best about that, because Luke says that of course you'll come and live with us."

It was two or three days after this that Rachel saw the Tappitt girls for the first time since the fact of her engagement had become known. It was in the evening, and she had been again walking with Luke, when she met them; but at that moment she was alone. Augusta would have turned boldly away, though they had all come closely together before either had been aware of the presence of the other. But to this both Martha and Cherry objected.

"We have heard of your engagement," said Martha, "and we congratulate you. You have heard, of course, that we are going to move to Torquay, and we hope that you will be comfortable at the brewery."

"Yes," said Augusta, "the place isn't what it used to be, and so we think it best to go. Mamma has already looked at a villa near Torquay, which will suit us delightfully."

Then they passed on, but Cherry remained behind to say another word. "I am so happy," said Cherry, "that you and he have hit it off. He's a charming fellow, and I always said he was to fall in love with you. After the ball of course there wasn't a doubt about it. Mind you send us cake, dear; and by-and-by we'll come and see you at the old place, and be better friends than ever we were."

CHAPTER XXX

Conclusion

EARLY IN NOVEMBER Mr. Tappitt officially announced his intention of abdicating, and the necessary forms and deeds and parchment obligations were drawn out, signed and sealed, for the giving up of the brewery to Luke Rowan. Mr. Honyman's clerk revelled in thinly-covered folio sheets to the great comfort and profit of his master; while Mr. Sharpit went about Baslehurst declaring that Tappitt was an egregious ass, and hinting that Rowan was little better than a clever swindler.

What he said, however, had but little effect on Baslehurst. It had become generally understood that Rowan would spend money in the town, employing labour and struggling to go ahead, and Baslehurst knew that such a man was desirable as a citizen. The parchments were prepared, and the signatures were written with the necessary amount of witnessing, and Tappitt and Rowan once more met each other on friendly terms. Tappitt had endeavoured to avoid this, pleading, both to Honyman and to his wife, that his personal dislike to the young man was as great as ever; but they had not permitted him thus to indulge his wrath. Mr. Honyman pointed out to Mrs. Tappitt that such ill humour might be very detrimental to their future interests, and Tappitt had been made to give way. We may as well declare at once that the days of Tappitt's domestic dominion were over, as is generally the case with a man who retires from work and allows himself to be placed, as a piece of venerable furniture, in the chimney corner. Hitherto he, and he only, had known what funds could be made available out of the brewery for household purposes; and Mrs. Tappitt had been subject, at every turn of her life, to provoking intimations of reduced profits: but now there was the clear thousand a year, and she could demand her rights in accordance with that sum. Tappitt, too, could never again stray away from home with mysterious hints that matters connected with malt and hops must be discussed at places in which beer was consumed. He had no longer left to him any excuse for deviating from the regular course of his life even by a hair's breadth; and before two years were over he had learned to regard it almost as a favour to be allowed to take a walk with one of his own girls. No man should abdicate,—unless, indeed, he does so for his soul's advantage. As to happiness in this life it is hardly compatible with that diminished respect which ever attends the relinquishing of labour. Otium cum dignitate is a dream. There is no such position at any rate for the man who has once worked. He may have the ease or he may have the dignity; but he can hardly combine the two. This truth the unfortunate

Tappitt learned before he had been three months settled in the Torquay villa.

He was called upon to meet Rowan on friendly terms, and he obeyed. The friendship was not very cordial, but such as it was it served its purpose. The meeting took place in the dining-room of the brewery, and Mrs. Tappitt was present on the occasion. The lady received her visitor with some little affectation of grandeur, while T., standing with his hands in his pockets on his own rug, looked like a whipped hound. The right hand he was soon forced to bring forth, as Rowan demanded it that he might shake it.

"I am very glad that this affair has been settled between us amicably," said Luke, while he still held the hand of the abdicating brewer.

"Yes; well, I suppose it's for the best," said Tappitt, bringing out his words uncomfortably and with hesitation. "Take care and mind what you're about, or I suppose I shall have to come back again."

"There'll be no fear of that, I think," said Rowan.

"I hope not," said Mrs. Tappitt, with a tone that showed that she was much better able to master the occasion than her husband. "I hope not; but this is a great undertaking for so young a man, and I trust you feel your responsibility. It would be disagreeable to us, of course, to have to return to the brewery after having settled ourselves pleasantly at Torquay; but we shall have to do so if things go wrong with you."

"Don't be frightened, Mrs. Tappitt; you shall never have to come back here."

"I hope not; but it is always well to be on one's guard. I am sure you must be aware that Mr. Tappitt has behaved to you very generously; and if you have the high principle for which we are willing to give you credit, and which you ought to possess for the management of such an undertaking as the brewery, you will be careful that me and my daughters shan't be put to inconvenience by any delay in paying up the income regularly."

"Don't be afraid about that, Mrs. Tappitt."

"Into the bank on quarter day, if you please, Mr. Rowan. Short accounts make long friends. And as Mr. T. won't want to be troubled with letters and such-like, you can send me a line to Montpellier Villa, Torquay, just to say that it's done."

"Oh, I'll see to that," said Tappitt.

"My dear, as Mr. Rowan is so young for the business there'll be nothing like getting him to write a letter himself, saying that the money is paid. It'll keep him up to the mark like, and I'm sure I shan't mind the trouble."

"Don't you be alarmed about the money, Mrs. Tappitt," said Rowan, laughing; "and in order that you may know how the old shop is going on, I'll always send you at Christmas sixteen gallons of the best stuff we're brewing."

"That will be a very proper little attention, Mr. Rowan, and we shall be happy to drink success to the establishment. Here's some cake and wine on the table, and perhaps you'll do us the favour to take a glass,—so as to bury any past unkindness. T., my love, will you pour out the wine?"

It was twelve o'clock in the day, and the port wine, which had been standing for the last week in its decanter, was sipped by Luke Rowan without any great relish. But it also served its purpose,—and the burial service over past unkindness was performed with as much heartiness as the nature of the entertainment admitted. It was not as yet full four months since Rowan had filled Rachel's glass with champagne in that same room. Then he had made himself quite at home in the house as a member of Mr. Tappitt's family; but now he was going to be at home there as master of the establishment. As he put down the glass he could not help looking round the room, and suggesting to himself the changes he would make. As seen at present, the parlour of the brewery was certainly a dull room. It was very long since the wainscoting had been painted, longer since the curtains or carpets had been renewed. It was dark and dingy. But then so were the Tappitts themselves. Before

Rachel should be brought there he would make the place as bright as herself.

They said to him no word about his marriage. As for Tappitt he said few words about anything; and Mrs. Tappitt, with all her wish to be gracious, could not bring herself to mention Rachel Ray. Even between her and her daughters there was no longer any utterance of Rachel's name. She had once declared to Augusta, with irrepressible energy, that the man was a greater fool than she had ever believed possible, but after that it had been felt that the calamity would be best endured in silence.

When that interview in the dining-room was over, Rowan saw no more of Mrs. Tappitt. Business made it needful that he should be daily about the brewery, and there occasionally he met the poor departing man wandering among the vats and empty casks like a brewer's ghost. There was no word spoken between them as to business. The accounts, the keys, and implements were all handed over through Worts; and Rowan found himself in possession of the whole establishment with no more trouble than would have been necessary in settling himself in a new lodging.

That promise which he had half made of sending bridecake to Mrs. Sturt before Christmas was not kept, but it was broken only by a little. They were married early in January. In December Mrs. Rowan came back to Baslehurst, and became the guest of her son, who was then keeping a bachelor's house at the brewery. This lady's first visit to the cottage after her return was an affair of great moment to Rachel. Everything now had gone well with her except that question of her mother-in-law. Her lover had come back to her a better lover than ever; her mother petted her to her heart's content, speaking of Luke as though she had never suspected him of lupine propensities; Mr. Comfort talked to her of her coming marriage as though she had acted with great sagacity through the whole affair, addressing her in a tone indicating much respect, and differing

greatly from that in which he had been wont to catechise her
when she was nothing more than Mrs. Ray's girl at Bragg's
End; and even Dolly had sent in her adhesion, with more or
less cordiality. But still she had feared Mrs. Rowan's enmity,
and when Luke told her that his mother was coming to Baslehurst for the Christmas,—so that she might also be present at
the marriage,—Rachel felt that there was still a cloud in her
heavens. "I know your mother won't like me," she said to Luke.
"She made up her mind not to like me when she was here before." Luke assured her that she did not understand his mother's character,—asserting that his mother would certainly like
any woman that he might choose for his wife as soon as she
should have been made to understand that his choice was ir-
revocable. But Rachel remembered too well the report as to
that former visit to the cottage which Mrs. Rowan had made
together with Mrs. Tappitt; and when she heard that Luke's
mother was again in the parlour she went down from her bedroom with hesitating step and an uneasy heart. Mrs. Rowan
was seated in the room with her mother and sister when she
entered it, and therefore the first words of the interview had
been already spoken. To Mrs. Ray the prospect of the visit had
not been pleasant, for she also remembered how grand and distant the lady had been when she came to the cottage on that
former occasion; but Rachel observed, as she entered the
room, that her mother's face did not wear that look of dismay
which was usual to her when she was in any presence that was
disagreeable to her.

"My dear child!" said Mrs. Rowan rising from her seat, and
opening her arms for an embrace. Rachel underwent the embrace, and kissed the lady by whom she found herself to be
thus enveloped. She kissed Mrs. Rowan, but she could not, for
the life of her, think of any word to speak which would be fitting for the occasion.

"My own dear child!" said Mrs. Rowan again; "for you
know that you are to be my child now as well as your own
mamma's."

"It is very kind of you to say so," said Mrs. Ray.

"Very kind, indeed," said Mrs. Prime; "and I'm sure that you will find Rachel dutiful as a daughter." Rachel herself did not feel disposed to give any positive assurance on that point. She intended to be dutiful to her husband, and was inclined to think that obedience in that direction was quite enough for a married woman.

"Now that Luke is going to settle himself for life," continued Mrs. Rowan, "it is so very desirable that he should be married at once. Don't you think so, Mrs. Ray?"

"Indeed, yes, Mrs. Rowan. I always like to hear of young men getting married; that is when they've got anything to live upon. It makes them less harum-scarum like."

"I don't think Luke was ever what you call harum-scarum," said Mrs. Rowan.

"Mother didn't mean to say he was," said Mrs. Prime; "but marriage certainly does steady a young man, and generally makes him much more constant at Divine service."

"My Luke always did go to church very regularly," said Mrs. Rowan.

"I like to see young men in church," said Mrs. Ray. "As for the girls they go as a matter of course; but young men are allowed so much of their own way. When a man is a father of a family it becomes very different." Hereupon Rachel blushed, and then was kissed again by Luke's mother; and was made the subject of certain very interesting prophecies, which embarrassed her considerably and which need not be repeated here. After that interview she was never again afraid of her mother-in-law.

"You'll love mamma, when you know her," said Mary Rowan to Rachel a day or two afterwards. "Strangers and acquaintances generally think that she is a very tremendous personage, but she always does what she is asked by those who belong to her;—and as for Luke, she's almost a slave to him." I won't say that Rachel resolved that Mrs. Rowan should be a slave to her also, but she did resolve that she would not be a slave to Mrs. Rowan. She intended henceforward to serve one person and one person only.

Mrs. Butler Cornbury also called at the cottage; and her visit was very delightful to Rachel,—not the less so perhaps because Mrs. Prime was away at a Dorcas meeting. Had she been at the cottage all those pleasant allusions to the transactions at the ball would hardly have been made. "Don't tell me," said Mrs. Cornbury. "Do you think I couldn't see how it was going to be with half an eye? I told Walter that very night that he was a goose to suppose that you would go down to supper with him."

"But, Mrs. Cornbury, I really intended it; only they had another dance, and I was obliged to stand up with Mr. Rowan because I was engaged to him."

"I don't doubt you were engaged to him, my dear."

"Only for that dance, I mean."

"Only for that dance, of course. But now you are engaged to him for something else, and I tell you that I knew it was going to be so."

All this was very pretty and very pleasant; and when Mrs. Cornbury, as she went away, made a special request that she might be invited to the wedding, Rachel was supremely happy.

"Mamma," she said, "I do love that woman. I hardly know why, but I do love her so much."

"It was always the same with Patty Comfort," said Mrs. Ray. "She had a way of making people fond of her. They say that she can do just what she likes with the old gentleman at the Grange."

It may be well that I should declare here that there was no scrutiny as to the return of Butler Cornbury to Parliament,— to the great satisfaction both of old Mr. Cornbury and of old Mr. Comfort. They had been brought to promise that the needful funds for supporting the scrutiny should be forthcoming; but the promise had been made with heavy hearts, and the tidings of Mr. Hart's quiescence had been received very gratefully both at Cornbury and at Cawston.

Luke and Rachel were married on New Year's Day at Cawston church, and afterwards made a short marriage trip to Penzance and the Land's End. It was cold weather for pleasure-travelling; but snow and winds and rain affect young married people less, I think, than they do other folk. Rachel when she returned could not bear to be told that it had been cold. There was no winter, she said, at Penzance,—and so she continued to say ever afterwards.

Mrs. Ray would not consent to abandon the cottage at Bragg's End. She still remained its occupier in conjunction with Mrs. Prime, but she passed more than half her time at the brewery. Mrs. Prime is still Mrs. Prime; and will, I think, remain so, although Mr. Prong is occasionally seen to call at the cottage.

It is, I think, now universally admitted by all Devonshire and Cornwall that Luke Rowan has succeeded in brewing good beer; with what results to himself I am not prepared to say. I do not, however, think it probable that he will succeed in his professed object of shutting up the apple orchards of the county.

A CATALOG OF SELECTED
DOVER BOOKS
IN ALL FIELDS OF INTEREST

A CATALOG OF SELECTED DOVER
BOOKS IN ALL FIELDS OF INTEREST

THE ART NOUVEAU STYLE, edited by Roberta Waddell. 579 rare photographs of works in jewelry, metalwork, glass, ceramics, textiles, architecture and furniture by 175 artists—Mucha, Seguy, Lalique, Tiffany, many others. 288pp. 8⅜ × 11¼.
23515-7 Pa. $8.95

AMERICAN COUNTRY HOUSES OF THE GILDED AGE (Sheldon's "Artistic Country-Seats"), A. Lewis. All of Sheldon's fascinating and historically important photographs and plans. New text by Arnold Lewis. Approx. 200 illustrations. 128pp. 9⅜ × 12¼.
24301-X Pa. $7.95

THE WAY WE LIVE NOW, Anthony Trollope. Trollope's late masterpiece, marks shift to bitter satire. Character Melmotte "his greatest villain." Reproduced from original edition with 40 illustrations. 416pp. 6⅛ × 9¼.
24360-5 Pa. $7.95

BENCHLEY LOST AND FOUND, Robert Benchley. Finest humor from early 30's, about pet peeves, child psychologists, post office and others. Mostly unavailable elsewhere. 73 illustrations by Peter Arno and others. 183pp. 5⅜ × 8½.
22410-4 Pa. $3.50

ISOMETRIC PERSPECTIVE DESIGNS AND HOW TO CREATE THEM, John Locke. Isometric perspective is the picture of an object adrift in imaginary space. 75 mindboggling designs. 52pp. 8¼ × 11.
24123-8 Pa. $2.50

PERSPECTIVE FOR ARTISTS, Rex Vicat Cole. Depth, perspective of sky and sea, shadows, much more, not usually covered. 391 diagrams, 81 reproductions of drawings and paintings. 279pp. 5⅜ × 8½.
22487-2 Pa. $4.00

MOVIE-STAR PORTRAITS OF THE FORTIES, edited by John Kobal. 163 glamor, studio photos of 106 stars of the 1940s: Rita Hayworth, Ava Gardner, Marlon Brando, Clark Gable, many more. 176pp. 8⅜ × 11¼.
23546-7 Pa. $6.95

STARS OF THE BROADWAY STAGE, 1940-1967, Fred Fehl. Marlon Brando, Uta Hagen, John Kerr, John Gielgud, Jessica Tandy in great shows—*South Pacific, Galileo, West Side Story*, more. 240 black-and-white photos. 144pp. 8⅜ × 11¼.
24398-2 Pa. $8.95

ILLUSTRATED DICTIONARY OF HISTORIC ARCHITECTURE, edited by Cyril M. Harris. Extraordinary compendium of clear, concise definitions for over 5000 important architectural terms complemented by over 2000 line drawings. 592pp. 7½ × 9⅜.
24444-X Pa. $14.95

THE EARLY WORK OF FRANK LLOYD WRIGHT, F.L. Wright. 207 rare photos of Oak Park period, first great buildings: Unity Temple, Dana house, Larkin factory. Complete photos of Wasmuth edition. New Introduction. 160pp. 8⅜ × 11¼.
24381-8 Pa. $7.50

LIVING MY LIFE, Emma Goldman. Candid, no holds barred account by foremost American anarchist: her own life, anarchist movement, famous contemporaries, ideas and their impact. 944pp. 5⅜ × 8½. 22543-7, 22544-5 Pa., Two-vol. set $13.00

UNDERSTANDING THERMODYNAMICS, H.C. Van Ness. Clear, lucid treatment of first and second laws of thermodynamics. Excellent supplement to basic textbook in undergraduate science or engineering class. 103pp. 5⅜ × 8.
63277-6 Pa. $3.50

CHILDREN'S BOOKPLATES AND LABELS, Ed Sibbett, Jr. 6 each of 12 types based on *Wizard of Oz, Alice,* nursery rhymes, fairy tales. Perforated; full color. 24pp. 8¼ × 11. 23538-6 Pa. $2.95

READY-TO-USE VICTORIAN COLOR STICKERS: 96 Pressure-Sensitive Seals, Carol Belanger Grafton. Drawn from authentic period sources. Motifs include heads of men, women, children, plus florals, animals, birds, more. Will adhere to any clean surface. 8pp. 8½ × 11. 24551-9 Pa. $2.95

CUT AND FOLD PAPER SPACESHIPS THAT FLY, Michael Grater. 16 colorful, easy-to-build spaceships that really fly. Star Shuttle, Lunar Freighter, Star Probe, 13 others. 32pp. 8¼ × 11. 23978-0 Pa. $2.50

CUT AND ASSEMBLE PAPER AIRPLANES THAT FLY, Arthur Baker. 8 aerodynamically sound, ready-to-build paper airplanes, designed with latest techniques. Fly *Pegasus, Daedalus, Songbird,* 5 other aircraft. Instructions. 32pp. 9¼ × 11¼. 24302-8 Pa. $3.95

SIDELIGHTS ON RELATIVITY, Albert Einstein. Two lectures delivered in 1920-21: *Ether and Relativity* and *Geometry and Experience.* Elegant ideas in non-mathematical form. 56pp. 5⅜ × 8½. 24511-X Pa. $2.25

FADS AND FALLACIES IN THE NAME OF SCIENCE, Martin Gardner. Fair, witty appraisal of cranks and quacks of science: Velikovsky, orgone energy, Bridey Murphy, medical fads, etc. 373pp. 5⅜ × 8½. 20394-8 Pa. $5.50

VACATION HOMES AND CABINS, U.S. Dept. of Agriculture. Complete plans for 16 cabins, vacation homes and other shelters. 105pp. 9 × 12. 23631-5 Pa. $4.50

HOW TO BUILD A WOOD-FRAME HOUSE, L.O. Anderson. Placement, foundations, framing, sheathing, roof, insulation, plaster, finishing—almost everything else. 179 illustrations. 223pp. 7⅞ × 10¾. 22954-8 Pa. $5.50

THE MYSTERY OF A HANSOM CAB, Fergus W. Hume. Bizarre murder in a hansom cab leads to engrossing investigation. Memorable characters, rich atmosphere. 19th-century bestseller, still enjoyable, exciting. 256pp. 5⅜ × 8. 21956-9 Pa. $4.00

MANUAL OF TRADITIONAL WOOD CARVING, edited by Paul N. Hasluck. Possibly the best book in English on the craft of wood carving. Practical instructions, along with 1,146 working drawings and photographic illustrations. 576pp. 6½ × 9¼. 23489-4 Pa. $8.95

WHITTLING AND WOODCARVING, E.J Tangerman. Best book on market; clear, full. If you can cut a potato, you can carve toys, puzzles, chains, etc. Over 464 illustrations. 293pp. 5⅜ × 8½. 20965-2 Pa. $4.95

AMERICAN TRADEMARK DESIGNS, Barbara Baer Capitman. 732 marks, logos and corporate-identity symbols. Categories include entertainment, heavy industry, food and beverage. All black-and-white in standard forms. 160pp. 8⅛ × 11. 23259-X Pa. $6.00

DECORATIVE FRAMES AND BORDERS, edited by Edmund V. Gillon, Jr. Largest collection of borders and frames ever compiled for use of artists and designers. Renaissance, neo-Greek, Art Nouveau, Art Deco, to mention only a few styles. 396 illustrations. 192pp. 8⅜ × 11¼. 22928-9 Pa. $6.00

TOLL HOUSE TRIED AND TRUE RECIPES, Ruth Graves Wakefield. Popovers, veal and ham loaf, baked beans, much more from the famous Mass. restaurant. Nearly 700 recipes. 376pp. 5⅜ × 8½.   23560-2 Pa. $4.95

FAVORITE CHRISTMAS CAROLS, selected and arranged by Charles J.F. Cofone. Title, music, first verse and refrain of 34 traditional carols in handsome calligraphy; also subsequent verses and other information in type. 79pp. 8⅜ × 11.
20445-6 Pa. $3.00

CAMERA WORK: A PICTORIAL GUIDE, Alfred Stieglitz. All 559 illustrations from most important periodical in history of art photography. Reduced in size but still clear, in strict chronological order, with complete captions. 176pp. 8⅜ × 11¼.
23591-2 Pa. $6.95

FAVORITE SONGS OF THE NINETIES, edited by Robert Fremont. 88 favorites: "Ta-Ra-Ra-Boom-De-Aye," "The Band Played On," "Bird in a Gilded Cage," etc. 401pp. 9 × 12.   21536-9 Pa. $10.95

STRING FIGURES AND HOW TO MAKE THEM, Caroline F. Jayne. Fullest, clearest instructions on string figures from around world: Eskimo, Navajo, Lapp, Europe, more. Cat's cradle, moving spear, lightning, stars. 950 illustrations. 407pp. 5⅜ × 8½.   20152-X Pa. $4.95

LIFE IN ANCIENT EGYPT, Adolf Erman. Detailed older account, with much not in more recent books: domestic life, religion, magic, medicine, commerce, and whatever else needed for complete picture. Many illustrations. 597pp. 5⅜ × 8½.
22632-8 Pa. $7.95

ANCIENT EGYPT: ITS CULTURE AND HISTORY, J.E. Manchip White. From pre-dynastics through Ptolemies: scoiety, history, political structure, religion, daily life, literature, cultural heritage. 48 plates. 217pp. 5⅜ × 8½. (EBE)
22548-8 Pa. $4.95

KEPT IN THE DARK, Anthony Trollope. Unusual short novel about Victorian morality and abnormal psychology by the great English author. Probably the first American publication. Frontispiece by Sir John Millais. 92pp. 6½ × 9¼.
23609-9 Pa. $2.95

MAN AND WIFE, Wilkie Collins. Nineteenth-century master launches an attack on out-moded Scottish marital laws and Victorian cult of athleticism. Artfully plotted. 35 illustrations. 239pp. 6⅛ × 9¼.   24451-2 Pa. $5.95

RELATIVITY AND COMMON SENSE, Herman Bondi. Radically reoriented presentation of Einstein's Special Theory and one of most valuable popular accounts available. 60 illustrations. 177pp. 5⅜ × 8. (EUK)   24021-5 Pa. $3.50

THE EGYPTIAN BOOK OF THE DEAD, E.A. Wallis Budge. Complete reproduction of Ani's papyrus, finest ever found. Full hieroglyphic text, interlinear transliteration, word-for-word translation, smooth translation. 533pp. 6½ × 9¼.
(USO) 21866-X Pa. $8.50

COUNTRY AND SUBURBAN HOMES OF THE PRAIRIE SCHOOL PERIOD, H.V. von Holst. Over 400 photographs floor plans, elevations, detailed drawings (exteriors and interiors) for over 100 structures. Text. Important primary source. 128pp. 8⅜ × 11¼.   24373-7 Pa. $5.95

THE MURDER BOOK OF J.G. REEDER, Edgar Wallace. Eight suspenseful stories by bestselling mystery writer of 20s and 30s. Features the donnish Mr. J.G. Reeder of Public Prosecutor's Office. 128pp. 5⅜ × 8½. (Available in U.S. only)
24374-5 Pa. $3.50

ANNE ORR'S CHARTED DESIGNS, Anne Orr. Best designs by premier needlework designer, all on charts: flowers, borders, birds, children, alphabets, etc. Over 100 charts, 10 in color. Total of 40pp. 8¼ × 11. 23704-4 Pa. $2.25

BASIC CONSTRUCTION TECHNIQUES FOR HOUSES AND SMALL BUILDINGS SIMPLY EXPLAINED, U.S. Bureau of Naval Personnel. Grading, masonry, woodworking, floor and wall framing, roof framing, plastering, tile setting, much more. Over 675 illustrations. 568pp. 6½ × 9¼. 20242-9 Pa. $8.95

MATISSE LINE DRAWINGS AND PRINTS, Henri Matisse. Representative collection of female nudes, faces, still lifes, experimental works, etc., from 1898 to 1948. 50 illustrations. 48pp. 8⅜ × 11¼. 23877-6 Pa. $2.50

HOW TO PLAY THE CHESS OPENINGS, Eugene Znosko-Borovsky. Clear, profound examinations of just what each opening is intended to do and how opponent can counter. Many sample games. 147pp. 5⅜ × 8½. 22795-2 Pa. $2.95

DUPLICATE BRIDGE, Alfred Sheinwold. Clear, thorough, easily followed account: rules, etiquette, scoring, strategy, bidding; Goren's point-count system, Blackwood and Gerber conventions, etc. 158pp. 5⅜ × 8½. 22741-3 Pa. $3.00

SARGENT PORTRAIT DRAWINGS, J.S. Sargent. Collection of 42 portraits reveals technical skill and intuitive eye of noted American portrait painter, John Singer Sargent. 48pp. 8¼ × 11⅛. 24524-1 Pa. $2.95

ENTERTAINING SCIENCE EXPERIMENTS WITH EVERYDAY OBJECTS, Martin Gardner. Over 100 experiments for youngsters. Will amuse, astonish, teach, and entertain. Over 100 illustrations. 127pp. 5⅜ × 8½. 24201-3 Pa. $2.50

TEDDY BEAR PAPER DOLLS IN FULL COLOR: A Family of Four Bears and Their Costumes, Crystal Collins. A family of four Teddy Bear paper dolls and nearly 60 cut-out costumes. Full color, printed one side only. 32pp. 9¼ × 12¼.
24550-0 Pa. $3.50

NEW CALLIGRAPHIC ORNAMENTS AND FLOURISHES, Arthur Baker. Unusual, multi-useable material: arrows, pointing hands, brackets and frames, ovals, swirls, birds, etc. Nearly 700 illustrations. 80pp. 8⅜ × 11¼.
24095-9 Pa. $3.50

DINOSAUR DIORAMAS TO CUT & ASSEMBLE, M. Kalmenoff. Two complete three-dimensional scenes in full color, with 31 cut-out animals and plants. Excellent educational toy for youngsters. Instructions; 2 assembly diagrams. 32pp. 9¼ × 12¼. 24541-1 Pa. $3.95

SILHOUETTES: A PICTORIAL ARCHIVE OF VARIED ILLUSTRATIONS, edited by Carol Belanger Grafton. Over 600 silhouettes from the 18th to 20th centuries. Profiles and full figures of men, women, children, birds, animals, groups and scenes, nature, ships, an alphabet. 144pp. 8⅜ × 11¼. 23781-8 Pa. $4.50

SURREAL STICKERS AND UNREAL STAMPS, William Rowe. 224 haunting, hilarious stamps on gummed, perforated stock, with images of elephants, geisha girls, George Washington, etc. 16pp. one side. 8¼ × 11.　24371-0 Pa. $3.50

GOURMET KITCHEN LABELS, Ed Sibbett, Jr. 112 full-color labels (4 copies each of 28 designs). Fruit, bread, other culinary motifs. Gummed and perforated. 16pp. 8¼ × 11.　24087-8 Pa. $2.95

PATTERNS AND INSTRUCTIONS FOR CARVING AUTHENTIC BIRDS, H.D. Green. Detailed instructions, 27 diagrams, 85 photographs for carving 15 species of birds so life-like, they'll seem ready to fly! 8¼ × 11.　24222-6 Pa. $2.75

FLATLAND, E.A. Abbott. Science-fiction classic explores life of 2-D being in 3-D world. 16 illustrations. 103pp. 5⅜ × 8.　20001-9 Pa. $2.00

DRIED FLOWERS, Sarah Whitlock and Martha Rankin. Concise, clear, practical guide to dehydration, glycerinizing, pressing plant material, and more. Covers use of silica gel. 12 drawings. 32pp. 5⅜ × 8½.　21802-3 Pa. $1.00

EASY-TO-MAKE CANDLES, Gary V. Guy. Learn how easy it is to make all kinds of decorative candles. Step-by-step instructions. 82 illustrations. 48pp. 8¼ × 11.
23881-4 Pa. $2.50

SUPER STICKERS FOR KIDS, Carolyn Bracken. 128 gummed and perforated full-color stickers: GIRL WANTED, KEEP OUT, BORED OF EDUCATION, X-RATED, COMBAT ZONE, many others. 16pp. 8¼ × 11.　24092-4 Pa. $2.50

CUT AND COLOR PAPER MASKS, Michael Grater. Clowns, animals, funny faces...simply color them in, cut them out, and put them together, and you have 9 paper masks to play with and enjoy. 32pp. 8¼ × 11.　23171-2 Pa. $2.25

A CHRISTMAS CAROL: THE ORIGINAL MANUSCRIPT, Charles Dickens. Clear facsimile of Dickens manuscript, on facing pages with final printed text. 8 illustrations by John Leech, 4 in color on covers. 144pp. 8⅜ × 11¼.
20980-6 Pa. $5.95

CARVING SHOREBIRDS, Harry V. Shourds & Anthony Hillman. 16 full-size patterns (all double-page spreads) for 19 North American shorebirds with step-by-step instructions. 72pp. 9¼ × 12¼.　24287-0 Pa. $4.95

THE GENTLE ART OF MATHEMATICS, Dan Pedoe. Mathematical games, probability, the question of infinity, topology, how the laws of algebra work, problems of irrational numbers, and more. 42 figures. 143pp. 5⅜ × 8½. (EBE)
22949-1 Pa. $3.00

READY-TO-USE DOLLHOUSE WALLPAPER, Katzenbach & Warren, Inc. Stripe, 2 floral stripes, 2 allover florals, polka dot; all in full color. 4 sheets (350 sq. in.) of each, enough for average room. 48pp. 8¼ × 11.　23495-9 Pa. $2.95

MINIATURE IRON-ON TRANSFER PATTERNS FOR DOLLHOUSES, DOLLS, AND SMALL PROJECTS, Rita Weiss and Frank Fontana. Over 100 miniature patterns: rugs, bedspreads, quilts, chair seats, etc. In standard dollhouse size. 48pp. 8¼ × 11.　23741-9 Pa. $1.95

THE DINOSAUR COLORING BOOK, Anthony Rao. 45 renderings of dinosaurs, fossil birds, turtles, other creatures of Mesozoic Era. Scientifically accurate. Captions. 48pp. 8¼ × 11.　24022-3 Pa. $2.25

JAPANESE DESIGN MOTIFS, Matsuya Co. Mon, or heraldic designs. Over 4000 typical, beautiful designs: birds, animals, flowers, swords, fans, geometrics; all beautifully stylized. 213pp. 11⅜ × 8¼. 22874-6 Pa. $6.95

THE TALE OF BENJAMIN BUNNY, Beatrix Potter. Peter Rabbit's cousin coaxes him back into Mr. McGregor's garden for a whole new set of adventures. All 27 full-color illustrations. 59pp. 4¼ × 5½. (Available in U.S. only) 21102-9 Pa. $1.50

THE TALE OF PETER RABBIT AND OTHER FAVORITE STORIES BOXED SET, Beatrix Potter. Seven of Beatrix Potter's best-loved tales including Peter Rabbit in a specially designed, durable boxed set. 4¼ × 5½. Total of 447pp. 158 color illustrations. (Available in U.S. only) 23903-9 Pa. $10.50

PRACTICAL MENTAL MAGIC, Theodore Annemann. Nearly 200 astonishing feats of mental magic revealed in step-by-step detail. Complete advice on staging, patter, etc. Illustrated. 320pp. 5⅜ × 8½. 24426-1 Pa. $5.95

CELEBRATED CASES OF JUDGE DEE (DEE GOONG AN), translated by Robert Van Gulik. Authentic 18th-century Chinese detective novel; Dee and associates solve three interlocked cases. Led to van Gulik's own stories with same characters. Extensive introduction. 9 illustrations. 237pp. 5⅜ × 8½.
23337-5 Pa. $4.50

CUT & FOLD EXTRATERRESTRIAL INVADERS THAT FLY, M. Grater. Stage your own lilliputian space battles. By following the step-by-step instructions and explanatory diagrams you can launch 22 full-color fliers into space. 36pp. 8¼ × 11. 24478-4 Pa. $2.95

CUT & ASSEMBLE VICTORIAN HOUSES, Edmund V. Gillon, Jr. Printed in full color on heavy cardboard stock, 4 authentic Victorian houses in H-O scale: Italian-style Villa, Octagon, Second Empire, Stick Style. 48pp. 9¼ × 12¼.
23849-0 Pa. $3.95

BEST SCIENCE FICTION STORIES OF H.G. WELLS, H.G. Wells. Full novel *The Invisible Man*, plus 17 short stories: "The Crystal Egg," "Aepyornis Island," "The Strange Orchid," etc. 303pp. 5⅜ × 8½. (Available in U.S. only)
21531-8 Pa. $3.95

TRADEMARK DESIGNS OF THE WORLD, Yusaku Kamekura. A lavish collection of nearly 700 trademarks, the work of Wright, Loewy, Klee, Binder, hundreds of others. 160pp. 8¾ × 8. (Available in U.S. only) 24191-2 Pa. $5.00

THE ARTIST'S AND CRAFTSMAN'S GUIDE TO REDUCING, ENLARGING AND TRANSFERRING DESIGNS, Rita Weiss. Discover, reduce, enlarge, transfer designs from any objects to any craft project. 12pp. plus 16 sheets special graph paper. 8¼ × 11. 24142-4 Pa. $3.25

TREASURY OF JAPANESE DESIGNS AND MOTIFS FOR ARTISTS AND CRAFTSMEN, edited by Carol Belanger Grafton. Indispensable collection of 360 traditional Japanese designs and motifs redrawn in clean, crisp black-and-white, copyright-free illustrations. 96pp. 8¼ × 11. 24435-0 Pa. $3.95

CHANCERY CURSIVE STROKE BY STROKE, Arthur Baker. Instructions and illustrations for each stroke of each letter (upper and lower case) and numerals. 54 full-page plates. 64pp. 8¼ × 11. 24278-1 Pa. $2.50

THE ENJOYMENT AND USE OF COLOR, Walter Sargent. Color relationships, values, intensities; complementary colors, illumination, similar topics. Color in nature and art. 7 color plates, 29 illustrations. 274pp. 5⅜ × 8½. 20944-X Pa. $4.50

SCULPTURE PRINCIPLES AND PRACTICE, Louis Slobodkin. Step-by-step approach to clay, plaster, metals, stone; classical and modern. 253 drawings, photos. 255pp. 8⅛ × 11. 22960-2 Pa. $7.00

VICTORIAN FASHION PAPER DOLLS FROM HARPER'S BAZAR, 1867-1898, Theodore Menten. Four female dolls with 28 elegant high fashion costumes, printed in full color. 32pp. 9¼ × 12¼. 23453-3 Pa. $3.50

FLOPSY, MOPSY AND COTTONTAIL: A Little Book of Paper Dolls in Full Color, Susan LaBelle. Three dolls and 21 costumes (7 for each doll) show Peter Rabbit's siblings dressed for holidays, gardening, hiking, etc. Charming borders, captions. 48pp. 4¼ × 5½. 24376-1 Pa. $2.00

NATIONAL LEAGUE BASEBALL CARD CLASSICS, Bert Randolph Sugar. 83 big-leaguers from 1909-69 on facsimile cards. Hubbell, Dean, Spahn, Brock plus advertising, info, no duplications. Perforated, detachable. 16pp. 8¼ × 11. 24308-7 Pa. $2.95

THE LOGICAL APPROACH TO CHESS, Dr. Max Euwe, et al. First-rate text of comprehensive strategy, tactics, theory for the amateur. No gambits to memorize, just a clear, logical approach. 224pp. 5⅜ × 8½. 24353-2 Pa. $4.50

MAGICK IN THEORY AND PRACTICE, Aleister Crowley. The summation of the thought and practice of the century's most famous necromancer, long hard to find. Crowley's best book. 436pp. 5⅜ × 8½. (Available in U.S. only) 23295-6 Pa. $6.50

THE HAUNTED HOTEL, Wilkie Collins. Collins' last great tale; doom and destiny in a Venetian palace. Praised by T.S. Eliot. 127pp. 5⅜ × 8½. 24333-8 Pa. $3.00

ART DECO DISPLAY ALPHABETS, Dan X. Solo. Wide variety of bold yet elegant lettering in handsome Art Deco styles. 100 complete fonts, with numerals, punctuation, more. 104pp. 8⅛ × 11. 24372-9 Pa. $4.00

CALLIGRAPHIC ALPHABETS, Arthur Baker. Nearly 150 complete alphabets by outstanding contemporary. Stimulating ideas; useful source for unique effects. 154 plates. 157pp. 8⅜ × 11¼. 21045-6 Pa. $4.95

ARTHUR BAKER'S HISTORIC CALLIGRAPHIC ALPHABETS, Arthur Baker. From monumental capitals of first-century Rome to humanistic cursive of 16th century, 33 alphabets in fresh interpretations. 88 plates. 96pp. 9 × 12. 24054-1 Pa. $3.95

LETTIE LANE PAPER DOLLS, Sheila Young. Genteel turn-of-the-century family very popular then and now. 24 paper dolls. 16 plates in full color. 32pp. 9¼ × 12¼. 24089-4 Pa. $3.50

TWENTY-FOUR ART NOUVEAU POSTCARDS IN FULL COLOR FROM CLASSIC POSTERS, Hayward and Blanche Cirker. Ready-to-mail postcards reproduced from rare set of poster art. Works by Toulouse-Lautrec, Parrish, Steinlen, Mucha, Cheret, others. 12pp. 8¼× 11. 24389-3 Pa. $2.95

READY-TO-USE ART NOUVEAU BOOKMARKS IN FULL COLOR, Carol Belanger Grafton. 30 elegant bookmarks featuring graceful, flowing lines, foliate motifs, sensuous women characteristic of Art Nouveau. Perforated for easy detaching. 16pp. 8¼ × 11. 24305-2 Pa. $2.95

FRUIT KEY AND TWIG KEY TO TREES AND SHRUBS, William M. Harlow. Fruit key covers 120 deciduous and evergreen species; twig key covers 160 deciduous species. Easily used. Over 300 photographs. 126pp. 5⅜ × 8½. 20511-8 Pa. $2.25

LEONARDO DRAWINGS, Leonardo da Vinci. Plants, landscapes, human face and figure, etc., plus studies for Sforza monument, *Last Supper*, more. 60 illustrations. 64pp. 8¼ × 11⅛. 23951-9 Pa. $2.75

CLASSIC BASEBALL CARDS, edited by Bert R. Sugar. 98 classic cards on heavy stock, full color, perforated for detaching. Ruth, Cobb, Durocher, DiMaggio, H. Wagner, 99 others. Rare originals cost hundreds. 16pp. 8¼ × 11. 23498-3 Pa. $2.95

TREES OF THE EASTERN AND CENTRAL UNITED STATES AND CANADA, William M. Harlow. Best one-volume guide to 140 trees. Full descriptions, woodlore, range, etc. Over 600 illustrations. Handy size. 288pp. 4½ × 6⅜. 20395-6 Pa. $3.50

JUDY GARLAND PAPER DOLLS IN FULL COLOR, Tom Tierney. 3 Judy Garland paper dolls (teenager, grown-up, and mature woman) and 30 gorgeous costumes highlighting memorable career. Captions. 32pp. 9¼ × 12¼. 24404-0 Pa. $3.50

GREAT FASHION DESIGNS OF THE BELLE EPOQUE PAPER DOLLS IN FULL COLOR, Tom Tierney. Two dolls and 30 costumes meticulously rendered. Haute couture by Worth, Lanvin, Paquin, other greats late Victorian to WWI. 32pp. 9¼ × 12¼. 24425-3 Pa. $3.50

FASHION PAPER DOLLS FROM GODEY'S LADY'S BOOK, 1840-1854, Susan Johnston. In full color: 7 female fashion dolls with 50 costumes. Little girl's, bridal, riding, bathing, wedding, evening, everyday, etc. 32pp. 9¼ × 12¼. 23511-4 Pa. $3.50

THE BOOK OF THE SACRED MAGIC OF ABRAMELIN THE MAGE, translated by S. MacGregor Mathers. Medieval manuscript of ceremonial magic. Basic document in Aleister Crowley, Golden Dawn groups. 268pp. 5⅜ × 8½. 23211-5 Pa. $5.00

PETER RABBIT POSTCARDS IN FULL COLOR: 24 Ready-to-Mail Cards, Susan Whited LaBelle. Bunnies ice-skating, coloring Easter eggs, making valentines, many other charming scenes. 24 perforated full-color postcards, each measuring 4¼ × 6, on coated stock. 12pp. 9 × 12. 24617-5 Pa. $2.95

CELTIC HAND STROKE BY STROKE, A. Baker. Complete guide creating each letter of the alphabet in distinctive Celtic manner. Covers hand position, strokes, pens, inks, paper, more. Illustrated. 48pp. 8¼ × 11. 24336-2 Pa. $2.50

HOW THE OTHER HALF LIVES, Jacob A. Riis. Journalistic record of filth, degradation, upward drive in New York immigrant slums, shops, around 1900. New edition includes 100 original Riis photos, monuments of early photography. 233pp. 10 × 7⅞. 22012-5 Pa. $7.95

CHINA AND ITS PEOPLE IN EARLY PHOTOGRAPHS, John Thomson. In 200 black-and-white photographs of exceptional quality photographic pioneer Thomson captures the mountains, dwellings, monuments and people of 19th-century China. 272pp. 9⅜ × 12¼. 24393-1 Pa. $12.95

GODEY COSTUME PLATES IN COLOR FOR DECOUPAGE AND FRAMING, edited by Eleanor Hasbrouk Rawlings. 24 full-color engravings depicting 19th-century Parisian haute couture. Printed on one side only. 56pp. 8¼ × 11. 23879-2 Pa. $3.95

ART NOUVEAU STAINED GLASS PATTERN BOOK, Ed Sibbett, Jr. 104 projects using well-known themes of Art Nouveau: swirling forms, florals, peacocks, and sensuous women. 60pp. 8¼ × 11. 23577-7 Pa. $3.00

QUICK AND EASY PATCHWORK ON THE SEWING MACHINE: Susan Aylsworth Murwin and Suzzy Payne. Instructions, diagrams show exactly how to machine sew 12 quilts. 48pp. of templates. 50 figures. 80pp. 8¼ × 11. 23770-2 Pa. $3.50

THE STANDARD BOOK OF QUILT MAKING AND COLLECTING, Marguerite Ickis. Full information, full-sized patterns for making 46 traditional quilts, also 150 other patterns. 483 illustrations. 273pp. 6⅞ × 9⅝. 20582-7 Pa. $5.95

LETTERING AND ALPHABETS, J. Albert Cavanagh. 85 complete alphabets lettered in various styles; instructions for spacing, roughs, brushwork. 121pp. 8¾ × 8. 20053-1 Pa. $3.75

LETTER FORMS: 110 COMPLETE ALPHABETS, Frederick Lambert. 110 sets of capital letters; 16 lower case alphabets; 70 sets of numbers and other symbols. 110pp. 8⅛ × 11. 22872-X Pa. $4.50

ORCHIDS AS HOUSE PLANTS, Rebecca Tyson Northen. Grow cattleyas and many other kinds of orchids—in a window, in a case, or under artificial light. 63 illustrations. 148pp. 5⅜ × 8½. 23261-1 Pa. $2.95

THE MUSHROOM HANDBOOK, Louis C.C. Krieger. Still the best popular handbook. Full descriptions of 259 species, extremely thorough text, poisons, folklore, etc. 32 color plates; 126 other illustrations. 560pp. 5⅜ × 8½. 21861-9 Pa. $8.50

THE DORÉ BIBLE ILLUSTRATIONS, Gustave Doré. All wonderful, detailed plates: Adam and Eve, Flood, Babylon, life of Jesus, etc. Brief King James text with each plate. 241 plates. 241pp. 9 × 12. 23004-X Pa. $6.95

THE BOOK OF KELLS: Selected Plates in Full Color, edited by Blanche Cirker. 32 full-page plates from greatest manuscript-icon of early Middle Ages. Fantastic, mysterious. Publisher's Note. Captions. 32pp. 9¾ × 12¼. 24345-1 Pa. $4.50

THE PERFECT WAGNERITE, George Bernard Shaw. Brilliant criticism of the Ring Cycle, with provocative interpretation of politics, economic theories behind the Ring. 136pp. 5⅜ × 8½. (Available in U.S. only) 21707-8 Pa. $3.00

THE RIME OF THE ANCIENT MARINER, Gustave Doré, S.T. Coleridge. Doré's finest work, 34 plates capture moods, subtleties of poem. Full text. 77pp. 9¼ × 12. 22305-1 Pa. $4.95

SONGS OF INNOCENCE, William Blake. The first and most popular of Blake's famous "Illuminated Books," in a facsimile edition reproducing all 31 brightly colored plates. Additional printed text of each poem. 64pp. 5¼ × 7.
22764-2 Pa. $3.00

AN INTRODUCTION TO INFORMATION THEORY, J.R. Pierce. Second (1980) edition of most impressive non-technical account available. Encoding, entropy, noisy channel, related areas, etc. 320pp. 5⅜ × 8½. 24061-4 Pa. $4.95

THE DIVINE PROPORTION: A STUDY IN MATHEMATICAL BEAUTY, H.E. Huntley. "Divine proportion" or "golden ratio" in poetry, Pascal's triangle, philosophy, psychology, music, mathematical figures, etc. Excellent bridge between science and art. 58 figures. 185pp. 5⅜ × 8½. 22254-3 Pa. $3.95

THE DOVER NEW YORK WALKING GUIDE: From the Battery to Wall Street, Mary J. Shapiro. Superb inexpensive guide to historic buildings and locales in lower Manhattan: Trinity Church, Bowling Green, more. Complete Text; maps. 36 illustrations. 48pp. 3⅞ × 9¼. 24225-0 Pa. $1.75

NEW YORK THEN AND NOW, Edward B. Watson, Edmund V. Gillon, Jr. 83 important Manhattan sites: on facing pages early photographs (1875-1925) and 1976 photos by Gillon. 172 illustrations. 171pp. 9¼ × 10. 23361-8 Pa. $7.95

HISTORIC COSTUME IN PICTURES, Braun & Schneider. Over 1450 costumed figures from dawn of civilization to end of 19th century. English captions. 125 plates. 256pp. 8⅜ × 11¼. 23150-X Pa. $7.50

VICTORIAN AND EDWARDIAN FASHION: A Photographic Survey, Alison Gernsheim. First fashion history completely illustrated by contemporary photographs. Full text plus 235 photos, 1840-1914, in which many celebrities appear. 240pp. 6½ × 9¼. 24205-6 Pa. $6.00

CHARTED CHRISTMAS DESIGNS FOR COUNTED CROSS-STITCH AND OTHER NEEDLECRAFTS, Lindberg Press. Charted designs for 45 beautiful needlecraft projects with many yuletide and wintertime motifs. 48pp. 8¼ × 11.
24356-7 Pa. $1.95

101 FOLK DESIGNS FOR COUNTED CROSS-STITCH AND OTHER NEEDLE-CRAFTS, Carter Houck. 101 authentic charted folk designs in a wide array of lovely representations with many suggestions for effective use. 48pp. 8¼ × 11.
24369-9 Pa. $1.95

FIVE ACRES AND INDEPENDENCE, Maurice G. Kains. Great back-to-the-land classic explains basics of self-sufficient farming. The one book to get. 95 illustrations. 397pp. 5⅜ × 8½. 20974-1 Pa. $4.95

A MODERN HERBAL, Margaret Grieve. Much the fullest, most exact, most useful compilation of herbal material. Gigantic alphabetical encyclopedia, from aconite to zedoary, gives botanical information, medical properties, folklore, economic uses, and much else. Indispensable to serious reader. 161 illustrations. 888pp. 6½ × 9¼. (Available in U.S. only) 22798-7, 22799-5 Pa., Two-vol. set $16.45

DECORATIVE NAPKIN FOLDING FOR BEGINNERS, Lillian Oppenheimer and Natalie Epstein. 22 different napkin folds in the shape of a heart, clown's hat, love knot, etc. 63 drawings. 48pp. 8¼ × 11. 23797-4 Pa. $1.95

DECORATIVE LABELS FOR HOME CANNING, PRESERVING, AND OTHER HOUSEHOLD AND GIFT USES, Theodore Menten. 128 gummed, perforated labels, beautifully printed in 2 colors. 12 versions. Adhere to metal, glass, wood, ceramics. 24pp. 8¼ × 11. 23219-0 Pa. $2.95

EARLY AMERICAN STENCILS ON WALLS AND FURNITURE, Janet Waring. Thorough coverage of 19th-century folk art: techniques, artifacts, surviving specimens. 166 illustrations, 7 in color. 147pp. of text. 7⅞ × 10¾. 21906-2 Pa. $8.95

AMERICAN ANTIQUE WEATHERVANES, A.B. & W.T. Westervelt. Extensively illustrated 1883 catalog exhibiting over 550 copper weathervanes and finials. Excellent primary source by one of the principal manufacturers. 104pp. 6⅛ × 9¼. 24396-6 Pa. $3.95

ART STUDENTS' ANATOMY, Edmond J. Farris. Long favorite in art schools. Basic elements, common positions, actions. Full text, 158 illustrations. 159pp. 5⅜ × 8½. 20744-7 Pa. $3.50

BRIDGMAN'S LIFE DRAWING, George B. Bridgman. More than 500 drawings and text teach you to abstract the body into its major masses. Also specific areas of anatomy. 192pp. 6½ × 9¼. (EA) 22710-3 Pa. $4.50

COMPLETE PRELUDES AND ETUDES FOR SOLO PIANO, Frederic Chopin. All 26 Preludes, all 27 Etudes by greatest composer of piano music. Authoritative Paderewski edition. 224pp. 9 × 12. (Available in U.S. only) 24052-5 Pa. $6.95

PIANO MUSIC 1888-1905, Claude Debussy. Deux Arabesques, Suite Bergamesque, Masques, 1st series of Images, etc. 9 others, in corrected editions. 175pp. 9⅜ × 12¼. (ECE) 22771-5 Pa. $5.95

TEDDY BEAR IRON-ON TRANSFER PATTERNS, Ted Menten. 80 iron-on transfer patterns of male and female Teddys in a wide variety of activities, poses, sizes. 48pp. 8¼ × 11. 24596-9 Pa. $2.00

A PICTURE HISTORY OF THE BROOKLYN BRIDGE, M.J. Shapiro. Profusely illustrated account of greatest engineering achievement of 19th century. 167 rare photos & engravings recall construction, human drama. Extensive, detailed text. 122pp. 8¼ × 11. 24403-2 Pa. $7.95

NEW YORK IN THE THIRTIES, Berenice Abbott. Noted photographer's fascinating study shows new buildings that have become famous and old sights that have disappeared forever. 97 photographs. 97pp. 11⅜ × 10. 22967-X Pa. $6.50

MATHEMATICAL TABLES AND FORMULAS, Robert D. Carmichael and Edwin R. Smith. Logarithms, sines, tangents, trig functions, powers, roots, reciprocals, exponential and hyperbolic functions, formulas and theorems. 269pp. 5⅜ × 8½. 60111-0 Pa. $3.75

HANDBOOK OF MATHEMATICAL FUNCTIONS WITH FORMULAS, GRAPHS, AND MATHEMATICAL TABLES, edited by Milton Abramowitz and Irene A. Stegun. Vast compendium: 29 sets of tables, some to as high as 20 places. 1,046pp. 8 × 10½. 61272-4 Pa. $19.95

REASON IN ART, George Santayana. Renowned philosopher's provocative, seminal treatment of basis of art in instinct and experience. Volume Four of *The Life of Reason*. 230pp. 5⅜ × 8. 24358-3 Pa. $4.50

LANGUAGE, TRUTH AND LOGIC, Alfred J. Ayer. Famous, clear introduction to Vienna, Cambridge schools of Logical Positivism. Role of philosophy, elimination of metaphysics, nature of analysis, etc. 160pp. 5⅜ × 8½. (USCO) 20010-8 Pa. $2.75

BASIC ELECTRONICS, U.S. Bureau of Naval Personnel. Electron tubes, circuits, antennas, AM, FM, and CW transmission and receiving, etc. 560 illustrations. 567pp. 6½ × 9¼. 21076-6 Pa. $8.95

THE ART DECO STYLE, edited by Theodore Menten. Furniture, jewelry, metalwork, ceramics, fabrics, lighting fixtures, interior decors, exteriors, graphics from pure French sources. Over 400 photographs. 183pp. 8⅜ × 11¼. 22824-X Pa. $6.95

THE FOUR BOOKS OF ARCHITECTURE, Andrea Palladio. 16th-century classic covers classical architectural remains, Renaissance revivals, classical orders, etc. 1738 Ware English edition. 216 plates. 110pp. of text. 9½ × 12¾. 21308-0 Pa. $10.00

THE WIT AND HUMOR OF OSCAR WILDE, edited by Alvin Redman. More than 1000 ripostes, paradoxes, wisecracks: Work is the curse of the drinking classes, I can resist everything except temptations, etc. 258pp. 5⅜ × 8½. (USCO) 20602-5 Pa. $3.50

THE DEVIL'S DICTIONARY, Ambrose Bierce. Barbed, bitter, brilliant witticisms in the form of a dictionary. Best, most ferocious satire America has produced. 145pp. 5⅜ × 8½. 20487-1 Pa. $2.50

ERTÉ'S FASHION DESIGNS, Erté. 210 black-and-white inventions from *Harper's Bazar*, 1918-32, plus 8pp. full-color covers. Captions. 88pp. 9 × 12. 24203-X Pa. $6.50

ERTÉ GRAPHICS, Erté. Collection of striking color graphics: *Seasons, Alphabet, Numerals, Aces* and *Precious Stones*. 50 plates, including 4 on covers. 48pp. 9⅜ × 12¼. 23580-7 Pa. $6.95

PAPER FOLDING FOR BEGINNERS, William D. Murray and Francis J. Rigney. Clearest book for making origami sail boats, roosters, frogs that move legs, etc. 40 projects. More than 275 illustrations. 94pp. 5⅜ × 8½. 20713-7 Pa. $1.95

ORIGAMI FOR THE ENTHUSIAST, John Montroll. Fish, ostrich, peacock, squirrel, rhinoceros, Pegasus, 19 other intricate subjects. Instructions. Diagrams. 128pp. 9 × 12. 23799-0 Pa. $4.95

CROCHETING NOVELTY POT HOLDERS, edited by Linda Macho. 64 useful, whimsical pot holders feature kitchen themes, animals, flowers, other novelties. Surprisingly easy to crochet. Complete instructions. 48pp. 8¼ × 11. 24296-X Pa. $1.95

CROCHETING DOILIES, edited by Rita Weiss. Irish Crochet, Jewel, Star Wheel, Vanity Fair and more. Also luncheon and console sets, runners and centerpieces. 51 illustrations. 48pp. 8¼ × 11. 23424-X Pa. $2.00

YUCATAN BEFORE AND AFTER THE CONQUEST, Diego de Landa. Only significant account of Yucatan written in the early post-Conquest era. Translated by William Gates. Over 120 illustrations. 162pp. 5⅜ × 8½.   23622-6 Pa. $3.50

ORNATE PICTORIAL CALLIGRAPHY, E.A. Lupfer. Complete instructions, over 150 examples help you create magnificent "flourishes" from which beautiful animals and objects gracefully emerge. 8⅛ × 11.   21957-7 Pa. $2.95

DOLLY DINGLE PAPER DOLLS, Grace Drayton. Cute chubby children. by same artist who did Campbell Kids. Rare plates from 1910s. 30 paper dolls and over 100 outfits reproduced in full color. 32pp. 9¼ × 12¼.   23711-7 Pa. $2.95

CURIOUS GEORGE PAPER DOLLS IN FULL COLOR, H. A. Rey, Kathy Allert. Naughty little monkey-hero of children's books in two doll figures, plus 48 full-color costumes: pirate, Indian chief, fireman, more. 32pp. 9¼ × 12¼.
24386-9 Pa. $3.50

GERMAN: HOW TO SPEAK AND WRITE IT, Joseph Rosenberg. Like *French, How to Speak and Write It.* Very rich modern course, with a wealth of pictorial material. 330 illustrations. 384pp. 5⅜ × 8½. (USUKO)   20271-2 Pa. $4.75

CATS AND KITTENS: 24 Ready-to-Mail Color Photo Postcards, D. Holby. Handsome collection; feline in a variety of adorable poses. Identifications. 12pp. on postcard stock. 8¼ × 11.   24469-5 Pa. $2.95

MARILYN MONROE PAPER DOLLS, Tom Tierney. 31 full-color designs on heavy stock, from *The Asphalt Jungle, Gentlemen Prefer Blondes,* 22 others. 1 doll. 16 plates. 32pp. 9⅜ × 12¼.   23769-9 Pa. $3.50

FUNDAMENTALS OF LAYOUT, F.H. Wills. All phases of layout design discussed and illustrated in 121 illustrations. Indispensable as student's text or handbook for professional. 124pp. 8⅛.× 11.   21279-3 Pa. $4.50

FANTASTIC SUPER STICKERS, Ed Sibbett, Jr. 75 colorful pressure-sensitive stickers. Peel off and place for a touch of pizzazz: clowns, penguins, teddy bears, etc. Full color. 16pp. 8¼ × 11.   24471-7 Pa. $2.95

LABELS FOR ALL OCCASIONS, Ed Sibbett, Jr. 6 labels each of 16 different designs—baroque, art nouveau, art deco, Pennsylvania Dutch, etc.—in full color. 24pp. 8¼ × 11.   23688-9 Pa. $2.95

HOW TO CALCULATE QUICKLY: RAPID METHODS IN BASIC MATHE-MATICS, Henry Sticker. Addition, subtraction, multiplication, division, checks, etc. More than 8000 problems, solutions. 185pp. 5 × 7¼.   20295-X Pa. $2.95

THE CAT COLORING BOOK, Karen Baldauski. Handsome, realistic renderings of 40 splendid felines, from American shorthair to exotic types. 44 plates. Captions. 48pp. 8¼ × 11.   24011-8 Pa. $2.25

THE TALE OF PETER RABBIT, Beatrix Potter. The inimitable Peter's terrifying adventure in Mr. McGregor's garden, with all 27 wonderful, full-color Potter illustrations. 55pp. 4¼ × 5½. (Available in U.S. only)   22827-4 Pa. $1.50

BASIC ELECTRICITY, U.S. Bureau of Naval Personnel. Batteries, circuits, conductors, AC and DC, inductance and capacitance, generators, motors, transformers, amplifiers, etc. 349 illustrations. 448pp. 6½ × 9¼.   20973-3 Pa. $7.95

READY-TO-USE BORDERS, Ted Menten. Both traditional and unusual interchangeable borders in a tremendous array of sizes, shapes, and styles. 32 plates. 64pp. 8¼ × 11. 23782-6 Pa. $2.95

THE WHOLE CRAFT OF SPINNING, Carol Kroll. Preparing fiber, drop spindle, treadle wheel, other fibers, more. Highly creative, yet simple. 43 illustrations. 48pp. 8¼ × 11. 23968-3 Pa. $2.50

HIDDEN PICTURE PUZZLE COLORING BOOK, Anna Pomaska. 31 delightful pictures to color with dozens of objects, people and animals hidden away to find. Captions. Solutions. 48pp. 8¼ × 11. 23909-8 Pa. $2.25

QUILTING WITH STRIPS AND STRINGS, H.W. Rose. Quickest, easiest way to turn left-over fabric into handsome quilt. 46 patchwork quilts; 31 full-size templates. 48pp. 8¼ × 11. 24357-5 Pa. $3.25

NATURAL DYES AND HOME DYEING, Rita J. Adrosko. Over 135 specific recipes from historical sources for cotton, wool, other fabrics. Genuine premodern handicrafts. 12 illustrations. 160pp. 5⅜ × 8½. 22688-3 Pa. $2.95

CARVING REALISTIC BIRDS, H.D. Green. Full-sized patterns, step-by-step instructions for robins, jays, cardinals, finches, etc. 97 illustrations. 80pp. 8¼ × 11. 23484-3 Pa. $3.00

GEOMETRY, RELATIVITY AND THE FOURTH DIMENSION, Rudolf Rucker. Exposition of fourth dimension, concepts of relativity as Flatland characters continue adventures. Popular, easily followed yet accurate, profound. 141 illustrations. 133pp. 5⅜ × 8½. 23400-2 Pa. $2.75

READY-TO-USE SMALL FRAMES AND BORDERS, Carol B. Grafton. Graphic message? Frame it graphically with 373 new frames and borders in many styles: Art Nouveau, Art Deco, Op Art. 64pp. 8¼ × 11. 24375-3 Pa. $2.95

CELTIC ART: THE METHODS OF CONSTRUCTION, George Bain. Simple geometric techniques for making Celtic interlacements, spirals, Kellstype initials, animals, humans, etc. Over 500 illustrations. 160pp. 9 × 12. (Available in U.S. only) 22923-8 Pa. $6.00

THE TALE OF TOM KITTEN, Beatrix Potter. Exciting text and all 27 vivid, full-color illustrations to charming tale of naughty little Tom getting into mischief again. 58pp. 4¼ × 5½. 24502-0 Pa. $1.50

WOODEN PUZZLE TOYS, Ed Sibbett, Jr. Transfer patterns and instructions for 24 easy-to-do projects: fish, butterflies, cats, acrobats, Humpty Dumpty, 19 others. 48pp. 8¼ × 11. 23713-3 Pa. $2.50

MY FAMILY TREE WORKBOOK, Rosemary A. Chorzempa. Enjoyable, easy-to-use introduction to genealogy designed specially for children. Data pages plus text. Instructive, educational, valuable. 64pp. 8¼ × 11. 24229-3 Pa. $2.25

Prices subject to change without notice.

Available at your book dealer or write for free catalog to Dept. GI, Dover Publications, Inc., 31 East 2nd St. Mineola, N.Y. 11501. Dover publishes more than 175 books each year on science, elementary and advanced mathematics, biology, music, art, literary history, social sciences and other areas.